"What are we going to do?" he asked at last.

Emily pushed away from him and walked over to the window. He knew the view she was afforded from the window. This place had been hard-earned. He'd worked just as hard as his siblings to make Montoro Enterprises into the success it was today.

"I just wanted you to know. Beyond that I don't need anything. Someday the kid is going to ask about you—"

"Someday? I'm going to be a part of this," Rafe said.

"I don't see how. You're going to be jetting off to Alma to take the throne. My life is here. The baby's life will be here."

He rubbed the back of his neck. The timing on this sucked. But he didn't blame Emily. He'd been running when he went to Key West, afraid to admit that he was in over his head. He was the oldest son. He was Rafael the Fourth, the future king. He should be in command all the time. But the truth was he was lost.

And somehow in Emily's arms he'd found something.

* * *

Carrying a King's Child
is part of the series Dynasties: The Montoros—
One royal family must choose between
love and destiny!

CARRYING A KING'S CHILD

BY
KATHERINE GARBERA

Published in Great Britain 2015
by Mills & Boon, an imprint of Harlequin (UK) Limited,
Eton House, 18-24 Paradise Road, Richmond, Surrey, TW9 1SR

© 2015 Harlequin Books S.A.

Special thanks and acknowledgment are given to Katherine Garbera for her contribution to the Dynasties: The Montoros miniseries.

ISBN: 978-0-263-25264-4

51-0615

Harlequin (UK) Limited's policy is to use papers that are natural, renewable and recyclable products and made from wood grown in sustainable forests. The logging and manufacturing processes conform to the legal environmental regulations of the country of origin.

Katherine Garbera is a *USA TODAY* bestselling author of more than fifty books and has always believed in happy endings. She lives in England with her husband, children and their pampered pet, Godiva. Visit Katherine on the web at katherinegarbera.com, or catch up with her on Facebook and Twitter.

One

Emily Fielding was shaking as she stepped off the elevator into the foyer of Rafael Montoro IV's penthouse in South Beach. The Montoros had settled in Miami, Florida, decades ago, when as the royal family of Alma, they had to flee their European island homeland because of a coup. Now the dictator who'd replaced them was dead and the parliament of Alma wanted the Montoros back.

With Rafe as king.

Great. Happy ending for everyone. Well, everyone except for Emily, the bartender who was pregnant with the soon-to-be-king's baby. Or at least that was what her gut told her. Her gut and three home pregnancy tests. She wasn't easy to convince.

She had debated not telling Rafe about the baby, but having grown up without knowing who her father was, she just couldn't do that to her own child. Sure, she'd had to lie to get up here to his very posh penthouse apartment, and she knew her timing sucked because Rafe had a lot of royal duties to attend to before his coronation, but she was still here.

Getting past security hadn't been that easy, but she'd made a few calls to friends and found that one of them had a connection to Rafe via a maid service. So she'd used Maria's pass to get into the gated community and her key to get into his building.

Sneaking around wasn't her style. Normally. But nothing about this situation was normal.

She was shaking as she stood on the Italian marble floor and let the air-conditioning dry the sweat at the small of her back. Luxurious and well appointed, the apartment was exactly the sort of place where she expected to find Rafe. His family might have fled Alma in the middle of the night, but they'd brought their dignity and their determination with them to the United States and this generation of Montoros had truly flourished.

Rafe was the CEO of Montoro Enterprises. He had been featured in *Forbes* long before the recent developments in Alma. He'd earned the wealth she saw around him, and the fact that he played as hard as he worked was something she could respect. She played hard, too.

She forced herself not to touch her stomach. Not to draw attention to the one thing that changed everything. Since she'd looked at that stick in the bathroom and realized she was going to have a baby, everything had changed.

Pretending that there was more to her visit than ensuring that her child would know who its father was would be stupid. A wealthy businessman she could have had a shot with, she thought. But not a king.

Still…

She'd seen photos of Alma. With its white sand beaches and castle that looked like something out of a dream, it was a beautiful place. The kind of place that she might have dreamed about as a little girl. A fairy-tale kingdom with a returning prince. Sounded perfect, right?

Except that Rafael Montoro IV was a playboy and they'd had a fling. She wrinkled her nose as she tried to come up with something else to call it, but a two-night stand didn't cover it, either. One weekend spent in each other's arms. She could lose herself in the memories if she wasn't careful.

Hell, she hadn't been careful. Which was precisely why she was here. Pregnant and determined. She walked down the hallway toward the sounds of Jay-Z playing in the distance. She paused in the doorway of his bedroom.

She'd had to charm her way upstairs, but no way could this wait another moment. Rafe needed to know before he left. She needed to tell him.

She felt queasy and swallowed hard.

There were right and wrong ways to deliver this news, and as appealing to her sense of outrage as it would be to throw up on his carpet, she was hoping for a little sophistication. Just a tiny bit.

After all, she'd seen pictures of his sister and jet-setting mother, though his mother wasn't really in the picture since her divorce from Rafe III. Still she was an elegant woman.

She cleared her throat.

She listened to Jay-Z and Kanye West singing about how there's no church in the wild. She almost laughed out loud as she watched Rafe stop packing his suitcase and start to rap along. She leaned against the doorjamb and admitted her anger was really fear. She wasn't mad at him. She just wanted him to be a different kind of guy so that she could have the fairy tale she wanted.

Not a castle and a title, but a man who loved her. A man who wanted to share his life with her and raise children by her side.

And no matter how fun Rafe was, his path lay somewhere else. He was duty-bound to become the constitutional monarch of Alma. She was determined to return to Key West and live out her life. She wasn't interested in being involved with a royal; besides, she'd read in the papers that the heirs would have to marry people with spotless reputations.

He was really getting into dancing around the room and rapping.

She applauded when he finished and he turned to look at her.

"What are you doing here?" he asked, shock apparent on his face.

His body was tense. She suspected he was a tiny bit embarrassed to be caught rapping. Nerves made her mouthy. She knew that. So she should just say she was sorry for using her friend's key to get into his penthouse.

But that wasn't her way.

"Hello to you, too, Your Majesty. Should I curtsy or something? I'm not sure of the rules."

"Neither am I," he admitted. "Juan Carlos doesn't

like it when I am seen doing something…well, so American but also undignified."

"Your secret is safe with me," she said. "Who is Juan Carlos?"

"Juan Carlos Salazar II, my cousin, head of the Montoro Family Trust and advocate of decorum at all times."

"He sounds like a stuffed shirt," she said. "I doubt I'd meet with his approval."

"Emily, what are you doing here? And how did you get up here? Security is usually very hard to get past."

"I have my ways."

"And they are?" he asked.

"My charm," she said.

He shook his head. "I'm going to have to warn them about feisty redheads."

"I actually used a key that I procured from your maid service."

"You've been reduced to criminal behavior. Curiouser and curiouser. Why are you here? Did you decide that you wanted to give me a proper send-off?" he asked. He strode over to her, his big body moving with an economy of motion that captivated her. The same way it had when she'd first glimpsed him in the crowded Key West bar where she worked as a bartender.

He was tall—well over six feet—and muscly, but he moved with grace and she could honestly watch him all day long.

"Why are you here, Red? You said goodbye was forever."

Goodbye.

She'd meant it when he'd left. He was a rich guy from Miami and experience had shown her they were only in Key West for one thing. Having given it to him she'd wanted to ensure she didn't give into temptation a second time.

"I did mean it."

"Help me, Red. I don't want to jump to conclusions," he said.

She chewed her lower lip. Up close she could see the flecks of green in his hazel eyes.

He was easily one of the most attractive men she'd ever seen. He'd make a killing in Hollywood with those thick eyelashes and those cheekbones. It wouldn't matter if he could act, just putting him on screen would draw the masses in.

She wished she were immune.

"I'm pregnant."

He stumbled backward and looked at her as if she'd just started speaking in tongues.

Pregnant!

He stepped back and walked over to the Bose speaker on the dresser to turn off the music. A baby. From what he knew of the tough-as-nails-bartender, he could guess she wouldn't be standing in his penthouse apartment if he wasn't the father. His first reaction was joy.

A child.

It wasn't something he'd ever thought he wanted. He hardly knew Emily so had no idea if she was here for money or something else. But knowing his child was growing inside of her stirred something primal. Something very powerful. The baby was his.

Maybe that was just because it gave him something to think about other than the recent decision that had been made for him.

He'd been dreading his trip to Alma. He was flattered that the country that had once driven his family out had come back to them and asked him to be the next king, but he had grown up here in Florida. He didn't want to be a stuffy royal.

He didn't want European paparazzi following him around and trying to catch him doing anything that would bring shame to his family. God, knew he worked and played hard.

"Rafe?"

"Yeah?"

"Did you hear what I said?" Emily asked.

He had. A baby. Lord knew his father hadn't been the best and as a result, Rafe had thought he'd never have kids. It wasn't as if either of his parents had set a great example. And he was still young, but damn if he wasn't feeling much older every day.

"Yeah, I did. Are you sure?" he asked at last.

She gave him a fiery look from those aqua-blue eyes of hers. He'd seen the passionate side of her nature, and he guessed he was about to witness her temper. "Would I be here if I wasn't?"

He held his hand up.

"Slow down, Red. I didn't mean are you sure it's mine. I meant…are you sure you're pregnant?"

"Damned straight."

"I get it. I had to take three at-home pregnancy tests and visit the doctor before I believed it myself. But trust me, Rafe. I'm positive I'm pregnant and that the baby is yours."

"This is a little surreal," he said.

"I know," she said, with just a hint of softening on in her tone. "Listen, I know you can't turn your back on your family and marry me and frankly, we only had one weekend together so I'd have to say no. But...I don't want this kid to grow up without any knowledge of you."

"Me either."

She glanced up, surprised.

To be honest, he sort of surprised himself. But he knew all the things not to do as a dad thanks to his own father. It didn't seem right for a kid of his to grow up without him. He wanted that. If he had a child, he wanted a chance to share the Montoro legacy...not the one newly sprung on him that came with a throne, but the one he'd carved out for himself in business. "Don't look shocked."

"You've kind of got a lot going on right now. And having a kid with me isn't going to go over well."

"Tough," he said. He still wasn't sure he wanted to be king of Alma. He and his siblings hadn't grown up with the attitude that they were royalty. They were regular American kids who'd never expected to go back to Alma. "I still make my own decisions."

"I know that," she said. She tucked a strand of hair behind her ear. "I've just been so crazy since I realized I was pregnant and alone. I didn't know what to do. You know my mom raised me by herself..."

He closed the gap between them again and pulled her into his arms. He hadn't realized she'd been raised by a single parent. To be honest, a weekend of hot sex didn't really lend itself to sharing each other's past like that. "You're not by yourself."

She looked up at him. That little pointed nose of hers was the tiniest bit red and her lip quivered as if she were struggling to keep from crying. That's when he realized how out of character it was for Emily to be unsure. The baby—his baby—had thrown her for a loop as well.

"Thanks. I just need…I have no idea. I mean, a kid. I never expected this. But we used protection."

"I didn't the third time, remember? I was out and we…"

She blushed and rested her forehead against the middle of his chest, wrapped her arms around his waist and held him. He'd thought he hated being trapped, but in Emily's arms this didn't feel constricting.

"Ugh. My mom was right."

"About what?" he asked. He looked over her head at the man in the mirror and remembered how many times he'd wanted to see some substance reflected back. Was this it? Of course it was. The baby would change things. He had no idea how or why, but he knew this moment was going to be the one that helped forge his future and the man he'd become.

"She said all it takes is a sweet-talking man and one time to get pregnant."

"I'm a sweet-talking man?" He tipped her head up with his finger under her chin.

"You can be."

"What are we going to do?" he asked at last. It was clear she'd run out of steam as soon as she entered the room. Marriage was the noble thing to do. He knew that's what Juan Carlos would suggest, but he and Emily were strangers, and tying their lives together didn't seem smart until they knew each other better.

She pushed away from him and walked over to the window. He knew the view she was afforded. This place had been hard-earned. He'd worked just as his siblings had to make Montoro Enterprises into the success it was today.

"I just wanted you to know. Beyond that I don't need anything. Someday the kid is going to ask about you—"

"Someday? I'm going to be a part of this," Rafe said.

"I don't see how. You're going to be jetting off to Alma to take the throne. My life is here. The baby's life will be here."

He rubbed the back of his neck. The timing on this sucked. But he didn't blame Emily. He'd been running when he went to Key West, afraid to admit that he was in over his head. He'd just gotten word that his family was definitely interested in returning to Alma and as the oldest son he was expected to take the throne.

He was the oldest son. He was Rafael the Fourth. He should have been in command all the time. But the truth was, he was lost.

He wanted his own life. Not one that was dictated by rules and the demands of running a country. If he'd made the decision to return to Alma on his own he might feel differently but right now he felt strong-armed into it.

But somehow in Emily's arms he'd found something.

Emily didn't really feel any better about her next steps, but now that she'd told Rafe her news she could at least start making plans. She didn't know what she expected… Well, the fairy-tale answer was that he'd profess his undying love—hey, their weekend together was pretty spectacular—then sweep her off her feet to his jet, and they'd go to Paris to celebrate their engagement.

But back in the real world, she was staring at him

and wondering if this was the last time she'd be alone with him. It didn't matter what the fantasy was or that she knew how he looked naked. They were still strangers.

Intimate strangers.

"You are looking at me in an odd way," he said.

She struggled with her blunt nature. Saying that she knew what he looked like naked but not how he'd react to their child would reveal too much insecurity. So she searched for something light. Keeping things light was the key to this.

"Well, I never heard you rap along with Jay-Z and Kanye before. Sort of changed my opinion of you."

"I'm a man of many talents," he said.

"I'd already guessed that."

"Did you?"

"Yes."

He walked over to her, all sex on a stick with that slow confident stride of his. His hazel eyes were intense, but then everything about him was. Last time they were together, she'd sensed his need to just forget who he was, but this time was different. This time he seemed to want to show her more of the man he was.

The real man.

"What else have you guessed?" he asked in a silky tone that sent shivers down her spine.

He had a great voice. She knew he had flaws, but as far as the physical, she couldn't find any. Even that tiny scar on the back of his hand didn't detract from his appeal. "That you are used to getting your own way."

"Aw, that's so easy it's almost like cheating."

"Have you figured out that I'm used to getting my own way, too?" she asked. Suddenly she didn't feel as if things were just happening to her. She was in control. Of Rafe, the baby and this entire afternoon. The pregnancy had thrown her. Brought up junk from her childhood she'd thought she'd moved on from, but now she was getting her groove back.

"Oh, I knew that from the moment I entered Shady Harry's and saw you standing behind the bar."

"Did you?" she asked. "I thought it was my Shady Harry's T-shirt that caught your attention."

The spicy scent of his aftershave brought an onslaught of memories of him moving over her. She'd buried her face in his neck. Damn, he'd smelled good. Then and now.

"Well, that and your legs. Red, you've got killer legs."

She looked down at them. Seemed kind of average to her. But she wasn't about to argue with a compliment like that.

"I like your ass," she admitted.

He winked at her, and then turned so that she could see it. He wore a slim-fitting suit that looked tailormade. Given who he was, it probably was.

He was going to be king.

She had no business flirting with him. Or even staying here a moment longer.

"Sorry."

"What?" he asked. "Why? What happened?"

She shrugged. No way was she admitting she was intimidated by his title. But that was the truth. She wasn't in control of that. No matter how much she wanted to be.

"This suit doesn't do anything for me, does it? I asked Gabe if these pants made me look fat but he said no."

She had seen pictures of his entire family in the newspaper and knew that the Gabe he referred to was Gabriel Montoro, his younger brother.

She laughed, as she knew he wanted her to. But inside something had changed. She no longer owned this afternoon. "I should go."

"Why? What happened just now?"

"I remembered that you aren't just a rich guy from Miami who came to Key West for the weekend. That your life isn't your own and I really don't have a place in it."

His expression tightened and he turned away from her. She studied him as he paced over to his bed and looked down at the expensive leather suitcase lying there. She'd interrupted his packing. He probably didn't really have time for her this afternoon.

"You said you never knew your father." With an almost aristocratic expression, he glanced over his shoulder at her. She had the feeling she was seeing the man who would be king. And she had to admit he made her a little bit nervous. Maybe it was simply the fact that she knew he was going to be a king now. But it seemed as if he was different. More regal in his bearing than he had been during their weekend together.

"Yes. I don't see what that has to do with anything."

"I did know my father and my grandfather and great-grandfather. From my birth I was named to follow in their footsteps. I've never deviated from that expectation, and to be honest, I took a certain pride in carrying on our family name and trying to set an example for my brother and sister."

"I'm getting a poor little rich boy feeling here. You have been given a lot of opportunities in your lifetime and now you have the chance to lead a nation," she said, but inside she sort of understood what he was getting at. His entire life had been scripted since birth. She understood from what she'd read in the newspapers that the Montoros may have left Alma in the middle of the night, but they hadn't left their pride behind.

"All my life I've done what is expected of me. I haven't shirked a single duty. I'm the CEO of Montoro Enterprises and now I will be king of Alma, but for this one afternoon, Red, can I be Rafe? Not a man with his future planned but your lover? Father of your baby?" he asked.

He came back over and dropped to his knees in front of her, wrapping his arms around her hips. Then he drew her closer to him and kissed her belly. "I want you to be able to speak to our baby about me with joy instead of regret."

She looked down at him as he rested his head against her body. Tunneling her fingers into his thick black hair, she understood that from this point on, when she left this penthouse they couldn't be this couple again.

She sighed, and the woman she'd always been, the one who lived by the motto Never Say Never, took over. Rafe and she might not have more than this time together. And she wanted this one last time with him.

She hadn't expected to be a mom this soon. She had made all these plans for her life and then when she'd taken those pregnancy tests it had all gone out the window.

But for this moment she could forget about tomorrow. She hoped this would be enough, but feared one more afternoon in his arms would never be enough to satisfy her.

Two

Rafe pushed aside all of his thoughts and just focused on Emily. It was amazing that she'd come to find him. She was strong enough, independent enough to keep the baby from him if she'd wanted. It embarrassed him a little, humbled him, too, that he would never have known about the baby if she hadn't shown up.

He'd been focusing on the royal legacy and managing everyone's expectations. Especially people he didn't even know and hadn't cared existed until last month. Funny how he'd gone from worrying about financial targets and managing a multinational company to worrying about a little thing like protocol.

But as long as Emily was here he could forget all that. Concentrate on being the man and not the king.

He held her tightly as he stood up, lifting her off her feet and letting her slide back down his body. She was curvy and light, his woman, and he wanted to be just her man. He carried her to the big brass bed and stood next to it, just waiting for a signal from her.

She owed him nothing.

She sighed and then lowered her head and brushed her lips over his, and something tight and frozen inside him started to melt. She kissed him not like the bold bartender she was when they'd met, but like a woman who wanted to relish her time with her lover.

They both knew without saying it that this was the last time they'd be together like this. Maybe if they'd met two years from now after he'd been on the throne and had time to figure out what being king meant, their path would have been different. But they hadn't.

They had this afternoon and nothing more.

He wanted these memories of the two of them to keep for himself as he moved into a life that was no longer his own.

He pushed his hands into her thick red hair, cradling her head as he took control of the kiss. He thrust his tongue deep into her mouth, tasted peppermint and woman. Her arms slipped lower and she stroked her hand down his back as he deepened the kiss.

Though he knew this long, wet kiss was just the beginning, he wanted to savor it. Dueling desires warred inside him as he wanted to make every touch last as long as possible. The intensity of his lust for her was almost unbearable; he needed to be hilt-deep inside her right now.

He lifted his head, rubbed his thumb along the column of her neck. Her pulse was racing and her eyes were half closed. Her creamy skin was dotted with freckles and the faint flush of desire.

He dropped nibbling kisses down her neck. She smelled of orange blossoms and sea breeze. She was like the wildest parts of Florida, and he felt as if he could hold her for only a fleeing moment and then she'd be gone. Tearing through his life like a hurricane.

He slid his hands down her back, tightening them around her waist, and lifted her off her feet again. She wrapped her legs around his waist and put her hands on his shoulders. Then she looked down into his eyes with that bright southern-Atlantic-blue gaze of hers. He felt lost. As if he were drowning in her eyes.

She nipped at his lower lip and then sucked it into her mouth and he hardened. He was going to explode if he didn't get his damned tailored pants off and bury himself in her body.

He reached for his fly but she shifted on him, rubbing her center over his erection. He shook, and the strength left his legs as he stumbled and fell back on the bed. She laughed and then thrust her tongue into his mouth again. And he gave up thinking.

She was like the wildest hurricane and all he could do was ride this storm out. She moved over him and made him remember what it felt like to be alive. The same way she had four weeks ago in Key West. She made the rest of the world pale, and everything narrowed to the two of them.

The heat flared between them and his clothes felt too constricting. He needed to be naked. Wanted her naked. Then she could climb back on his lap. He tore his mouth from hers, his breath heavy as he drew her T-shirt up and over her head and tossed it aside.

She wore the same beige lace bra she'd had on the last time they'd had sex. He traced his finger over the seam where the fabric met skin, saw the goose bumps spread from her breast over her chest and down her arms. Her nipple tightened and he leaned forward to rub his lips over it as he reached behind her back and undid the bra.

The cups loosened, but he didn't lift his head from her nipple. He continued teasing her with light brushes of his tongue over it until she reached between them and undid his tie, leaving it dangling around his neck as she went to work on his shirt buttons.

He shifted back, taking the edge of her bra between his teeth and pulling it away. She laughed, a deep, husky sound he remembered so well. And he got even harder. He had thought there was no way he could want her more, but he'd been wrong.

She pushed the fabric of his shirt open and peeled it down his arms, but she hadn't undone his cuffs so his own shirt bound him. His hands were trapped.

"Undo my hands."

"Not yet, Rafe. Right now, I'm in charge," she said. She scraped her fingernail down the side of his jaw to his neck and then over his pectorals. He sat there craving more of her touch, but damned if he was going to ask her for it. Control and power were two things he always maintained. But with Emily it was as if they'd flown out the window.

She took what she wanted, and though he'd never admit it out loud, he didn't want to stop her. It felt good to just let go.

Flexing her fingers, she dug her nails into his chest and then shifted forward so that the long strands of her hair brushed against him. He shuddered with need, turning his head to try to catch her mouth with his, but she just laughed again and shifted back on his thighs, looking down at him with those eyes that were full of mysteries he knew he'd never really understand.

She drew one finger down the center of his chest, following the path of the light dusting of hair. She swirled her finger around his belly button in tiny circles that made everything inside him contract.

She stroked his erection through the fabric of his pants, and he canted his hips.

She rocked against him and smiled when he moaned her name. Wrapping her arms around his shoulders, she caught the lobe of his ear between her teeth and bit it lightly before whispering all the things she was going to do him. He felt his control slipping with each thrust of her tongue as she flicked it into his ear and then shifted backward on his thighs to reach between them, stroking his length through his pants again.

Cursing, he tried to reach for her but his bound arms wouldn't let him. She rotated her shoulders and rubbed her nipples against his chest. She closed her eyes as she undulated against him, and this time he pulled his arms forward with all of his strength and heard the tear of fabric. She opened her eyes and then started laughing.

He grabbed her waist and rolled to his side, pulling her with him. He rolled over top of her, carefully keeping his weight on his elbows and knees so she wasn't crushed under him. He took both of her hands in his and stretched them high over her head and then rubbed his chest over hers and heard her moan.

Damn, she felt good. Better than he'd remembered her feeling, and that said a lot because he still had erotic dreams of their weekend together.

He lowered his head and sucked her nipple into his

mouth, holding both of her wrists above her head with
one of his hands. He reached lower between their bodies and undid her jeans, pushing them down so that he
could cup her in his hand. He rubbed her mound, and
then traced the seam of her panties. Her legs scissored
underneath his and he shifted until he lay between
them. He let go of her wrists as he slowly kissed his
way down her body.

She was covered in freckles; up close he could see
that they were all different sizes. He flicked his tongue
over each of them as he moved lower and lower until
he found her belly button ring. The small loop had a
starfish dangling from it. He tongued it and traced the
circumference of her belly button.

He moved lower, catching the top of her bikini panties with the tip of his finger and drawing them slowly
down. She shifted her hips and he pushed her jeans
and panties down to her knees. She kicked them the
rest of the way off.

He traced the pattern of freckles from her thigh
to her knee, circling her kneecap and the small scar
there before caressing his way back up the inside of
her thighs. He felt the humid warmth of her body and
traced her feminine core with his fingertip. She shifted
on the bed, her hands reaching for him, but it was his
turn to tease her. Plus if she touched him, he feared
his control would splinter into a million pieces and this
would be over too quickly.

He parted her folds and then leaned down to taste
her. He closed his eyes as he sucked her intimate flesh,
causing her to draw her legs closer around him and her
hands to fall to the back of his head. She gripped his

hair as her hips lifted upward toward his mouth and his tongue.

She was addicting. He couldn't get enough of her. He pushed one finger into her body and heard her call his name. She was wet and ready for him. He fumbled, trying to free himself from his trousers. He lifted his head, looked up at her and saw that she was watching him. Her eyes were filled with passion and desire.

He stood up, shoved his pants and underwear off in a move that definitely couldn't be called graceful, and then he lowered himself on top of her. He slowly used his chest and body to caress hers as he moved over her. She shifted her legs so that her thighs were on either side of his and he moved his hips forward, felt the tip of his erection at the opening of her body. He hesitated. This time was different from their weekend in Key West, but the passion in her eyes was the same.

Slowly he entered her, trying to make it last because she felt so damned good. She gripped his rock-hard flesh as he entered her and drove himself all the way home and then forced himself to stay still once he was fully seated in her body.

Her hands were on his shoulders, running up and down his back and then reaching lower to cup his butt and try to get him to move. But he needed a moment before he did that. A moment to make sure that she was with him. He lowered his head to her neck, and then bit her lightly before moving lower, kissing the full globes of her breasts.

She tightened as she arched underneath him. She looked up at him and whispered dark, sexual words that made his control disappear along with his willpower, and he found himself thrusting deeper into her body. Driving toward his climax and carrying her along with him.

He pushed her legs higher, putting her feet on his shoulders so he could go deeper, and pounded into her faster and faster until he heard her calling out his name and he spilled himself inside her. He thrust into her three more times before he let go of her legs and fell forward, bracing himself on his arms. He kissed the pert pink nipple on her left breast as he rested his head on her shoulder and tried to catch his breath.

He got up and left her for a few moments to wash up and then came back and lay down next to her on the bed. He was aware of the time and knew he should already be at the private airport and getting on his family's jet so he could travel with them to Alma, but he couldn't make himself leave.

He knew that this wasn't love. He wasn't going to lie to her or himself. But she was pregnant with his child and this fired him with an enthusiasm he just couldn't muster when he thought of being king. He didn't want the throne, but his father, who couldn't inherit it because he'd never had his marriage annulled after divorcing Rafe's mother, had been very clear that he thought Rafe needed to do his duty.

He stroked his hand down Emily's arm. She had turned on her side and had her head on his shoulder.

"What are you thinking?"

"That I'm glad you came here today. Did you ever think of not telling me?" he asked.

He suspected he knew the answer, but wanted to hear it from her.

"No. It wasn't easy to track you down—you're pretty secretive about this penthouse bachelor pad, aren't you?

But Harry has lots of friends who have connections. It only took him six hours to find you."

"Harry scares me," Rafe admitted. The owner of Shady Harry's bar had been fun and gregarious when Rafe had been partying and buying rounds for the entire place. But the next morning when he'd spotted the older man as he'd left Emily's cottage, Harry had given him a look that said to watch his back. "What's he to you?"

"He and my mom dated for a while," Emily said. "He's sort of like my stepdad. Why?"

"I have a feeling if I show up in Key West he's going to be waiting with a shotgun."

"You're not going to Key West, you're going to Alma. I've seen pictures. It's really beautiful," she said.

Not as beautiful as she was, Rafe thought. He leaned up on his elbow, put his hand flat on her stomach and realized he couldn't control this any more than he could say no to the people in Alma who'd asked his family to come back and rule the country.

"It is. They've had a rough time since the revolution and I guess…I have to go," he said.

"I know. I told you I wasn't here to ask you to stay. I just needed you to know."

"Why?"

"I didn't know my dad. My mom has never mentioned his name to me. I asked her one time about him and she started crying. I want more than that for our baby. It's not that I had a deprived childhood, but I always wonder. I have this emptiness inside me that nothing can fill. It's that empty spot where everyone else has a dad."

He was humbled by her explanation. He knew he wanted to be more than a name and a face to their kid, though. "We need to figure this out."

There was a knock on the bedroom door.

"Rafael? Are you in here? Your father is in a car waiting downstairs and if you're not down in ten minutes he's coming up here and getting you." It was his personal assistant, Jose.

Jose was his right-hand man at Montoro Enterprises and at home. He took care of all the details.

"I have company," Rafe said. But Emily was more than just company. She was his lover. The mother of his unborn child.

"I am aware of that," Jose said.

"Tell Father I'll be down when I'm down," Rafe said.

But the mood was broken and Emily was getting up and putting her clothes on. She had her jeans on and buttoned, but he stopped her before she put her T-shirt on. He pulled her into his arms. It seemed the sort of gesture that would reassure her, but since he was already thinking of everything he had to do, it felt hollow. He knew she noticed it, too, when she pulled back and shook her head.

The mantle of being a Montoro was tightening around him. "I—"

"Don't. No excuses and definitely no lies," she said. She reached into her back pocket and pulled out a business card for Shady Harry's; he turned it over and saw she'd written her name and number on the back. "If you want to know about our child, contact me."

"I do. I will," he said.

She smiled up at him. "I know that the next few weeks are going to be crazy for you, so no pressure."

She pulled her shirt on and then tucked her underwear into her purse and started for the door. He watched her walk out. Part of him wanted to run after her and make her stay so he could talk her into trying a relationship or maybe even marriage. Another part wanted to scoop her up and run away with her to some Pacific island where no one would know their names, far enough away from his family and everyone they knew.

But Emily was a brave sort of woman, and running had never been his style, either, so he had no choice but to get dressed and head down to the car.

His father didn't speak to him the entire way to the airport. Rafael III had wanted the throne enough to try to convince his ex-wife to come back, but Rafe's mother wasn't interested in doing anything to help out her former husband. To say the two of them had a strained relationship was putting it mildly.

They were a prime example of how getting married to the wrong person didn't make for a happy family. Rafe had the childhood to prove it.

During the ride, his cousin Juan Carlos spoke too much. Telling him what was expected of the next king of Alma.

Juan Carlos had been orphaned and seemed to be fixated on the monarchy as a way of proving to himself and the rest of the family that he could carry on his parents' legacy. Perhaps if Rafe's parents hadn't divorced and been horrible to each other, he'd have felt the same way about the family honor.

Rafe freely admitted to himself that if Emily's preg-

Three

Key West was a tourist town and there was no getting around that. The atmosphere was laid back and everyone had a sort of hungover look. There was something about being on the edge of the ocean that inspired indulgence in sun, sand and drinks.

Emily sat on the front porch of her flamingo-pink and white cottage with her feet propped on the railing, desperately needing to absorb that laid-back attitude. She'd left Miami and Rafe behind. She'd done what she'd set out to do, namely tell him he was going to be a father. That had gone well—differently than she'd expected, but the end result was the same. She was back here.

Alone.

"Em. Your mom asked me stop by," Harry said as he walked around the side of the house.

He was tall, at least six five, and wore middle age well. His reddish-blond hair had thinned a little but was still thick enough, and he wore it cut short in a military style. His beard was equal parts red, blond and gray, and he had an easy smile. He was the closest thing she had to a dad. So she was glad to see him.

"Why?" Emily asked. Though she knew why her mom had sent Harry. If anyone could make her forget her troubles it was the jovial bar owner.

"She thought you might need some company. She's on her way back to port but won't be here until tonight."

Emily sighed. "I don't really want any company."

"Figured you might say that, so I brought you a cup of decaf and a blueberry bagel. We can both sit here and eat and pretend we're alone."

Decaf.

Seemed like a little thing, but she always drank full-on caffeine. Now she knew that her mom had spilled the beans about her being preggers. Harry handed her a bakery bag from Key Koffee with the bagel and the coffee.

"You know?"

"I know. It was that slick guy from South Beach, right?"

She tipped her head back and closed her eyes. "He's not that slick."

Harry laughed. "They never are. Talk to me, kiddo. Do I need to take my .45 and head to Miami?"

She opened her eyes and lifted her head. "You would have made a really good dad," she said, smiling at him.

"I think I have been to you," he reminded her.

"You have. But no to the .45. Besides, you'd have to fly to Europe to find him."

Harry took a bite out of his everything bagel and settled down on the top step, turning sideways with his back against the railing to face her.

"Europe? He seemed American to me," Harry said.

"He's Rafael Montoro IV. Part of…I'm not sure what to call him. But his family was royalty in a tiny Mediterranean country called Alma. They were kicked out decades ago but now they want them back. He's the oldest son and heir apparent to the newly restored monarchy."

"Complicates things, doesn't it?" Harry said.

"You have no idea," she said. "But I didn't expect him to do anything when I gave him the news. You know?"

Harry took a sip of his coffee and then gave her one of those wise looks of his that she hated. He knew when she was lying, especially to herself.

"Okay, fine, I wanted him to be, like, we'll do this together. Instead, I got…he was sweet but clearly torn. He can't let his family down. And he and I only had one weekend together, Harry."

"Sometimes that's all it takes," he said.

"It wasn't enough for the guy who fathered me," she said. "Please don't tell Mom I said that. But really, that complicates everything. I've always thought I was okay with the fact that I don't know who he was, but this baby…" She put her hands on her stomach. "It's making me realize I'm not."

Harry didn't say anything. And after a few minutes Emily looked away from him and back to the foot traffic on the street near her house. What could he say? He was her substitute dad who'd stepped up when he didn't have to. Harry must have thought that she was making a mess where there didn't need to be one.

"I get it, kiddo. It's hard to not want the best for your baby. We all do that," he said. "Try to fix the problems in our past so that our kids don't have to experience them."

"Did you do that for Rita and Danny?" she asked. Harry had two kids who were both more than fifteen years older than her and lived in Chicago. They came down for two weeks each spring to visit Harry.

"I tried. But I ended up making my own mistakes and they have done the same. It's all a part of being human," he said.

"I'm getting Zen Harry this morning," she said. But his positive attitude helped take her mind off Rafe and the sadness she'd been feeling.

It wasn't that she'd expected anything else from him, but that she'd wanted something more. She shook her head as she realized that what she'd wanted was to be wanted.

For him to want to stay with her.

It was unrealistic, but a girl could dream.

"Well, I do have all this wonderful advice and no one to share it with," Harry said with a wink. "You'll be okay, kiddo. You'll make decisions and choices and some of them are going to be fabulous and others you're going to regret. But I do know one thing."

"What's that?" she asked.

"You're going to love that baby of yours, and in the end that's all that really matters."

"You think so?"

"I do. Your own mom did that for you. Look how you turned out," he said.

"Not bad," she admitted. She liked her life. She could have followed her mom into a similar career—

she was a marine biologist—but Emily liked being on the land and not out at sea. She had a degree in hotel and restaurant management and one day hoped to open her own place. She knew she had a good life, but a part of her still missed Rafe.

Another part of her knew she just missed the idea of Rafe. So far every time they'd been together they'd ended up in bed. It wasn't as if he was even a friend.

She wanted that picture-perfect family that she kept in her head. She wanted that for this baby she was carrying. She didn't want her child to have the piecemeal family that she did. No matter that she loved her mom and Harry fiercely. For her child she wanted more.

And being the bastard of a European king probably wasn't what her child would want. She was going to have to be very protective. Raise the baby to know its own strength and place in the world.

She noticed Harry watching her, realized she wasn't alone and that made the loneliness she felt when she thought of Rafe a little less painful.

Alma was breathtakingly beautiful. The island was surrounded by sparkling blue seas and old world charm seemed to imbue every building. They'd landed at a private air field and were driving to the royal palace in the urban capital of Del Sol.

Rafe had heard there was a lively nightclub scene and before Emily's visit had sort of thought of checking it out. But now that he had the dual mantle of monarchy and fatherhood hanging over him, he figured he should rethink that.

Del Sol was even more striking than the black and white photos he'd seen in the albums his *tia* Isabella kept. While there were modern buildings dotted throughout the city many of the old buildings remained. Tia Isabella had been a young woman when she'd been forced to flee Alma with the rest of their family. When Rafe and his siblings and cousin had been growing up they'd been entertained by her stories. Tia Isabella had spent a lot of time talking about the old days and what it had been like to grow up on Alma. But Rafe thought he understood why his grandfather hadn't talked that much about it. Rafe would have been sad to leave this homeland, too.

As the royal motorcade made its way into Del Sol, Alma's capital, people on the streets craned their necks to get a glimpse of the Montoros. Rafe was used to a certain level of fame and notoriety in Miami, but not this. There he was one of the jet-set Montoros. The young generation who worked hard and played harder.

Here he was the future monarch. He'd be the face of Alma to the world. And while his ego was sort of jazzed about that, another part of him wasn't.

"Maybe you should put the window down and do that princess wave," his sister Bella said with a sparkle in her blue eyes. Their father and the rest of their party were in a separate vehicle.

"Princess wave? That's more your cup of tea," he said. "Maybe I'll throw up the peace sign."

She giggled. He'd always been close to his little sister, and making her laugh helped him to relax.

Bella looked like a fairy-tale princess with her pretty blond hair. Not anything like Emily. He wondered what Emily would think of Alma. It was an island not that unlike her hometown of Key West, but the laid-back attitude in the Keys was a world away from this charming European nation.

For a country that had been ruled by a dictator for decades, the people in the streets seemed happy and prosperous and the buildings were clean and well-maintained. Rafe didn't see any signs of financial ruin. But economic danger lurked whenever there was a change of regime. And if there was one thing he was good at, it was making money.

But would the government here listen to him?

To be honest he wasn't the kind of person to negotiate for what he wanted. That was one of the reasons Montoro Enterprises had thrived under his leadership. He made bold decisions. Sometimes they didn't pay off, but most of the time they did.

"You okay?" Bella asked.

He started to shrug it off. There was no way he was going to mention Emily or the fact that she was pregnant to his sister. Not until he had a chance to figure it out for himself. But the family stuff was also getting to him, especially how Juan Carlos was going really crazy about protocol and proper image and all that.

"This return to Alma is throwing me," he admitted to her.

"How?" she asked. "You've always handled whatever the family has dished out. This will be no different. Pretend you're the CEO of the country."

As if. Being the king was a "name only" position. No power. Maybe that was why he hesitated to fully embrace it. He was a man of action. Not a figurehead.

"Good suggestion," he said, glancing out the window as they approached the castle. Surrounded by glittering blue water on three sides, it rose from the land like a sand castle at the beach. He groaned.

"What?"

"I was hoping the castle would be in disrepair."

"Why?"

"So I could hate it."

Bella laughed again. "I love it. It's everything I thought it would be," she said.

"What if there's not a hopping club scene? Will you still love it then?" he asked. Bella liked to party. Hell, they all did. They hadn't been raised to assume the throne. They were all more likely to show up in the tabloids in a compromising position than on the society pages at a formal tea. The closer he got to the throne the less sure he was that he wanted to be there.

He felt Bella's hand on his shoulder. "You're going to be fine. I think you'll make a great king."

"Why? I'm not sure at all."

"You've been a great big brother and always ensured our family's place in business and in society."

"Business is easy. I understand that world," Rafe countered.

"I never thought the day would come when you'd admit that you aren't sure of yourself," she said, taking her phone from her handbag.

"What are you doing?"

"Texting Gabe that you have feet of clay."

"He already knows that."

"We all do," Bella said. "Why are you acting like you are just figuring it out?"

"I'm going to be a king, Bella. It's making me nutty," he said.

"You weren't as thrown by it a week ago," she said.

"What happened yesterday to make you delay your flight?"

Nothing.

Everything.

Something that could change the man he was. If he let it.

"Business. Running Montoro Enterprises does take a lot of time," he said.

The car pulled to a stop and an attendant in full livery came to open the door for them. Bella climbed out first but looked back at Rafe.

"Lying to me is one thing. You can keep your secrets if you want to," she said. "But I hope you aren't lying to yourself."

He followed her out of the car, and the warm Mediterranean air swept around him. She had a point. He knew in his gut that this didn't feel right. He should be in Miami with Emily. He missed her.

The porte-cochere led to an inner brick-lined courtyard. There was a fountain underneath a statue of Rafe's great-grandfather Rafael I. He was surprised it hadn't been torn down when the dictator had taken over. Bella stopped walking and spun around on her heel, taking in the beauty of the palace.

For the first time he felt a sense of his royal lineage settling over him. If their family hadn't been forced to flee he would have grown up in this palace. His memories would be of this place that smelled wonderfully of jasmine and lavender. Where was the scent coming from?

His father came up beside him and put his hand on his shoulder not saying a word. Something passed between them. An emotion that Rafe didn't want to define. But Alma became real to him. In a way that it hadn't been before. In Miami it had been easy to say he wasn't sure if he wanted to be king but seeing this palace—he felt the history. And he sort of understood Juan Carlos's perspective for once. Rafe didn't want to let down their family line.

If Alma wanted the Montoros back on the throne than Rafe would have to put aside the feelings he felt stirring for Emily and figure out how to be their king.

That surprised him. He hadn't expected to feel this torn. He was isolated from the rest of his family who seemed to think this return to royalty was just the thing they needed. They were all caught up in being back in the homeland. But as much as he felt swept up in the majesty of their return to Alma he knew he was still trying to figure out where home really was.

Emily worked the closing shift at Harry's and walked home at 2:00 a.m. Key West wasn't like the mean streets of Miami, but she moved quickly and kept her eyes open for danger. It was something she'd teach her kid.

She was starting to find her bearings with this pregnancy more and more as each day passed. Being a mom was going to take some getting used to, but as her own mom had said, she had nine months to make the adjustment.

Her cell phone vibrated in the pocket of her jeans and she reached back to pull it out. Glancing at the screen, she saw it was an international call. She only knew one person who was traveling internationally right now. She did some quick math and figured out that it was early morning in Alma.

"Hello?"

"Hey, Red. Figured you'd be getting off work. Please tell me I didn't wake you." Sure enough, it was Rafe.

"You'd think you'd be more careful about disturbing a pregnant woman's rest," she teased. She didn't want to admit it but she'd missed him. Three days. That was all it had been since she'd seen him, but it had felt like a lifetime. His voice was deep and resonated in her ear, making her feel warm all over.

"Well, maybe I did call the bar earlier to determine if you were working tonight," he admitted.

That sounded like Rafe. He was a man who left little to chance. "What can I do for you?"

"How are you feeling?" he asked. "How's Florida?"

"I'm feeling fine," she said. "I have had a little bit of morning sickness, and it's not just limited to mornings. I've been getting sick midafternoon."

She saw her house at the end of the lane and got her keys out. She'd left the porch lights on and it looked so welcoming. The only thing that would be better was if Rafe was waiting for her. And to be honest, as he talked to her on the phone, it was almost as if he was there with her.

"Makes sense since that's when you wake up," he said. "Is there anything you can do to help that?"

"No," she said. "It's not too bad. How's Alma?"

"Nice. You'd like it. It's all sand and sea for as far as the eye can see and quaint little villages. Not as laid back as Key West but still nice."

"Any places to go paddleboarding?"

"Not yet. Why, do you think you'd move here and start a business?" he asked.

It was the closest he'd come to suggesting that she

be near him in the future, and she felt numb even contemplating it. She had her own plans to open a restaurant around the corner from Harry's. Not to be Rafe's hidden mistress in some far-off European country.

"Not at all. I've got a place picked out for my future restaurant," she said.

"Is that what you want to do?"

Once again she realized how little they actually knew of each other's lives.

"Well, I can't be a bartender forever."

"I guess not. Tell me about your dreams," he said.

She thought she heard the sound of footsteps on a tiled floor on his end. "Where are you?"

"Not ready to share that much with me?" he asked, countering her evasion.

In a way she wished they were playing a game. It would make everything easier. She could concentrate on winning and not really have to think about the emotions. But the truth was she was tired and still a little unsure of what she was doing. Sure, just hearing Rafe's voice made her feel not so alone. But she didn't want to allow herself to become dependent on him.

Not to turn her life into one big sob story, but usually when she started to feel comfortable with someone they left. It wasn't that they abandoned her, just moved on and left her to her independent self. Even her mom and Harry. And she didn't want that with Rafe.

"Nope. I want to hear about Alma. I read a little online yesterday. Seems like the change of regime is going to have a big impact on the economy. I know you are good at making money. Is that why they chose you and your family to come back and lead the country?" she asked.

"Our family ruled the country before the coup that installed the late dictator, Tantaberra. That's why we were chosen. But my parents are divorced so Dad, who would be next in line, can't assume the throne. They want someone with the right pedigree and the right reputation."

"Um…I'm guessing if they found out about me that could put a wrench in things."

"Possibly. I'm not going to deny you exist, Emily."

"Really?"

"Yes. Would I be on the phone with you if I didn't care?" he asked.

"I don't know," she said honestly. "We're strangers."

"Who are about to be parents to a baby," he said. "Let's get to know each other. And while we have half the world between us maybe I can talk to you without being distracted by your body and that sexy way you tilt your head to the side. You always make me forget everything except wanting to get you naked."

Her breath caught as she sank down into the big armchair where Rafe had sat the one time he'd been to her place. They'd made love in the chair and she felt closer to him now. She tucked her leg up underneath her and let those memories wash over her.

"Red? You still there?"

"Yes. Dammit, now you've got me thinking about you naked."

"Good. My evil plan worked," he said. "Tell me something about yourself."

"What?"

"Anything. I want to know the woman who's going to be the mother of my child."

She thought about her life. It was ordinary: nothing

too tragic, nothing too exciting. But it was hers. "When I was six I thought if I spent enough time in the ocean I'd turn into a mermaid. My mom's a marine biologist and we were living on her research vessel, *The Sea Spirit*. She made me a bikini top out of shells and sent me off every day to swim."

"I'm glad you didn't turn into a mermaid," he said with a quiet laugh.

They talked on the phone until Emily started drifting to sleep. She knew she should hang up, but she didn't want to break the connection. Didn't want to wake up without Rafe.

"Red?"

"Yes?"

"I wish I was there to tuck you into bed," he said.

"Me, too," she admitted. Then she opened her eyes as she realized that she was starting to need him.

"Good night, Rafe," she said, hanging up the phone before she could do anything stupid like ask him what he'd wanted to be as a boy. Or to come back to Key West.

Four

Rafe secluded himself from the rest of the family in the office area of the suite of rooms he'd been given. The deal he'd struck for Montoro Enterprises to ship Alma's oil was taking a lot of his time.

Alma was a major oil producing country to the north of Spain. Montoro Enterprises would be shipping the oil to its customers in North and South America where the bulk of their business interests were. It made good business sense but he also wanted it because he'd get a chance to explore the country of his ancestors. When he'd first done the deal he'd anticipated his father becoming King not himself.

Plus truth be told, he'd been so focused on work because he was avoiding his family and the coterie of diplomats who seemed to be lurking whenever he stepped out of his suite. He didn't want to talk about his coronation or about the business of running the government. Yet.

But sitting around and hiding out went against the grain, so he'd been working nonstop. He hadn't shaved in the three days, and Mozart had replaced Jay-Z and Kanye on the stereo because no one would ever be tempted to stop working and rap to Mozart. He hadn't even contacted Emily, though he'd thought of her night and day.

She was an obsession. He knew that. He had the feeling that if he were in Miami maybe it wouldn't be as fierce, but he was far away from her and thinking of her was nice and comforting in the midst of this storm that was brewing around him.

He banged his head on the desk.

"I can see I'm interrupting," Gabe said as he entered without knocking.

"I'm working."

"Yeah, I noticed," Gabe said, nodding toward the empty cans of Red Bull that littered the desk and the floor. He walked to the window and pulled back the drapes.

Rafe blinked against the glare of the sunlight. "What time is it?"

"Four in the afternoon. You're expected for dinner tonight and if you don't show up Juan Carlos is going to have a stroke. I know he's been a pain lately with all this royal protocol, but we don't want our cousin to have a stroke, do we?"

Rafe shook his head. "No." He scrubbed his hands over his face. His eyes felt gritty and the stubble on his jaw felt rough. He was a mess. Truly. "This sucks."

Gabe laughed that wicked, low laugh that Rafe had

heard women found irresistible. He just found it annoying.

"Yeah, it does. Not so cool being the older brother now, is it?"

Not at all. "I should walk away…that would leave you holding the bag."

A fleeting glimpse of panic ran across his brother's face. "Dad would disown you. I'm pretty sure the board would fire you from Montoro Enterprises. Then what would you do?"

Run away to Key West.

Seemed simple enough, but to be fair he wasn't sure what type of reception he'd receive if he just showed up on Emily's doorstep.

"I think I'm too American to want to be a royal, you know? Maybe Dad still wants it, but it feels weird to me. I don't want to be called 'Your Majesty' or 'Your Highness.'"

Rafe watched his younger brother. If there were the slightest sign that Gabe was interested in being king, Rafe would just walk away and let his brother have it. But Gabe rubbed the back of his neck as he paced over to the window. "Me neither."

"Then I guess I'd better stop acting like a jerk and get out there," Rafe said. "What's the plan?"

"Dinner with some supporters. And a family who'd love for you to meet their daughter," Gabe said with a wry smile.

Rafe shook his head. He'd do his duty to his family, but he was already involved with a redhead who wouldn't take kindly to him catting around. He was getting to know her, starting a relationship with the woman who was going to be the mother of his child.

What if she didn't feel possessive toward him the way he did toward her? And he did feel possessive. Emily was his. "I'm not interested."

"Are you interested in someone else?"

"It's complicated, Gabe."

"I never thought I'd see the day when you said that. Is she special?"

"She could be," Rafe said. Or at least that was what his gut was saying. The rest of him wasn't too sure.

Once his brother left and Rafe had wrapped up what he was working on for the day, he started getting ready for the state dinner. When he got out of the shower, he saw that he had a text message from Emily.

It's official. Just got word back from the doctor's office. I'm due in January.

Would he be able to get back to the States in January?

Being with Emily would mean giving up the monarchy... and possibly his job, depending on how much it pissed off his family. Montoro Enterprises and Alma were now all linked together. Could he walk away from one without walking away from them all?

But what kind of man walked away from his own child?

Not one that Rafe wanted to be. He knew that but as he'd said to Gabe earlier, it was complicated.

He braced his hands on the bathroom counter and looked into his own hazel eyes searching for answers or a solution. But there was nothing there.

And that really pissed him off. He needed to take control of his personal life the way he did the boardroom. No more doing what everyone else wanted unless it fit with his own inner moral compass.

Except that he'd been a playboy for so long he wasn't too sure he had one. Everyone had one, right? Then shouldn't the answer be clearer than this?

When he was finished shaving, he took the towel off his hips and tossed it at his image in the mirror before he walked into the bedroom to dress.

He hit the remote for his sound system and switched from Mozart to "The Man" by Aloe Blacc . He stopped in his tracks. Right now it seemed as if everyone had a piece of him and the man Rafe had always wanted to be had been lost.

He knew what he had to do. No use pretending he was going to do anything else. It wasn't that he thought the path would be easy, but then when had he ever taken the easy path? It was simply that spending time with his siblings made him realize that family was important to him.

His mind made up, he grabbed his phone and began typing, hitting Send before he could have second thoughts.

I'll be there. When is your next appointment? I'd like to go with you if I can.

He owed it to himself and to his child to at least see if he could be a real partner to Emily. And be a real part of the baby's life.

Really? Okay. If you do this then I don't want you making promises you can't keep.

That right there showed him how little she knew of him. Hell, what did he know about her? He knew how she looked in his arms. He knew that she had wanted to be a mermaid when she was little. He smiled at that one. He knew she was having his baby.

I'm a man of my word, Red. I'll be there.

Two days later Emily woke up to a beautiful sunny morning. Since it was her day off, she decided to take her paddleboard and head to a quiet cove on Geiger Key where there weren't many tourists. She'd been too much in her head since she'd found out she was pregnant and needed to forget for a few hours.

After she'd had her daily bout of morning sickness, she took the prenatal vitamins the doctor had prescribed and then got dressed in her usual bikini. She stood in front of the full-length mirror mounted on the back of her walk-in closet door and looked at her body. No signs of her pregnancy were visible. In fact, she looked a little bit thinner than she had before. Her boobs were getting a little larger, though.

She'd always sort of been…well, smallish, but now she was actually filling out the top. Not bad, she thought. She patted her stomach and shook her head. She definitely needed today for herself.

Someone knocked on her front door. She grabbed her board shorts, putting them as she went to answer it.

There was a man in a suit waiting there.

"Hello, Ms. Fielding. I have a package for you from Rafael Montoro. He asked me to deliver it to you personally."

She took the package from him. "You look a little fancy for a deliveryman."

"I'm Jose, his assistant at Montoro Enterprises," Jose said.

"That explains the suit," she said.

She wanted to ask more questions, debated it for a moment, and then decided to heck with looking cool. "So when will he be back in the US?"

"I'm not at liberty to say."

"Really? He sent you here but you can't tell me that?" she asked. "I know it's your job to protect his privacy, it's just that he said…never mind. Thank you for getting up early to deliver this. Are you driving back to Miami?"

"Nah. I took the company chopper."

Of course he did. Men like Rafe—and his assistant, for that matter—didn't drive almost four hours to Key West like other mere mortals.

"Safe travels," she said, turning around to go back inside.

What had he sent her?

"Ms. Fielding?"

She glanced over her shoulder at Jose. "He's hoping to be back next week but that all depends on the people in Alma."

She smiled at him. "Thank you."

"Don't rat me out," he said with a wink, and then left.

His assistant was nice. She wondered if that was a reflection of Rafe as a boss, but she knew no matter who worked for him he might still be a jerk at work. "Jose!"

"Yes."

"What kind of man is Rafe to work for?"

"Demanding. He won't settle for a job half done. But he's also very generous when a project is over. He's a good man," he said.

"Thanks," she said.

He walked away and she thought about it. A good man. Was she a good woman? Hell, yes, she was. She sat down on what she was now calling the Rafe chair and opened the package. When she pulled back the sides of the cardboard box there was a pretty paper inside with the words *Handcrafted in Alma* printed on it in scrolling letters.

She carefully pulled the sides of the paper back to reveal something in Bubble Wrap. Lifting it from the box, she carefully removed the Bubble Wrap and caught her breath as she saw that it contained a stained glass mermaid that looked a lot like her.

She traced her finger over the details and tried to downplay the importance of the gift. But she couldn't avoid the fact that he'd taken her childhood dream and given it to her.

She took a picture and then attached it to the text message.

She's even prettier than I imagined a mermaid could be. Thank you for this wonderful gift.

The response was almost instantaneous.

I'm glad you like it. I'm just coming out of a meeting. Do you have time to chat with me?

She thought about the paddleboarding she'd planned

for the day, but as her mom always said, the ocean wasn't going anywhere. Plus a part of her realized she'd been running away from her house and her situation so she didn't have to deal with it on her own. Talking to Rafe was a solution. She didn't want it to be, because she'd always prided herself on being independent and handling anything life threw at her. But she knew she wanted him by her side.

Yes. I can talk.

Good. I'll call in a few minutes.

She paced around her living room and ended up back in the kitchen. She took the stained glass mermaid and held her up to the back window, where she got the light from the morning sun, and realized she'd fit perfectly there.

She jotted down the supplies she'd need and then made herself a mango and passion fruit smoothie. By the time she was finished with it, he still hadn't called.

He was a man who would be king, she thought. Obviously his time wasn't his own. She waited another thirty minutes before she turned the ringer off on her phone, got into her car and drove to Geiger Key.

She tried to shake it off. She'd known that the only one she could count on was herself, but it stung just the tiniest bit that he hadn't messaged her back to say he'd been delayed.

Rafe was in a bad mood by the time he escaped the royal palace in Del Sol and drove down the winding coastal road to his family's beach compound in Playa del Onda. He'd spent the entire day either in meetings or being cornered by Dita Gomez.

Dita was the oldest daughter of one of the best families in Alma. Her parents were part of the newly forming royal court and they were hoping for a royal match. Dita was a lovely lady, no doubt, but as his man Kanye might say, she was a gold digger. Rafe wasn't entirely sure how she had access to his schedule but everywhere he went, she was there.

He'd been so busy dealing with getting rid of Dita that he hadn't been able to call Emily. And he knew her well enough to know that giving the excuse that he'd been dodging the advances of a beautiful blonde wasn't going to go over well.

Wanting to punch something, he shoved his hands in his hair. This was too restricting. He hadn't felt a connection to Alma or to the people the way that Bella seemed to. While he was busy plotting ways to get back to Miami early, she was happy to stay for a little while longer.

He wondered if something had happened to make Bella so happy with the land that time forgot. He made a mental note to talk to her, but he had no idea when he'd get a chance. His schedule was grueling.

He glanced at his watch; it had been seven hours since he said he'd call Emily. That meant it was probably midafternoon in Key West. He dialed her number and waited. It rang twice before he got a text message that had obviously been tailored for him saying she didn't want to talk to His Majesty.

First he was angry. Screw her. He was doing his best to keep all the balls in the air. Family, business, kingdom. He'd expect her to understand.

Then he remembered what she'd said to him a few days ago. *Don't make promises he couldn't keep.*

So he dialed her number again and this time she answered. But she didn't say anything—all he heard was the rush of wind and the faint sound of music in the background.

"Don't hang up. I'm sorry. My days over here are insane and I ended up being cornered by someone from the royal court. This is the first time I've been alone since I texted you."

After an excruciating pause, she finally spoke. "It's okay. I know you're busy. But even busy men can take a moment to text."

"Point taken. Honestly, Em, I feel like I'm running from one thing to the next and I can't catch up. I'm not used to this. And I feel like I have to play nice and by their rules. This means a lot to my family."

That was the problem. He wanted to tell them what he'd do and then say take it or leave it. But that wasn't an option. Tia Isabella was so excited to be returning home. He couldn't and wouldn't disappoint his great-aunt or any of his other relatives by ruining this for them. They'd looked to him for leadership and he was stepping up.

But he was losing himself.

"I'm trying to figure this out."

"Who says you have to do it all?" she asked. "Being the monarch and the head of a huge company is a big task for anyone. I think in most countries that isn't allowed."

"I know. But I like running the company. There I'm only answerable to the board and I have a certain degree of anonymity to deal with problems on my own.

Here…I sat in a meeting today about what color napkins we should have at the coronation."

She laughed. "What color did you decide?"

"I have no idea. I tuned out," he said. "I'd never do that at a board meeting."

"Well," she said at last. "I'm no expert on that sort of thing but I think you're going to have to find what makes being king exciting to you. I bet at Montoro Enterprises there are tasks that would normally bore you but you do them because you want to be successful."

She was right. "Good advice."

"Thanks. And thank you again for the mermaid. I hung her up after I got back from paddleboarding and am looking forward to seeing my kitchen lit up when the sun sets tonight."

"I wish I was there with you," he said.

"Don't."

"Don't what?"

Don't say things like that. Let's keep this light," she said. "That way I don't start thinking something else and you don't have to worry about calling me."

Hell. "I do want to call you, Em. I like talking to you and you make me…you're the only thing that feels real right now."

"That's because I have nothing to do with Alma or the throne. And you know with me it's just about the baby and getting to know each other. But that's running away from your obligations in Alma. And I think that for a little while that might suit you, but eventually it won't."

"I'm not sure what you mean by that," he said. Afraid very much that he did know what she meant.

"That once you decide to commit to Alma and the

people there, you will realize that you can't have me. I'll have been the distraction you needed to make the decision, and then I'll be left by the wayside."

Damn. He knew she was right. He didn't want to admit it to her, but then with Emily he didn't have to. "That's not my intention."

"Whether that's true or not, you can't change who you are and with you, Rafael Montoro IV, it's all about your family legacy. And we both know you aren't going to turn your back on it."

She was right. She'd taken the debate he'd been having with himself and boiled it down to its essence. He was a man who was all about family; it was the compass he used in every decision he'd ever made. Now he just had to decide if he could shift away from the Montoro legacy to pursue his own future with Emily and their child. And the decision would be a tough one.

After he hung up with her he went to his office to work. He put on a little Jimmy Buffett because he needed to hear some sounds of home.

There was a knock on the door and he rubbed the back of his neck. "Come in."

"Sir, I have a few more questions for the coronation," Hector said as he entered. Hector was the head of the Coronation Committee. Since Alma hadn't had a monarch in several decades, they were anxious to make sure the coronation had all the bells and whistles.

"Please have a seat," Rafe said. This was what he'd be giving up, he thought as Hector talked about where foreign dignitaries would be seated. Alma was going to be a world player. Lots of countries were interested in doing business with them since their previous ruler had kept the country isolated. Rafe's skills in business made him uniquely suited to help Alma get the most from their entry into the global marketplace.

"Do you like that?"

Rafe had to start paying attention. As Emily said, he needed to find the things about it that excited him. "You know better than me, Hector. No offense, but I'm not at all interested in color schemes or seating arrangements."

"None taken. You're a man of action and need to be doing something," Hector said.

"True. I'm going to let you make all the choices. If something doesn't look right then I will tell you."

"Thank you, sir."

"Clearly you know what you're doing," Rafe said.

Hector stood up to leave, but turned back when he got to the door. "I mean, thank you for coming back here. It means a lot to our people."

Hector left.

Rafe felt humbled. He knew that he wasn't going to find it easy to choose between Alma and Emily. He needed her and the people needed him.

Five

"I toured the countryside today. I have to say that it is beautiful. There's a little cove that I know you would like," Rafe said.

It was 10:00 a.m. Emily sat at one of the corner tables in the coffeehouse on Duval Street talking to Rafe. It had become their date. He hadn't missed calling her one time since the day he'd sent the stained glass mermaid a week ago. She hated to admit it, but she looked forward to his calls every day.

She took a sip of her herbal tea and looked out the window, but she didn't see Key West. Instead she saw the countryside of Alma as he described the rolling hills and hedgerows. The sheep on the hillside munching on grass.

"How's the weather there?" she asked. "I've never been farther north than Georgia."

"It's nice. The island isn't that big and so the sea breezes keep it cool. I think you'd like it."

He said that almost every time they talked, but she'd read the papers and online articles and knew there was no way she could ever visit him there. There was even speculation online that he'd chosen a bride from one of Alma's aristocratic families. She knew that came with the territory of being a monarch.

"Met any nice locals?" she asked before she could stop herself.

"A few. The head of the Coronation Committee is a great guy. He's helped me find things I like to do," he said.

She noticed he didn't mention any women, even though she'd seen his picture with more than one. It still made her sad.

Not sad enough that she stopped taking his calls or looking forward to talking to him.

She suddenly understood how a woman could willingly become a man's mistress. Because she had the feeling that if he asked her to, she'd be tempted to say yes. She was falling for him and he wasn't even here with her. But the silly thing was it was more intense by not actually having him physically here. They didn't argue over the little things like what to get for dinner because they only had a few hours together each week, and then it was only by phone.

"You still there?"

"Yes," she said. "Just imagining Alma."

"What's your view like today?"

"Sunburned tourists in swimsuits and flip-flops. There was a guy last night at the bar who had a few too many and kept coming on to this group of coeds.

They ignored him and so he started stripping. Can you imagine? I was laughing because he was harmless. A sunburned middle-aged man. I wanted to see how far he'd go. But Harry put an end to it."

"Sounds interesting. Did you think he'd look good naked?" Rafe asked.

"Nah. He didn't look anything like you. It was the expression on his face that had me hooked. He wasn't going to stop until those women acknowledged him."

"So he didn't look like me... Does that mean you like the way I look naked?" Rafe asked. "Because I haven't slept a single night without remembering how you felt in my arms that last time in Miami."

She took a sip of her tea and put her feet up on the chair across from her. She'd thought of little else but the way Rafe looked with his shirt off or how he'd moved when he'd been rapping to Jay-Z in his bedroom at the penthouse. She hadn't realized that she could be so lusty with this pregnancy, but she was.

"Tell me about it," she said.

"I will tonight. Why don't you call me when you get off work? I'll be waiting up for you."

She liked the sound of that. She glanced around the coffeehouse and noticed a man watching her. He looked away as she spotted him. Weird.

"Okay. I'm working an early shift because Harry is worried that late nights aren't good for me."

"They probably aren't. As a matter of fact, why don't you quit your job there?"

"Why would I do that?" she asked. She'd be bored stiff if she had nothing to do, and her savings would only last her three months. Then she'd have to look for another job. Though she knew Harry would take her back.

"I don't like the idea of you working late nights," he said. "I can support you so you don't have to work."

She put both feet on the floor and leaned forward as a wave of annoyance swept over her. "I don't need your money, Rafael. I'm not about to become your kept woman."

"Slow down, Red. I just meant that if you are tired, I'd help you out. It's nothing any man wouldn't do for the woman carrying his baby."

"That's not true," she said. Her own father had done a lot less. He'd just walked away and left her mom and her alone. "I guess you hit one of my triggers. I don't do needy."

"Hell, I know that. I don't do overprotective usually, but with you I want to. I know that's not what you want from me, so I'm keeping my distance," he said.

"Yeah, right, you're 'keeping your distance' because of your obligation to your family. You're just as afraid of committing yourself to me as you are of committing yourself to the throne."

There was silence on the line and she wondered if she'd gone too far. A part of her almost wished she had because then he'd just break it off with her and she'd know she was on her own.

These calls, this bond that was developing between them couldn't last. She knew it and if Rafe was being honest he'd admit to it too. The way things stood, they couldn't co-parent their child. Didn't royal babies have nannies or something?

She was going to be a hands-on mom and every time

she talked to Rafe she fell a little more for him, started to picture him as a hands-on dad.

"You're right," he said. "But I'm also not rushing back to your side because if I do I'm not sure what sort of reception I'll get."

"What sort do you want?" she asked. She had no idea how she'd act if he showed up on her doorstep, but frankly she imagined she'd be tempted to throw herself into his arms. And she had no idea how he'd react to that.

"You."

She caught her breath. "You don't have to keep this much distance between us, you know."

"I know. But you are unpredictable and I'm not on solid ground right now. Just know I wouldn't be calling you this often if you weren't important to me."

He didn't have to keep quite as much distance as he was for her sake. But getting to know him this way was safer. That was one of the issues she kept pushing to the back of her mind. "Okay, sorry for overreacting. It's just…a lot of things are changing in my body. You know how scary that is for a control freak like me?"

"I do. Red, that's how I feel about this entire constitutional monarchy thing in Alma."

She laughed. He was the only man she knew who'd compare being king to being pregnant. Mainly because he was the only man she knew who wasn't afraid to admit that he had doubts. That he liked to control things. That he was human. He didn't front with her and she knew that was one of the reasons she liked him.

"Okay, so about this late-night call. What do you say we use that video chat function? I miss seeing you," she admitted.

"Finally. I thought you'd never admit to missing me."

"I guess you're not as smart as everyone gives you credit for being," she said.

"Probably not," he said. "But I'm not concerned with what anyone thinks about me but you."

Those words made her heart beat a little faster and made her feel all warm and fuzzy inside. It wasn't love. Not yet. But she knew if he kept calling her every day she was going to start really falling for him, and she was starting to struggle to remember why that was a bad idea.

After hanging up with Emily, Rafe left the royal palace in Del Sol and walked around the well-manicured gardens. As he walked, he had his iPod set to his Key West playlist, which was really his Emily playlist. But he knew better than to actually name it that—he didn't want to leave any evidence of his affair for others to observe.

He listened to Jack Johnson sing about waking up and making banana pancakes together. Pretending the world outside didn't exist. And Rafe wanted that. But then as the days went by and he met more people in Alma he started to see how much the country needed him, or at least his family, here, too. Rafe guessed they were all so relieved to have the monarchy back.

After years under a dictator he understood that. It was sort of how he'd felt when he'd turned eighteen and left his father's house. He had acted like a wild man in college for about three months before he realized that he wanted his life to be about more than tabloid headlines. So he'd gotten serious and proven to himself that he could stand outside of his father's shadow and still be a part of the family.

"Hey, big brother," Bella said, coming up behind him and linking her arm through his. He pulled his earbuds out and smiled down at his baby sister. She'd really thrived in Alma and had an affinity with the people here that bordered on mutual admiration. For the Montoros, and Juan Carlos in particular, it was as if they'd come home. They were a part of Alma and Juan Carlos was busy bringing them back into the fold. There was sincere joy in all of them at being here. Even Rafe. Though he was torn, with his love of Miami and his lover in Key West.

"Hello, Bella. What's up?"

She led him to one of the wrought iron benches nestled next to a flowering jasmine bush and sat down. He sat down next to her and looked at his sister for the first time in days. She smiled easily.

"You seem distracted lately and I'm going to do the meddling kid sister thing and ask why."

"I'm trying to figure out how to be royal after years of being so ordinary," he said. It was his pat answer, and he'd been saying it to himself for so long that when he finally heard it out loud he realized how hollow the words were.

Maybe Bella wouldn't notice.

"Yeah, right," she said. "I'd think you'd have a better excuse than that."

He wasn't in the mood to discuss this with her and started to get up. But she stopped him with her hand on his sleeve.

"I think you have someone back home," she said.

"A woman who isn't from here and can't fit into this world."

"I have a lot of women back home," he said.

"Lying to me is one thing," she said with that honesty that made him feel exposed. "But lying to yourself is something else. If you have a woman, then marry her. Then take the throne."

If it were as simple as that he'd do it. But he knew from the meetings he'd been in that a smooth transition was needed. He was expected to marry someone who'd strengthen the Montoros' claim to the throne. Someone who'd make the people of Alma and its enemies believe that the restored monarchy would be around for a long time. That they were the only ones who could return Alma to its former glory.

And a bartender from Key West who didn't know who her father was wasn't going to be approved by the committee.

"Thanks, Bella, but it's not that simple," he said.

"It is if you know what you want."

He realized anew that he was lost. Hearing his little sister boil down his problems and come up with a solution was humbling. But he couldn't do what she suggested. He hadn't even seen Emily since he'd learned he was going to be a father. Their daily calls were great, but he needed to hold her in his arms again. Look into her eyes and see what, if anything, she felt for him.

Aside from lust. Sex between them had been raw and electric since the moment they'd met, and now he had to figure out if what he felt for her was more than that. Was he just using her as an escape to get away from the mantle of kingship that he didn't want? And he *really* didn't want it.

Because if he did it would be easier to make a decision about Em. Force her to take some money from him and set her and the baby up and then keep his distance. But he wanted more than that.

"I...thank you," he said.

"For what? I didn't say anything that you don't already know for yourself. Tell me what's going on."

He shook his head. "You've done enough."

"I have?"

"Yes. I just needed to hear someone else say it. I've been afraid of screwing up and embarrassing the family so I've stopped being myself. I've been trying to be regal and we both know I'm not."

She laughed and punched his shoulder. "You're not succeeding at being regal. I saw you roll your eyes when the Gomezes mentioned what beautiful babies you and Dita would have."

"I thought I showed a lot of restraint by not mentioning that the babies would probably be born with a tail and cloven hooves."

Bella laughed. "You're not that evil."

"Imp, you think it's funny having someone come after you because of your position? Wait until the princess royal or whatever title they decide on for you has to make a good marriage."

"Don't even joke about that, Rafe. I'm too young and pretty to be tied down to a man." She batted her eyelashes.

He hugged her close. "Damned straight. Besides, only one of us should be shackled by this monarchy thing. I'll do what's needed to protect you, Gabe and the rest of our family."

"Don't sacrifice yourself for us. We're stronger than you think we are."

"I know that. But I want you both to be happy."

Emily's shift was long. Her feet hurt and she felt as if she was going to be sick until she stepped outside into the balmy June air. It was only eleven—so not that late—as she walked through the crowds toward her cottage.

She had been looking forward to chatting with Rafe all evening. But once again she'd seen him on the local news on one of the televisions at the bar. He was with a blonde woman and she hoped like hell that it was just for publicity purposes. But a part of her realized that she had no hold on the king of Alma.

But that Rafe was different from the man who she spoke on the phone with and she hadn't asked about the woman because she really didn't want to hear that his obligation to his family might force him to marry someone else.

The US press, especially the local Miami reporters, loved anything to do with royalty and since the Montoros were raised in America, the media were obsessed with them. It seemed she didn't have to try too hard to find out about Rafael, Gabriel and Bella. She learned about the private schools they'd gone to and had seen Rafe's college roommate on CNN talking about how the Montoros were all about family.

She got it. As far as the media were concerned Rafe was going to make a great king. It had been a long time since an American had claimed a foreign throne, and despite the fact that most patriots were all about democracy they did like a fairy-tale story like this now and then.

She rubbed the back of her neck as she let herself into her house. She kicked off her Vans and left the lights off as she walked to her bedroom. She'd wanted him all day. Looked forward to the time when she could be alone and talk to him, and now she wasn't sure.

She wasn't sure how much more of Rafe she could take before he became so embedded in her soul that she wouldn't be able to survive without him.

She was sure part of it was the hormones from being pregnant with his baby. The other part was that she'd never had this kind of interaction with a guy. They talked every day. Most of her boyfriends had been busy with their own lives and had called only when they were horny or lonely.

Which had suited her.

She'd never wanted anything solid and lasting until now.

Until Rafe. And he wasn't available for her to claim.

Her phone rang. She glanced down at the Skype icon and knew that it was Rafe doing what she'd asked: calling her for a video chat this time.

She missed him. She didn't want to.

But she swiped her finger across the screen, unlocking the phone to answer the call. The image on the other end was dark with just a pool of light in the background.

Her own image popped up as a dark square in the bottom corner of the screen. She hadn't turned on the light.

"I guess you changed your mind about seeing me," he said.

"I just got home," she said. She fell backward on her bed and reached over to flick on the lamp on her nightstand. "I can't see you, either."

He turned the phone and she saw him sprawled on his back on a big bed with some sort of padded brocade headboard behind him. His shirt was unbuttoned and he had one arm stretched up over his head. He was holding the phone up above him with his other hand.

"Better?"

She sighed. She shouldn't do this late at night when her defenses were down. And they were down. She was feeling mopey and alone. Her mom was due back tomorrow and maybe that would help. But for tonight she had Rafe.

"I miss you."

"You do?"

"I do. You look like you had a formal event tonight," she said. She'd seen him on the news entering a gala with the blonde on his arm earlier this evening.

"I did. Listen, if you saw any pictures on the news of me with a woman, it was just state business. She's nothing to me."

"Does she know that?" Emily asked. Because that woman had seemed as though she had her claws sunk into him.

"Would I be here with you if she didn't?" he asked.

She looked at him in the shadows. "Would you?"

"No. I thought you knew me better than that," he said.

She had made him angry but she needed to know if he was the kind of man who'd cheat on her. "We don't have anything official between us. I…are you a one-woman man?"

He leaned in toward the camera, so close she could see the green and dark brown flecks in his hazel eyes. "I am."

"Then stop having your picture taken with foreign blondes," she said.

He sighed. "It's not that easy. She keeps showing up everywhere I am."

Emily was tempted to go to Alma and—

Do what?

She was Rafe's baby mama, not his fiancée.

This was something she had no idea how to handle. But she wanted him to be hers. For the world to know that he belonged to her. But she didn't want to say that to him. Admit that all these late calls had made her start to fall for him.

"How was your day?" She toed off her socks and grabbed a second pillow to prop her head up.

"Interesting. My baby sister is worried about me."

"Why?"

"She said I don't seem happy," Rafe said.

"Are you?"

"Happy isn't exactly something I aspire to. I think that is a path to crazy," he said. "I'd like to be content."

"Happiness equals crazy?" she asked. "I've never thought that."

"I mean trying to be happy all the time. Life isn't about always being happy. There are quiet moments and the normal grind. That's what makes the happy times memorable."

"So is this a quiet moment?"

"It's so much more than that, Red. You're my reward for being the good son and doing what's expected of me here in Alma."

It wasn't what she wanted to hear, but it warmed her up and made the feelings that had been dogging her all night dissolve. She realized that she'd been edgy and mopey because she didn't like seeing Rafe with that blonde woman.

"I was jealous."

"Of?"

"That blonde." She made a face and put her thumb over the part of her phone that showed her end of the video chat. She didn't want to see her own face.

"Don't be."

"I want this to be light and easy, Rafe. But it's not. It hasn't been for a while."

"You want the truth, Red?" he asked, rolling to his side and propping his phone up on something so that he wasn't holding it any more.

"You know I do."

"This hasn't been light or easy since the moment I first kissed you. I'm not a one-night-stand guy and we both know you don't take guys home all the time. We've both been trying to pretend that it was nothing more than a moment, but I think it's time we stopped pretending."

She swallowed hard. Had she been pretending? Was that why she'd been jealous and lonely?

"What do you suggest?"

"That we figure out what we both want. I know I want you. Not just for sex."

"Me, too."

Six

It was somehow easier to talk to her when he saw her face. She looked good, with that smattering of freckles across the bridge of her nose and the weary hope in her blue eyes. She seemed to want him to be the man he wasn't sure he could be.

He wanted to be a man of his word, but that was complicated. Making promises to her was out of the question because he had to figure out a solution that would take care of his family's future. Or did he? He was tired of walking on the tightrope between what he wanted and what he should do.

He thought of his mom, who'd divorced their father when Bella turned eighteen. It was as if his mother had served her time raising them and was ready to do something for herself. He didn't want to wait like that... Besides, assuming the throne was for life.

"What are you thinking? You got all intense all of a sudden," Emily said.

"I was thinking about my mom," he admitted quietly. "How she raised us until Bella was eighteen and then moved on with her life. What kind of mom will you be?"

"Not that kind. But I'm independent," she said. "I imagine my child will be too."

"It's our child."

"You're going to be ruling Alma, Rafe. I'm the one who will raise our child."

He didn't like her point. But he knew better than to argue it. He wasn't in a position to win. And he was tired of losing.

"You look nice. No sign of the pregnancy yet," he said.

"Thanks. A Shady Harry's T-shirt and jeans aren't exactly haute couture but they suit me."

They did suit her. He wanted to suit her as well. Be a part of that life. Yet he was torn. How could he be?

"I've got to get changed. I smell like the bar."

"Can I watch?" he asked. Seeing her brought all of his senses into sharp focus and made the life he'd been living these last few days look as if it were in black and white. He had been on autopilot doing what was expected of him and doing it well, but now he truly felt the first spark of excitement…of life.

"Is that what you want?" she asked. There was a teasing note in her voice and he caught a glimpse of the woman who'd bound him with his own shirt in South Beach.

If she only knew the power she wielded over him.

"It is."

"Well okay then," she said. "It's not going to be very exciting. I mean I've never worked in a high-end strip club or anything."

He shook his head. "I didn't think you had."

"Have you been to one?" she asked.

"Are you going to go on a feminist rant if I say yes?" he asked.

"No, I'm not. The women who work in places like that usually earn a good living. And it's their choice to make," she said. "So you have been to one."

He shrugged. Some nights that was where the crowd he ran with back in Miami had ended up. "It's not my favorite place to hang out."

"That's good to know. You should know I've only gotten undressed in front of a few guys."

"You should know I have no interest in any of the other men in your life," he said. "I want to be the only one."

He knew he had no right to say that. That he might not even be able to claim Emily but, hell, this was the twenty-first century and he wasn't going to marry another "suitable" woman when he felt this strongly about her.

She touched her finger to the screen and he imagined he felt her light touch on his face. "As of right now you are."

She got to her feet and his screen was filled with the image of her ceiling until she got to the bathroom. She flipped on the light switch and she propped the phone up on the counter. "I need a shower, too."

"How about a bath? If I were there, I'd fill that big claw-foot tub of yours with warm water and bubbles and have it waiting for you when you got home."

He wanted to take care of her. She was the first person outside of the circle of his family he'd ever felt this way about.

"Okay. Give me a few minutes."

"Don't take your clothes off until I can see you."

"Do you have a bathtub in your big palace?" she asked. "I saw some pictures of your entire family walking around the gardens on CNN last night. Looked nice."

"I do have a very nice bathroom here. The tub is controlled by a computer," he said.

"Join me in the bath?" she asked. There was a hint of vulnerability in her words. He found it both enchanting and a little bit unnerving. Emily was a very strong woman who didn't really need anyone. But tonight he caught a glimpse behind that attitude and saw that she did need him.

That made him feel like Atlas, strong enough to carry the weight of the earth on his shoulders. And like the mythological being he couldn't simultaneously protect Emily and shoulder his burden. He had no idea where any of this was going. He was used to being the strong one. The one who knew exactly what needed to be done—

And he did this time. He needed to let her go, but for once wanted to be selfish and keep her. For tonight he was going to do just that.

"Okay," he said, getting up and going to his own opulently appointed bathroom. He selected the temperature from a computerized keypad on the wall and soon the water started flowing into the tub. He flicked on the overhead light that just illuminated the tub and then glanced back at his phone screen to see where Emily was.

She was sitting on the edge of her tub biting her lower lip as she fiddled with the taps.

Then she stood up and undid her jeans.

"Hey. Not so fast, Red. I want to see every inch of you," he said.

"Fair enough. Take your shirt off. Not that you don't look sexy with it unbuttoned and your chest showing."

He'd undone his shirt earlier because he felt uncomfortable and hadn't really known what to wear for a video call with her. He lifted his arms. "You see these buttons?"

"Yeah?"

"You're supposed to undo them first. That way I don't have to rip the shirt," he said.

"I like it when you rip your shirt," she said with a wink. "In fact the next time I see you I've got a new shirt for you to try on. One that is made of tougher material."

Arching one eyebrow at her, he tossed his shirt toward the corner and then stood there, feeling a bit ridiculous.

"Damn, you look good," she said.

The open admiration in her eyes as she looked at him made him feel ten feet tall. He rubbed his hand over his chest. And then flexed his muscles for her. He heard her intake of breath. And suddenly all those reps he did at the gym were worth it. He worked out because he lived in South Beach and owned a very successful business. He wasn't about to have a photo of himself looking like a sloth turn up anywhere. But knowing she liked his body gave him another reason to do it.

"Your turn. I want to see your…muscles."

She laughed. "I did help unload a beer delivery this afternoon, so I think my arms are looking a little buffer than usual."

He frowned. "Why are you unloading anything? Harry should know better."

"He does. He was pissed when he got there. But the delivery guys weren't our usual ones and they were piling the beer in the sun…no one else was there. Harry ripped them a new one and they apologized to me."

Good. Still, Rafe didn't like that she'd had to deal with those guys. She should be pampered while she carried his child.

She pulled the Shady Harry's T-shirt up over her head and he immediately noticed her breasts swelling around the sides of the cups of her bra. She reached behind her back and unhooked the bra and let it slid down her arms and onto the floor. Her nipples looked bigger and a darker shade of pink than he remembered. Signs of the changes his baby was having on her body. She skimmed her hand down to her stomach and he noticed just the smallest bump there.

She unhooked her jeans and pushed them down her legs with her panties. And just like that, she was standing there naked.

He touched the image on his phone and realized that seeing her like this was a double-edged sword. He wanted to be there with her.

And that's when he came to his decision. He was going home first thing in the morning. He didn't care what the parliament thought; he needed to be back in Florida with Emily. Even if it was just for a few days.

"Dammit, Red. You get more beautiful each time I see you naked."

She blushed, and he observed that the color started at the top of her breasts and swept up her neck to her cheeks. She shook her head. "I had to unbutton my jeans at work tonight. It's not like they are too tight... well, okay, they are, but it was uncomfortable for the first time."

"I can see the little bump," he said. He traced his finger over her body on the screen. The changes were small, but this was their child making itself known in their lives. Well, mostly hers as of right now. He was missing out.

"I see a little bump in your pants as well," she said with a wink.

He guessed she didn't want to talk about the pregnancy, and he let her change the subject. "Little? Woman, look again."

He undid his pants and carefully shoved them down his legs until he stood there naked. He heard her sharp intake of breath and then her wolf whistle. She was good for his ego. And she kept things light. Was he ever seeing the real woman?

"Not so little."

"Not around you," he said.

"I didn't mean for this to be phone sex," she said.

"I never mean for it to turn into sex with you, but damn, Red, you turn me on like no one else ever has."

She smiled at me. "I feel the same. But I smell like the bar."

"Not to me. To me you smell like Florida sunshine and a day at the beach."

She walked over to the tub with the phone, her heart-shaped face filling the screen. Her eyes were sparkling, and unless he missed his guess, she was happy. While he might not think happiness was a good goal for every second of his life, he was glad to see her smiling.

She propped her phone up on the ledge of the tub and then climbed in. She closed her eyes and let her head fall back against the pillow she had there. The edges of her long hair fell into the water. She looked like his mermaid.

His.

He climbed into his tub, balled a towel up behind his head. The water felt hot and luxurious against his sensitive skin.

"This is nice. But I'm always by myself," she said.

"Me, too."

"Even in that crowd that's always with you?" she asked.

"Yeah."

"If I was there, I'd climb in behind you and rub your shoulders," she said. "You seem stressed."

"I'd like that. But only because I'd feel your naked breasts against my back."

"Maybe I'd lean over you and kiss your neck. Nibble on your earlobe. I know you like that, too."

He stretched his legs to make room for his growing erection and rubbed his hand over his own chest. He wished she were here so he could touch her. But his imagination was doing a good job of filling in the gaps.

"I'd probably pull you around in my arms and kiss you. I can't resist your mouth," he said.

"That's good. I like the way you taste, Rafe. No other guy I've kissed has tasted so right."

Damned straight. He wanted to be the only guy who

felt right to her. In all things. A wave of pure posses-
siveness overwhelmed him and he knew he wanted to
claim her as his. But this damned situation with his
family was keeping him from doing it.

"I'd put my hands on your waist and lift you up a
bit until I could reach your breasts. Are they more sensitive now?"

She nodded.

"Show me."

"How?" she asked. She shifted up on her knees and
leaned toward the phone. "I like your mouth on me."

Damn. He did, too. Her nipples felt so right in his
mouth, and nothing made him harder than when he
swirled his tongue around them and she gripped the
back of his head.

"Touch yourself. Run your finger around your nipple and pinch it. Pretend I'm biting you," he said as she
shifted back. "Just talking has made your nipples hard."

She nodded and gave him a slow smile. "I've been
thinking about you touching me. Remembering how
your mouth felt against my nipple."

"Show me," he said again.

She brought her hand up from the water, the droplets
sparkling in the light as they fell from her arm. Then
she cupped her breast and trailed her finger around her
nipple. It puckered as she touched it, and he got even
harder watching her as her head fell back and she let
out a moan.

"Feel good?" he asked, his voice husky and low.
His skin was so sensitive that each lap of the water
brought him closer to the edge. He was going to come.
But he didn't want to until she did. He wanted to keep
watching her for as long as he could. And draw out the

pleasure so he could feel as if they were together. He needed this. Needed her.

He'd been trying to deny it, but there it was. The truth that he'd been afraid to admit to himself.

She was cupping both of her breasts and he groaned as he reached for the screen of his phone and touched it. He remembered the way she felt underneath him. How her limbs felt wrapped around his.

"Not as good as when you do touch me," she said. "If I were there I'd caress your chest and then slowly tease you by working my fingers lower."

"When you do that it makes it difficult for me to think," he admitted.

"Really?"

He nodded. Words were sort of beyond him at this moment.

"Are you hard for me?" she asked.

"I am." He stroked himself, remembering how she fit him like a glove when he thrust into her.

"Show me," she said. "Let me see how hard you are."

Her words were like a velvet lash on his skin and he shuddered. This was excruciating. He wanted to come inside her and each time she said something so sexual he couldn't contain his groans.

"Red…"

"Show me, Rafe. I want to see you. See how much you want me."

He groaned, but did as she asked, shifting until he was out of the water and she could see him. He stroked his hand up and down his shaft.

"Swipe your finger over the top," she said. "Pretend it's my tongue on you."

He did as she instructed and then shuddered as he realized how close to the edge he was.

"Are you ready for me? Show me," he said.

She parted her legs and showed him. Pushed her finger up inside and moaned as she did so. "It's not the same as when you do it."

"Does it feel good?" he asked.

"It does."

"Come for me, Red."

This was too intimate and yet not intimate enough.

"I want to touch you, Rafe. If I were there I'd take you inside me. I need you," she said.

"Me, too, Red."

She moaned. "I'm so ready for it. For you."

He was, too. He remembered the way it had felt the last time they were together. How she'd gripped him as soon as he entered her body. How deep he'd gone and the way her eyes had opened and he'd met her gaze. Felt her wrapped around him all the way to his soul.

"Rafe."

Hearing her name on his lips made him come. He closed his eyes and put his head back as his orgasm washed over him. He opened them to see her doing the same. She gave him a slow, sexy smile.

"That's my kind of bath," she said, smiling.

"Mine, too," he said. "When I get home I want to do this again."

"But together in the same tub."

He hit the button to drain the tub and got to his feet. She stayed where she was, watching him, and he realized that in her eyes he was enough. He didn't have to prove anything to her. Or at least he hoped he didn't have to. Because he was coming to realize he didn't know who he was anymore. He hadn't known in a long, long time.

"Come to bed with me, Red. Let's talk until we both fall asleep."

She nodded. She got out of the tub and dried herself off and he just watched, absently toweling himself dry. He caught his breath when she padded naked back to her bed and climbed between the sheets. She'd washed the sheets but not the pillow case he'd slept on.

"This pillow smells like you," she said.

"It does?"

"Yes. I've been pretending you are here with me every night… Tomorrow I'm going to deny that. But tonight I need you here with me."

He understood. When the sun was out there were oceans between them and problems that wouldn't be easily solved. And while he wanted to do what Bella said and put himself first—maybe marry Emily so that the rest of the world would have to accept her—he knew she wouldn't go for that. She didn't want a man who could be hers only halfway.

And that was all he could offer right now. But he knew he wanted to call her his and he needed to figure out a way.

He climbed into his own bed and curled on his side. "I don't have a pillow that smells like you."

"Sorry, babe."

She smiled sleepily at him and he watched her as she started to drift off to sleep. "Thank you for being here tonight."

"You're welcome, Red."

He watched over her until he knew she was sound asleep and snoring slightly. Maybe he kept the line open for longer than he should have before disconnecting the call.

He knew he couldn't do this any longer. He was tired of making do with phone calls to Emily. He'd thought that the video call would make it easier but it hadn't. Instead it made him long to touch her. Really touch her.

He got out of his bed, pacing to the window and looking out at the sea. The ocean was endless and as he glanced up at the moon that was almost setting he realized that in Emily's part of the world the moon was rising. He wanted to be in the same place she was. See if there was anything really between them.

Honestly he knew this wasn't real. How could it be? He was painting her the way he wanted her to be. And not to be oedipal or anything, but he was making Emily into the woman he wanted while imagining her as the mother he never had.

He got dressed and walked out of his room down the hall to Gabe's. He figured Gabe would be easier to talk to than Juan Carlos. But there was no answer when he knocked.

He rubbed the back of his neck.

Damn.

He walked to Juan Carlos's room and wasn't surprised when his cousin answered the door wearing a dressing gown with the Alma royal seal monogramed on the breast.

"What is it?"

"I…I have to return to the States."

"Why? You know that royal protocol states—"

"Screw royal protocol, J.C. I had a life before Alma came to us and I can't just walk away from it."

"You gave your word. Our family gave our word. You are the oldest."

"I wish I wasn't."

"Stop being so selfish. This country needs a leader. It needs someone who can take it from the isolated kingdom it's been into the twenty-first century. You are the man."

"I didn't choose this," Rafe said. "I'm not sure I want this."

"Too bad, Rafael, you're birthright has brought you to this. Sure, it would have been easier if we'd been brought up on the island but that doesn't make our legacy any less important."

Juan Carlos would be so much better at this than him, Rafe thought. But he wasn't from the right family line and Rafe really couldn't—

"I have to return to the States," he said again. "I'm the one who will be king so my decision is final."

"This is ridiculous."

"Why?"

"Because already I can see that your loyalty isn't to your people. And they will see it too."

"I can't take care of the people of Alma until I figure out this part of my life."

"Is there a woman?"

"Yes. Yes, there is, and I haven't had a chance to resolve anything with her."

"Is she…would the court approve a marriage to her?"

Rafe doubted it. Hell, he wasn't even sure he wanted to marry her. He had to get back to her and figure this all out.

"I have no idea if I want to marry her or not. I need some time to myself to figure this out."

"Hell. I'll go with you."

"I don't want the entire family to know," Rafe said. "Why would you come with me?"

"As you said, you can't be a good ruler until you know where you belong. I want that, Rafe. I know I seem all tied up with royal protocol, but I want what is best for all of us. You're like a brother to me."

"You are to me as well," Rafe said. Juan Carlos had grown up in their home after his parents had died. "I do need to be in Miami to take care of the details of the new shipping deal I just signed. I will let the court and the coronation committee know that's why I'm returning."

"I will back you up," Juan Carlos said. "Just be sure you make the right decision."

Rafe nodded. His impromptu decision to leave had to be delayed until he could talk to the court advisors and his family. Since it was early morning it would take time for the entire Montoro clan who were in Alma to be ready to go.

But sure enough, later that day, they were all on the plane and headed toward Miami.

Seven

Emily went to Key Koffee for a cup of decaf and sat at the corner table again. Last night with Rafe had been different. It had been fun, but also, in the safety of the darkness and with the distance between them, she felt he'd shared more of himself than he had before.

Caution, she warned herself.

Her mom was always warning her about racing headlong into action before thinking about it first. But she felt as if it was too late to change. And last night had made her fall a little more for Rafe.

Which was probably why she was up early even though she had to work later. But her mom was also due to dock at the marina at nine, and Emily wanted to be there to greet her.

"Give me a double espresso and a lemon poppy-seed muffin to go as well as my usual order," Emily said to Cara behind the bar.

"Sure thing. Feeling hungry this morning?"

"A little, but the extra stuff is for my mom. She's back in port today," she told Cara.

"How about your man?" Cara asked.

Emily shook her head. "I don't have a man."

She couldn't claim Rafe as her own until he indicated he was ready for that. And she knew despite their closeness when they were alone that he wasn't. That knowledge sort of tinged her day. She frowned a little. The smell of the espresso was strong this morning, and she felt bile rising in the back of her throat.

She swallowed hard to keep from getting sick and then realized it wasn't going to work. She ran for the bathroom but made it only as far as the hallway before she began retching. She forced herself to keep moving into the bathroom and threw up. She was heavy and aching and knew this wasn't one of the times when she could say she was enjoying her pregnancy.

Cara followed her into the bathroom with a wet towel. After Emily rinsed her mouth and splashed water on her face, Cara walked her back to her table. Emily felt as if everyone was staring at her. Cara just smiled at them.

"She's pregnant. You don't worry about our food."

Everyone nodded and went back to their papers and electronic devices.

"I sort of wasn't planning on telling anyone yet," Emily said.

"Sorry, Em. But I can't have people thinking it's my food."

"It's okay," Emily said.

"Your man should be here with you," Cara said in

a kind way. "I saw you two together. He's not the kind of man who'd just walk away."

Cara tucked a strand of Emily's hair behind her ear. "Have you told him?"

She wasn't that close to Cara, but they were friends. They'd gone to the same high school and had even taken a road trip to Georgia together one time. But she didn't want to discuss Rafe with her. "Yes. It's complicated."

"Fair enough. Park yourself right there. I'm going to get your order for you."

Emily looked up and noticed a man watching her. The same guy who had been eavesdropping on her telephone conversation with Rafe the other day.

"How you feeling?" he asked, coming over with a packet of Club crackers that they kept on the tables for when Key Koffee serve conch chowder in the afternoon. "These always helped my wife when she was expecting."

She smiled her thanks and took them, weakly opening the pack and taking out a cracker. She munched on one and tipped her head back as her body stopped rioting and started to calm down.

"Are you reading this?" he asked.

She glanced down at the *Miami Herald,* which was flipped open to the society page with a picture of Rafe and his family in Alma.

"No."

"I can't believe how obsessed everyone is with that family," the guy said. "I'm Stan, by the way."

"Emily," she said. "Well, it's a fairy tale, isn't it? American royalty becomes real royalty."

"True enough. I've heard that Rafe comes down to Key West," Stan said.

It seemed to her that he was fishing for information. She didn't know if he was some obsessed royal watcher or just making conversation. "I guess he does. It's not that uncommon."

"No it's not. But surely now that he's going to be king he won't be," Stan added.

"I have no idea," Emily admitted.

"Mind if I take this paper?"

"Be my guest," she said.

"Thanks," he said, walking out.

"Here's your breakfast to go," Cara said, coming over. "What did he want?"

"The newspaper," Emily said. She started to get up but Cara pushed her back down. "Sit for a little while. I called Harry to come and get you."

"Cara."

"What? You're family, Em. We take care of our own here," she reminded her.

She felt tears burn the back of her eyes and blinked so they didn't fall. She'd always felt as if Key West was her home, ever since she was three years old and her mother moved them there. The people she knew were like family to her, but she had always figured it was a one-way street. The feelings of a girl left too many times by a mother whose job was her life, her obsession.

"Thanks, Cara. But I'm a big girl."

"Even big girls deserve to be looked after," Harry said, walking into the coffee shop and approaching their table. "We got time for me to grab a cup of coffee?"

"No need to wait, Harry," Cara said, handing him a cup and a bakery bag.

Unless Emily missed her guess, that bakery bag would have a toasted everything bagel in it. Cara was right. They were all family.

This place was as much a part of her as the baby growing inside her. And though she didn't need the re-assurance, it was nice to know that she wasn't alone. That if Rafe made the choice that any sane man would and took the throne of Alma half a world away from her, she'd still have family around her. Her baby would grow up with the family she'd chosen for herself and not the one she'd been born into. The family her mother had chosen for them when she'd moved them to Key West.

"You okay, kiddo?" Harry asked.

"Just morning sickness."

"Another thing that I will bring up to Rafe Montoro the next time he shows his face here."

Rafe stretched his long legs out in front of him as he settled in for the flight. His cousin Juan Carlos—the one in the family who was the best suited for royal life since he seemed to know so much about it—sat across from him reading a book on the history of Alma from the 1970s to today.

His father, brother and sister were all sitting in the back of the plane talking quietly amongst themselves. They were happy enough to follow his lead especially when he mentioned that the oil deal needed his attention in Miami.

Rafe had been surprised by Juan Carlos's understanding but now he realized he shouldn't have been.

He knew his cousin as well as he knew Gabe…though he had to admit that he'd known both men better when they were children. But the bond among all of them was still strong. And Rafe felt less isolated that he had before. Felt a little more as if his family had his back.

Rafe read the book last week, since the government people wanted to make sure that everyone in the Montoro camp was familiar with the past. The common consensus being that maybe then they wouldn't make the same mistakes again. Rafe didn't want to have to flee the country in the middle of the night and start over with nothing.

At least his great-grandfather had his wife by his side, and his family. Something that was becoming more and more important to Rafe.

"Juan, what would you do if you were going to be king?" Rafe asked. "I'm tempted to invest Montoro Enterprises money into the manufacturing sector so that Alma isn't just reliant on oil."

"That's a start. They really need stability so that Alma's citizens will start staying on the island instead of emigrating to countries in the EU. I think we should try to become a member of the EU as well," Juan Carlos said.

"It's one of the prime minister's top priorities. He has me scheduled to go to Brussels next month for meetings on the subject," Rafe said, rubbing the back of his neck.

"I can go with you if you like," Juan Carolos said. "I'm not as impatient as you are at the negotiating table. Of course, you are always very shrewd at getting the best deal for Montoro Enterprises."

"That would be great. I'd love to have you there with

me," Rafe said. One thing about his family that had been made clear during the last few weeks as they'd traveled to Alma and gotten a handle on their new lives was how they all banded together. "When is Tia Isabella going to join us in Alma?"

"Soon, I hope," Juan Carlos said. Juan Carlos's grandmother suffered from Parkinson's and had her good days and her bad days. "We are waiting for her doctors to okay the visit."

"How is she doing?" Rafe asked. "You talk to her nurse every day, don't you?"

"Yes, I do. I think the thought of returning to Alma has rallied her spirits, and though medically I'd have to say there have been no changes, she seems healthier."

Rafe smiled to himself. The very thing that felt like a burden to him was a dream come true to Tia Isabella. She had longed to return to her home for decades and now it was possible.

That almost made his royal sacrifice worthwhile. But there was also a lot to be said for the old-world charm of Playa del Onda. And for Juan Carlos's excitement over their all being part of the royal aristocracy again as well.

It just made everything more difficult for Rafe. He wanted to keep his family happy. He was the eldest and had the power to do it. But then he remembered Emily and he was torn.

Had been torn for too long. When he got to Miami he needed to see her and figure this entire thing out.

"Do you think that the government would accept a commoner as my wife?" Rafe asked his cousin. They were still negotiating the constitution that Alma's parliament had brought to them. Rafe had been asking for little changes because he wanted to see how far they would go to get him and his family back in the country.

"Is your woman a commoner?" Juan Carlos asked.

"Not many royals in the States, Juan Carlos." He didn't want to talk about Emily with anyone else. Not yet. Why then did he keep bringing her up? He clearly needed to talk even if he didn't want to. Not until he had her sorted out. God, she'd kill him if she knew he thought that way about her.

"I don't know. I think they want you to marry a woman who will reinforce the monarchy, and a commoner wouldn't do that," Juan Carlos said at last.

Rafe nodded at his cousin and then leaned back and closed his eyes. He'd figured as much. There was no way to have it both ways. Why was he still trying to?

Because he couldn't walk away from Emily.

There it was: the truth he'd been trying to pretend didn't exist for too long. And letting his family down, well, that wasn't something he was prepared to do, either. He wasn't even sure if he walked away from the throne that they would let him keep his job at Montoro Enterprises. Though truth be told, he was a genius at making money, so he had no doubt he could start his own company and make it a success.

But that would mean walking away from everything and everyone. His family was so deeply rooted in his life, he truly wasn't sure what he'd do without them. When they'd lived in the Miami area, he saw them every day at their Coral Gables compound. He worked hard for all of them so that they wouldn't have to worry.

That was why he hesitated. Then there was Tia Isabella. With her deteriorating health, Rafe didn't really want to do anything to upset her. If he walked away, would he find a way to make peace with the family before her illness got the better of her? Bella would be forced into a difficult position as well. His father would more than likely try to come between her and Rafe, and that would cause her stress. She liked to keep the peace.

Gabriel would be none too pleased with him. Gabe lived a nice and easy lifestyle, enjoying the many beautiful women who flocked to Miami. No-strings relationships were his MO.

Rafe laughed to himself. Gabe always did whatever the hell he wanted. He'd be plenty pissed at Rafe if he walked away from the throne and Gabe had to take it. That would be a nightmare for all concerned. His younger brother was a player. Not the image that Alma wanted for their new king.

So Rafe was back to the exact same position he'd been in since he left Miami. Except this time he was leaning more toward Emily. Hell, last night had changed something between them.

He no longer saw her as the fun-loving bartender who had gotten pregnant, but more as Emily, the woman who was going to be the mother to their child.

Their child. If he had a son he'd be Rafael V. Or would he? Would Emily want to name him something else? There was still so much for them to discuss.

He closed his eyes, trying to picture what their child would look like. Would the baby have his dark hair and eyes or Emily's bright blue ones? He tried to picture the little tyke, maybe with her red hair and his hazel eyes.

He wanted to be a part of that. Be a part of his child's life. He had to find a way to have it all. Perhaps he needed introduce Emily to his family so they could start to get to know her. Once that happened, they would be on his side. And marrying a commoner wouldn't be such a big issue.

At first Emily might be reluctant about this plan of action, but Rafe was confident he could change her mind and bring her around to his way of thinking.

He'd seen that look in her eyes as she'd drifted off to sleep last night. She cared for him. He was gambling that she wanted him in her life as much as he wanted to be there.

He'd never been much of a gambling man. He preferred to take risks where he could control the outcome. But there was no controlling Em. She was a force unto herself and no matter what happened, she was never going to be coerced into doing anything she wasn't comfortable with.

Emily, her mom and Harry spent a pleasant day together at her house. It was nice to forget about everything and just enjoy having her mom home.

Jessica Fielding had the same blue eyes as Emily but her hair was blond and cut short in a low-maintenance bob. She'd had a look of mild concern on her face ever since she docked earlier today. "So how far along are you?" she asked.

"About eight weeks. I'm not really showing yet but have lots of morning sickness," Emily said as her mom got up and brought her a glass of homemade lemonade and a gingersnap. Emily had been ordered to sit on the padded chaise longue in the shade of a big magnolia tree in the backyard while Harry manned the grill preparing fish for their dinner and her mom bustled around doing things for Emily that she could do herself. She'd protested at first, but then figured her mom was only in town for a few days and it was okay to let her spoil her. Well, fetching drinks and fixing dinner was probably going to be the extent of the spoiling. Her mom wasn't one of those in-your-face, hands-on parents.

"Tell me about the father," her mom said. "Is he totally out of the picture?"

Emily took a sip of her lemonade. "Not entirely. Was my dad when you were pregnant?"

"Em," Jessica said.

"Mom, I want to know more about him. I'm not going to suddenly show up on his doorstep—how could I? Is he even alive?" These were the questions she'd kept hidden away for years but the truth was, she needed to know now more than ever. She'd always wanted to know for herself but really felt as if she had to know the answers to share with your child.

"No, you can't show up on his doorstep, Emily. He's dead. He died when you were three," Jessica said at last. She rubbed her hand over her forehead and Emily almost felt bad for asking about him.

But she had a right to know. Someday her child was going to want to know about Rafe, and Emily planned to have the answers ready.

"Why didn't you ever tell me this?"

"You never asked."

"I didn't ask because you seemed sad whenever I said anything about my father," Emily said.

"Sorry, sweetie, I just thought you were too young to understand and then as you got older you never brought it up so I kept quiet."

"Is that why we moved here?" Emily asked.

"That was part of it. Also, I had the grant so I needed

to live someplace where I could do my work and be home every night for you," Jessica said

She got that. Work had always been her mother's driving force. Emily had been swimming before she learned to walk and had understood boat safety by the time she was six. Her life had been on the water and as an assistant to her mother's work. The work always came first, and Em had understood that at a very early age.

Emily was beginning to think of what she would do once her baby was born, and though she hadn't talked to Harry yet, she was pretty sure she wouldn't be tending bar.

"Did he want me?" Emily asked. It was the question that had weighed on her mind for a long time.

"He did, sweetie, but he had another family. He was a married man," Jessica said at last. "He saw you from time to time before he died. But really he knew that he couldn't leave his wife."

That wasn't what she'd expected. A married man. Had her mother known he was married? It didn't fit the picture she had of her mother, of the woman she'd always thought her mother was. Then the thought struck her that she might have another family.

"Do I have siblings?" she asked, mildly alarmed by the thought of strangers who might share her DNA.

"No. His wife was infertile and they never had children. He offered to adopt you and raise you with his wife, but I couldn't let you go."

Harry left his position by the grill and went over to her mother, putting his hand on her shoulder. Emily realized now why her mom had never spoken of her father. But she was glad to finally know something about him.

She went over to her mom and hugged her tightly. Her mom hugged her back, and then kissed the top of her head.

"I love you, Mom."

"I love you too, honey. I'm sorry I never talked about him."

"It's okay," Emily said. "Thank you."

"For what?" she asked, tucking a strand of hair behind Emily's ear.

"Telling me. I hated not knowing. I always felt… Well, that doesn't matter now," Emily said. But she'd always felt an emptiness inside her where a father should be. Now she knew. Their situation had been complicated. More so than her own?

She wasn't too sure.

"Tell me about the father of your child," Jessica said.

"He's Rafael Montoro IV," Emily said. Then she realized that she always used his full name when she told people about him so they'd get why he wasn't with her. She was sort of making excuses for coming second in his life. "We had a weekend together and then I got pregnant. His family got called back to Alma to restore the monarchy before I knew I was going to have his baby."

"Harry filled me in on a few of the details via our calls on the satellite phone."

Jessica sat down on the end of the chaise longue and lifted Emily's legs, drawing them over her lap. "Well, I can see why you said it was complicated. What did he say when you told him about the baby?"

"I caught him on his way out of town, Mom. We

really didn't have any time to talk. I wanted him to know he had a kid coming but I never expected anything from him."

Her mom nodded. "You're strong enough to raise the baby on your own, and you have me."

"And me," Harry said.

Emily smiled over at Harry. "I know. But I think he wants to be a part of the baby's life."

"And yours?"

She bit her lower lip. She'd been telling herself that he did, but what if she was just seeing something that wasn't there? Emotions and bonds that she wanted to see because she'd started to care about him. And not just because he was her baby's father.

"I don't know. He's been calling me every day while he's in Alma. He sent me that beautiful mermaid that's hanging in the kitchen."

Her mom smiled. "Remember when you wanted to be a mermaid?"

She nodded.

"You told him?" her mom asked. "Oh, baby, I'd hoped you wouldn't fall for a man who wasn't available."

She had, too. Of course until this afternoon she'd had no idea how much her own life might parallel her mother's, but it was clear now that the Fielding women always seemed to go for men who were already spoken for.

"I'm not sure I've fallen for him."

"You are starting to," her mom said.

"Mom." Her mom always had to push her when she wasn't ready.

"Dinner's ready, ladies," Harry said, interrupting the fight that he could sense brewing.

They went to the table and Harry served the fish her mom had caught that morning and fresh mango with grilled green onions. It was delicious and Emily forgot her ire at her mother as they finished eating.

This was turning out to be one of the best days she'd had in a while. She'd talked to Rafe this morning and felt closer to him than ever. She'd learned the details of her own parentage and felt closer to her mom than ever before.

Her mom picked up the dishes and went into the kitchen to watch the evening weather forecast, something she did every night so she'd know what to expect on the water the next day.

"You better come in here and see this," her mom said as she leaned out the window.

Emily got to her feet, looking up at the evening summer sky and wondering if it looked similar in Alma.

She stepped inside and noticed that that instead of the local fishing report the television was tuned to E! News. She'd been watching *Keeping up with the Kardashians* earlier. Now the words *Montoro Baby Mama!* were on the screen and Emily felt as if she was going to be sick.

Eight

Rafe turned his phone to flight-safe mode once they were getting ready to land. There was a tingle of excitement in the pit of his stomach as he made plans to bring Emily to his family. She was stubborn, so he knew it wouldn't be easy to convince her to leave Key West, but he was fairly confident that he had his ways of persuading her.

They landed at the private airfield the Montoros always used. As Rafe got off the plane and started walking across the tarmac, he noticed there seemed to be a swarm of reporters waiting. Had something happened in Alma in the last ten hours while he'd been on the plane? He slowed down, as did the rest of the party, all looking at one another as they flicked on their phones and scanned headlines.

Gabe was the first one to spot it and cursed under his breath.

"Your baby mama is headline news," Gabe said.

His baby mama.

Damn.

"It's not like that," he said.

Juan Carlos looked pissed but he was quiet as he simply turned away from Rafe and walked toward the hangar. He couldn't have known that the press would find out about Emily while they were in the air. Rafe shoved his hands into his pockets and rocked back on his heels.

Gabe clapped a sympathetic hand on his shoulders before following the rest of their party into the hangar. Rafe's phone finally connected and he saw he had a dozen missed calls from Emily along with seven text messages that all said the same thing. Call me.

She'd already seen the news.

Of course she had. For a brief moment he wondered if she'd leaked the news, but then he remembered how fierce she was about keeping to herself. It was doubtful that she'd rat herself out.

When Rafe got into the hangar, Gabe immediately introduced him to a tall, dapper man in a white linen suit. Geoff Standings was a British press agent who'd once worked for the British royal family. Apparently he'd been sent by the royal advisers back in Alma to meet Rafe's plane and start doing damage control.

Gabe didn't look as amused as he had a few minutes ago.

"We need to fix this," Gabe said.

"Duh."

"No, I mean if the people of Alma decide that you are too hot to touch, then I'm going to have to take your place as king. We need to fix this. Now."

"Fine. Geoff, what do you recommend? I have been planning to introduce Emily to the family, and was even thinking of having a dinner next week where she could meet the members of my family who came with me on the trip. Do you think we should get engaged? Should I marry her?"

"Well, marriage usually is the right step for an illegitimate baby. But in your case I'm going to have to figure this out. I have already sent my assistant to start researching her lineage. Maybe we can find a relation—however distant—to a royal somewhere."

"If that doesn't work?" Rafe asked.

"I think we can make a case for you as a love match. Prince William married a commoner and perhaps Alma won't mind so much if we can make her into a style icon the way Kate is."

Style icon? Rafe doubted Emily would go for that. He loved her style but it was bohemian and beachy. Not exactly what Geoff was talking about.

Geoff was frantically typing away on his smartphone. "Either way, I'm going to book you some shows so you can get out there. Yes, you need to be engaged to her. I'd like to send a press release out that says she's your fiancée, not just your 'baby mama.' Who do you think leaked this?"

Good question.

"I have to ask her before you say she's my fiancée. She might get stubborn if she sees that online or in a paper before I ask," Rafe said.

"Fair enough. Any ideas on the leak?"

"None," Rafe said. "I think she's told her mom and her boss and that's it. Neither of them would tell a reporter."

"Let me look into it and see if I can find out where the information came from. Where will you be?"

"Key West. You've got my cell number, and here is Jose's as well. He's my assistant based at Montoro Enterprises headquarters in Miami and he's at your service."

Juan Carlos returned. "I'll take the family out the front of the airport. I've had your car brought around. Resolve this, Rafe. This needs to be made right."

"I know," he said. "I'll be back in the office in a couple of days to take care of the details of the Alma shipping deal, but I need to go to Key West."

He didn't like answering to his cousin and normally wouldn't have but if Juan Carlos was upset Rafe knew the court advisors in Alma would be as well.

"I was trying to keep this under control," Rafe said.

"I realize that. That's why I'm going to help you as much as I can. Alma needs the Montoros back on the throne."

Juan Carlos gathered the rest of their family. Bella gave Rafe a hug and Gabe shook his head but clapped him on the shoulder before they headed toward the main airport area and the waiting reporters.

No one said another word as Rafe strode out of the airport to his waiting Audi. His phone rang as soon as he was inside. He synched it to Bluetooth and hit the button to answer it.

"Jose here. Have you seen the news? I'm getting calls from morning news shows asking you to come on and tell your story. What should I do?" Jose asked.

"Coordinate with Geoff. He's the PR expert that the Alma court hired to make the scandal go away. I need some media prepared and he's the expert. They are all going nuts over this. Any idea where the leak came from?"

"No, sir. She wasn't visibly pregnant when I delivered your gift and I didn't see any reporters hanging around her place."

"Thanks, Jose. I'm going to leave the phone off while I drive to Key West.

"Why don't you take the chopper? I already have it ready and waiting at the Coral Gables compound."

"I'm trying to decide if I need more time alone to clear my head," he said.

"It's up to you, sir."

If he took the chopper he'd cut his travel time in half and be at Emily's side that much sooner. But he was still not sure what he was going to say when he got there. The plans he'd been hatching as he flew back from Alma were all moot now. He was in damage control, and so was the rest of the family.

"I'll take the chopper."

"I'm turning around and will be in Coral Gables with your bag in a few minutes."

"Where were you headed?"

"Key West," Jose said. "I also have procured two jewelers to meet you. They are waiting in Coral Gables."

"Thanks, Jose." Rafe disconnected the call.

Jose had thought of everything, which was why Rafe paid him the big bucks. Still, Rafe was uncertain. Having the chopper and his bag and even a ring might make going to Key West easier for him, but he had no idea what kind of reception he was going to get when he saw Emily. How was he going to tell her that they had to be engaged? He knew he needed to have that conversation in person and not over the phone. In fact, the sooner he could get to her the better. He needed to think about what he was going to do.

With Em he tended to react first and then do damage control later. This was one time when he needed to plan with his head and not his groin. He wanted her, but he needed the details to be right. There was no more choosing between the throne and Emily.

What kind of king would the people of Alma think he was if he abandoned his child? In a way it was the perfect solution to the debate he'd been having with himself. There was no more keeping Emily and the baby hidden.

Emily gave up trying to call Rafe and convinced her mom and Harry to go home around 11:00 p.m. She changed into a big T-shirt she'd gotten during the last hurricane to hit the Keys with the slogan It Takes More Than a Little Breeze to Shake Me on it.

Harry had called his buddies at the Key West Police Department and together they'd cleared the reporters from her yard and were keeping them at the end of the street. She'd heard a chopper fly over and hadn't turned on the local news because she was afraid she'd see her home on it.

She felt as if this story about being Rafe's "baby mama" was enough to shake her though. She had an idea that the source might be that creepy guy from the coffee shop who'd watched her and made awkward conversation with her. But how had he known about Rafe?

Not that they'd done much to keep it secret. They had been flirting at the bar that weekend he'd been on Key West. Everyone had seen them together. She guessed it wouldn't take Sherlock Holmes to figure out that she and Rafe had hooked up.

But baby mama? That was insulting. She guessed it was meant to be. If it was that creep from the coffee shop, did that rat bastard have a vendetta against Rafe? She vowed to get to the bottom of it tomorrow. She rolled to her side feeling very alone as she stared out the window.

She'd done everything to pretend that it was normal. That she wasn't bothered by the fact that he hadn't called her back.

Why hadn't he?

Surely he knew she hadn't gone to the papers. Didn't he?

There was nothing in it for her if she did. Or maybe he hadn't heard about it yet. But that seemed far-fetched to her, even if she wanted it to be true.

What if he'd decided he'd had enough and the paparazzi were the last straw? It didn't seem like the man she knew to just retreat. More than likely he was coming up with some plan. Maybe he'd ask her and the baby to leave town. Disappear for a while so he could get on with his coronation plans.

Tired of listening to her own thoughts, she got out of bed and wandered through her empty house to the kitchen. She found the carton of frozen yogurt she'd shoved into the back of the freezer when she got home from the grocery store earlier. She'd been trying to hide it from herself because the last time she'd opened a pint of the key lime pie flavor, she'd eaten it in one sitting.

But if ever she needed the cold comfort of fro-yo, it was tonight.

She didn't want to leave Key West, to start over on

her own. But she wasn't alone, was she? She had this little pod in her belly.

She dipped her spoon into the carton and took a big scoop, putting it in her mouth as she leaned against the counter. Letting the frozen dessert melt on her tongue was bliss.

She didn't care what was happening outside her little cottage. She'd just stay here with her fro-yo until she figured out how to fix this.

She'd never met a problem she couldn't solve. It was just late-night loneliness making her feel blue. That and the fact that she was getting total radio silence from Rafe. Why didn't he return her call?

She had a feeling this was going to be one of those nights when sleep evaded her. Part of it she blamed on the habits formed by spending her entire adult life working nights, but the other part was worry. She never admitted she was scared. But she was very afraid that this thing with the news might have helped Rafe decide he didn't need her or their baby in his life.

She wasn't thinking that because he was a jerk or anything. It was just that she understood that royals, especially those in a volatile newly reestablished monarchy, probably needed to be above reproach.

Her mind went to the video chat they'd had two nights ago. He hadn't exactly been staid on that call. She guessed that was what appealed to her about him.

She rubbed her stomach as she walked into the living room. Without turning on the lights, she went to her couch and turned on the television and the DVR to watch her comfort movie. But there was a knock on her door before the opening credits started to roll. She paused it and put her frozen yogurt container on the coffee table, grabbing her baseball bat from the hall closet before she went to the front door.

She pushed aside the curtain on the small, narrow window next to the door and peeked out, not sure what she'd find.

Rafe.

Illuminated by her front porch light, he stood there in faded jeans that fit in all the right places and a T-shirt that molded to his chest like a second skin. Not very regal tonight, was he. Very American and very real, though, she thought.

She unlatched the door and let it swing open, keeping her bat in one hand.

"Rafe."

Was he really here?

"Red. Planning to hit me with that bat?" he asked, pulling her into his arms and hugging her tightly. "I'm sorry I didn't return your calls."

"Why didn't you? When did you get back to the States?" she asked. She felt shell-shocked after everything that had been going on this evening. She hated to admit it but she was very glad to see him.

"No. The bat is not for you. I thought if I found that rat bastard reporter snooping around I might take it to him. I was afraid he might have slipped past the patrolmen."

"We don't need it tonight," he said. "Can I come in?"

She stood there feeling a little aggrieved now that she knew he wasn't a threat. That Rafe was here.

"How long have you been back in the States?"

"I got in this afternoon, right about the time the baby story broke," he said.

"And you came here? But not straight here," she

said. "It doesn't take that long to get here and I know you've got a helicopter."

"Can we do this inside?" he asked.

She felt the need in him to get his own way but she wasn't threatened by him at all. She stepped back and he walked in, closing the door and leaning back against it. First thing he did was take the bat and drop it on the floor. Then he lifted her off her feet with his hands on her waist.

"I missed you, Red," he said, lowering his mouth to hers and taking a kiss that left no doubt that he wasn't going to walk away from her. She had no idea what he thought their future would be, but she realized as she wrapped her arms around his shoulders that she wanted him by her side.

Rafe took his first deep breath since he'd stepped off the plane in Miami. He was with Em, and right now that was enough. His family, who had always been his stalwart supporters, weren't really there for him now. He tucked that away for further analysis later. He knew it was important, but right now he needed to figure out this threat and convince Emily that his plan to move forward was the best one.

"I thought coming home to you was going to be the first peace I've felt in a few days," he said as he lifted his head and stepped back from her.

"I didn't realize you were coming back to me," she said.

"Are you kidding me? I've been calling you every day. What else did you think that meant?"

She bit her lower lip, reaching behind him to bolt

the door before picking up her baseball bat and leaning it against the wall. "I didn't know."

She walked down the hallway lit only by little nightlights plugged into the wall sockets, and he followed her.

All this time he'd thought he was courting her...wait a minute. Was that what he'd been doing?

Yes.

No matter how he'd tried to rationalize it, that was exactly what he'd been doing.

"That's my bad. I was trying to be cool and see if you liked me," he said as he entered her living room. The television projected a soft blue glow into the room and he noted the opened container of frozen yogurt on the coffee table.

She sat in the chair that he had fond memories of making love to her in, with her legs curled under her body. With a quick economical movement she reached over and flicked on the light on the side table.

"I think we both know I *like* you," she said.

He sat down on the ottoman in front of her and put his hands on the arms of the chair. "I'm not talking about lust. I'm talking about whether you like me for the man I am. I don't think I did much but show off the last time I was in Key West. Trying to catch your eye and show you I wasn't like all the other men in the bar."

"You did that," she said softly. "If that was you showing off, you did it very well."

He winked at her. "After all this time I do know how to present a good image."

"It worked. So is that what you were doing in Alma with the people? I saw some of the press coverage from your trip. It looks like you were falling in love with the country and the people."

"You're talking about the blonde, right?" He laughed softly when she frowned and shook her head in denial. "Her family is nuts. They want her to marry the next king. She's not…real. It's not like when I'm with you," he said. Dita was a beautiful woman, but all the scheming with her mother made him edgy. And it was impossible to think of anything other than getting away from her.

"So what do you want from me?" Emily asked.

There it was. The million-dollar question. He had been debating it for so long and still had no answer. "Right now, I need to figure out how the media found out you were pregnant."

She nodded. "The easy stuff first."

It was interesting that she thought finding the source of the leak was going to be easy. "How is that the easy stuff? Do you know who broke the story?"

"Let's just say I have some suspicions, and if that little weasel is at the coffee shop tomorrow morning I intend to confirm them," she said. "I pretty much caught some guy eavesdropping on me when you and I were talking on the phone the other day. And yesterday…I had really bad bout of morning sickness at the coffee shop and Snoopy was right there talking to me about you. Seems odd, right?"

Rafe didn't like the idea that Emily had been targeted. How had the reporter been alerted to her presence? The community in Key West was a close-knit one and Rafe couldn't for the life of him imagine any of them talking about Emily.

It must have been someone who knew him. He remembered the way she'd sneaked into his penthouse. Maybe that was where the reporter had picked up the thread of the story. Maybe he'd followed her.

Hell, he had no idea.

He rubbed the back of his neck. He was tired.

"You're not confronting anyone," he said. "I'll go tomorrow and take care of it."

She put her hand on his chest and shoved him back so she could get up from the chair. Standing next to him, she put her hands on her hips and arched one eyebrow at him.

"One—you're not the boss of me. Sorry, I'm just not going to take orders. Two—that rat bastard played me and I want to make sure that doesn't happen again," she said. "So I'll take care of it."

It was late and he was tired of being pulled in too many directions, so perhaps that was why he let his temper slip as he stood up, towering over her. He put his hands on her shoulders and realized all he wanted to do was protect her, and that was the one thing that Emily didn't seem to want from him.

"Dammit, woman. I'm trying to keep you safe. I don't want any of this dirty press to affect you. I need to know that you aren't harmed by it."

"Why?" she asked. "Because you think I can't handle it?"

"Hell, Red. You can handle anything. I am doing this because I care about you and if anything hurt you I wouldn't be able to live with it."

Nine

Rafe pulled her to him and slammed his mouth down on hers, backing her up against the wall. The moment their mouths met his anger died. It felt like too long since he'd held her in his arms. She did that thing with her tongue where she twirled it around his, and he instantly got hard.

He cupped her butt and flexed his fingers, lifting her up until he could rub his erection right over the center of her body. She was naked under her shirt, and he liked the feel of her cool buttocks in his hands. She moved against him and he feathered his finger in a circle around the small of her back. She moaned and arched against him before tunneling her fingers into his hair and holding him to her while she plundered his mouth.

There was too much pent-up emotion between them.

They'd been in the same room together three times and each time it hadn't been enough. He wanted her. The way she got to him was unlike anything else he'd ever experienced, and his gut was starting to say he wouldn't find it with anyone else.

He sank to the floor when she sucked his bottom lip between her teeth and bit him lightly. Once he was on the floor, he pushed his hands up her back, felt the way her body arched over his. He rubbed his hand up her delicate spine, finding the sensitive nerves at the back of her neck, tracing a pattern over the skin of her nape.

She pulled back and looked up at him. Her lips were swollen, her face slightly flushed pink, making her freckles more prominent. Her eyes were brilliant in the dim light and he realized he'd never seen anything more beautiful.

He wanted her so much at this moment he couldn't think of anything but getting inside her.

"The other night was a pale imitation of this," she said, her husky voice turning him on.

"Damned straight," he said. He pulled her shirt up over her body and tossed it aside.

He set her back on his thighs as he stretched his legs out and held her there so he could look at her. He took in her breasts, which were slightly larger since her pregnancy, and those darker, fuller nipples. He lightly caressed them, running his finger over first one, then the other. She reached between them and pushed his T-shirt up his body.

He let go of her to rip it off and toss it carelessly to the side. She put her fingers on his pectorals and he flexed them. She sighed and traced her finger around each of his nipples before leaning forward to nip each of them in turn.

He brought his hands back to her breasts, but she took one of them and drew it slowly down the side of her body. He reached around behind her and grabbed her ass, bringing her closer. She rocked her pelvis over the ridge of his erection where it strained against the front of his jeans.

He brought one of his arms up behind her and held her with his hand on the back of her neck as he lowered his head and kissed his way down her neck to her shoulder blade. There was a large strawberry birthmark on her left shoulder and he kissed it, laving it with his tongue before he nibbled his way lower. He dropped small kisses around the full globe of her breast and then moved lower to the underside, biting lightly at the spot where her breast rested against her chest.

She moaned his name and rocked against him as she gripped his sides, trying to bring him closer to her. But he held her where she was. He wasn't ready to let her have free rein over his body. She'd been tormenting him for days with her conversations and the little pieces of her soul that she shared with him almost as if they were an afterthought.

He had her in his arms, but she was hard to hold. So hard to keep. And he was determined that he would keep her.

He sucked at the smooth skin between her breasts and then moved on to her other breast. This one was slightly smaller than its mate. He wanted to know everything about her, to know all these details instead of just being satisfied with sex. He needed more than the physical from her this time. He wanted to lay her completely bare so that maybe he'd have the answers that he'd been seeking.

He brought one of his hands up and slowly drew his finger in circles around her areola. He felt the texture of her nipple changing as it tightened under his finger and then he rubbed his finger back and forth against it until she leaned forward, catching the lobe of his ear between her teeth and biting down hard.

He lifted his head to look into her blue eyes. He swore he could see the same desire in her eyes to get rid of all the questions and doubts that remained between them. But he knew he might just be projecting what he wanted to see. He needed something from her that he couldn't define.

She swiped her tongue around the rim of his ear and he got even harder. Uncomfortable now, he reached between their bodies, distracted by the feel of her wet sex against the back of his fingers. He turned his hand and palmed her. He liked the feel of her springy curls as he rotated his palm against her.

She arched her back and shifted against him. He teased the opening of her body with his finger and then slowly pushed it up into her. She tightened around him. And he felt as if he were going to explode. He wanted to feel her naked flesh against him.

Though he did like her naked on his lap while he was still clothed. He pulled back and looked down at her, wanting to keep this moment in his mind forever.

He used his thumb to find her clit. He tapped it lightly and then made a small circle. She responded instantly. He felt the minute tightening of her body around his finger as he continued to rub his thumb in a circle over her center.

He lowered his mouth to her breast and took her nipple between his lips, swirling his tongue over it and then sucking. Her hands were on his shoulders, nails digging into them as she rocked against his hand. She arched her shoulders and pulled her breast from his mouth.

Their eyes met and all the things he'd been afraid to say seemed to hover in the air around them. He opened his mouth and she leaned forward and kissed him.

She started to rock more quickly. She sucked his tongue deep into her mouth and plunged it back and forth to the same rhythm of his finger inside her body. Her thighs tightened around his hand and he pulled his mouth from hers.

"Come for me," he said, whispering the words against her ear.

Her hips moved more frantically and he added a second finger inside her body as she cried out his name. She thrust her hips rapidly against him and then she shuddered and fell forward, resting her head on his shoulder. Her breath was warm against his neck as she reached her hand down between them and unzipped his jeans.

Her touch through the opening of his pants almost made him come. He felt a drop leak out of him and slowly pulled his hand from her body and got to his feet, lifting her up into his arms. He didn't want this to end too quickly

He carried her down the small hallway and into her bedroom, setting her down on her feet next to the bed. She had wrapped one arm around his shoulder, holding on to him and idly toying with the hair at the back of his neck, while her other arm was awkwardly wedged between them, her hand wrapped around his length.

She stroked him up and down, her finger swirling over the top of him. His hips jerked forward and no matter how much his mind said that he was going to take this slowly, his body had different plans.

He let her body slide down his. She moaned as her hardened nipples rubbed over his chest, and he closed his eyes as he felt the dampness of her core against the front of his boxers.

He stepped back and shoved his pants and underwear down his legs and then nudged her forward until she fell back on the bed. Her legs sprawled apart slightly, her hair fanning out around her head, one brilliant dark red curl falling over her shoulder. She had her hands on the top of her thighs and she watched him with hungry eyes.

He wanted to say something profound because the emotions he felt for her welled up inside him, but instead all he could think about was touching and tasting every inch of her.

"Are you just going to stand there and stare at me?" she asked, a tinge of wry amusement visible on her face.

"I'm debating where to start. Every time we've been together I want to make it last…I haven't had the chance to taste you or to explore every one of those lovely freckles of yours."

"There's plenty of time for that later. I want you now," she said.

Her words lanced through him and his erection jumped. He shook his head. Every time he thought he had the upper hand with Emily she did something to remind him that he was putty in her hands. Now and always.

She reached for his length, circling him with her thumb and forefinger at the root. She slowly drew her hand up, closing the circle of her fingers around him as she did so. Involuntarily he thrust closer to her and she smiled up at him as a drop of precome glistened on the tip of his erection. She swiped her finger over it and then brought it to her mouth.

He groaned and crawled up over her body, and then put his hands on her hips and forced her to move back on the bed. He took her hands in his and drew them up over her head as he settled his hips between hers and the tip of his erection found the moist center of her body.

He drew his hips back and then thrust forward again, entering her slowly. She arched underneath him and yet still he resisted the urge to plunge his way all the way home. She turned her hands under his, laced their fingers together and looked up at him.

"Take me," she said.

He nodded as he drove himself hilt-deep into her body. She sighed and arched against him again and he started to thrust in and out, taking them both closer and closer to the edge. He pulled his hand free of hers and drew it down her side as he rocked back and forth. Going deeper each time and taking them higher and higher.

She ran her finger down his back and he jerked his hips forward as he came. Then he felt her legs tighten around his hips and heard her calling his name as she climaxed.

He kept driving into her until she bit him softly on

KATHERINE GARBERA   125

the shoulder and sighed. She turned her head to face him and he saw the completion on her face. He found her lips with his and gave her a soft, gentle kiss.

Rafe wanted to believe that everything was okay between them but he knew that sex hadn't made it so. From the beginning their bond had been strong and physical. That created its own sort of problems. He wanted to just keep making love to her and pretending that was enough, but he knew it wasn't. And there were things he had to say that she might not want to hear.

But for this moment he wanted to just hold her, look up at the moon and pretend that everything was okay.

Emily woke up in the middle of the night having to go to the bathroom. This was something that had only started in the last week. She had read in one of her prenatal books that things like this were only the beginning.

Rafe was cuddled behind her and propped himself up on an elbow as she climbed from the bed. "You okay?" he asked.

"Yes. Be right back."

He fell back down on the pillow and she knew he was tired. They'd resolved nothing except that they still wanted each other. But she felt as if this time they'd done more than just have sex. Rafe meant more to her than any other guy she'd ever dated, and she acknowledged that it had nothing to do with the fact that he was the father of her child—and yet at the same time had everything to do with that.

He made her feel more alive than anyone else ever had, and that was dangerous. She didn't want to rely on him. He could sleep in her bed and come to her bar.

Hell, he could even be involved with their baby, but she didn't want to care for him.

She washed her hands and leaned forward to look at herself in the mirror.

"Don't fall for him," she warned herself. But she sort of already knew that it was too late.

That falling for Rafe was a foregone conclusion now.

He'd come to her in the middle of the night. Wanted to defend her. Everyone knew she could take care of herself, but he still wanted to protect her.

That made her feel so safe. So cherished.

Things that had never mattered to her before tonight.

She shook her head.

He had to want something. There had to be a reason he was here tonight. She wanted it to be for her, but maybe it was about the baby. Now that the world knew about their child, the decisions they'd been making together took on a different quality. Whatever he did could impact his people back in Alma.

She knew that. She wanted it to not matter, but she knew it did.

And she also was very aware that she wasn't cut out to be a queen or consort or whatever the hell they had in Alma.

Maybe that was why he was here.

She left the bathroom and stood in the doorway leading back into the bedroom, watching him as he lay sleeping, his big, strong, sexy body taking up too much of her bed, his face relaxed in sleep. He didn't seem as if he had an agenda. He didn't act as if there were some reason he was in her bed other than that he wanted to be there.

But she knew there had to be more.

She lived in the real world, and stained glass mermaid aside, Rafe had always been very real with her. . When they'd spent their one weekend together, he'd made it clear that would be it. As had she. And when she'd barged in on him in Miami and told him she was pregnant he hadn't pretended they were suddenly a couple.

"I thought you got lost, Red."

She thought she did, too. The first time she'd looked into his hazel eyes.

"I almost did. Why are you here, Rafe?" she asked.

"Come back to bed," he said.

She walked over and sat on the edge of the bed, but he lifted the sheets and gestured for her to come closer. She wanted to. She started to lie down in the curve of his body but stopped herself.

"I need some answers. So far all we've done is establish what we both already knew. We want each other. We have some kind of lust that won't be denied. But I need some answers."

"Okay."

"Okay?"

"Sure. Ask your questions," he said, sitting up and propping his back on the headboard. "I figured we'd do this in the morning."

"I don't think I can sleep until I know if you are going to take my child from me."

She hadn't meant to say it that way. But it was 3:00 a.m. and her guard was down. Her fears were all around her. Rafe was a powerful man before she even factored in the fact that he was about to become the ruler of a foreign land.

"Hell. No. I'm not going to take our child from you,"

he said. "Why would you think I'd do that? I'm not an asshole."

She swallowed hard. "I know you aren't. But we both know I'm not the kind of woman your family has been hoping you'll marry. And now that the world knows I'm carrying the king of Alma's child, I think the stakes have changed."

He reached for her. Took her hand in his and brought it to his mouth. He dropped a warm kiss in the center of his palm before placing her hand on his chest right over his heart.

"I haven't changed, Red. I'm still the man you know. I'm not going to let anything change me."

She wanted to believe him. But the monarchy was bigger than Rafe, whether he wanted to admit it or not.

He tugged her off balance and into his arms. Rolling until she was tucked underneath him. He kissed her long and slow, and she felt her fears for the future disappearing slowly.

In his embrace she felt as if things would work out, but she feared that was false hope until she knew how he felt about her. Until she had some promises… But she'd never had a man make her promises. Never wanted them until now. Until Rafe. She needed something from him, but she was afraid to admit that even to herself.

How the hell was she going to tell him that she wanted him to be by her side? Not because of the baby, but because she needed him.

She tipped her head, closing her eyes and pretending that she had the answers she needed. But she knew that things were even more complicated now than they had been before.

Ten

Rafe woke with the sun, since he was still on European time, and left Emily sleeping quietly in her bed. Last night he'd almost lost her. He still wasn't sure he'd said the right thing or even done enough to keep her. But today he intended to change all of that.

He went out to his car and retrieved the bag that Jose had packed and brought it into the house. He scanned the street while he did so, but saw no reporters hanging around, which was reassuring. As were the two cop cars parked at each end of her street. There was no foot traffic on her block today either.

He found eggs and the fixings for an omelet in Emily's fridge and set to making breakfast for her. His hands were sweating when he put it all on the breakfast tray he'd found in her pantry. He dashed outside to pick a hibiscus from the flowering bush in her backyard and put it in a small teacup with some water. Then he patted his pocket to make sure the ring hadn't disappeared and walked back to her bedroom.

With any other woman this kind of gesture might be enough to make her swoon. But Rafe suspected it might not be enough with Red.

She was still asleep on her side with his pillow tucked up against her. She looked small and vulnerable as she slept. During the day she was a virago, constantly moving and challenging everything in her path. But like this it was easy to see she wasn't as invincible as she wanted the world to believe. Feeling like a voyeur, he put the tray on her dresser and snapped a quick photo of her with his iPhone.

Then he walked over to the bed and sat down next to her. He was tempted to slide back under the sheets with her. Make love to her again, but sex was tearing away layers that he usually used to insulate himself against women. And he couldn't afford to let Emily any closer to him than she already was.

Love was a fairy tale, one he wasn't too sure existed. He'd seen what his father had done for love and how that had torn their entire family apart.

"Em…"

"Um…"

"Wake up, sleepyhead."

She blinked up at him and shoved her hand through her thick red hair, pushing it back off her face. She sat up, ran her tongue over her teeth and then looked at him. "Aren't you chipper in the morning."

He was. He'd always been a morning person, but he sensed that she wasn't and decided silence was the better part of valor. "I'm still on a different time zone. I brought you coffee."

"I can only have decaf," she said.

"That's what I made since it was on the counter next to your machine," he said.

"Thank you," she said, reaching for the mug. Blowing on the surface of the hot liquid before taking a sip, she closed her eyes, seeming to savor it as that first swallow went down.

He felt himself stir and shook his head.

Really. Was there nothing she could do that wouldn't turn him on?

"You haven't tried the omelet yet," he said as he knelt on the bed and settled the tray over her lap.

"No. For trying to protect me. For doing this," she said. "I'm just not the kind of woman men usually do this kind of thing for."

"Yes, you are," he said.

She wrinkled her brow as she stared over at him. He took off the lid that he'd used to cover her plate so it wouldn't get cold and smiled over at her.

"Are you arguing with me?"

"Yeah, I am. I made you breakfast in bed, so clearly you are the right type. The other guys in your life haven't measured up."

She put her coffee on the tray and leaned over to kiss him. It was a little clumsy and tasted of sleepy woman and coffee. He wanted more but she pulled back.

"You're saying all the right things this morning."

"I try. How's your stomach?" he asked. "I didn't even think about your morning sickness."

"I'm not sure I can eat too much, but the coffee seems okay right now."

"That's good. I had Jose get me a bunch of books on pregnancy but haven't had a chance to read them yet," he said.

He wanted to know what was going to be happening to her so he could anticipate her needs. Make everything easier for her.

They shared the breakfast he made and then he set the tray to the side and lay next to her on the bed. "Do you have to work today?"

"No. Do you?"

"No. I'm supposed to lie low," he said. And make everything with Emily right in the eyes of the world. But that part was still better left unspoken for now.

"Good. What do you want to do?"

"Well…"

He pulled her into his arms and then rolled over, bracing his body on top of hers. He put his hand on her stomach and dropped a quick kiss there before looking up at her. He worked his free hand into the pocket of his pants and pulled out the ring box.

"I'm hoping that you'll agree to marry me, Red."

He put the ring box on her stomach and then opened it up so she could see the thin band with the pear-shaped diamond. He'd chosen the band lined with aquamarine because that stone reminded him of her eyes. He shifted to his side, knelt next to her and stared down into her heart-shaped face. "I hope you'll say yes."

She stared up at him for a long moment and he had the feeling she wasn't going to say yes. What had he done wrong? He'd made the big romantic gesture; he'd purchased a ring that reminded him of her.

He was being a good guy. Doing everything by the book of romance. He'd seen his sister reading fairy tales and *Cosmo* so he knew that he had to come across as modern and thoughtful but also deliver on all Emily's secret dreams.

It was a big ask of a man who was used to women falling for him. Especially after the time he'd spent on Alma with Dita and her ilk fawning over him.

"What did I do wrong?"

"Nothing," she said. "I like the ring and the breakfast, but I like my mermaid, too."

He processed that.

The mermaid had been a stroke of genius. Well, really it had been the gesture of a man who missed his woman.

"Doesn't matter if you wear the ring, you're mine."

"I'm yours?"

"We both know it. There isn't a wannabe debutante in all the world who can compare to you, Red."

She gave him a haughty look and then ruined it by laughing. "I know it."

"What about you?"

"Huh?"

"Is there anyone else in your life?"

"Would I be with you if there was?" she asked. "I like you way more than I should, Rafael. Your life is literally worlds away from here but I can't help letting you into my house and my bed. I'm just trying to keep us both from making a mistake."

Maybe he could convince her to say yes. This was the opening he needed. "It's not a mistake. Trust me. Together, we can take on anything."

"For now. But what happens when the newness of being lovers wears off and we have a baby who doesn't sleep through the night? And you have to run a kingdom?"

He saw where she was coming from. And realized the fears she had stemmed from the fact that she didn't know him. Didn't realize how unstoppable he was once he made his mind up.

"I said I'd give you time to get to know me, and once you do, you will know that isn't going to be an issue," he said.

Frankly this shocked her. Rafe didn't strike her as all that traditional. And she knew that he was still trying to figure out the next few months of his life. She wasn't going to be his lifesaver. His safety valve. And that's what this felt like.

"No." The little girl who never had a mom and a dad desperately wanted her to say yes. But she'd learned long ago that the things she wanted most were the ones that made her make the dumbest decisions. And marriage wasn't something to be entered into lightly. Rafe was going to be king. He should have a wife who was in it for the long haul.

He was going to have to do a lot of work to make the monarchy stick in Alma. *Alma.* She wasn't even sure where it was. Maybe she should have looked that up on the internet instead of ogling pictures of Rafe as he toured the island nation. But she hadn't.

"No?" he asked. "Red, think this through."

"I can't marry you," she said. She could, but it wasn't under these circumstances. If he'd asked her the first time she'd shown up on his doorstep pregnant she might have said yes. But too much had happened since then and she couldn't trust his motives.

They knew each other so much better now than they had a mere two weeks earlier, but still not well enough. Or from her perspective, maybe too well. She wanted that man who sent her the stained glass to fall down on his knees and beg her to marry him.

That wasn't going to happen. Rafe liked her. He wanted her but he didn't love her.

"Are you asking me because I'm pregnant?" she asked at last.

He rolled off the bed and got to his feet. He put his hands on his lean hips and stood there as if he could will her to change her mind. She wished he'd put a shirt on, because his bare chest was a tempting distraction.

But not enough of one that she'd say yes to this. She knew if she said yes she'd want him to love her. Why? She'd been fine with lust until this moment, and now she wanted professions of deep emotion from him. Emotion she wasn't prepared to admit she felt for him.

They didn't love each other. She had never thought she was one of those women who needed it, but in her heart she knew she did. She wasn't as practical as she'd expected to be when it came to Rafe. He was arguing that they'd be stronger together, and she thought if they loved each other then he might be right. But a couple who married for the sake of a child? That seemed like a steep hill to climb.

Maybe it was because her mother had never compromised and married that Emily felt so strongly about this. But she couldn't help it. She wasn't going to marry him for any reason. Unless he fell in love with her and proved it in some way that would convince her. She liked him. She cared about him and she had no intention of isolating him from his child. But marriage?

No. Definitely not.

"Partly. I'm traditional, Red. You know that. I want our baby to have my name. And to know who I am. We can do that so much better together," he said. He scrubbed one hand over his eyes and then sat down on the edge of the bed with his back toward her. "Every child needs a mom and a dad. Didn't you miss having a dad?"

"I did," she said. "But I found my way without one. And Harry's sort of filled the role for me. It's all I needed."

"I don't want our kid to have a relationship with some future boyfriend of yours," he said.

"Don't. Don't think of any of that. We are going to get to know each other. We will figure this out."

She crawled over to him and wrapped her arms around his shoulders, leaning her head on his chest to look at him. "Marriage like this isn't a solution. We'd have to be more businesslike and we aren't. The way you get to me…it's all I can do to remind myself every day that you belong on the throne of Alma and I have no place by your side."

He covered her hands with his and clasped them to his chest. "You might."

She shook her head and slid around on the bed next to him. He was so serious, this man of hers. "Is that why you are asking me?"

"Yes. I care for you, Emily," he said. "I want what's best for you and our child. And if you are my fiancée I can protect you from the media. I can bring the full force of the Montoro name and reputation to bear against these people. I can do it now, but they will just glom onto the fact that I'm not marrying you or taking you to Alma. Being my fiancée will make everything easier."

She felt the sincerity in his words. Understood that he was willing to tie his life to hers to keep her safe. But for how long? Because she knew that she didn't want to leave Key West, and there was no way he could rule from here.

"I can't."

"Don't say no. Think about it. Let's see if I can change your mind," he said.

She had no doubt that he could. If she spent time with him and fell any deeper for him then she'd say yes. She'd exchange her life for his. And she knew herself well enough to know that she'd be angry with that.

"How?"

"Let's date and get to know each other. In a few weeks I'll ask you again," he said.

"How will we do that? Do I have to fly to Alma?"

"No. I'm in Miami to wrap up a few business deals. So while I'm here let's date."

"Okay. But what if the answer is still no. What then?" she asked.

"I'm pretty determined it won't be," he said. "And I've never lost a challenge."

"Never?"

"Nope. I'm not afraid to do whatever I have to in order to win you over."

She believed him but she also knew this decision wasn't his alone. "What about your family?"

"Leave them to me. I'd like you to come to Miami Beach next week, stay at my place and meet everyone who's here with me at a dinner. Would you do that?"

She pursed her lips but then nodded. "What day? I'll have to check my schedule at the bar."

"I was hoping for Friday night. But I know that's one of your busiest nights and this relationship isn't all about me. So you tell me which day works for you," he said.

She reached for her phone on the nightstand and checked her work schedule. Harry was going to transition her to the daytime shift starting next week since her pregnancy had really started showing.

She texted Beau, the other bartender, to see if he'd fill in for her on Friday and Saturday. He was always looking for more money and immediately responded that he could.

"Friday is fine," she said.

"Great. Now what should we do today?" he asked.

"I have a few ideas," she said. "But you're going to need swim trunks."

"I packed for a couple of days. I'm good."

The beach that Emily took him to later that afternoon was deserted and well off the beaten path. They had to carry the paddleboard from her car through a stand of mangroves to the water's edge. There were cicadas chirping and the smell of salt water mixed with ripe vegetation. It was so Florida.

The heat beat down on his back and he wore a baseball cap and large sunglasses to protect his face from the sun. Emily had surprised him by giving him a lecture about the dangers of skin cancer even to someone with his olive complexion. So he'd donned her SPF 50 sun cream and the hat even though he never burned.

Her mothering had charmed him. And it was mothering. She'd kind of ensured he had the cream on and taken her time rubbing it on his back, which had led them back to the bedroom. Hence the late start at the beach.

She'd also packed a cooler of fruit juice, sandwiches and veggies. He'd seldom—okay, never —taken a day like this. It was a Monday. He should be in Miami getting ready for the weekly management meeting where he should be discussing the new shipping deal and getting all the routes worked out for their customers, but truth be told he wouldn't trade this for anything.

The way his family had reacted when they'd landed had worried Rafe. He had the sinking feeling in his gut that they were going to make him choose between Emily and their baby and the throne. And as usual when he got his back up that meant he got stubborn. He wasn't too sure he wanted the throne, but he wasn't about to let his family force him out of it.

He had the Coleman cooler in one hand and the paddleboard under his other arm. She'd said she could help carry stuff but he'd said no. He found that he liked making gallant gestures. This morning when she'd turned down his proposal, he'd realized she hadn't had a lot of men doing that for her. And he was determined to convince her that he was the right guy for her.

On that front, he wasn't backing down.

"This spot looks good. We can leave the cooler here. Actually," she said with a blush, "we could have left it in the car. It's not that far to walk back for a snack."

"Then why did I carry it down here?"

She crossed her arms over her chest and gave him a chagrined look. "Because you were so stubborn about me helping carry the board. I hate being bossed."

"You mentioned that. But this isn't bossing, it's pampering. Like when you insisted I wear sunscreen."

She started to argue but then stuck her tongue out at him. "You're right. But don't make a habit of it."

He threw his head back and laughed. She kept him on his toes no matter how much he didn't want to admit it. He liked the challenge of being with her.

"So you've never been on a paddleboard before?" she asked.

"Nope. Never even surfed. I am scuba certified though. Want to do that instead?"

"Yes but the water around here isn't that deep. Snorkeling would be better. We could do that tonight. I know a gorgeous place where we can go at sunset. In fact, if my mom doesn't mind, we can take her boat," she said.

"I'd like to meet your mom," he said.

She got really still. "Why?"

"Because she's your mom," Rafe said. "Why else?"

"Don't try to get her on your side with this engagement thing, okay?"

He put the board on the sand and walked over to her, putting his finger under her chin and tipping her head back so he could see her eyes under the bill of her baseball cap. "When you say yes—and I'm betting you eventually do—it will be because you've decided you want to marry me. Not because I pressured you into saying yes. Got it?"

She punched him playfully in the shoulder and ran down toward the waterline. "I've got it. Get that board and come on, Your Majesty. It's time for your first lesson."

Rafe followed her to the water and they spent the

next thirty minutes with her showing him how to get his balance on the board. Finally Emily decided he could take a turn rowing and he got about two strokes in before he fell into the warm Atlantic Ocean.

He glanced at the shore to find her standing there laughing.

"I bet it wasn't easy for you at first," he said as he swam back to shore with the board.

"I don't remember. I've been on the water since before I could walk," she said.

"So you grew up here?"

"Since I was three, so I think that counts, doesn't it?"

"Pretty much. I was born in Coral Gables and grew up there," he said.

"Florida native."

"Well, just my generation," he said.

He looked at her and the future suddenly didn't seem as nebulous as it always had. The future was real and it was staring back at him with red hair and blue eyes. And that made Alma seem farther away than ever.

"Why don't you stand on the end of my board and look studly and I'll take you on a tour of this inlet?" she asked.

"Studly?"

"Yeah. Oh, is that an insult to your masculinity?" she teased. "I figured after that dunking you gave yourself you might like to play it safe."

He rushed her, scooping her up in his arms and carrying her into the water. "I never play it safe, Red. And I'm not the only one who's going to get a dunking."

He fell backward into the water, keeping her in his arms and drenching them both. She swiveled in his arms and when they both surfaced she kissed him. One kiss led to another and Rafe realized he was having the best afternoon of his life.

He told himself it was just the relief at being away from the pressures of leading Alma and Montoro Enterprises, but his heart said his future was tied to this woman.

Eleven

Emily had felt more at ease staring down a belligerent drunk at Shady Harry's than she did standing in the formal dining room of the Montoros' Coral Gables mansion holding a tonic water with lime in one hand. Rafael III had turned his back on her when she entered the room with Rafe, who had been called away by Jose. He'd seemed reluctant to leave her but she'd urged him to go. She was rethinking that opinion now.

Juan Carlos looked less than pleased to actually meet her and the PR guy Geoff had muttered under his breath that she was no style icon. Well, who was? She was a real person. She wasn't going to apologize for who she was.

Tia Isabella had been feeling well enough to be up with the family. She and her nurse were in one corner with Rafe's sister Bella. Tia Isabella was in a wheelchair and her hands and head kept shaking because of her advanced Parkinson's. When her nurse invited Emily over to join the women, she was grateful. Isabella had beautiful white hair and was the only one to smile at Emily and make her feel truly welcome.

"Hello, Emily," Bella said, coming up behind her and putting her arm around her.

"Bella right? Or should I call you Lady Bella?"

"Just Bella is fine. You look like you are about to bolt."

"I am."

"Well, don't. I've never seen Rafe like this before."

"Like what?"

"Unsettled."

"That's good. He's too sure he knows it all," Emily said.

Bella laughed and Emily noticed that her brothers smiled at the sound. "Rafe mentioned going out on your mother's boat...Is it a yacht?"

Emily realized that Bella was really in a different world. "No. She's a marine biologist. Her boat is like the station wagon of the sea."

"Did you grow up on it? Like Jacques Cousteau's family?"

"No. She had a grant that enabled her to return to Key West every night," Emily said.   ,

"Sounds fascinating."

They were called to dinner and Rafe rejoined her. "How'd it go?"

"Most of your family hate me. If they could make me disappear they would," she said.

"They don't hate you," Rafe said.

"Don't lie to me," she retorted.

"Well, it's not you. It's the fact that I am putting our family's return to Alma and the throne in a very delicate state. No one, not even me, wants that."

Emily wanted to apologize but she couldn't. She wasn't sorry she was having his baby or that she'd gotten to know him. But she was sorry that they'd met now when his life wasn't his own. And when his family would never approve of her.

The next two weeks were busy and though Rafe would be happy to stop flying back and forth between Key West and Miami, he enjoyed every second he spent with Emily.

Tonight he was cruising toward the setting sun with Jessica, Harry and Emily. His first meeting with Emily's mom had been tense but ever since Emily had wrapped her arm around his waist and given her mom a stubborn look, Jessica had been sort of friendly toward him. Harry on the other hand looked as if he was going to need more than a stern look from Emily.

If he didn't know that they were going night diving, he'd have been worried.

"Beer?" Harry asked, walking up to him where he sat on a padded bench at the stern of the boat.

"Nah, I'm good."

Harry sat down next to him and took a sip of his Corona. Emily and her mom were at the helm of the boat talking and laughing as they got out of the no-wake zone. Suddenly Jessica hit the throttle and they were flying full speed across the ocean.

As the wind buffeted Rafe, Harry leaned forward, shouting a little to be heard over the noise. "What are your plans with our girl?"

"None of your business," Rafe shouted back. "No disrespect but you and I both know she'll skin us alive if we discuss it behind her back."

Harry threw his head back and gave a great shout of laughter. The other man was big and solid, but no taller than Rafe. And he'd noticed over the past couple weeks how Harry watched out for Emily as no other adult in her life had.

Her mom, though sweet and loving toward Emily, spent most of her time thinking about her research and reapplying for grants. Her entire world was the ocean and the creatures in it.

It had been startling to realize that in essence Emily had raised herself. That was probably why she was so tough, so feisty and so damned independent. She had a lifetime of doing things on her own. How the hell was he going to convince her that she needed him by her side?

But he understood why the arguments he'd been making hadn't worked. What was it that she needed? The one thing she couldn't give herself, he suspected, was the key to bringing her around.

His phone buzzed. He'd hoped they'd be out of range but no such luck. He looked down and saw he had received a text from Geoff Standings once again asking again if he could run with their release announcing Rafe's engagement to Emily.

He texted back no and then shut his phone off. His family didn't get how delicate the situation was and thought that he could order her to marry him.

As if.

"Just know if you hurt her, bud, I'm coming after you," Harry said with that slightly maniacal grin of his.

"That's the last thing I want to do," Rafe said loudly.

Jessica killed the engines and his words sort of echoed around the boat as everything went quiet.

"What's the last thing you want to do?" Emily said, coming over and sitting on his lap. She wrapped her arm around his shoulders and reached over to take Harry's beer. "No drinking and diving, Harry. That's dangerous."

"It was one beer, kiddo. And barely that," Harry said, getting up and going over to Jessica.

"What is the last thing you'd do?" she asked Rafe when they were alone. He heard the sounds of Jessica and Harry getting the scuba gear ready behind them.

"Hurt you," he said, looking down into her pretty blue eyes.

"No promises, remember?" she said, standing up.

He grabbed her wrist, keeping her by his side as he had a sudden flash of insight into what it was she needed but was afraid to ask for. She needed promises and she needed them to be kept.

"I'm making this one, Red. And I'm keeping it," he said.

"What about Alma and your family?" she asked.

"What about them? That has nothing to do with you and me."

She snorted and shook her head. "It has everything to do with us. I'm complicating things. I think we both know that dinner with your family didn't go very well because of it. They think…heck, I have no idea what they think. But they don't like me much."

He wondered if that were true. He believed his family didn't feel one way or another about Emily. It was him they were frustrated with. They needed him to make her his fiancée or get her out of the picture. They needed him to clean up his act so they could continue with the coronation plans. But he wasn't playing their game.

"It's me they're pissed at," he said. "I'm sure they will like you once they get to know you."

She gave him an incredulous look. "I thought you were going to be a king of Alma, not fairy-tale land."

He laughed. "I am."

"You two done flirting?" Harry called, interrupting their argument. "Ready to do some diving?"

"Yes, we are, Harry," Emily said, walking over and getting her gear on.

Rafe followed her, wishing things were as simple as flirting. But nothing with her ever was.

He joined her family and went over the side of the boat after they'd put the diver down flag in the water. He noticed that everyone scattered in their own direction.

He followed close by Emily's side and reached for her hand, linking them together. She looked at him for a moment, her face not very clear behind the glass of her scuba mask, and then led him through the underwater world. She pointed out different species of fish and coral, and caught up in the natural beauty of his surroundings, he forgot his troubles. There was something very peaceful about snorkeling. But when they surfaced, he knew that nothing had changed in their world.

But he felt strongly that he and Emily had crossed a bridge into new territory.

"That was nice," she said, treading water next to him.

"Yes, it was. Exactly what I need after a day full of

meetings and demands," he said as they took off their tanks and put them in the boat.

"What is?"

Time with the woman he loved.

Shock held him in place as he realized that he did love her.

Versailles was the most famous Cuban restaurant in Miami. Hell, probably the world. Rafe had a night away from his family planned for himself and Emily. And grabbing Cuban sandwiches at his favorite restaurant was exactly the right sort of tone he wanted to set.

He needed Emily to accept his proposal, but pressuring her wasn't the way to get the job done. So he'd been as smooth as he could be, trying not to pressure her into making a decision that he needed from her. And the sooner, the better.

Every day she waited just made his family more anxious. At first it was just the inner circle of his father, brother and cousin, but now his more distant relatives—even his ill Tia Isabella—were asking him when he was going to announce his engagement.

He suspected Tia Isabella was being egged on by his cousin Juan Carlos, the one who wanted the family's return to the throne of Alma to be...triumphant. Not mired in scandal.

Rafe got that.

He'd even had a meeting with Montoro Enterprises' board of directors today. They had been pretty threatening; the upshot was, if he screwed up things in Alma he might not be CEO for much longer.

But the more his family pushed, the less he responded. None of that mattered tonight. The dinner with Emily hadn't gone well. And they'd called a "family" meeting to discuss the matter tomorrow.

Tonight he was going to seduce the hell out of Emily and secure her as his fiancée and then go into the meeting with his family he had scheduled for tomorrow and take control of the situation.

Waiting on Emily, waiting on his family—he felt shackled on all sides. He couldn't take action the way he needed to so that he could move forward.

He and Emily were seated against the wall in the glass-and-mirrored main room of the restaurant. All around him he heard people talking in Spanish. The Cuban dialect was different from the Castilian Spanish that many of the people of Alma used. Cuban Spanish was much more familiar to him.

"So what's on the agenda tonight?" Emily said after they had placed their order.

"Dinner, dancing and then I'll show you the harbor from my rooftop patio. I think you will be impressed."

"I'm never not impressed by you, Rafe."

"Thank you. Perhaps I should ask you that question again?"

She shook her head and her face got a little pinched. "Please don't. Can we have tonight and just be Emily and Rafe, not the future king and his errant pregnant lover?"

He realized that she was facing a different kind of pressure. She'd agreed to come to Miami for a few days after a group of paparazzi had staked out Shady Harry's in Key West. It was either take the security offered by staying in his penthouse or go out on the boat with her mother.

He was pleased she'd chosen to come to him. He

felt as if they had gotten so much closer over the last few weeks together.

"Yes, we can," he said.

"Great. So tell me why you picked this restaurant. I know it's famous and all that, but I wouldn't expect you to be a regular here."

He leaned back in the chair. "Well, the food is the best. You can't find a better Cuban sandwich anywhere in the city. But when I was younger, about ten or so, our mom used to bring Gabe, Bella and me here for dinners on the nights when our dad was in one of his moods and ranting all over the place. And later it was the first place she took us when we got Gabe back."

"Where'd he go?" Emily asked.

"In his early twenties, he was kidnapped while working for our South American division. He ultimately escaped. When we got him back, Mom packed us all up and brought us here. I always associate this place with happy times."

"Where is your mom?" she asked.

"She's remarried and pretty much enjoying her life now that she's out from under the burden of her marriage to our father."

"Do you see her at all?"

"I don't see her very often. But we text. It's enough for me," he said.

She nodded. "It's like that with my mom. I know other people have these crazy-close relationships with their parents but that was never us. She raised me to think for myself and do things for myself."

"Same," Rafe said. "My father gave me the legacy… that sort of feeling of pride in being a Montoro, and my mom gave me the strength to stand on my own while I carry out my version of what that means."

Emily reached across the table and linked their hands together. "I wonder what we will give our baby?"

"Probably everything we never had and always wanted," Rafe said.

Their food arrived and their conversation drifted to lighter topics like bands and books and movies. Everything but the one thing Rafe wanted to discuss. But she'd asked for time, for an evening where they were like every other young couple out on a date.

And he struggled to give it to her. This felt like a game she was playing, and if he wasn't so sure of her confusion about what to do with him, he'd demand an answer. But he knew she wasn't acting maliciously. She was pregnant by a man she hadn't intended to get to know better. The fact that they liked each other as much as they did was fate.

Fate.

Was that what this was?

They weren't like everyone else. They never were going to be. And the fact that Emily wanted them to be didn't make him feel confident for their future together. It started a niggling bit of doubt in the seat of his soul where he'd been confident until now that he could have it all. The throne, his child and Emily by his side.

The rhythm of Little Havana pulsed around them as they walked up Calle Ocho. Rafe reached out and grabbed her hand, lacing their fingers together. Tonight they were pretending that nothing else existed.

But she was aware of the reporters who had followed them from Rafe's South Beach penthouse and were now probably taking photos of them. She wore a Carolina Herrera dress she'd found in a vintage shop earlier in the week. It was a cocktail number in turquoise that hugged her curves on top and had a plunging neckline that gave way to a full skirt that masked her small baby bump.

Everything had been different between her and Rafe since earlier in the week when he'd come diving with her in Key West.

She couldn't put her finger on it, but she knew a lot of it had to do with the new feelings she had for him. It was silly to call it anything but love. Except that she wasn't too sure what love was.

Her mom and she had a relationship based on mutual respect and caring. She could count on one hand the times her mom had told her she loved her. It wasn't that Emily felt unlovable before this; it was just that she struggled to believe these feelings were real.

"Have you been here before?" he asked as they approached the club.

"Little Havana?" she asked.

He nodded.

"Yes. This club—no. I'm not usually on the celebrity radar…though in this dress, I bet I could get in without you tonight."

"You might be able to," Rafe agreed. "The owner and I went to school together."

"The hottie baseball player?"

"He's married. And you're spoken for," Rafe said.

"Am I?"

"You are. We could make it official. I've been carrying your ring around in my pocket."

"Not tonight," she said. She was closer to saying

yes. The more time they spent together, the more she realized that being his wife was…well, exactly what she wanted.

"Prepare to be amazed," he said. "They pulled out all the stops with this club."

Emily's breath caught as they were waved past the line of waiting guests and through the grand entrance. The Chihuly chandelier in the lobby was exquisite. But then when wasn't a Chihuly glamorous?

The club was divided into several different areas. The main floor in front of the stage was a huge dance area surrounded by high-stooled tables and cozy booths set in darkened alcoves. On the second floor, where they were headed tonight, was a mezzanine that overlooked the main club and featured a Latin-inspired dance floor. The hottest Latin groups performed there. Regular people and celebrities mingled, brought together by the sexy samba beats of the music.

"Rafael! Hey, dude," said a tall, broad-shouldered man coming over to them. "Do I have to genuflect now?"

Rafe grabbed the man's hand and did that guy hug that was part shoulder bump, part slap on the back before they stepped apart. "Only you do."

The other man shook his head. "I'm going to pass on that. Why don't you introduce me to your lovely lady?"

"Emily Fielding," Rafe said. "Eric Rubio. He owns this place."

Emily held her hand out to Eric, who took it in his, winked at Rafe and then kissed it. Emily laughed at the easy camaraderie between the two men. As they made their way upstairs to the dance club, she real-

ized that this was the first time she'd seen Rafe so relaxed in Miami.

Emily suspected it was because he was away from
the Montoros and the decisions they wanted from him.
She knew that she felt the pressure, and it wasn't even
directed at her.

She should just say yes to his proposal. She wanted
to make everything easier for him, and her taking her
time and trying to figure out what she felt for him and
if he would always be there when she needed him to
be was just making everything harder for Rafe.

Eric left them as the music started, and Rafe held his
hand out to her and led her to the dance floor.

They spent the night dancing to salsa music, their
bodies brushing against each other, fanning the flames
of the desire that was always there between them.

She wished for a moment they could go back to the
people they'd been when they'd first met. Just two lusty
twentysomethings instead of a man and woman who
knew too much about each other.

"You okay?" Rafe asked.

She nodded, but as she looked into those hazel eyes
of his she realized she'd probably never be just okay
again. All the debating in her mind about whether she
loved him or not had been another diversion.

She went up on tiptoe and kissed him, pouring the
emotions that she was too scared to admit to into that
embrace. His hands skimmed down her sides to her
hips and he held her pressed close to him. It felt as if
everything dropped away but the two of them.

"Let's get out of here," Rafe said, taking her hand
and leading her out the door.

Twelve

Emily wasn't having a good morning. When Rafe's alarm went off, she sprang out of bed and ran to his bathroom to throw up. The morning sickness, which had been waning, was back with a vengeance today. But then she was still in the first trimester. It had seemed as if months had passed, but in reality it was only four weeks since she'd confronted Rafe here in his penthouse. Ten weeks since she'd gotten pregnant.

Yet her entire world had changed.

She suspected it was partially nerves, since Rafe had a big meeting with his family this morning. One that she wasn't invited to attend. He hadn't said much but it had put a damper on their evening once they'd gotten home and he'd finally read all the texts from his cousin and brother reminding him about the meeting. She thought of her little family and how her mom was never one to pressure her into making a decision. But knew she was comparing apples and oranges. Rafe was in line to become king of Alma. There was nothing in Fielding family history that even came close to that.

Both of them knew that this time of dating and getting to know each other was over. She'd overheard a very tense conversation between Rafe and his cousin Juan Carlos last night that didn't sound too promising. She rinsed her mouth out and splashed some water on her face, looking up in the mirror to see Rafe standing there. Simply watching her.

"You okay?" he asked, a gentle smile on his face. He wore only a pair of boxer briefs and she was struck again by how handsome he was. How much she loved every inch of his strong muscled body. "I didn't know what to do. I hate that you get sick in the mornings."

"Yes," she said, taking a hand towel and drying her face. "How are you?"

"I'm fine," he said. "Will you accompany me to the office? We can take the helicopter back to Key West after my meetings are over."

She nodded. "Sounds great."

"I need to shower and shave," he said.

There was an awkwardness between them this morning that hadn't been there in a long time. She wondered if he'd changed his mind about marrying her. Wondered if he wished that he'd just paid her off when she'd come here to tell him that she was pregnant. She just hoped that he didn't regret coming to Key West and Shady Harry's bar and spending that first weekend with her. But the man she'd come to know was now hidden away behind his official Montoro facade.

She knew his attitude had everything to do with his

family. He seemed angry and a little bit hurt. And she was scared. For the first time she faced the very real possibility that she might be losing him.

She thought it telling that he hadn't asked her again to marry him this morning. She assumed the time for that had passed. Maybe he wasn't in the mood to pacify his family anymore.

He turned the large shower on and she watched him get into it. For a long minute she stood there before the pain she felt radiating from him made her move.

She undressed and got into the shower cubicle with him. He was facing the wall with his face turned upward to the spray and she just wrapped her arms around him and put her face between his shoulder blades.

She held him to her, trying to give him her strength and that love she hadn't found the words to express yet. Even in her own heart and head.

He turned around, put his hands on her waist and brought his mouth down on hers. She felt the desperation in the embrace, the feeling that after this moment everything would change. He caressed her back, his palms settling on her butt as he pulled her closer to him, anchoring her body and his together.

She kissed him back, wrapped her legs around his hips and trusted that he'd hold her. And he did. He took a step forward and she felt the cold marble wall at her back. Then Rafe adjusted his hips and thrust up into her.

He filled her completely and just stayed still for a moment while her body adjusted to having him inside her. She ran her hands up and down his back, pushing her tongue deep into his mouth. She needed more and the way he was rocking into her sent sparks of sensation up her body.

He palmed her breasts and broke the kiss, lowering his head to take one of her nipples in his mouth. His strong sucking made everything inside her clench. She felt the first waves of her orgasm roll through her.

She grabbed his shoulders and arched her back to try to take him deeper and he started thrusting harder and faster into her. His mouth found hers again; he tangled his hand in her hair and pulled her head back as he thrust deeper into her.

She dug her nails into his shoulders, felt her body driving toward climax again and moaned deep in her throat as a second, deeper orgasm rolled through her. Rafe ripped his mouth from hers and made a feral sound as he thrust his hips forward and came inside her.

He turned and leaned against the wall. She rested her head on his shoulder as her pulse slowly returned to normal. She let her legs slide down his and stood there in his arms. He didn't let her go. Just kept stroking her back and not saying a word.

She realized she was crying and really didn't understand why. Maybe it was because she had the answer to the question about her love for him. It was true and deep. And she understood that now because she was willing to walk away from him if that was what it took for him to have all he wanted.

Jose was waiting in Rafe's office when they got to the headquarters of Montoro Enterprises. His trusty assistant had a cup of decaf coffee waiting for Emily and a Red Bull for Rafe. He also had a file that needed Rafe's attention before he went into the meeting.

"Jose, I've heard there is a sculpture garden in the building," Emily said, as Rafe skimmed his papers. She was dressed in a scoop-neck blouse, a pair of white denim capris and two-inch platform sandals. She'd left her hair down to curl over her shoulders.

Rafe thought she looked beautiful, but there was a hint of vulnerability to her. One that had been there since she'd dashed to the bathroom from their bed this morning. Nothing he'd done had taken it away. And that was a horrible feeling for a man to know he wasn't able to protect his woman.

"There is the Montoro collection and exhibit. It's on the third floor. Would you like me to show you to it?" Jose asked.

"If Rafe doesn't need you," she said.

"I'm good," Rafe said. Emily gave him a little wave and then walked out of the room with Jose.

The papers that Jose had given him to review showed him the main points of the new constitution of Alma. And he noticed that the part Jose had highlighted dealt with royal marriage. Since they were just reestablishing the monarchy, the rules were strict. Of course, existing marriages would be honored. In cases of divorce, the marriage must be annulled, which was why Rafe's father couldn't inherit the throne. The final stipulation was that the only suitable matches for a single heir to the throne were members of other royal families or the European nobility.

But since Rafe had yet to assume the throne, and this was still a new, untested document, there might still be room to maneuver. Or at least that was what Rafe hoped.

Rafe walked into the boardroom to find Gabe already there.

"I've been trying to get in touch with you all morning," Gabe said.

"Sorry. I had to turn the phone off. I needed time to think," Rafe said.

"Well, I'm the one that the family elected to talk to you. Juan Carlos has been on the phone with the prime minister and the court advisors. They are insistent that we have a scandal-free transition back to the monarchy."

Rafe shoved his hands deep into his pockets and strove for the calm he'd always had when dealing with delicate business situations. And this was the most delicate merger of his entire life. He had to keep calm and not lose his temper.

"Thanks."

"Thanks. That's it? You're losing control of the situation and that's not like you," Gabe said.

"You think I don't know that? Emily is still trying to figure out if marrying me is a good idea. She's got morning sickness and looks more vulnerable every time I see her. The entire family desperately wants me to make this right and for once, Gabe, I truly have no idea how I'm going to do it."

Gabe clapped his hand on Rafe's shoulder. "You always make things work. I've seen you pull off deals that everyone else thought were lost."

Rafe nodded. He wished it were that easy. But from the first, this entire situation had too much emotion in it. There was Tia Isabella and her emotional plea for them to consider the offer from the Alma government to return to the throne. His father's bitter disappointment that he couldn't be the next king and his determination that his eldest son and namesake would be. All of it reeked of emotion, not common sense.

His chest felt tight and for once he needed that legendary coolness he was known for.

The rest of his family trickled in. Juan Carlos led the way. His expression read loud and clear: Rafe needed to act like a monarch and not a jet-setter.

Bella gave him a sad sort of smile as she came in. And his father's glare was icy to say the least. Gabe was sort of in Rafe's corner but he knew his brother didn't want to have to give up his lifestyle if Rafe abdicated.

Right now, he knew that was the only way for them to get him out of the picture.

After his family, the Alma delegation filed in. They had their lawyer and PR agent with them and quickly sat down on one side of the big walnut boardroom table.

His family settled in on the other side and Rafe took his customary seat at the head of the table.

"Rafael, has the girl agreed to marry you?" his father asked without preamble.

"We're not even sure he can marry her without the approval of this board," one of the members of the Alma delegation said.

"I think he should be allowed to marry. Look at the surge of popularity in the British monarchy after William and Kate tied the knot," Bella said with a wink at Rafe.

He gave his little sister a smile.

"A royal wedding would be grand. But we need to settle the subject of her being a commoner first."

"Did she say yes?" his father asked again. "If she's accepted then there is nothing more for this committee to consider. He's a Montoro and she's carrying an heir. The heir to the throne. I think that if he's engaged before the coronation that should be good enough for your council."

It was the first time Rafe could remember his father being on his side. Rafe was grateful to have his family's support for once in this situation.

"We can all appreciate that, Uncle Rafael," Juan Carlos said. "But Rafe has already let our family down and not just with the baby scandal. He's been very cavalier toward royal protocol and taking over the throne."

All of the voices at the table rose as everyone kept arguing their points until Rafe stood up and walked out of the room. He needed to come back to them when he'd made his decision and no sooner. Because they were going to keep fighting and tearing into each other, and in the end they'd tear him and Emily apart if he let them.

Emily wandered through the sculpture garden, admiring the eclectic collection. Famous sculptures stood next to pieces by unknown artists that reflected the Montoro taste.

As much as she'd enjoyed the few days she'd spent in Miami with Rafe, she was ready to go back to Key West. She'd be happy to grab her baseball bat and get rid of the reporters who'd been hanging around Key West hoping for a glimpse of her and then go back to normal.

She'd heard that life changed when a woman got pregnant, but this was more than she could deal with. She wanted things to work out for her and Rafe. For his family to just let her continue to try to figure out if marriage was a good idea or not.

"Emily?"

"Over here," she said, standing up from the bench where she'd been sitting and walking up the path toward Rafe's voice.

One look at his face and the turmoil of his expression and her heart sank. There was no way she could keep doing this to herself or to him. She knew in her heart that she would always love him, but she wasn't going to move to Alma. It hadn't taken more than a night in Miami to remind her how much she loved living in Key West.

"What'd they say?"

"They are still arguing about everything."

"Like what?"

"Whether I can I marry you, whether a royal wedding would be the PR coup of the year, whether I'm an embarrassment," he said.

"You're not an embarrassment," she said, taking a deep breath.

"My cousin Juan Carlos would disagree with you on that score. But none of that matters. I know I promised you time to make a decision but I do need your answer now, Red. Will you marry me? Be my partner on the throne in Alma?"

She bit her lower lip. Hesitating as she warred between what she knew was right for Rafe and what she'd started to believe she could have for herself. But he'd nailed it when he said they weren't sure he could marry her. She wouldn't be the reason he was ostracized from his family. She wouldn't be the reason he had to give up being king.

Her stomach roiled and she was afraid she was going to be sick again, but then realized it was nerves, not morning sickness. She took another deep breath.

Rafe cursed and gave her a hard look.

"Seriously?"

"I can't marry you," she said. "While I'm sure that Alma is a lovely place, I can't imagine living there."

"It is lovely. You can have your own bar and do whatever you like once you are there."

"We both know that's not true. And I can't ask you to choose between me and the throne. I won't be the reason you aren't king, and there is a very real possibility of that happening. You'd resent me."

He shoved his hands in his hair and turned away from her.

She knew she'd made the right choice, but it hurt way more than she expected. "I know you'll support our child, but I'll be okay raising him or her on my own. I think I'll be good at that."

"I bet you do," he said, turning back around to face her. "No one there to interfere with any of your decisions."

"Don't get like that with me, Rafe. You know this is the only smart decision."

He stalked over to her and she realized he was truly mad at her. She'd done the noble thing. She was sacrificing her love and her dream of a family for him.

"I only know that you've hesitated from the moment you learned about our baby to involve me in your life. You keep pushing me away. I have given you space and tried to let you have the time you needed to see that we should be together. I know I seem angry. Hell, I am angry, but I really feel like you are making a mistake."

"And I know that you are. There is no world where you and I get to be together and raise this baby as we want to. I don't want our child to be raised with a bunch of rules on how to behave. You know that would happen. And I'm not good at conforming to them myself. It would be a constant headache."

"You're not going to change your mind, are you?"

"No."

"Fine. Go ahead and leave. You're good at being on your own. You said your mother let you be independent, but it's more likely that you pushed her away so you'd feel nice and safe with only yourself to be concerned over."

His words were mean and cut her to the core.

"You're just a spoiled man who can't handle the fact that he's not going to get his way in all things. That's what this is about. Not me or the baby, but you and your pride. They said you can't have me and the throne so you're trying to shove that down their throats. And to what end?" she demanded.

"Spoiled? You wrote the book on that, Red. I think you're describing yourself and not me. Normal couples, the ones you're always going on about, trust each other, depend on each other. And have each other's backs. They don't give themselves halfway to a relationship to try to keep from getting hurt the way you do. You don't care about anything or anyone other than yourself."

"Well, if that's how you feel I'm surprised you asked me to marry you."

"As you said, I just wanted to have it all. Make you

mine for some ulterior motive. Never because I cared about you or wanted a family of my own."

She was too angry to listen as she stormed past him out of the sculpture garden and out of his life. But later she'd remember his words and cry.

Because at the end of the day, all she really wanted was to have a family with him.

Thirteen

Rafe watched Emily go and he was so angry that he didn't even contemplate going after her. Instead he thought sarcastically that at least his family would be happy. They wouldn't have to worry about him marrying a commoner any more.

But he needed time to calm down before he walked back into the boardroom, or he had the feeling he'd say something he regretted. He'd always been the one who was in control. Calm when he needed to be. Decisive. A man of action.

But then Emily stormed into his life and no matter what decisions he made he still couldn't achieve the results he needed. He remembered how he'd felt on the boat in Key West when he'd looked over at Emily and realized he loved her. He'd been so focused on everything else that the love part seemed to have gotten lost.

His mom had told him when she left to never compromise with himself, because once that happened true happiness would never be his own. As a young adult he'd taken that to mean that he should live by his moral compass and not make business deals that were underhanded. But since meeting Emily he had the feeling that his mom had meant that sometimes making the right decision in society's eyes would be the wrong choice for the person he was.

He stood up and walked slowly back to the boardroom. He opened the door to find everyone still sitting around the table, but they were no longer all talking at once. Rafe knew that they had settled something while he'd been gone and he realized as king his choices were never going to be his own. He was always going to have to compromise and go to the committee before he could do anything.

"Good, you're back," Juan Carlos said.

"I am. What have you all decided?" Rafe asked as he walked to the head of the table and took his seat. "I think you should know that Emily and I will not be marrying."

"See, this just underscores my point," one of the officials from Alma said. "He can't control his personal life. He's a PR liability."

PR liability? He'd always played by the rules. He had a double degree in business management and geology—because of Montoro Enterprises' interests in oil—and he'd always known that without a good understanding of where they got their product he wouldn't be able to lead the company.

He'd worked hard for his family to build up the company so that there was no fear that this generation or the ones that followed would ever want for anything, and this was the thanks he got.

"A liability?" he asked. "Do you all feel this way?"

Juan Carlos nodded; Bella looked down at her fingers; his father just tightened his jaw. Gabe wouldn't make eye contact with him. Screw them. But he knew he was angry in general. He'd tried to please everyone—his family, the Alma delegation, Emily—and ended up not doing a good job of it for anyone.

He stood up and walked out of the boardroom and straight to his office. Jose was waiting there as always. "What do you need, sir?"

"I need to get to Key West. I'm afraid the chopper might not be a good option," Rafe said. He didn't want to take the company helicopter in case his services were no longer needed as CEO. "Can you have my car brought around?"

"Right away."

"Jose?"

"Yes, sir?"

"You've been a great assistant," Rafe said. "I'm not sure what is going to be happening at Montoro Enterprises. Please know that I will always have room for you on my staff wherever I am."

"Yes, sir."

Jose didn't ask any further questions and Rafe was grateful. He really didn't know how to explain anything other than that.

There was a knock on the door and he looked up to see Gabriel standing there. "Damn, I've never seen a man say so much with just a look."

Rafe shook his head as he finished gathering personal effects from his desk.

"There wasn't really anything else to say. I mean when your entire family thinks you've let them down, that's a horrible place to be."

Gabriel came farther into the room and leaned his hip against the desk. "You haven't let me down. I've never seen you so…alive as you've been in the last few weeks. I think that's because of Emily. If you can have her and be happy, you should go for it. That is what you're doing, right?"

"Yes," Rafe said. It had felt wrong to just let her walk away and now that he knew there really was no pleasing everyone, he was going to take care of himself and Emily first. He loved her and he was determined to convince her of it.

"Are you abdicating?"

"I am."

Gabriel cursed.

"I can't be king of Alma when my heart is here. I guess it never felt right to me being a monarch. I'm not aristocrat material."

"I'm sure as hell not either, but I think this means I'm going to have to clean up my act."

"I probably didn't make things any easier for you," Rafe admitted. "But you are a good man, Gabriel. I think you will make a very good king."

"Truly?"

"Yes. Better than me."

"No, I know you're lying. I'm going to pretend you're not. But I'm happy you have found someone."

"Don't be happy yet. She's stubborn and ticked off. I think it's going to take me a while to make her come around."

Gabe smiled at him. "I'm confident you're just the man to do that."

Rafe was, too.

He wished Gabe luck with his royal predicament and left Miami without talking to anyone else. Traffic wasn't too heavy in the midafternoon, but the drive was a long one and left Rafe time to think.

Deciding he wanted Emily was all well and good, but he knew he had his work cut out convincing her that she still wanted him.

Emily arrived in Key West just in time to shower and get dressed for work. It was a typical day in late June. There were too many tourists in town and she knew that she was cranky.

She started her shift with attitude. The first kid who presented her with a fake ID got it confiscated, then had a stern lecture from her before she had him escorted out of the bar.

The waitress and other bartender were all giving her a wide berth, which suited her. She didn't want to talk. She didn't want to think. She simply wanted to forget everything that happened today, get through her shift and then get home.

Harry had looked at her once or twice and made as if he was going to come over and talk to her, but she shut him down with one hand in the air that told him she wasn't ready to talk. Tonight she had no idea whether she would ever be ready to talk about Rafe and the baby or anything.

Tonight all she needed to worry about was mixing drinks and keeping the tourists happy. She didn't even have to worry about reporters sniffing around any-

more. Cara had told her this afternoon that another sus-
picious reporter had shown his face over at the coffee
shop one more time. Cara and a few other locals had
explained that he wasn't welcome in Key West anymore and told him to get the hell out of town.

It made Emily feel really good to know that these
people had her back. She was home. This was where
she and her child would live the rest of their lives together.

They would be fine. She knew that they would. It
didn't matter that her heart was breaking right now.
And that someday she might have to answer uncomfortable questions about where her baby's father was.

For tonight she was doing what she was good at.
Rafe had accused her of being too self-sufficient and
now she knew she couldn't deny it. She did get her
guard up and isolate herself when things got uncomfortable.

Even when faced with love. But there was no way
she was going to be the reason Rafael Montoro IV
didn't become king of Alma. His great-grandfather Rafael I had been king when the family fled. She knew
how important it was to the people of Alma and to the
Montoros that Rafe sit on the throne.

Another kid came up to the bar and she gave him
a hard stare. He looked as though he was eighteen if
he was a day. "Kid, think twice before you place your
order."

"What are you talking about, honey? I need a tube
of LandShark for that table over there."

"Let's see your ID," she said, ready to rip him a new
one.

But he pulled out his real ID and it showed he was

nineteen. Off by two years. "I can't serve you beer, Alfred."

"It's for my dad and his buddies," Alfred said. "Dad, you're going to have to come over here."

Alfred's dad came over and got the beers and the rest of the night settled into a routine. This was going to be her life.

This was what she'd chosen. She could have been with Rafe wherever he was…but she'd chosen the safety of the only home she'd ever known over him. Not because she loved Key West so much but because it was safer to love a place than a man.

Key West wasn't going to leave her.

Rafe could.

"Why don't you take a break?" Harry said. "I've got some conch fritters on my desk and a nice fruit salad."

It was really a nice gesture from Harry. His way of saying that he was there for her. She walked over to him and gave him a hug. He hugged her back.

"You okay, kiddo?"

"I screwed up."

"Want to talk about it?"

She shook her head. "I think I'll start crying and maybe never stop."

"Go eat your dinner. That will make you feel better."

She went into Harry's office and found not only dinner waiting but Rafe.

Her breath caught and her heart felt as if it skipped a beat. She wanted to believe he was here for her, but what man would give up a throne for a woman like her?

"What are you doing here?" she asked. So afraid of his answer but she had to know.

"I abdicated."

"Oh, Rafe. Are you sure?"

"Very," he said, getting up and coming over to her. "I can't rule a country when my heart is somewhere else."

"Your heart?" This was more than she'd hoped for. She had dreamed that he'd come for her but she'd never let herself believe it. She wasn't the kind of woman who a man like Rafe would give up everything for.

Yet she knew now that she was. She could see it in his hazel eyes and his wide grin. Only love made a person grin like that. She knew because she was grinning the same way.

"I love you, Red. I've never met another person who completes me the way you do. I know that sounds cheesy, but I'm new to this kind of thing."

She shook her head. "You can't abdicate. I don't want to be the reason you gave up the throne—"

"You aren't the only reason I abdicated, Em. My time in Alma was constraining. I didn't like having to follow all the rules or answer to a committee. That's not my way. I want to focus on you and our child. And I can't rule without you by my side. Plus, it wasn't really a choice when it came down to picking between you and Alma. You were miles ahead."

"Really?" she asked. "Miles?"

"Yes," he said, getting down on one knee in front of her. "Will you marry me?"

She got down on her knees in front of him and wrapped her arms around him. "I love you so much. I'm sorry for all the mean things I said today."

"Me, too," he said. "I think I knew even as you walked out that I was never going to be king of Alma. I didn't want it, especially given the way I needed you. So are you going to be Mrs. Rafael Montoro IV?"

"Yes."

He took the ring box from his pocket and put it on her finger.

"You should know that there is some question as to whether I will remain CEO of Montoro Enterprises…I might buy you that restaurant you were talking about after all."

"We can see about that. Am I dreaming this? Are you really here?"

"I am."

She still couldn't believe it. She was just so happy to have Rafe in her arms and to know that he was going to be hers. She put her hands on his jaw and kissed him with all the love she'd been afraid to admit she felt for him. He held her close and whispered softly that he was never letting her go again.

There was a knock on the door and Rafe got to his feet, lifting her up, too. "You better eat your dinner."

She went over to the desk and sat down to her meal while Rafe opened the door. It was Harry. The two men exchanged a look before Harry smiled at her.

"Everything better now?" he asked.

She nodded. "I'm engaged."

Harry let out a whoop. "Drinks on the house. And you can take the rest of the night off."

Fourteen

The moon shone brightly down, warming them as Rafe led her toward the hammock in her backyard. The grass path under her feet was soft.

He stopped, turned her around and drew her into his arms from behind. His head rested on her shoulder and his big hands spanned her waist. She stood still, feeling the heat of his body against hers.

They fit perfectly together, which was something she'd rarely experienced in real life before Rafe. There was something about him that made everything sweeter. But this was a dream. She found it hard to believe that she'd found a man she could trust with her heart and soul. But he was that man. She could just let go of everything and enjoy it. But a part of her was afraid to.

He turned her in his arms and she let him. He kept

his hands at her waist and when she was facing him she was struck again by how he was quite a bit taller than she was. He gave her a half smile before he leaned in closer.

"You have a very tempting mouth," he said.

"I don't… Thank you?"

He gave a small laugh. "You are very welcome. It was one of the first things I noticed about you when you told me to wait in line at the bar. But I knew that you wanted something more from me."

"What?"

"You seemed to be begging me to kiss you," he said.

"Perhaps I was," she admitted.

His mouth was firm on hers as he took his time kissing her. He rubbed his lips back and forth over hers lightly until her mouth parted and she felt the humid warmth of his exhalation. He tasted so…delicious, she thought. She wanted more and opened her mouth wider to invite him closer.

She thrust her tongue into his mouth. He closed his teeth carefully over her tongue and sucked on her. She shivered and went up on her tiptoes to get closer to him.

His taste was addicting and she wanted more. Yes, she thought, she wanted much more of him, not just his kisses.

She put her hands on his shoulders and then higher on his close-cropped hair and rubbed her hands over his skull. He was hers now. Something that she could finally admit she'd wanted from the moment they met.

For a moment she felt a niggling doubt… There was something she should remember, but he tasted so good that she didn't want to think. She just wanted to experience him.

His hands moved over her shoulders, his fingers tracing a delicate pattern over the globes of her breasts. He moved them back and forth until the very tip of his finger dipped beneath the material of her top and reached lower, brushing over the edge of her nipple.

Exquisite shivers racked her body as his finger continued to move over her. He found the zipper at the left side of her top and slowly lowered it. Once it was fully down and the material fell away to the ground, he took her wrists in his hands and stepped back.

She was proud of her body and the changes that pregnancy had wrought in it. She could tell he was, too. His gaze started at the top of her head and moved down her neck and chest to her nipped-in waist.

He wrapped his hands around her waist and drew her to him, lifting her. "Wrap your legs around me."

She did and was immediately surrounded by him. With his hands on her butt and his mouth on her breasts, he sucked her gently, nibbling at her nipples as he massaged her backside. When he took her nipple into his mouth she felt everything inside her tighten and her center grow moist.

Then she felt as if she was falling and soon found herself lying on the hammock while he knelt over her. His mouth…she couldn't even think. She could only feel the sensations that were washing over her as he continued to focus on her breasts.

One of his heavy thighs parted her legs and then he was between them. She felt the ridge of his erection rubbing against her pleasure center and she shifted against him to increase the sensation.

She wanted to touch him, had to hold him to her as his mouth moved from her breast down her sternum and to her belly button. He looked up at her and for a moment when their eyes met there was something almost reverent in his eyes.

"My fiancée," he said. "Finally you and the baby are officially mine."

"Yes, we are."

He lowered his head and nibbled at the skin of her belly, his tongue tracing the indentation of her belly button. Each time he dipped his tongue into her it felt as if her clit tingled. She shifted her hips to rub against him and he answered her with a thrust of his own hips.

His mouth moved lower on her, his hands moving to the waistband of her jeans and undoing the button and then slowly lowering the zipper. She felt the warmth of his breath on her lower belly and then the edge of his tongue as he traced the skin revealed by the open zipper.

The feel of his five o'clock shadow against her was soft and smooth. She moaned a little, afraid to say his name and wake from this dream where he was hers. She thought she'd learned everything she needed to about Rafe, but it seemed there was still more for her to experience.

"Lift your hips," he said.

She planted her feet on the hammock and did as he asked. She felt him draw her jeans over her hips and down her thighs. She was left wearing the tiny black thong she'd put on this morning.

He palmed her through the panties and she squirmed on the hammock. She wanted more.

He gave it to her. He placed his hand on her most intimate flesh and then his mouth as he drew her underwear down by pulling with his teeth. His hands kept moving over her stomach and thighs until she was completely naked and bare underneath him. Then he leaned back on his knees and just stared down at her.

"You are exquisite," he said.

His voice was low and husky and made her blood flow heavier in her veins. Everything about this man seemed to make her hotter and hornier than she'd ever been before.

"It's you," she said in a raspy voice. "You are the one who is making me…"

"I am making you," he said. "And I'm not going to be happy until you come harder than you ever have before."

She shuddered at the impact of his words. He spoke against her skin so that she felt them all the way through her body.

"This is the one thing I should have done when you came to my penthouse in South Beach."

"Sex? Um, we did that."

"I should have taken you to bed and kept you there until you agreed to never leave me."

He parted her with the thumb and forefinger of his left hand and she felt the air against her most intimate flesh, followed by the brush of his tongue. It was so soft and wet, and she squirmed wanting—no, needing—more from him.

He scraped his teeth over her and she almost came right then, but he lifted his head and smiled up at her. By this time she knew her lover well enough to know that he liked to draw out the experience.

She gripped his shoulders as he teased her with his mouth and then tunneled her fingers through his hair, holding him closer to her as she lifted her hips. He moaned against her and the sound tickled her clit and sent chills racing through her body.

He traced the opening of her body with his other hand, those large deft fingers making her squirm against him. Her breasts felt full and her nipples were tight as he pushed just the tip of his finger inside her.

The first ripples of her orgasm started to pulse through her, but he pulled back, lifting his head and moving down her body and nibbling at the flesh of her legs. She was aching for him. Needed more of what he had been giving her.

"Rafe…"

"Yes?" he asked, lightly stroking her lower belly and then moving both hands to her breasts and cupping them.

"I need more."

"You will get it," he said.

"Now."

He shook his head. "That's not the way to get what you want."

She was shivering with the need to come. She had played these kinds of games before, but her head wasn't in it. She just wanted his big body moving over hers. She wanted him inside her. She reached between their bodies and stroked him through his pants, and then slowly lowered the tab of his zipper. But he caught her wrist and drew her hand up above her head.

"That's not what I had in mind," he said.

"But you are what I want."

"Good," he said, lowering his body over hers so the soft fabric of his shirt brushed her breasts and stomach before she felt the masculine hardness of his muscles underneath. Then his thigh was between her legs, moving slowly against her engorged flesh, and she wanted to scream as everything in her tightened just a little bit more.

But it wasn't enough. She writhed against him but he just slowed his touch so that the sensations were even more intense than before. He shifted again and she felt the warmth of his breath against her mound. She opened her eyes to look down at him and this time she knew she saw something different. But she couldn't process it because his mouth was on her.

Each sweep of his tongue against her clit drove her higher and higher as everything in her body tightened, waiting for the touch that would push her over the edge. She shifted her legs around his head, felt the brush of his silky smooth hair against her inner thighs, felt his finger at the opening of her body once again and then the delicate biting of his teeth against her pleasure bud as he plunged that finger deep inside her. She screamed his name as his mouth moved over her.

Her hips jerked forward and her nipples tightened. She felt the moisture between her legs and his finger pushing hard against her G-spot. She was shivering and her entire body was convulsing, but he didn't lift his head. He kept sucking on her and driving her harder and harder until she came again, screaming with her orgasm as stars danced behind her eyelids.

She reached down to claw at his shoulders as pleasure rolled over her. It was more than she could process and she had to close her eyes again. She reached for Rafe, needing some sort of comfort after that storm of pleasure.

He pulled her into his arms and rocked her back and forth. "Now I feel that we are engaged. That you and I are going to be okay no matter what else happens in the world."

She shivered at his words and knew that she'd found the one man she'd never realized she'd been searching for. A man who could be her partner and respect her independence. The kind of man who'd be a good father and build a family with her.

"I've been meaning to ask you something," she said.

"What is it?"

"What did you want to be as a little boy? I never got to ask you," she said. She wondered about the man he'd become. Would his dreams have been to be a sports star or business tycoon? Well, he'd become that. Surely, he hadn't wanted to be king.

"I wanted to be your man," he said.

She punched him the shoulder. "Stop making fun."

"I didn't know that you would be the woman, Emily, but I always wanted a family of my own. The chance to have someone who was always by my side."

"Well, you've got that," she said, kissing him.

* * * * *

"You really are a stickler for rules, huh?" Darcy said.

Before he could say anything, she added, "Children need room to grow, to flourish. Yes, they need schedules, but they also need to learn to be flexible."

Colin met and held her stare. There was no way this nanny was going to come in here and wreck everything just for the sake of making memories.

"I'll take her up for her nap," he told Darcy, picking up little Iris and heading to the nursery, Darcy following. With her little arms around his neck, his daughter still clutched the new doll Darcy had given her. Iris had taken to Darcy exactly how Colin wished his little girl would take to a new nanny.

Yet everything about Darcy hadn't measured up to anything he thought he'd be getting into.

Colin stepped into the pale green and pink nursery. A room fit for a princess...or duchess as the case might be.

He glanced at beautiful Darcy. The woman had no idea who he was...

And yet the pull between them was undeniable. Somehow he'd have to resist his sexy new nanny.

* * *

What the Prince Wants
is part of Mills & Boon® Desire™'s No.1 bestselling
series, Billionaires and Babies: Powerful men…
wrapped around their babies' little fingers.

WHAT THE PRINCE WANTS

BY
JULES BENNETT

MILLS &
BOON

Published in Great Britain 2015
by Mills & Boon, an imprint of Harlequin (UK) Limited,
Eton House, 18-24 Paradise Road, Richmond, Surrey, TW9 1SR

© 2015 Jules Bennett

ISBN: 978-0-263-25264-4

51-0615

Harlequin (UK) Limited's policy is to use papers that are natural, renewable and recyclable products and made from wood grown in sustainable forests. The logging and manufacturing processes conform to the legal environmental regulations of the country of origin.

Printed and bound in Spain
by CPI, Barcelona

Award-winning author **Jules Bennett** is no stranger to romance—she met her husband when she was only fourteen. After dating through high school, the two married. He encouraged her to chase her dream of becoming an author. Jules has now published nearly thirty novels. She and her husband are living their own happily-ever-after while raising two girls. Jules loves to hear from readers through her website, www.julesbennett.com, her Facebook fan page or on Twitter.

One

The curves, the expressive green eyes, rich brown hair the color of his favorite scotch—all made for a punch of primal lust Mikos Colin Alexander hadn't experienced in years. This sure as hell was not the woman he'd expected to see on his doorstep.

Woman? No, she couldn't be more than twenty years old. She looked as if she'd just stepped out of a photo shoot for some popular American teen magazine. With her pink T-shirt, body-hugging jeans and little white sandals, this was not the image he'd had in mind when he'd gone on-line seeking a nanny.

Iris's angry cry drew his attention back to the point of this meeting. The lady at his door immediately shifted her gaze from him to the child on his hip.

"Aww, it's okay, sweetheart." Her voice, so soft, so gentle, got Iris's attention. "What's a beautiful princess like you crying about?"

Princess. He cringed at the term, hating how dead-on

this stranger was. But he was in LA now, not Galini Isle, a country so small that nobody here knew who he was. Which was just how he preferred it.

His wish to be free from his royal heritage had carried him through life, but the urge had never been stronger than after the accident that nearly took his life. Between that, his failed marriage, Karina's death and his being a widowed prince, the media was all over him. There wasn't a moment's peace back home and he needed to get away, to regroup…and maybe to never return.

Now more than ever he wanted independence—for him and his daughter.

"I'm sorry." Extending her hand, the lady offered him a wide, radiant smile. "I'm Darcy Cooper. You must be Mr. Alexander."

Darcy. The woman he'd emailed, the woman he'd spoken to on the phone. The woman he'd all but hired sight unseen to be his live-in nanny because of her impressive references and the number of years the agency had been in business.

Na pari i eychi. Damn it.

What happened to the short, round, bun-wearing grandmother type he'd seen pictured on the website? He'd been assured the woman coming to care for his daughter was the owner. No way could this curvaceous beauty be in charge of Loving Hands Childcare Agency. Perhaps they'd sent someone else at the last minute.

Colin shifted his irate daughter to his good hip. Damn accident still had him fighting to get back to normal… whatever normal was after nearly dying and then losing your wife. "You're not what I expected."

Quirking a brow, she tipped her head as a smile spread across her face. Her eyes ran over him, no doubt taking in his running shorts, T-shirt and bedhead.

"That would make two of us."

Her sparkling eyes held his. Was she mocking him? Of course she was. She had no idea who she was speaking to…not that anybody here knew of his royal status, but still. Nobody mocked him except his brother.

Iris's piercing wails grew louder, more shrill in his ear. Between lack of sleep and the constant pain in his back and hip, he was done trying to be Father of the Year. The fact that he'd had no choice but to find assistance still angered him. Iris was the only reason he was giving in. Her needs had to come before his pride—which is why he now found himself staring down at the petite, yet very shapely, nanny.

This is what he'd wanted, right? To be free from all the servants, the media, the people ready to step in and practically raise his child for him while thrusting her into the limelight? Hell, he'd even been running his own vacuum here. Among other domestic tasks like dusting and putting the trash out at the end of the driveway. His brother would die laughing if he saw Mikos wielding a dust mop.

Colin. He had to keep thinking of himself as Colin now that he was in the United States. His middle name would help him blend in so much better. He was here to see who he was as a man, not a prince. To rediscover a piece of himself he was afraid he'd lost.

He just wanted these next six months to be free of all things involving his royal status. He was tired of being home where pity shrouded the faces of everyone he came in contact with. Yes, he was a widower, but so many people didn't know he and his wife had been separated for months before her death. They'd had to keep putting up a good front for the sake of their reputations.

Pretenses. That word pretty much summed him up. He wanted this freedom, wanted to see how he and Iris could live without being waited on hand and foot. He'd promised his brother, King Stefan, that he would only be in the United States for six months, the maximum time a member of the royal family could be away from the island for personal reasons. Then Colin would have to decide whether to renounce his title of Prince Mikos Colin Alexander of Galini Isle or return to the island and resume his royal duties.

Colin was first in line to take over the throne if something ever happened to his brother. If he gave up his position, the crown would be passed to their oldest cousin, who'd rather chase skirts and make scandalous headlines than run a country. That fact had guilt coursing through Colin every time he thought about the situation.

He'd temporarily lost his title when he'd married Karina because she had been divorced once. Their land had archaic rules, but that was one he hadn't been about to fight.

Now that his wife had passed on, he was thrust back into the royal limelight whether he wanted to be there or not. And with his daughter being the next generation of royalty, that automatically made her a duchess. The entire situation was a complicated mess. Added to that, he faced years of ramifications if he chose to walk away from his title.

Colin was determined to be a hands-on father. Being in a new country, still adjusting to this lifestyle and trying to cope with this damn inconvenient handicap forced him to admit he might need just a bit of help. This short-term arrangement would give him good insight into whether or not he could fully care for Iris on his own and if he and his baby should stay here.

When Iris arched her back, screaming as if someone had taken her most prized possession, Darcy instantly reached for the girl.

Without asking, the woman swiped away Iris's tears and gently lifted her from his arms.

"Now, now," Darcy said, patting Iris's back and lightly bouncing his eighteen-month-old. "I'm not a fan of Monday mornings, either."

Colin crossed his arms over his chest as Darcy continued to speak in a calm, relaxing tone. Yeah, like that was going to work. Iris couldn't hear this woman for all the screaming. No way would Darcy's sweet, soft voice penetrate the power of a toddler's lungs.

Darcy stroked a finger across Iris's damp cheeks again. Little by little she started to calm as this virtual stranger kept talking in the same soothing tone, never raising her voice to be louder than Iris. Colin watched as his daughter stared at the stranger.

Within a minute or two, Iris had stopped fussing and was pulling Darcy's ponytail around. Strands of rich, silky hair instantly went to Iris's mouth as she sniffed, hiccupped and finally settled herself.

"Oh, no." He reached for the clump of hair that was serving as Iris's pacifier, but Darcy shifted her body away.

"She's fine," Darcy assured him in the same delicate voice she'd used moments ago to get Iris under control. "Babies put everything in their mouths. I promise it's clean."

Colin watched as Iris gripped the strands in her tight fist and gave a swift yank. Darcy only laughed and reached up to pat the baby's pudgy little hand. "Not so hard, little one. That's attached."

Colin couldn't believe this. Iris had cried off and on all night—more on than off—and had been quite angry all morning. How the hell did this woman calm his child in the span of a few minutes? With a ponytail?

Darcy tapped a fingertip to Iris's nose before turning her attention to him. "May I come in?"

Feeling like a jerk for leaving her on his porch, Colin stepped back and opened the door wider. As Darcy passed by him, some fruity scent trailed her, tickling his nose in a teasing manner.

If he thought she looked good from the front, the view from behind was even more impressive. The woman knew how to wear a pair of jeans.

Perhaps she was older than he'd first thought, because only a woman would be this shapely, this comfortable with her body. He'd assumed all women in LA wanted that waiflike build, enhanced with silicone as the perfect accessory.

Darcy Cooper was anything but waiflike and her curves were all natural.

Colin gritted his teeth and took a mental step back. He needed to focus. The last thing he needed was to be visually sampling a potential nanny. He had to blame his wayward thoughts on sleep deprivation. Nothing else could explain this sudden onset of lust. His wife was the last woman he'd slept with and that was before his near-fatal rock climbing accident two years ago. Between the accident, the baby, the separation from his wife and then her death...yeah, sex hadn't been a priority in his life.

Years ago he'd been the Playboy Prince of Galini Isle and now his life revolved around diapers, baby dolls and trying to walk without this damn limp. Oh, and his glamorous life now included housework.

Yet a beautiful stranger had showed up in his house only moments ago and he was already experiencing a lustful tug. He wasn't sure if he should be elated by the fact he wasn't dead and actually had hormones still ready to stand up and take notice, or if he should be angry because sex was the last thing he had time for.

He and Darcy had agreed on the phone two days ago that today would be a mostly hands-on type of interview. It was important that Iris connect with her potential caregiver. However, he had nobody else lined up because there wasn't another agency that had measured up to this one.

Darcy had been here for all of five minutes. How the hell did he expect her to live here for six months if his attraction had already taken such control of his thoughts? His life was already a jumbled mess without a steamy affair to complicate things further.

Colin watched Darcy as she walked around the open-concept living area, bouncing the baby on one hip as if they'd known each other for some time. Iris started fussing a bit, but just like moments ago, Darcy patted her back and spoke in those hushed tones.

He'd never seen anything like this. He'd tried all damn night to calm his daughter.

Karina would've known what to do. Even though he and Karina had been separated for nearly a year before she died of a sudden aneurism, he still mourned the loss. The rock-climbing accident had changed him, had him pushing her away due to his stubborn pride and fear of not being the perfect husband and father, but a part of him would still always love her. She'd been a loyal wife and an amazing mother.

When Darcy bent over the sofa and picked up a stuffed lamb, Colin clenched his fists at how the denim pulled across her backside. Why couldn't he tear his eyes away? Why couldn't he concentrate on something other than her tempting shape? No, she couldn't stay.

What he needed was someone old enough to be his grandmother, with many years of experience, a woman with silver hair in a bun and ill-fitting clothing. What he did *not* need was a woman who could kick-start his libido without even trying. But, damn it, she'd calmed Iris and had done so with the ease of an expert.

"What is her daily routine?"

Colin blinked as he stared back at the woman who

was trying to be professional when his thoughts had been anything but.

"Routine?"

Dancing the lamb toward Iris's nose and then pulling it back, Darcy simply nodded without even looking at him. "Yes. Naps, eating schedule, bedtime."

Since coming to LA only days ago, he did what worked best for them and he was still adjusting. As hard as this change was, he wasn't sorry he'd made the move.

Colin glanced at Iris's smile, the prominent dimple in her cheek that matched his own. Sure, she'd smile for the stranger, but not for him? He loved his little girl with every bit of his soul. He'd give anything to be able to care for her on his own without the fear of his handicap harming her, but he had to face his own limitations to keep her safe.

"Mr. Alexander?"

Colin returned his gaze to Darcy who was actually staring at him. Oh, yeah, she'd asked him a question. Unfortunately, he was going to have to end this trial before it started. Having someone like Darcy here would be a colossal mistake.

Holding those bright green eyes with his, Colin took a deep breath and said, "I'm afraid I can't use your services."

Darcy swallowed her shock. What had he just said? The very survival of Loving Hands was contingent on her landing this job. She refused to take no for an answer. She couldn't afford to.

She also couldn't afford to keep making eye contact with Mr. Alexander's baby blues. No, *blue* wasn't the right word. What was the proper description for a set of eyes that were so mesmerizing they nearly made her forget all her troubles? The power he possessed when he held her gaze was unlike anything she'd ever experienced, so she kept her focus on the sweet little girl in her arms.

Holding onto a squirming Iris was difficult enough without the added impact of desire. Though she'd certainly take a dose of lust over the ache in her heart from holding such a precious child. She'd avoided working with babies for years, giving those jobs to her employees. Unfortunately, the entire staff of Loving Hands had been let go and Darcy had to face her demons head-on if she wanted to save her grandmother's company. So, his "no" wasn't an option.

This would be the first job caring for a young child she'd taken on since having been told at the age of twenty-one she couldn't have kids due to severe endometriosis. She could do this…she had to do this. No matter the heartache, Darcy had to pull through.

But first she had to convince Mr. Alexander she was the one for the job.

Turning to fully face the sexy father, Darcy kept her hold on Iris, who was nearly chewing the ear off the poor lamb. A sweet smell wafted up from the child's hair, no doubt from whatever shampoo her father used for her.

Darcy had learned from the emails and phone conversations that Mr. Alexander was a single father and new to the area. She also knew his wife had died suddenly just a few months ago. What she didn't know was what he did for a living or where he was from. The sexy, exotic accent that made her toes curl in her secondhand sandals clearly implied that he wasn't American.

Honestly she didn't care where he was from as long as he was here legally and the job posting was legit. He'd offered her a ridiculous sum to live here for the next six months and care for his daughter, and that money would help her save her grandmother's dying agency…the agency

Darcy's ex had pilfered money from, nearly leaving Darcy on the street. Oh, wait, he *had* left her on the street.

Darcy didn't know what happened at the end of the six months, and with the amount of money he'd offered, she didn't need to know.

"You can't use me?" she asked, not ready to admit defeat. "Do you have another nanny service lined up?"

"No."

Shoulders back and chin up, Darcy used all of the courage she wished she possessed to cross the room. Closing the gap between them only made her heart pound even more. She would do whatever it took to pay tribute to the grandmother who'd given up everything to raise her.

Darcy's nerves had kicked into high gear before she'd even arrived here because so much was riding on this one job. Being turned away by the client hadn't been her biggest concern, either. Darcy had truly feared she'd take one look at the child and freeze…or worse, break down and start sobbing.

Yet here she was, holding it together and ready to fight for what her ex had stolen from her. Darcy had already given up her apartment and had slept in her car those first two nights until her best friend discovered what happened. Now Darcy found herself spending nights on the sofa in her bestie's overpriced, undersized studio apartment. This live-in nanny position would secure a roof over her head and a steady income to help get Loving Hands back up and running.

As if all of that weren't stressful enough, her would-be employer had opened his door and all coherent thoughts had completely left her mind. A handsome man holding a baby was sexy, no doubt about it. But this man with his disheveled hair and piercing eyes had epitomized sexy single dad. Those tanned muscles stretched his T-shirt in ways that should be illegal. Not to mention the flash of ink peeking from beneath his sleeve.

The man who all but had her knees trembling and her stomach in knots was trying to send her on her way. Not going to happen.

"So you have nobody else lined up," she repeated, praying she came across as professional and not pushy. "I'm here, your sweet little girl is much happier than when you answered the door, and you're ready to usher me back out."

When he continued to stare as if trying to somehow dissuade her, Darcy continued.

"May I ask why you're opting to not even give me a chance?"

His intriguing set of eyes roamed over her face, sending spears of tingles through her body just as powerfully as if he'd touched her. It was as though he was looking straight into her soul.

Iris squealed and smacked Darcy on the cheek with the wet, slobbery stuffed lamb's ear that had been in her mouth. Still, nothing could stop Darcy from trying to maintain some sort of control over this situation…if she'd ever had any to begin with. She had a feeling Mr. Alexander was a man who was used to being in charge. That thought alone had arousal hitting hard.

Focus, Darcy.

"Mr. Alexander?"

"Colin." That husky voice slid over her. "Call me Colin."

A thread of hope started working its way through her. "That would imply I'll be here long enough to call you by your first name."

The muscle clenched in his jaw, the pulse in his neck seemed to be keeping that same frantic pace as hers.

Before he could comment, she kept going, more than

ready to plead her case. "We discussed a trial period over the phone. Why don't we agree on a set time? That way if this arrangement doesn't work for either of us, we have a way out."

She'd care for Lucifer's kids to get the amount of money she and Colin had agreed upon.

"May I be honest?" he asked, taking a step back as if he'd just realized how close they were.

"Please."

Iris wiggled in Darcy's arms. Darcy set the toddler on the floor to play then straightened to see Colin's eyes still fixed on her.

"I wasn't expecting someone so young."

She was always mistaken for someone younger, which was normally a lovely compliment. "I turned thirty two weeks ago."

His eyes widened as he raked that gaze over her body once more. At one time she'd been self-conscious of her slightly fuller frame. Being surrounded by so much surgically enhanced beauty in Hollywood would wreak havoc with anybody's self-esteem.

She could still hear her grandmother's words on the subject: *Be proud of who you are, your body and your spirit. Nobody can make you feel inferior without you allowing it.* So Darcy had embraced her curves and her size twelve wardrobe, meager as it may be. Besides, who was in charge of dictating what was and wasn't socially acceptable?

Her ass of an ex had mentioned her weight. She should've known then he wasn't The One.

When Colin was done taking his visual journey, he rested his hands on his hips and shifted his stance. With a slight wince, he moved in the other direction. That was the second time she'd caught him moving as if he couldn't stand on one leg for too long.

"Are you okay?" she asked before she could stop herself.

"Fine," he bit off. "You don't look more than twenty-one."

With a smile, she shrugged. "It's hereditary and I'll take that as a compliment."

His eyes narrowed as he tilted his head. "It wasn't meant to be one."

Crossing her arms, Darcy glanced down just as Iris gripped Darcy's jeans and pulled herself up. The little girl with bouncy dark curls started toward the other side of the living area, which was immaculate.

Where were the toys? The random blanket or sippy cup? Other than that stuffed lamb, there were no signs a child even lived here. Even if they had moved in just a few days ago, wouldn't the place be littered with baby items?

Beyond that, from what she could see, the house was perfectly furnished, complete with fresh flowers on the entryway table and the large kitchen island she could see across the open floor plan.

"Perhaps you have an older, more experienced worker?"

The man was testing her patience. Withholding a sigh, Darcy focused her attention back on the sexy, albeit frustrating, guy. "I'm the only one available for the job at this time."

Not a lie. She was the only one—period. Just last month she'd had to lay off her final employee. Letting her grandmother's staff go had been heartbreaking, but the money simply hadn't been there after several of her clients had changed agencies. They had been like family and had all worked so well together. Fortunately, everyone understood Darcy's predicament and Darcy happily gave each of them glowing recommendations for other jobs. Hopefully she'd be able to get Loving Hands back on its feet and slowly bring her workers back.

"Listen," she told him, steeling herself against any

worry or doubt. She wasn't going to borrow trouble yet. "I realize I look young. I understand how you only want the best for your daughter. However, everything I do will be monitored by you since I'd be staying here. You see something you don't like or you believe her care is not up to par, let me know. That's what the trial period is for."

Colin glanced from her to Iris, who was now smacking her hands on the coffee table as if playing the drums. Darcy wasn't about to give him a chance to answer, because she might not like the one he gave.

"I'm here now and from the dark circles under your eyes, you need to rest." Darcy smiled, hoping he was not going to put up a fight. "I can take over while you take some time for yourself."

She waited a beat, her heart pounding. Would he send her away simply because she wasn't an old lady wearing an apron and sensible shoes?

Colin rubbed his eyes then raked a hand over his face, the stubble on his jaw bristling beneath his palm. Why was that sound so…erotic? His eyes settled on her again and she refused to look away, refused to step back or show any fear. This was her livelihood, her only option of getting out of the depths of hell she'd fallen into. Though being thrust into a lifestyle she'd dreamed about for years, a lifestyle that was completely impossible for her to have, was a whole other layer of hell.

When the silence stretched between them, hovering in the air like an unwelcome guest, Darcy was convinced he was going to show her the door. After what seemed like forever, Colin nodded.

"I'll give you today to prove yourself."

Two

Never before had he allowed someone to steamroll him into going against his instincts. Yet a determined woman with enough killer curves to fuel any man's fantasy for every lonely night had done just that.

Perhaps it had been her sensual body that had him caving and ignoring common sense. But Darcy had something else he admired—tenacity. She wasn't giving in and she made very valid points as to why he should keep her around.

Such as the fact that he would be monitoring her every move while she was here. Perfect, just what he needed. Watching her every move might very well be his undoing. He'd wanted to figure out who he was as a man while he was here in LA, but this unexpected lust was an angle he hadn't considered.

Colin clasped his hands behind his head and continued staring up at the vaulted ceiling in his master suite. Sunlight spilled in through the sliver of an opening in his blackout blinds. He hadn't even bothered getting beneath his navy duvet because he knew his mind simply wouldn't shut down, and getting too comfortable didn't really matter. Napping in the middle of the day really wasn't something he did, but he was exhausted.

Rest wouldn't be his friend for some time, he feared. He'd needed a nanny fast. Based on previous families his assistants had interviewed, Darcy was the best option. Unfortunately he hadn't had time to do a full background check on individual people, so he'd just placed a quick call to one of his assistants. Hopefully more information would come back within a few hours, but his gut said he could trust her.

When he told her she'd gotten the job, at least provisionally, she'd returned carrying one tattered old duffel bag. Didn't women have two bags just for makeup alone and another two for shoes? How the hell did she fit everything into one bag that looked as if it would fall apart if accidentally bumped the wrong way or dropped too hard onto the floor?

Before he'd come up to his room, Colin had offered to help her inside with her things, but she'd dismissed him. When she came in with so little, he'd assumed she had more in the car. She assured him she had it all under control and she only had the one bag. There was a story there, and if she was staying around he'd get to the bottom of it. Money was apparently an issue, so he'd be interested what her background check showed.

The cell on his nightstand vibrated. Glancing over he saw his brother's name lighting up the screen. Not what he needed right now.

With a grunt, he rolled to his side and reached for the device. "Yeah," he answered.

"I assume by your chipper greeting you're still on the nanny hunt and not resting?"

"I may have found someone," he replied, not adding that this someone would most likely keep him awake at night.

Stefan laughed. "As usual you're not going into details. Fine. I figured you'd have given up by now and be ready to return home."

"I've only been gone a few days. I think you know I wouldn't give up on anything that soon."

Returning home only meant going back to the life of status he'd never wanted, raising his daughter in a setting that would consume her and stifle her growth. As the current duchess, she'd be in the spotlight at all times. He remembered how irritated he'd been growing up when he couldn't just go out and spend a day at the beach. He'd always been escorted by bodyguards, which seriously put a damper on his teen years and his ability to sneak out to have some alone time with friends—not that he didn't invent some pretty creative ways to lose the guards.

His parents had been wonderful, but still they'd had duties to fulfill, which often kept them away for weeks at a time. Then his mother had passed away from a tragic car accident and his father had been even busier, pouring himself into work and serving the people of the island in an attempt to fill the void.

Colin wanted to be there fully for his daughter. He wanted to form a bond that was so strong she would know just how much he loved her and that he would always put her needs first. Even before the crown. Which reminded him, his brother was still on the phone.

"I know you've never wanted this title," Stefan continued. "You do realize that no matter where you live, you're still a prince, but if I die and you've renounced the title, our cousin will assume the position? He's the last person Galini Isle deserves."

Why couldn't he just have a simple life? A life without

the worry of an entire country on his shoulders? A small country, but still.

Again, it was times like this that he wished Karina were still alive. Colin knew his daughter needed a woman's guidance through life and he needed assistance with these major decisions.

"Listen, if an emergency arises, you know I wouldn't turn my back on you or Galini Isle. But I may have to renounce my title if I think that's the best decision for Iris." Colin sat up and swung his legs over the side of the bed. "Maybe I am making a mistake, but for now I need the distance. I need to figure out what the best plan is for Iris and for me. I'm all she has right now."

Stefan sighed. "If you came home, she'd have many people to love and care for her."

"I really need this time. Iris and I don't need to be surrounded by servants who look at us with pity. That's not what I want for myself or her."

"What about Victoria and me? We miss you guys."

Guilt had already eaten away at Colin's conscience, so Stefan adding another layer was pointless. He missed his brother, but they had their own schedules, their own lives. Years ago the two had been inseparable, often rock climbing or kayaking together. Stefan had stepped up when their father had passed from a heart attack and had scaled back his need for adrenaline rushes.

"When are you coming to the States for a visit?" Colin asked. "Isn't it time for Victoria to see her family?"

Colin's sister-in-law was from LA and was a member of the prestigious Dane family of Hollywood.

Stefan chuckled. "I knew you'd say that. Actually we're not coming for several months, but the annual royal celebration ball is in just over two months and we'd really like you here for that. No pressure, just throwing that out there."

Coming to his feet, Colin twisted from his waist in an attempt to loosen his back, which had wanted to tighten up and spasm a bit more lately. He'd slowed down on the therapy he was supposed to be doing at home. After this long he figured the prescribed exercises were a waste of time. Apparently not.

"I haven't even thought about the ball," Colin told his brother.

"The media will not be allowed inside the palace," Stefan assured him. "I can always smuggle you in via one of the underground entrances, just like when we were teens."

Colin laughed, remembering the numerous times they'd covered for each other so they could sneak out and meet up with their girlfriends at the time.

"Will you at least think about this?" Stefan asked. Colin knew he wasn't just referring to the ball. "Think about how hard life will be for you with no family and no one to help you with Iris."

Colin's mind flashed to the woman who had shown up earlier full of confidence and curves. She was helping his daughter, no doubt. It was what she was doing to Colin that had him questioning his judgment.

"I've got everything under control," Colin assured him. "I need to go check on Iris."

He disconnected the call and slid the phone into the pocket of his shorts. Stefan had wanted Colin to think about this decision to leave the royal title behind, as if Colin had thought of anything else. The moment he'd discovered his wife was pregnant he'd done nothing but try to get out of that damn wheelchair in order to live for his child and be the sole supporter and provider—not in the monetary way, but in the fatherly bonding way.

Growing up with maids, butlers, personal assistants and even people who picked out your daily wardrobe was a bit ridiculous. Just because his family happened to be titled, because they had a certain last name and were wealthy, they had every single material thing at their disposal.

But money could only do so much. Colin still worried about the pressure and responsibility that came with being a member of the royal family. He knew he was projecting his fears onto his daughter, but he was her main source of stability now and he'd rather be overprotective than to pass along something that would overwhelm her.

Raking a hand through his hair, Colin opened his door and stepped out into the hallway. The twelve thousand square foot home was large, not as large as the palace by any means, but big enough that he'd had video monitors installed in most rooms so he could watch the feeds from his bedroom. He'd also had sound monitors wired throughout the house so he could hear Iris no matter where he was. There were alarms on the doors and windows, so he definitely would've heard had Darcy tried to take Iris from the house. He might be paranoid, but he would never take a chance with the safety of his child.

Colin was headed for the steps when his back started twitching.

Damn it. He gripped the railing as he stood on the landing and breathed deeply, waiting for the crippling pain to pass. Total agony he could tolerate, but being in a wheelchair and rendered helpless he could not.

Immediately following the accident, the doctors had indicated he might not ever be able to walk again, but the moment he'd heard those words he'd made it his mission to prove them wrong. Granted, he was walking, but the spasms in his back and piercing pain in his hip and down through his leg would blast him at the most inopportune times. Another reason he needed a nanny. Back home he had a driver, but he needed someone for that task here, too. Damn it, he hated being dependent on others for help, but he couldn't risk his daughter's safety if his pain hit while he was behind the wheel.

Colin needed to start making use of that home gym he'd had put in before arriving. He couldn't put off the physical therapy any longer, because he refused to be at the mercy of this injury.

Once the pain ceased, Colin headed down the steps carefully, in case the sensations returned.

Just as he reached the last step, squeals carried through the foyer. Colin followed the sound and stopped short when he spotted the carnage that used to be his spotless living room. He'd seen Darcy and Iris on the screen in his bedroom just before Stefan had called, but he sure as hell hadn't see this disaster.

"What the—"

Darcy sat on the floor surrounded by toys. Her hair, which had been pulled back earlier, was now down and in complete disarray, as if her hands—or the hands of a lover—had been running through it. Dry cereal was strewn across his coffee table and had trickled down to the rug beneath. From the looks of things some of the pieces had been trampled on and ground into the carpeting. A sippy cup sat on its side, but, fortunately, no liquid appeared to puddle beneath due to the spill-proof lid. There was one blessing in this chaos.

While Darcy was smiling, her eyes on his, Iris was playing with the hair on a doll. Doll? That wasn't one of her dolls. Colin had only shipped her favorite things and this wasn't part of Iris's collection.

"Did we wake you?" Darcy asked, smiling as if this scene were absolutely normal. "We were trying to be quiet."

He'd turned the sound down in his bedroom, hoping sleep would come.

"You didn't wake me." He took a cautious step into the room, almost afraid to look for any more destruction. "Is this typically how you watch children? You let them destroy a house?"

Shoving her hair back, Darcy pulled a band from her wrist and secured the dark mass into a low, messy style. As she came to her feet, she wiped her hands on her pants.

"This is far from destroyed, Colin."

The second his name slid through her lips, his eyes locked onto that unpainted mouth. He'd been told numerous times how intimidating his stare could be, yet she hadn't blinked or even shied away from him. Granted, he didn't want to intimidate her, but he was pretty impressed by how strong she seemed to be. One more aspect of American women he found intriguing. So independent, so strong-willed. As if he needed another reason to be drawn to Darcy.

"Iris and I are playing, and when we're done we'll pick it up." Her arms crossed over her chest, sending the swell of her breasts up to the opening of her V-neck. "There were no toys in here at all so we quietly snuck to her room and I grabbed a few things. Then I wasn't sure what her eating schedule was and she was hungry. Took me a second to figure out what nack-nack was, but I figured it meant snacks when she tugged me toward the kitchen."

As she defended herself, Colin couldn't help but slide his gaze to the way the V of her shirt twisted toward one side, showcasing the swell of her breasts, all but mocking him. Then there was the way her rounded hips filled out her jeans in such a way that would make any man beg.

Prince Mikos Colin Alexander had never begged for anything in his life and he sure as hell wasn't about to start now because of some punch of lust to his gut that he couldn't get under control.

Darcy was quite a captivating woman. He still couldn't get over the fact she wore no jewelry or makeup whatsoever. The woman oozed simplicity and for some reason he found that to be utterly sexy and ridiculously arousing. She wasn't out to impress him in any way other than relating to the care of his daughter.

Iris squealed when she spotted him. With her little arms out wide, she ran across the hardwood, over the rug, crushing even more cereal pieces beneath her bare feet before she collided with his legs. Colin cringed when she reached for him. He wanted to scoop her up, but with his back just coming off a muscle seizure, he opted to take a seat in the closest armchair and pull her into his lap instead.

Iris's little hands smacked up and down his arm and he placed a kiss on top of her head, where her wayward curls always tickled his nose. The smile she offered him had him returning her five-toothed grin. How could he look at her and not smile instantly? She was his every reason for being, the motivation behind all decisions he made.

"How long will the living room be a war zone?" he asked, turning his attention back to Darcy.

She glanced around then back to him with a laugh. "You do realize you're raising a toddler, right? They will make messes, they will make memories and they will learn to clean up later. I assure you this area will be spotless once she lays down for a nap."

Iris wiggled right off his lap and headed toward the coffee table covered in a buffet of snacks. Weren't kids supposed to eat in high chairs? Had his assistants at the palace let Iris be so carefree when he hadn't been around?

"She's been playing in her room," Colin informed Darcy when she continued to stare at him. "That's why the toys are kept there."

A wide smile spread across Darcy's face, making her look even younger. "You really are a stickler for rules, huh? Children need room to grow, to flourish. Yes, they need schedules, but they also need to learn to be flexible."

Even though she stood above him, Colin met and held her stare. There was no way this nanny was going to come in here and wreck everything just for the sake of making memories or whatever the hell else she'd babbled about.

Colin wasn't stupid. He knew he owed his not-so-sunny disposition to the fact that he couldn't get a grip on his attraction. Why this woman? Why now? And why the hell were her breasts right at eye level?

"By flourish do you mean grinding cereal into the floor?" he asked, focusing on the mess. "Or maybe you mean throwing toys around the room without a care of what may break?"

"That was another point I was going to bring up." Darcy stepped over a stuffed animal and sank down on the edge of the sofa. Lacing her fingers over the arm, she brought her eyes back to his. "All of these breakables should probably be put away for now, or at least placed higher where she can't pull them down. She'll get used to what she can and can't touch, but for now I'd try to avoid unnecessary injuries."

The home had come fully furnished. Colin had simply paid a designer to get everything set up so he only had to bring their clothes and personal belongings. All the breakables and any other knickknacks sitting around meant nothing to him. He'd replace whatever was broken, if need be.

Colin glanced across the mayhem on the floor. Iris sat on her beloved lamb while playing with the new doll.

"Where did that come from?"

Darcy glanced over as Iris gripped the doll's long, dark hair and started swinging it around. "I brought it for her."

So in the single bag she'd brought, Darcy had managed to squeeze a doll in among her belongings?

"Is that something you normally do? Bribe potential clients?"

Darcy's eyes widened. "I've never had to bribe anybody. Your daughter was being introduced to a stranger and I used the doll as a way to talk to her and make her comfortable. I can take it back if it offends you."

Colin gritted his teeth. In the span of a few hours his house had been taken over by this free spirit who seemed oblivious to the mess surrounding them and was trying to tell him how to raise his child. She'd calmed Iris in a way he'd never seen and now his new nanny was stomping all over his libido. And he was paying her for every bit of this torture.

Iris started whimpering as she rubbed her eyes.

"Is this nap time?" Darcy asked.

"She tends to nap once a day." He smoothed a wayward curl from Iris's forehead and slid his finger down her silky cheek. "There's no set time. I just lay her down when she seems ready."

Darcy came to her feet, crossed the room and lifted Iris into her arms. "Come on, sweetheart. Let's get you down for a nap. I'll clean the mess today and you can help tomorrow."

Colin rose. Now that he didn't have to bend over and pick Iris up, he figured he could carry her to her bedroom. He hadn't felt even a twinge in his back since he'd been downstairs.

"I'll take her up." Colin took Iris from Darcy's arms, careful not to brush against any part of her tempting body. "You can work on this."

Holding his daughter tight, he headed up to the nursery. With her little arms around his neck, she still clutched the new doll and with each step he took it slapped against his back. Iris had taken to Darcy exactly the way Colin hoped his little girl would take to a new nanny. Yet some things about Darcy didn't add up. He'd picked her agency because of its reputation and level of experience. Okay, so she was older than he'd first thought. But why did she have so few belongings and why were her clothes a bit on the cheap, hand-me-down side?

With Iris nuzzling his neck, Colin stepped into the pale green and pink nursery. This was the one room he'd had painted before they'd moved in. Every other room had just been furnished as he'd requested. He'd wanted something special for Iris and the designer really went all out with the round crib in the middle of the spacious room, sheer draping suspended from the ceiling that flowed down over the bed and classic white furniture complete with all things girly, pink and just a touch of sparkle. The floor-to-ceiling window also had sheer curtains that were tied back with some pink, shimmery material, and toy bins were stacked neatly against the far wall.

A room fit for a princess…or duchess, as the case may be.

When he sat Iris in her bed, she quickly grabbed her little heart pillow, hugged her new doll to her chest and lay down. Colin watched until her eyes closed, her breathing slowed.

Darcy might be a bit of a mystery, but with his status, he had to be extremely watchful. She seemed trustworthy so far. If she just wanted privacy that was one thing. Who was he to judge? Wasn't he lying and pretending to be someone else right now?

The fact that there was more to figure out with the alluring, frustrating nanny left him no choice but to head back downstairs and talk with her now that they were alone.

Of course, he was hiding the fact that he was a prince, one who found her to be sexy as hell. Still, he needed help with Iris. For now he'd have to keep Darcy around, but that didn't mean she'd be here for the full six months. They needed to pin down a suitable trial period. In the meantime, he could be researching a backup in case Darcy didn't work out.

Regardless of the end result, he had to ignore how enticing she was. Romance, whether short- or long-term, was not on his agenda, and he sure as hell wouldn't be so trite as to fall into bed with his baby's nanny.

Three

Darcy had picked up the living room, piling all the toys and infant blankets neatly in the corner. The rogue cereal pieces were in the trash, except for the crushed bits. She'd have to ask Colin where the vacuum was kept to get the rug back in order. She'd work with Iris and her cleaning skills next time. The girl needed a nap more than she needed a lesson.

Playing with Iris, truly feeling a bond starting to form, was both a blessing and an ache she couldn't begin to put into words. For so long she'd had that little-girl dream of having her own family, but such things were not meant to be. Darcy hadn't thought this job would be so intense, yet maybe it was the combination of the baby and the man that had her stomach in knots. As grouchy as he was, Colin was still very sexy, there was no denying the obvious.

At first, the instant attraction to Colin had layered over her anxiety of working with an infant. The man was hot, hot, hot, and that was just the physical packaging. When he spoke with that accent he only rose another notch on the sexy scale. But there was nothing like seeing him holding his beautiful daughter, the way he looked at her with all the love in the world. Something about watching him with his guard down had Darcy melting even more.

As Colin's footsteps pounded down the steps, she stood at the kitchen sink rinsing the sippy cup. Quickly placing it on the drying mat, she wiped her hands on her jeans. She had no clue what mood Colin would be in or how he might react once they were alone.

Would he ask her to leave simply because of the mess? A good first impression was everything and she'd probably blown it. He'd told her she had until the end of the day to prove herself, but she may not make it that far. She stood to lose her pride and her grandmother's legacy. There was no plan B, there was no knight who would ride to her rescue. So if Colin was angry enough to ask her to go, she wouldn't have much choice.

Darcy couldn't get a good read on him. When he looked at her she couldn't tell if he was angry or turned on. Ridiculous to think a piece of eye candy like Colin Alexander would find her attractive, but he volleyed between being pissed and raking his eyes over her.

No way would she bring up the fact he turned her inside out. She'd always been a professional and this job was no different...except for the fact she needed this one more than any other.

Just as Darcy turned, Colin was rounding the large center island. Even in the openness of the kitchen, the man seemed to dominate the room. She stepped back, the edge of the counter biting into the small of her back.

"Is she asleep?" Darcy asked, trying to keep her voice steady, though she felt anything but.

"Yes." His eyes pinned her in place as he rested one

hand on the granite counter. "We need to talk while she's down."

Swallowing, Darcy nodded. This was like the equivalent of the breakup in a business setting. Still, she wouldn't go down without a fight.

"I need to clean the rug first," she told him, knowing he probably recognized the stalling tactic. "I wasn't sure where you kept your vacuum."

"There's a handheld one in the utility room. I'll get it later."

Oh, this wasn't good. An image of her grandmother flashed through her mind. Darcy had promised Gram before she passed that Loving Hands would stay up and running. Then love had entered the picture…or what Darcy had thought was love. How could she have been so naive as to trust a man with her life and her family business, and not see that he was a lying, greedy user?

Colin leaned against the island and crossed his arms over his broad chest. "Why only one bag?"

His question jerked her from her thoughts. That's what he'd initially wanted to talk about? Her luggage?

"How many bags do I need?" she countered.

A sliver of a tattoo peeked out from beneath the hem of his T-shirt sleeve. Darcy's belly clenched. She'd always been a sucker for ink. But shallow lust is what got her into a mess of trouble the last time. A sexy, smooth-talking man and tats over solid muscles…she refused to go down the same path again, when all she'd met at the end of her journey was a broken heart. Not that Colin was a smooth talker. He was more of a blunt, grumpy, irritable talker.

"Will you be sending for more belongings?" he asked.

Still stunned that this was what he'd wanted to discuss, she shook her head. "I have all I need. Does this mean I'm staying?"

When he raked a hand through his tousled hair, a masculine, woodsy scent slid across the gap and straight to her. How did the man positively reek of sex appeal when he looked like he'd spent days without sleep?

"I want to discuss the trial period," he told her, shifting his weight with a slight wince. "The contract we mentioned on the phone was for six months. I'll give you one month to prove that you're the right fit for the job. Anytime in that month we can decide to terminate the agreement."

Relief spread through her in waves. She would definitely win him over in a month. She was good at her job, she'd been raised helping her grandmother care for children and, honestly, raising kids was all she knew. The irony of the situation as it related to her personal struggles was not lost on her.

And, actually, caring for kids wasn't all she knew, just all she knew to pay her bills. Cooking was her hobby, her therapy, really, but it wouldn't keep her afloat financially no matter how much she enjoyed it.

"That sounds fair." She rested her hands on either side of her hips, gripping the edge of the counter with her palms.

"I know we agreed on compensation," he went on as if conducting a business meeting and not standing in his kitchen with sexual tension vibrating between them. "I'll give you half now and the other half at the end of the six months, if you stay. Between now and the sixth month, there may be incentives along the way. Bonuses, if you will."

"And if I leave at the end of this month?"

Colin's bright eyes held hers as he lifted a shoulder. "Then take the first half of the money and go. No incentives."

Half the money was better than no money. Still, she

needed the full amount to pay off Thad's debt and jump-start the agency again. This job would save her business and get her back where she needed to be so she would make sure she impressed him with her skills.

She was an excellent cook, if she did say so herself. Surely that would be another check in her favor. What single man wouldn't want someone who had hot meals ready for him every single night?

"I expect you to care for Iris during my working hours which I already went over with you on the phone," he went on. "I don't expect you to cook every meal, that's a duty we can share. I do need you to drive if we go out, as I'm still recovering from an accident that has limited my activities. If all of this is fine with you, then you can stay."

Darcy nodded, though she wanted to ask about his injury. But now wasn't the time and if she stayed on as nanny, she'd most likely discover what had happened to him.

"I'm fine with that deal."

She held out a hand to shake. He darted his gaze down to her hand, then back up to her face. With an emotionless expression, Colin slid his warm, strong hand into hers and an electric sensation shot straight up her arm. His eyes widened for the briefest of moments. The grip on her hand tightened.

This wasn't happening. No way could an attraction form so quickly, be so intense. She'd been convinced the tension and fascination was one-sided. Apparently not.

Darcy swallowed, wondering what he was thinking, feeling. She didn't want the awkwardness to settle between them. This was only day one, though, so she'd chalk it up to them getting a feel for each other...not the chemistry that was growing and already causing problems.

"Do you want to give me a tour of the house?" Darcy asked, needing to remove herself from temptation.

Colin blinked, dropped her hand and nodded. "Of course. I also wanted to let you know that if you need an evening off to go out or have some personal time, just give me notice. I don't expect you to put your life on hold and work twenty-four hours a day."

Laughter bubbled up and Darcy couldn't keep it contained. Colin's brows drew together.

"You find that funny?"

Waving a hand in the air, Darcy shook her head. "I have no social life. I won't require any time off."

He tipped his chin down slightly, causing a longer strand of dark hair to fall over his eye as he studied her. "You keep surprising me."

Besides his striking looks, Colin had a voice that would make any woman tremble with need. She didn't want to tremble, didn't want to have any type of unexpected attraction toward this man or any other. From here on out, until her agency was back in business, Darcy vowed to stay focused. No men, regardless of how lonely she was. She didn't need someone to complete her, not by any means. But there were those nights she missed being held, missed the powerful touch only a man could provide.

"I'm really pretty simple," she told him. "My work keeps me happy so I don't need anything else."

"What about friends? Boyfriends?"

Okay, that wasn't subtle. Was he asking as an employer or as a man?

Pulling her self-control up front and center, Darcy stepped away from him and headed out of the kitchen. "How about that tour while Iris is sleeping?"

Two weeks and a great deal of sexual tension later, Colin led Darcy down the hall toward the back of the house, well aware of her closeness behind him and even more aware of the unspoken attraction that seemed to be hovering between them. He'd been struggling to keep any emotions hidden. He didn't want her to look at him and see any sign of lust. Colin had no room for such things, not when he and his daughter were desperate for help.

But each time he'd seen Darcy with Iris, something had moved in him. Something he couldn't identify. He assumed at this point she had no boyfriend. She'd made no mention of one even though she'd never come out and answered him when he'd grilled her on the subject her first day.

She'd managed to put him in his place without a word. Fine. He didn't have time to get involved in her personal life and he sure as hell shouldn't want to.

Earlier today, when he'd mentioned working out, he'd seen a brief interest pass over her face. He figured if he showed her the gym and they both made use of it, maybe they could work through…whatever this was brewing between them. He couldn't speak for Darcy, but fourteen days of strain and sexual tension was taking its toll on him.

Colin headed toward the back of the house where the first floor bedroom had been turned into a gym. He'd specified to his designer all the equipment he'd need to continue his therapy on his own and to keep in shape. He had to keep his workouts inside now since his injuries prevented him from going out for a run or rock climbing. He'd never rock climb again. His one main passion in life had been stolen from him.

Shoving aside unwanted anger and frustration, Colin eased the French doors open and stepped inside.

"I know you're busy with Iris, but I wanted you to know this is available to you any time you want to use it. I have weights, a treadmill, elliptical, bike, all top of the line."

"Wow, you certainly take the meaning of home gym

to a whole new level." Darcy glanced through the room and smiled. "I've never had much time to devote to a workout before."

Colin didn't think she needed to work out at all, but he wanted to extend the offer since he'd been using the gym and he hadn't invited her to make use of the space yet. Darcy's shapely body was perfect from every angle… and he'd studied it at every opportunity since the moment she moved in.

"You're more than welcome to everything in here if you decide you'd like to try," he told her.

"I've never used any of these machines before," she muttered. "But I'm sure I could muddle my way through."

Or he could offer to show her.

Colin cursed himself. If they were both going to use this space, he knew they had to do so at different times. The last thing he needed to see was a sweaty, flushed Darcy because that would conjure up a whole host of other images and fantasies.

At this point, he had to get something out in the open. They'd gone two weeks with passing glances and innocent touching as they worked with Iris. Each day he found it more difficult to quash his desires. And Darcy was a damn good nanny, so getting rid of her was not an option.

"I need to be honest with you," he told her.

Tucking her long hair behind her ears, Darcy nodded. "Okay."

"You're a beautiful woman," he began, hoping he wasn't making a mistake. "There's a pull between us and I don't think I'm being presumptuous when I say that. However, I plan to remain single and I have every intention of keeping our relationship professional."

Darcy's mouth had dropped open. For a moment he wondered if he'd gone too far or if his imagination had taken over.

Upfront and honest was how he preferred everything. Okay, obviously there were exceptions since he was keeping a colossal truth from her. But his royal status wouldn't affect her life. She was a nanny, she'd get paid, they would part ways in less than six months and their personal lives could remain private, for the most part.

"Then I'll be honest, too." She laced her fingers in front of her and lifted her chin. "I won't deny the attraction. I mean, you have to know what you look like, but that's just superficial. I still don't know you very well because you're so quiet and brooding, but my main focus is Iris. I promise I'm not here looking for anything other than a job. I've had enough difficulties in my life the past few years. Does that help ease your mind?"

Part of him wanted to know what she'd been through, but the other part told him to shut up and deal with his own issues. Had she just called him brooding? He suppressed the urge to smile at her bluntness. Admiration for this woman who wasn't afraid to speak her mind mixed right along with his arousal where she was concerned. The combination of the two could prove to be crippling if he didn't keep a tight rein on his emotions.

Still, Darcy wasn't like any woman he'd ever known. She wasn't blatantly sexual, she wasn't throwing herself at him even though she'd admitted to being attracted, and she'd been in his house ample time to try her hand at seduction. Not once had she come out with skimpy pajamas or purposely been provocative to try to capture his attention. Perhaps that was just another reason he found her so intriguing and refreshing.

Would she be so controlled if she knew who he really was, how much he was worth?

Being a member of royalty had always made him an instant magnet for women. His late wife hadn't cared about his status, which was one of the things that had initially drawn him to her. But then reality had hit, and the accident that nearly claimed his life wedged between them at the same time she'd discovered her pregnancy. Months of stress and worry had torn them apart and for once in his life, money couldn't fix his problems.

"You okay?" Darcy asked.

Her delicate hand rested on his bare arm and Colin clenched his teeth, fighting away the memories. He couldn't live in the past, trying to pinpoint the exact moment his marriage went wrong. Like everything else, little things started adding up to bigger things and, slowly, the marriage had just dissolved.

Iris was his main concern now. He needed to relax, work on being a regular father giving his daughter the best life possible.

And to decide whether to renounce his title. The pressure of knowing that their wayward cousin, who didn't deserve the title, would have it if something happened to Stefan was overwhelming. He hated being in this position, but ignoring it wouldn't make the situation go away.

"Colin?"

Nodding, he let out a sigh. "I'm fine," he assured her, hating when her hand slid away. Those gentle fingertips trailed down his arm before leaving him wanting more than just an innocent touch. "Anything you want to ask about the equipment while I'm here with you?"

Her eyes roamed over the apparatus in the workout room. An image of her sweating with him flashed through his mind which led to other images of them sweating and he cursed himself. If he didn't get control over his libido he'd have more trouble on his hands than he could possibly handle.

"If I wanted to start working out, what would you recommend? The treadmill? I'm pretty out of shape."

Out of shape? Everything about her shape screamed

perfection. He never was one of those guys who needed his woman to be supermodel thin. He preferred having plenty of curves to explore.

When her eyes came back to his, he fought the urge to pull her inside and get that sweat going. He'd bet his royal, jeweled crown she would look even sexier all flushed, with a sheen of perspiration across her body.

"Do you really want to work out?" he asked. "I don't want you to feel pressured. I'm just offering the room to you."

Darcy shrugged. "I could stand to lose a few pounds."

Anger simmered beneath the surface. "Who told you that?"

Darcy entered the room and checked out the elliptical, the treadmill, the free weights. "He's no longer in the picture, but that's not what matters. What matters is that I've let myself go, and with all of this at my fingertips I don't see why I shouldn't take advantage of it while I'm here."

Colin stepped in and came up behind her, close enough to touch. He clenched his hands at his sides. "If you want to feel better about yourself, that's one thing. If you're doing this because some bastard told you you're overweight, then I have a problem."

Her shoulders stiffened as she turned. The second she realized how close they were, her eyes widened, but she didn't step back. Their bodies were only a breath apart and with each inhale, the tips of her breasts brushed against his chest. He was playing with fire and damn if he could stop himself. He'd always lived for the adrenaline rush and Darcy got his blood pumping.

Being this close he noticed a sprinkling of freckles across her nose. There was so much innocence in this woman, yet in some ways she seemed too tough to be innocent. She'd gone through hard times, according to her. Even if she hadn't said so, he could tell by the way she was headstrong, determined and focused. How the hell could he not find that completely sexy?

"My weight may have been mentioned in my last relationship," she told him, keeping her eyes on his. "But he's history and I want to do this for me. Will you help me or not?"

Would he help her? Close quarters, alone without Iris as a buffer and having Darcy's body as his sole focus for hours? He may not want this attraction, but it was there nonetheless and only an idiot would turn her down.

"I'll help you," he told her. "We'll start tonight after Iris goes to bed. That work for you?"

Her smile spread across her face, lighting up those expressive eyes. "It works if you take it easy on me."

Oiktirmon. Mercy.

"Oh, I plan on giving you just what you need."

Four

What had she been thinking? Darcy had been so impressed by the gym she'd opened her mouth before she could even think about what she was saying. Now she'd committed to exercising with someone who should be posing for calendars sans shirt, while she looked like the before picture on a Weight Watcher's ad.

She'd been taken with Colin and his blunt declaration of attraction. Apparently a lust-filled haze had clouded her mind and hindered her common sense. He'd called out the obvious and now they both had to deal with the tension that would no doubt envelop them every time they were together.

Dinner had been comfortable, though. Iris as the focal point certainly helped. Now she was bathed and in bed, and Darcy had pulled on her favorite yoga pants and an old Loving Hands T-shirt. After pulling on her worn tennis shoes, she headed toward the gym.

The whirring of the treadmill filtered out of the partially open doors and into the hallway. When Darcy peeked around the corner, she was so, so glad she had the advantage of being behind him. Obvious eye-candy images aside, she was thankful no one could see her because there was no way she could take in this male form, all sweaty, shirtless and in action, and not stand here with her mouth open, eyes wide.

The full view of his tattoo caught her attention. A dragon started over one shoulder blade, swirled down one biceps and disappeared over his shoulder to the front. Her fingers itched to trace the pattern, to feel all that taut skin beneath her fingertips. Surely there was some meaning behind the image. Most people had tattoos based on something personal in their lives. She couldn't help but wonder if she'd ever uncover anything beneath the surface with him.

Just as Darcy eased the door open, Colin stumbled, shouted a curse and smacked the red emergency button on the treadmill. Gripping the sides of the machine, he panted, head hanging between his shoulders.

"Are you all right?" she asked, crossing to the piece of equipment in case he needed help.

Colin jerked his head around, wincing as he caught sight of her. "I thought you'd be longer with putting Iris down."

As he turned completely and started to step down, his leg went out from under him and he collapsed, landing hard on the belt of the machine.

Darcy squatted beside him, her hands resting on his bare knee. "Colin, are you okay?" she repeated.

Stupid question, as he'd obviously hurt himself and was trying to hide the fact. Still, she couldn't just stand here and not do or say something.

"Fine," he bit out through gritted teeth. "I'm supposed

to walk every day, but the doctor says if I feel like it I can try jogging."

"Is that why you were running full speed on an incline when I came in?"

His eyes met hers. There went that click once again when this man stared at her. The intensity of his gaze couldn't even be put into words because she'd never experienced such a force in her life.

"I'm not going to be held prisoner by this injury." His tone left no room for argument. "And I don't want your pity."

Colin's eyes held hers another second before they dropped to her hands on his knee. The dark hair on his leg slid beneath her palms as she started to remove her hands. Instantly, his hand covered hers, holding her in place.

"I wasn't feeling pity," she whispered. "Attracted, intrigued, yes. Not pity."

His thumb stroked the back of her hand. "This can't be an issue."

She knew he wasn't referring to his injury or the fact that she'd found him in a state of pain.

"It's already an issue," she retorted, not even trying to pretend she had no idea what he was referring to. "We just have to take control of the tension instead of it controlling us."

His eyes held hers, the muscle ticked in his jaw. "Are you ready to get sweaty?"

Darcy swallowed, then took her own advice and tried to get a grip. Offering a smile, she said, "If you're trying to keep this attraction on the backburner, I think you probably shouldn't ask questions like that."

Laughing, Colin started to rise. "Just wanted to see the look on your face."

The man actually laughed. And there went that zing of desire shooting through her again, because a brooding Colin was sexy, but a smiling Colin was flat-out ir-resistible.

Darcy came to her feet. "I'm sure I didn't disappoint," she joked.

As Colin got his feet beneath him, Darcy took a step back. "So what are you recovering from?"

Raking a hand through his hair, Colin sighed and shook his head. "A life I've left behind," he muttered.

Curiosity heightened, she wanted to know more about this mysterious man who'd so easily and swiftly captured her attention.

"Tell me what your goal is," he said, resting a hand on the rail of the treadmill. "Are you wanting to lose weight, tone up or just work on feeling better about yourself?"

"All of the above."

A wide smile stretched across his face. The combination of those bright blue eyes and that knee-weakening smile could have any woman throwing all morals and professional behavior out the window.

"Let's get started," he said, clasping his hands together.

An hour later, Darcy was questioning her sanity and wondering why she'd let those sexy, dark-skinned muscles sway her judgment. How in the world did she think she could keep up? This man was obviously in shape and she was obviously...not.

She resisted the urge to bend over and pull in much-needed air to her overexerted lungs.

"Ready for more?" he asked, hands on his hips, dev-astatingly handsome smile on his face.

She sent him a glare. "I'm not a masochist."

"You're honest," he replied, using his T-shirt to wipe the sweat off his brow. "I prefer honesty."

"That makes two of us."

He moved over to the small refrigerator in the corner of the room and pulled out two bottles of water. After handing her one, they both uncapped the drinks and took long pulls. Water had never tasted so good.

"So why the nanny business?" he asked, propping his foot upon a workout bench. His elbow rested on his knee, the bottle of water hung between two fingers. "Because you're an amazing cook. Dinner was pretty damn delicious. All of the meals have been great, but tonight's was my favorite."

Stunned and flattered at the compliment and his openness, Darcy screwed the lid back on her bottle. "I've never known anything other than taking care of children. I went to work with my grandmother every single day and fell in love. Cooking is a fun hobby and I love trying out new things. I guess if I weren't a nanny, I'd like to be a chef or a caterer."

She'd quickly steered the conversation to cooking. Anything to avoid talking too much about babies. The facts that children of her own weren't in her future and that anything she'd saved toward adoption had disappeared with Thad cut deep. Still, taking care of others was what she was meant to be doing, of that she was sure.

"Hey." Colin tipped his head to the side, searching her face. "You all right?"

"Oh, yeah." Darcy pushed a sweaty strand of hair that had escaped her ponytail behind her ear. "Just tired."

Pushing off the bench, Colin stalked closer, his focus solely on her. "Tomorrow we'll do weights and skip cardio."

"Tomorrow?" she asked. "You mean we're going to do this every day?"

The corner of his mouth twitched. "Only if you want to. I'm here every night after Iris goes to bed. If you want to join me, you are more than welcome. If you don't want to, no pressure. Personally, I think you're perfect the way you are."

"You haven't seen me naked," she muttered, realizing her mistake the second the words were out of her mouth. "Sorry. I'm—forget I said that."

"When a woman as sultry as you says the word *naked* it's impossible to keep certain images from flooding my mind."

Darcy held onto her bottle, thankful for the prop because her hands were shaking, as were her knees, and her entire body was responding to that low, sexy, heavily accented voice.

"Where are you from?" she asked.

"Greece."

Of course he was. Someplace beautiful and exotic, much like the man himself.

"So, dinner requests for tomorrow?" she asked. "I'll probably need to run to the store at some point, if that's okay."

"Not a problem." He turned toward the doorway, motioning her to exit ahead of him. "I have no requests. You obviously know what you're doing in the kitchen, which is more than I can say for myself."

Stepping into the hallway, she waited until Colin reached in and turned off the light. Darkness enveloped them, save for the slash of light at the end of the hallway shining down from the chandelier in the foyer.

"What's your favorite food?" she asked, trying to focus on his face in the dark, though neither of them had made a move to walk into the light.

"I haven't had too many American dishes," he replied. "I normally eat a lot of fish and vegetables."

Which would further explain why he was so buff and polished, and she had more dimples than a newborn baby's backside.

"I know just what to serve," she replied.

Her vision had adjusted to the darkness enough to see

the flare of heat in his baby blues just as he stepped in closer. "You claim I can't deliver loaded statements." His rich, low voice washed over her already heated body, ironically sending shivers all through her. "I'd say that goes both ways."

Before she could respond, Colin trailed a fingertip along the side of her face.

"Wh—what are you doing?" she asked, cursing her stammer, knowing it was a sign of weakness.

"Putting my curiosity to rest."

"Curiosity?"

That finger kept stroking, causing every pleasure point in her body to tingle.

"I needed to know if you are as silky as you appear," he murmured.

Warmth radiated from his broad body as he leaned in even closer, close enough to brush against hers and have her backing up into the wall.

Her gaze held his. "Am I?"

"Here you are," he whispered. "I wonder about here."

His lips covered hers in an instant, leaving her no choice but to reply to his demands. Okay, she could've chosen to push him away, but…why?

His tongue swept inside her mouth just as his hand curved around her chin, his thumb and forefinger on either side of her face as if to hold her in place. Darcy arched into him, wanting more and taking all he delivered. So many promises wrapped in that one kiss and all she had to do was let go.

Hadn't they both agreed to keep this professional? There was nothing professional about the spiral of arousal coursing through her or the need she so desperately wanted to cave in to.

Colin lifted only to shift his stance, pressing her further against the wall and his very hard, impressive body.

Whoever Colin Alexander was, the man possessed power and control. He demanded so much without words and his actions proved he was used to getting what he wanted.

Just like Thad.

Darcy jerked her head to the side, causing Colin's lips to slide against her jaw, his hand falling away.

She closed her eyes, trying to ignore the devil on her shoulder telling her to turn back and let Colin continue whatever it was he had in mind.

"Colin…"

He dropped his forehead to her shoulder, sighed, then took a step back. "Darcy, that was inexcusable."

Holding her hand to her moist lips, Darcy risked glancing back to Colin. "No, no. We're both to blame."

He propped his hands on his narrow hips and stared up at the ceiling. Darcy had no idea what to say, what to do.

"I've never been in this position before," she told him, clutching her water and wrapping her arms around her waist. "You need to know that I don't kiss employers and I've never, ever had a relationship with any of them beyond a professional one."

"I believe you."

When he offered no further comment, Darcy couldn't take the uncomfortable silence any longer. She turned and started walking down the hallway, when he called her name. She froze, but didn't look back.

"You need to know the last person I had a relationship with was my wife." His soft words floated down the wide hall, enveloping her. "I know we aren't taking this any further, but I didn't want you to think I made a habit of coming on to beautiful women."

Beautiful women.

Darcy threw him a look over her shoulder, nodded and carried on. She didn't stop, didn't slow down until she was in her room with the door shut behind her. Her heart still pounded just as fiercely as it had when she'd been in the darkened hall with Colin, the same as when she'd been sweating in the gym with him and the same as when he'd opened the door first thing that morning looking all rumpled and sexy.

With baby monitors in every room, there was no way she'd miss it if Iris needed something. Which was a very good thing because when Colin had been kissing her, for the briefest of moments, she'd forgotten her sole purpose for even being here. Her mind had traveled to a selfish place and all she wanted was more of that talented, demanding mouth on hers.

Dropping her head back against the door, Darcy groaned. This was the last thing she needed. If she didn't straighten up and focus, she'd have to resign and she needed the full amount of money Colin was paying her if she wanted to keep the agency afloat in any way. Not to mention if she wanted to ever get an apartment or a reliable vehicle.

The video monitor on the white nightstand showed a very peaceful Iris hugging her new doll to her chest. It was in the quiet, serene moments like this that Darcy truly felt that void in her heart. Growing up around other children and loving families, Darcy had always assumed she'd have a family of her own one day.

With the way she worked herself now, though, she didn't even have time for a date, much less a husband. Losing her entire savings had only pushed her dream of adopting further back, making her wonder if she just wasn't meant to be a mother.

There were worse things in the world than not having children...though from her perspective not many. She truly wished with all her heart that she had the ability to conceive like nearly every other woman, but that wasn't meant to be and she had to quit dwelling on it and move on. She wanted to be happy, so she had to focus on happy things and things that were in her control…infertility was certainly not one of them.

Tomorrow, she vowed, she would be one hundred percent professional. She just had to figure out a way to become immune to those striking blue eyes, that sultry accent and forget the way his lips basically assaulted hers in the best, most arousing way possible.

Hysterical laughter escaped her. Sure. No problem.

Five

The alarm chimed throughout the house, indicating that someone had triggered the gate and was coming up the drive. Colin lifted Iris in his arms and headed to the door to help Darcy with her grocery bags. She'd been gone for quite a while and he wondered if she'd run away or if she was stockpiling for the next month.

He'd just gotten off the phone with his assistant who informed Colin of some rather interesting information regarding Darcy and her financial situation. Apparently she was much worse off than he'd first thought. He wasn't sure whether to bring it up or let it slide. The last thing he wanted to do was make her uncomfortable or embarrassed, but at the same time, he wanted to do…something.

He was definitely going to have to bring up the fact her business was basically failing, but he needed to figure out the delicate matter.

Colin didn't know her personal issues, and he had no doubt she had them with her financial situation. All he knew right now was that her business had hit hard times in the last year and had fallen from one of the most sought out to an agency with only Darcy as the worker. There was definitely a story there.

When he opened the door, he didn't see her car. Instead, Darcy was walking up the drive, her arms weighted down with reusable grocery sacks bulging with food.

He sat Iris on the stoop. "Stay here, baby. Daddy needs to help Darcy."

With the gated property, Colin wasn't concerned about Iris wandering off. Worst-case scenario, she'd pluck all the vibrant flowers in the beds before he could get back to her. There was a pool around back, but he'd watch her and make sure she didn't toddle around the house.

Quickly moving toward Darcy, Colin felt his blood pressure rising. "What the hell are you doing?" he asked once he'd closed the gap. "Where's your car?"

"Broke down about a half mile back."

He pulled several bags off each arm, narrowing his eyes at the red creases on her delicate skin caused by all the weight. She wasn't some damn pack mule.

"Why didn't you call me?" he demanded as he curled his hands around the straining handles. "I would've come to get you."

Left with only two lighter bags, Darcy smiled and started up the drive. "By the time you could've gotten Iris in the car seat and gotten to me, I would've been here. Plus I didn't want to bother you guys in case you were playing or she was getting fussy and ready to lie down for a nap."

Even though Darcy's hair was pulled up into a high ponytail, Colin noted the damp tendrils clinging to her neck. The heat of the California sun could be relentless.

"Where exactly is your car?" he asked, trying to keep his voice controlled.

She explained what street she'd left it on, which really

didn't mean much to him since he knew little about the area or the street names. He'd call to have it towed and then he'd work on getting her proper transportation. No way was any employee of his going to be stranded again.

What if Iris had been with Darcy? Then what would she have done? The mishap was frustrating on so many levels.

Not only was she his employee, he refused to see any woman working herself to the point of sweaty exhaustion and that's exactly where Darcy was at. A sheen of perspiration glistened across her forehead and upper lip, her cheeks were red and she had circles beneath her eyes.

Where he was from the women would never leave their homes without full makeup, perfectly styled hair and flashy clothes...much like LA. Still, Darcy didn't seem to care that she wasn't completely made up for an outing. He actually found the quality quite refreshing and incredibly hot.

As if he needed another reason to be aroused by her. He needed to nip this sexual urge in the bud and stay focused.

Once they reached the stoop, Iris had indeed plucked up a variety of flowers, clutching them in her tight little hand.

"Pitty," she exclaimed, thrusting them toward Darcy. "You pitty."

Darcy laughed. "Oh, honey. You're so sweet."

Colin looked at Darcy and saw an alluring, determined and resilient woman. How could any man not be attracted to those qualities? And her sexuality was stealthy. You didn't see the impact coming until it hit you hard. Each day that passed made him realize just how much power she was beginning to have over him.

By the time they got all the bags inside and onto the wide center island in the kitchen, Colin had worked up quite a sweat of his own.

"I'll put these away," Darcy told him as she opened the pantry. "I need to walk back to my car after and see if it's the transmission. I've been having issues with that thing, but a transmission would cost more than the old car is worth."

Colin stood amazed. "*You* plan on looking to see if the transmission is shot?"

Over the stacks of bags, Darcy met his gaze. "Yeah, why? Who else is going to look at it?"

Iris patted his leg and Colin leaned down to lift her up. She still clutched those colorful flowers in her hand so he moved to the cabinet to get down a small glass to use as a vase.

"I'd call a mechanic," he replied, filling the glass with water.

With a soft laugh and shake of her head, Darcy turned her attention back to pulling the groceries from the sacks. "Well, mechanics charge just to come look at the car, then there's the labor to fix the problem, plus the part."

As she listed all the costs associated with getting the vehicle fixed, Colin had to remind himself he wasn't back at the palace. He wasn't talking to someone who would just pay someone else to take care of the issue and move on. Darcy was obviously a hard worker and she didn't need to tell him her funds were lacking.

Taking the flowers from Iris's hand, he sat them in the glass. "There, sweetheart."

She clapped her hands together and wiggled in an attempt to get away. Carefully, he put her back down and watched her move to Darcy. The easy way Iris had taken to the new nanny made him happy he'd allowed her to stay. The incident in the hall last night, though, had kept him up questioning his decision. They were still on a trial and he really didn't want to start the process of finding someone else. That was one thing he wouldn't do to Iris.

Even though they'd moved across the globe, he wanted Iris to have as much stability in her life as possible until he was absolutely certain of their future.

"Hey, cutie." Darcy pulled out a bag of flour and glanced down to her side, a wide smile stretching across her face. "I'm almost done and then you and I can play a little game."

"I'll take care of getting your car picked up."

Darcy's eyes flashed back to his. "That's not your job."

Crossing his arms over his chest, ready for the battle she so obviously thought was coming, Colin replied, "Cooking every single meal and going to the store isn't your job, either. I'm trying to help. We agreed on sharing these responsibilities."

"You can help by letting me do what works for me with my personal circumstances. Fixing my car wasn't included in our agreement."

As Darcy ignored him to focus on putting the last of the groceries away, Colin didn't know if he was pissed to be dismissed so easily or if he was elated that she wasn't walking on eggshells around him because he was a prince. How would she react if she knew just how wealthy he was? Would she even care about his royal status? Darcy didn't seem the type to be attracted to money or power. She seemed to be doing just fine on her own.

And that was the main problem he was having. She shouldn't have to do everything on her own.

"How about I fix lunch and you can make dinner?" he suggested.

Bundling all the reusable sacks into one neatly folded pile, Darcy raised a brow and grinned. "And what are you making for lunch, oh great chef?"

"You're mocking me," he laughed. "I know I'm not as good as you in the kitchen, but I think I can give you a run for your money. Isn't that the expression you Americans have?"

Her lips pursed as she continued to stare. "It is, but I don't think you can hold your own against me."

"Challenge accepted," he told her, ready to prove her wrong.

Damn it. Now he needed to search on the internet for something easy, quick and delicious. He'd been thinking of throwing sandwich stuff together for lunch, but given her instant doubt, Colin had to raise his game. And he would, just as soon as he took care of the car. She was getting his assistance whether she liked it or not.

The shrill alarm had Darcy jumping to her feet and pulling Iris with her. They'd been coloring on the floor in the living room when the ear-piercing noise came out of nowhere.

Darcy knew that sound and it was all she could do not to laugh. Calmly, though, she rested Iris on her hip and headed toward the kitchen where lunch was probably not going to be happening anytime soon.

Standing in the wide, arched doorway, Darcy took in the scene and had to literally bite her lips to keep from laughing.

There were dirty bowls littering the island, opened packages of random ingredients spread about and Colin was currently slapping a kitchen towel at the small flame coming from the burner. Smoke billowed through the open space as Darcy moved into the kitchen. She eased Iris into her high chair and wheeled it over near the patio door, which Darcy opened to let some fresh air in. She made her way down the wall, opening each window as she passed.

Colin turned, still holding the charred dishtowel, and shrugged. "I'm not admitting defeat."

"Of course not," she replied, not even bothering to hide her smile. "Why would you?"

"Lunch will be just a few more minutes."

"I'm sure it will be wonderful." Darcy shrugged. "No rush."

Poor guy was still trying to save his pride. She wasn't about to say more. Their easy banter seriously helped take the edge off the sexual tension. Playfulness, even a little flirting she could handle. Anything beyond that… she glanced to the tiny flame Colin was smacking. Yeah, that flame signified her life right now. If she got too close to Colin she'd get burned. The signs were literally in front of her face.

Darcy had just grabbed a handful of puffed snacks to hold Iris over until lunch was ready when another alarm sounded through the house. This one was announcing a visitor.

The darn house was wired so tight with security and monitors and alarms, Darcy's head had practically spun in circles when Colin had explained the entire system to her. Who was this man that he needed so much security?

"Are you expecting company?" she asked, laying the snacks across the highchair tray for Iris.

"Actually, I am." Colin turned off the burner, sat the pan on a cooler one and turned to her. "Don't touch anything. I've got it under control. This won't take long."

He rushed from the room and out the front door.

"Your father is one mysterious man," Darcy muttered to Iris. "And apparently not a chef."

Smoothing the dark curls away from the baby's face, Darcy really studied how much Iris looked like Colin. All bronzed skin, dark molasses eyes and striking features. Iris would be an absolute bombshell when she grew up. Darcy couldn't help but wonder if Iris's mother had been a Greek beauty as well. Most likely Colin wouldn't have married someone who was an ogre.

Moments later, Colin breezed back into the house.

"Sorry about that. Lunch will be ready in five minutes if you'd like to get some plates out."

"Are you going to tell me what we're having now?"

"You'll see," he told her before he went back into the foyer.

On a sigh, she crossed the room and pulled out two plates and one smaller plate for Iris. She resisted the urge to stroke the beautiful cabinets and the quartz countertops. This kitchen alone cost more money than she made in a year...during the good times. Having a home and a gourmet kitchen with a family to cook for was a dream she honestly didn't see coming true. That was okay, though. For now she was here, working and making money to save her agency, and in the end that's all that truly mattered. And the fact she was caring for a baby was a great form of forced therapy she'd desperately needed to face her fears.

Moments later, Colin came back into the kitchen wearing a mischievous grin, but he said nothing as he dished out whatever he'd managed to salvage from the burning pan. Apparently he'd removed the pot before the flames consumed their entire meal.

"I admit, after the fanfare with the smoke alarm, this actually smells delicious."

He threw her a glance over his shoulder. "I have a whole host of surprises for you."

Those words held a plethora of meanings, but when said while holding her gaze beneath heavy lids, her mind instantly traveled to the darkened hallway last night and how her body still ached after such a gloriously arousing kiss.

Could such an experience be labeled by one simple word? A kiss was something that could be given from a parent to a child, from a child to a pet, from a peasant to the hand of a diplomat. The word *kiss* blanketed a lot of ground.

"Ready?"

Darcy blinked, realizing Colin stood in front of her with two plates of...

"You made shrimp Alfredo?" she asked, more than amazed.

"You think I can't boil noodles and melt some butter?" he asked, feigning shock.

Taking her plate, inhaling the garlicky goodness, she laughed. "I had my doubts."

Darcy sat her plate on the table and went to move Iris's highchair over.

"I've got her," Colin said, holding his hand up. "You eat while it's hot."

Darcy stared as Colin wheeled Iris closer to the table. She then sat in amazement as he cut up the noodles, blew on them and offered small bites to his daughter.

"You're not eating," he commented without turning his head in her direction.

"I'm surprised." Darcy slid onto the built-in bench beneath the wide window. Grabbing her fork, she started pushing the noodles and shrimp around on her plate. "I'm the nanny, so eating a hot meal isn't something I'm used to. I'm also not used to the parent doing my job while I'm sitting right here."

He tossed her a glance. "I'm not like most parents. She's my daughter and I'm not paying you to raise her so I can prop my feet up and watch her life go by. I'm paying you to help for a few months. There's a huge difference."

Darcy swallowed, hating how her observation instantly made him defensive and how she was reminded again how little time she would actually have here.

"I apologize," she said, stabbing a plump shrimp coated in Alfredo sauce. "I should know by now that every family, every circumstance is different."

"Don't apologize," he replied. "Actually, as soon as you're finished eating, I have something for you."

Intrigued, Darcy stared across the table. "You made lunch, you're forcing me to eat instead of feeding Iris and you have something else up your sleeve? You've got to be kidding."

The muscle in his jaw ticked, his eyes held hers. "I don't joke too often."

The man was intense, she'd give him that. He went from super dad to sexy employer in the span of one quick blink. Regardless of his demeanor, Colin Alexander exuded sex appeal.

Darcy didn't ask any more questions. She didn't know Colin well, but she was positive anything she'd ask would be dodged or ignored. He was a man of absolute control, absolute power. She had no clue what he did for a living, she only knew he worked from home. However Colin made his money, Darcy was positive he dominated every facet of his life, and was even more controlled and possibly ruthless in whatever business he was in.

They finished lunch in silence, except for the cute noises and random words coming from Iris. When Darcy was finished, she took the plates to the sink, rinsed them and put them in the dishwasher.

"This is a really nice dishwasher."

Inwardly she groaned. What sane person coveted someone else's kitchen appliances? Talk about pathetic. She was showing her lower-class side…which was the only side she knew lately.

Pulling the tray out, Colin lifted Iris and carefully set her on the tile. In an instant she darted off toward the living room. Thanks to the mostly open-concept design of the house, they could still keep an eye on her through the wide, arched doorway.

The little girl picked up the doll Darcy had given her,

sat on the floor and started rocking her. That familiar ache spread through Darcy. But there were plenty more blessings in her life to count. Each day with Iris was a blessing. The child was sweet, always happy and fun-loving, when she got her naps in, and Darcy was lucky to be working under such amazing circumstances.

"Get Iris and meet me out front."

Darcy glanced back to Colin. "You're making me nervous."

One corner of his mouth kicked up. "Baby, that's the best compliment anyone has ever given me."

He strode away without another word and Darcy had a gut feeling she'd just stirred the hornet's nest of hormones.

Darcy crossed into the living room and slid her hands beneath Iris's little arms. "Come on, sweetheart. Bring your dolly and let's go see what your daddy is up to."

"Doll," Iris repeated. "Pitty."

Laughing, Darcy kissed the dark head of curls. "Yes, baby. Your dolly is pretty."

Stepping outside, Darcy immediately spotted Colin with a wide grin on his face.

"What is that?" she asked, glancing over his shoulder at the big, black SUV, all shiny and brand-new.

"Yours."

Six

Colin watched Darcy as her eyes widened, her face paled.

"You—what…"

Her stuttering and the fact she was rendered speechless had him confused. "Your car isn't worth fixing and you need viable transportation. Consider this a very late birthday present."

Her eyes darted to his and instead of gratitude he saw… anger? Seriously? He didn't know a woman that didn't fawn all over gifts, especially a new car. He didn't know where he'd gone wrong here, but he'd seriously miscalculated her response.

"You said you'd call someone about my car," she explained.

"I did. I had it removed from the road and now you have a new vehicle that you won't have to worry about."

Darcy didn't look nearly as excited as he'd figured she would. In fact, she looked downright angry.

"I can't accept this," she stated, still remaining on the

concrete stoop holding onto Iris. "I want my own car fixed, not a replacement that cost more than I could ever afford. And I don't need a birthday present from you."

"If you don't want it as a late present, then just use the vehicle while you work for me," he said slowly, moving toward her as he made sure she understood this wasn't any form of bribery or something more. "Consider it one of the incentives I mentioned on your first day. The vehicle is not up for debate. You need to have reliable transportation because you're watching my daughter and had she been in your car earlier, you both would've been stranded."

Darcy rolled her eyes. "Don't be so dramatic. I wasn't stranded. I walked here. Had Iris been with me, I would've called for help and you could've been there in no time. I was only a half mile away."

"What happens when you're ten miles away?" he countered, slipping Iris from Darcy's arms. "You can't walk that far with a toddler and you can't stay in the car in this heat."

Darcy crossed her arms over her chest and glanced away. "I can handle myself."

"Do you even want to go look at the car?" he asked.

"I can see it just fine." She brought her eyes back up to meet his. "I would like to know where my car is and I want it back."

Spinning on her heel, she went back inside, slamming the door. Colin glanced to Iris who was now chewing on the small stuffed doll's hair.

"Where did I go wrong?" he asked.

Colin knew whatever had just happened had little to do with the vehicle in his drive and everything to do with something that was personal to her. Did her old broken car hold some sentimental value?

"We better go see if she's sticking around," he told Iris as he headed toward the door.

By the time he found Darcy, she was in her room, standing at the floor-to-ceiling window looking out onto the backyard. Her room was neat and tidy. She'd plumped the pillows on her perfectly made bed and her single piece of luggage sat on the floor at the foot of it. Other than a small pair of flip-flops, there was no sign she'd even made herself at home. He knew she was orderly around the house, but he assumed in her own room, she'd be a little more laid back.

"Are you quitting?" he asked from the doorway. Even though this was his house, the bedroom was Darcy's for as long as she was here and he wasn't about to infringe on her territory.

Without turning around, Darcy let out a laugh that held no humor. "I have nowhere else to go and I need this job. I'll use the car while I'm here, but I really just want mine back. I have my reasons."

"Down," Iris said, squirming against him.

"Can we come in?" he asked.

Darcy glanced over her shoulder. "It's your house, Colin."

He stepped into the room and closed the door, confining Iris to an area where he could still watch her and talk to Darcy at the same time.

"Listen, I had no idea getting you a car would set off so much emotion." Slowly closing the space between them, he came to stand in front of her. "I'll get your car fixed and have it delivered back here. But you will still be using the new one. No arguments."

She eyed him for another minute before tipping her head to the side. "One of these days someone is going to tell you no."

"No, no, no, no," Iris chanted as she toddled around the room waving her doll in the air.

Darcy laughed and Colin couldn't stop himself from smiling. "She's the only one who can get away with it," he informed Darcy.

Truly focusing on Darcy, he crossed the room. As he neared, her eyes widened. He liked to think it was from the attraction, but that was his arrogance talking. More than likely she was trying to figure him out, same as he was doing with her.

But he would get through her defenses. He knew without a doubt her secret had everything to do with the fact that she had nowhere else to go.

As the space between them minimized, Colin kept his gaze locked on hers. The closer he got, the more she had to tip her head back to hold his stare.

"I can't help but feel you're hiding something," he started. "Your background check told me your business has hit a rough patch and you are on your own now."

Darcy nodded, her lips thinning. "There are challenges I'm facing privately, but nothing that will affect my job with you. I promise. I just don't want to be indebted to you for fixing my car."

Money wasn't the root of all evil as the old saying went. The evil was the person holding the purse strings who did nothing to help others.

"I think I'll take Iris outside for a walk." Darcy skirted around him, careful to shift her body so she didn't even brush against him. "Feel free to join us if you want."

Colin laughed as he turned to face her. "Not very subtle, the way you dodged my question."

"Subtlety wasn't what I was going for." She lifted Iris in her arms and smiled. The way she headed straight out the door as if she hadn't just put him in his place really annoyed and amused him at the same time. Damn, she was fun, yet prickly.

Darcy was perfect with Iris, independent and she turned him inside out at every move.

When his marriage had started failing, Colin blamed himself. He'd put Karina through hell with his injury, his surgeries, not being there for her as a husband should be. He'd never imagined he'd feel a desire for another woman again, but here he was, pining after his temporary nanny, of all people.

If he didn't keep his head on straight, he'd be losing focus on why he was in LA to begin with. He was no closer to deciding if staying away from Galini Isle was best for him and Iris or if returning to the secure, enclosed, yet exposed, lifestyle of the royals was the way he should go.

Here he had more freedom to take her out in public. They'd walked to the park last week and it had been so refreshing not to have guards hovering nearby. The longer he stayed in the United States, the more he worried he'd never want to leave.

There was only one right decision…he only wished he knew which one it was.

Playing outside in the yard was always so much fun for Darcy. She loved hearing Iris's squeals of delight and seeing her little carefree spirit. Darcy had been here for a full month now and had easily passed the trial period. Each second she spent with Iris only had Darcy more thankful she'd fought for this position. Holding onto Iris's tiny little hand just felt right. Everything about being with this sweet child felt right.

Not to mention that working for a man who oozed sexiness, power and control was one giant glob of icing on the proverbial cake.

Talk about landing the job of a lifetime. Still, Darcy couldn't help but wonder what happened to Colin's late wife. He didn't mention her, didn't even have any photos around the house. The man seemed as if he was running away or hiding from something, but she truly had no clue what. She could easily research him online, but she wasn't going to snoop into his life. That would be sneaky and Darcy prided herself on honesty. If he wanted to discuss his life, he would when the time was right.

Iris pulled away from Darcy and started running toward the landscaping framing the patio. Shielding her eyes with her hand, Darcy stared ahead as the little girl ran after a butterfly that had landed on one of the vibrant flowers. By the time Iris got there, the butterfly had flown away.

Iris looked around and when she realized the insect was no longer nearby, her chin started quivering. Closing the space between them, Darcy knelt down in front of the toddler and smoothed the curls away from her forehead, making a mental note to pick up some hair accessories for Iris.

"It's okay, sweetheart," Darcy consoled. "Miss Butterfly had to go home for a nap. I bet she'll be back another time. Would you like to go in and lie down? I saw a butterfly book in your room. How about we read that?"

"No," Iris cried, shaking her head. "No, no, no."

The one word kids learned early and used for nearly every reply, especially when they were in need of a nap. Darcy may have been working with older children these past several years, but certain things she would never forget.

When Darcy scooped her up and headed toward the house, the tears instantly transformed from sad to angry, and Iris's arms started flying as the instant tantrum went into full swing. Maybe Darcy shouldn't have taken Iris on that walk. Apparently the window of opportunity was missed and the nap should've come first.

Patting her back and trying to dodge the whirlwind arms, Darcy took Iris into the house. Of course, inside, the cries seemed to echo into surround sound. Colin came running from the office off the kitchen, his cell to his ear, worry etched across his face.

"What happened?" he said, holding the device away from his mouth.

"She's just tired," Darcy explained. "Sorry we disturbed you."

Colin didn't resume his call as Darcy walked by. Maybe he was waiting for them to pass because of Iris's ear-splitting screams, but the way he studied them, Darcy worried he was wondering why his daughter was so unhappy. This was the first time Iris had truly thrown a fit around Darcy, but every kid had their moments and as a nanny, one just had to learn how to adjust to that child's needs accordingly.

And right now, little Miss Iris needed her bed and a couple of hours of peace and quiet.

As she reached the top of the stairs, Darcy didn't have to glance over her shoulder to know that Colin was staring at her.

"Come on, little one," Darcy cooed.

After walking around the room, shutting the blinds, turning on the small fan for white noise and grabbing Iris's blanket and doll, Darcy settled into the cushy rocking chair and began to hum, occasionally adding in a few lyrics to "You Are My Sunshine." Iris's eyes started to grow heavy. Darcy knew the rule of thumb was to lay young children down while they were still awake, but holding and rocking a baby was a temptation she couldn't avoid. Today Darcy justified it by telling herself she was just waiting for Iris to calm down.

Darcy held onto the precious bundle in her arms and

came to her feet. Iris still clutched the silky blanket and stuffed doll as Darcy eased the sleeping beauty into her bed.

With her hands resting on the rail, Darcy stared at the spiky, damp lashes resting on Iris's reddened cheeks. Moments ago this child was throwing a fit and now she slept peacefully. When she woke she wouldn't remember she'd been upset, and that was how Darcy wanted to live her life.

Moving forward was the only way to prove there was life after the death of a dream. She couldn't allow endometriosis to define her. Discovering that the family she'd dreamed of having one day wouldn't happen had been a crushing blow, but Darcy had persevered, forcing herself to become stronger than her disappointments.

Swallowing the lump in her throat, Darcy turned from the bed and headed into the hall. She'd just pulled the door closed when she turned and ran straight into Colin's hard chest.

The instant force of colliding with him threw her off balance. Colin's hands immediately gripped her bare arms to steady her. Breath caught in her throat, her heart beat a fast, bruising rhythm against her chest. An instant flash of their heated kiss flooded her mind and all Darcy could think of was how perfectly they fit together.

Down girl.

Colin's eyes studied her face, her mouth. Tingles shot through her…tingles she shouldn't be feeling for her boss.

"We need to talk."

The statement, laced with such authority, delivered a punch to her stomach. Were they going to talk professionally? Personally? Was he upset with her for something she'd done?

Or did he want her alone for purely selfish, carnal reasons?

The second he turned and walked away, Darcy followed.

Seven

Fisting his hands at his sides, Colin cursed himself as he went downstairs and into his office. He had to keep reminding himself that the woman he'd hired to care for Iris was an employee, not an object to be lusting after. He'd never been sexually attracted to an employee—before, during or after his marriage.

Not once had his professional and personal needs ever crossed paths, but every single time he looked at Darcy he felt that kick to the gut that demanded he take notice of the all-American beauty.

Added to that, she was the only woman since Karina to have any connection to Iris. Colin would be lying to himself if he didn't admit that seeing Darcy around his daughter in all her youthful, vibrant glory had something tugging on his heart.

Damn it, he didn't want his heart tugged. He had too much on his plate right now and craving a woman, his nanny, for pity's sake, was not an option.

"You wanted me?"

Grinding his teeth to keep from saying what he really wanted, Colin turned to face Darcy. He'd assumed coming to his office would make this conversation easier, less personal.

"I want you to stop rocking Iris before you lay her down to sleep."

Darcy blanched and Colin cursed himself for the rough tone he'd taken.

"She was always used to just being laid down," he went on, trying to lighten his voice. It wasn't Darcy's fault he was fighting a losing battle with his attraction for her.

Darcy straightened her shoulders, tipped her chin and gave a quick nod. "I apologize. I'll be sure to lay her down right away next time."

Stiffly, she turned toward the door and Colin hated himself for making her feel bad about herself. Damn it. He didn't want this. He didn't want the chemistry or the awkward sexual tension, and he sure as hell didn't want to have to mask his arousal by being snippy and gruff with her. He wanted Iris to have that loving touch, to be wrapped in the arms of someone who cared for her, and it was obvious Darcy cared for his little girl.

Maybe he wasn't capable of being happy anywhere if this was any indication. He'd taken out his frustrations with himself on Darcy. If he wasn't happy here, though, did that mean he wasn't happy stepping away from his duty? Is that what all of this boiled down to?

Colin had been in a great mood moments ago as he'd been talking on the phone with his best friend, Prince Luc Silva. He hadn't spoken to him in months, other than texts or emails. As soon as they'd hung up, Darcy's soft voice had filtered through the monitor system in the home and damn if hearing all of that softness wasn't like being wrapped in her sweet embrace.

He couldn't afford to be wrapped up in anything that didn't involve his country, his loyalty and the decision he needed to make regarding his and Iris's future in the kingdom.

"Darcy," he called out before she could clear the doorway.

She froze, but didn't turn around. "Yes?"

Anything he wanted to say would be a bad idea, rocking their already shaky relationship. "Nothing," he said, shaking his head.

Regardless of the attraction, Colin was glad he'd decided to let Darcy stay on after they'd verbally battled that first day. He couldn't imagine anyone else with Iris.

Each day brought them closer to the six-month mark, closer to his staying or going. And, to be honest, he was growing too fond of having her here, in his life. He was finding an inner peace he hadn't expected. He was almost angry at himself for allowing his emotions to get the better of him, but where Darcy was concerned, he was finding he had little say in the matter.

Stefan was putting the pressure on, but Colin couldn't deal with Galini Isle and Darcy simultaneously. Both issues were overwhelming and threatened to take over his life. Right now, though, he wanted to concentrate on Darcy. Even though he knew Galini Isle should come first, he needed to see if there was more to their attraction than pure lust.

After dinner, Colin wanted to give Iris her bath so Darcy took the opportunity to sew a button back on her only dress shirt. The button right at the breast had popped off after a big inhale. In order for this top to fit properly, she either needed to lose a few pounds or stop breathing. She was thankful Colin had been nowhere around to witness the mishap.

Threading the needle, Darcy quickly fixed the shirt and was putting her small sewing kit away when a knock sounded at her door.

"Come in," she called as she wound the unused thread back around the spool.

Colin stepped in, holding Iris who was wrapped in her thick terrycloth monogrammed towel. Darcy didn't even want to know how much that plush towel cost…she'd seen the designer label.

"I need to make a phone call," Colin told her, taking in the shirt in her lap and the supplies spread over the bed. "Am I interrupting something?"

"Oh, no." Darcy scooted everything out of the way and came to her feet, smoothing down her pink T-shirt. "I was just sewing a button back on my shirt."

Colin's brows drew together. "Just buy a new shirt."

Yeah, why didn't she think of that? Between being technically homeless, nearly ready to shut the doors on the business barely keeping food in her mouth and trying to keep her car running, why hadn't she just hit the mall in her spare time for a new wardrobe?

But he didn't need her sarcasm. A man like Colin wouldn't understand because if anything in his life was broken, he could just pay to have it fixed or snap his fingers and have people at his beck and call.

Another layer of division between them, showing her just how vast their differences were.

Ignoring his question, because anything she would reply with would most definitely be snarky, she came to her feet, crossed the room and reached for Iris.

"Go on and make your call." The sweet scent of freshly bathed baby always made her heart weep just a little. "I'll take care of this sweet princess."

"Don't call her that."

Jerking her attention from the wrapped, squirming

bundle in her arms to Colin, Darcy jerked. "Call her what? Princess?"

"I don't like that term," he stated, crossing his arms and leveling her gaze.

"It's a simple term of endearment," Darcy defended herself, shifting Iris to settle her more comfortably on her hip. "I'm not sure what you think I'm implying when I say it, but—"

"No more. I don't want her to be a spoiled child and that term suggests too much."

"Colin—"

He held up a hand, cutting her off once more. "She's my daughter. She will not be called princess."

Feeling her blood pressure rise through the onslaught of confusion, Darcy took a step forward. "Yes, sir. If you'll excuse me, I need to get Iris ready for bed."

She pushed by him and exited her room, headed into the nursery next door and closed the door. What on earth had gotten into him? He was still in a mood and Darcy had no clue why. Darcy quickly dressed Iris in a pair of yellow footed pajamas with little bunnies on each of the toes. Every single baby item the toddler possessed was adorable. Darcy was getting more and more used to being surrounded by everything baby. The only thing she worried about now was how she'd leave at the end of the term they'd agreed upon. Staying away from babies for years had helped to soothe her ache somewhat, but being thrust into the world of all things tiny and pink brought Darcy's wishes back to the surface. To think all of that would be taken from her again in a few months.

She had no clue what he'd do when her term was up. Perhaps he just wanted to get his feet back on solid ground since he was a widower with a baby. Maybe he thought he could take it from there. Darcy had learned long ago not to question her clients' intentions.

She couldn't get too used to the weight of Iris in her arms, or the way Iris would clutch that ugly old doll Darcy had given her or the way she had started to reach for Darcy. But such simple things had already infiltrated Darcy's heart.

And Colin, as grouchy and moody as he'd been, had also managed to capture her attention in a way she hadn't expected. She couldn't get the image of him dominating her, kissing her, demanding more, from her mind.

As Darcy turned off the lights and clicked on the projector that danced stars across the ceiling, she knew she needed to find him and figure out what was going on. The man was a walking mystery, and if she was going to stay, and she really had no choice, she needed to clear the air. He obviously had something on his mind. Now all she had to do was let him know she was here if he wanted to talk and try to prevent anymore kissing episodes from happening.

Because kissing Colin had turned into another one of those fantasies leaving her wanting more. But Darcy was a realist by default. She may want a man to love her and a family to go right along with him in her perfect world, or the image she had of perfection, but the truth was Colin and Iris were out of reach.

Darcy had to keep reminding herself of that or she'd be severely crushed when time came to leave…alone.

Oh. My.

There was a reason Darcy had made her way through the house searching for Colin, but right at this moment she had no clue what it was. In fact, she had no thoughts whatsoever because her mind and her sight were filled with a glorious image of Colin doing one-armed pull-ups, shirtless, displaying that tattoo in a sweaty way that had her all but panting.

Dark skin wrapped around taut muscles flexing with each movement had Darcy gripping the doorframe. She wasn't about to interrupt this free show. There was no way she could miss the chance to see her boss in all his sexy glory. She wasn't dead, after all. She just couldn't think clearly when he was around…an issue she'd never had with any other man.

With a grunt, he pulled himself up one last time before dropping back to the floor. Hands resting on his hips just above his low-slung shorts, Colin's shoulders shifted up and down as he pulled in deep breaths. Then he stilled, turned his head over his shoulder and spotted her.

Busted.

He held her gaze. It was now or never.

"We need to talk," she informed him, bolstering her courage by tamping down her girlie parts and stepping into the gym.

"If you want to work out, fine. I'm not in the mood to talk."

Darcy crossed her arms over her chest. "Seems like your mood is flat-out grouchy."

Colin turned fully to face her, but continued to stare. Darcy wondered if she'd crossed a line. But, boss or not, he shouldn't take his attitude out on her.

"I came to see if you wanted to talk about whatever has you brooding," she went on, trying her hardest to keep her eyes on his and not on the sweaty pecs and the ink that had her heart racing. "This tension is something I prefer not to work around and it's not good for a child because they can sense such things even at an early age."

Colin took a step forward, eyes locked on hers. "Is that right?"

Swallowing, Darcy nodded. "Yes."

He took another step, then another, eventually closing the gap between them. Darcy inhaled that musky, male scent, took in those muscles that were within striking distance and blinked up at Colin.

"If you're trying to intimidate me, you'll have to try harder." She had to keep the upper hand here because her control was slowly slipping and she had to at least put up a strong front. "If you don't want to talk, I'll leave you to your workout so you can take out your frustrations that way."

His stunning blue eyes traveled over her face. "Go change and join me."

"I don't think that's a good idea."

"Because of my mood?"

Darcy took in a deep breath. "Among other things."

"Like the pull between us?"

Why deny the obvious? She'd never been one to play games, though she did do her best to avoid uncomfortable situations. So how did she find herself here?

"Whatever has made you all surly is the main issue," she stated. "But the attraction is something we already discussed and agreed to ignore."

The muscle in Colin's jaw ticked, his nostrils flared. "Discussing and ignoring our chemistry isn't going to make it go away. As far as my mood goes, I had a disagreement with my brother on the phone and I'm dealing with some family things. That's all you need to know and more than you're entitled to."

Shaking her head, Darcy took a step back. "Obviously it was a mistake to come down here."

She turned, set on heading up to her room and figuring out new recipes for the coming week. She'd barely taken a step out the door before one strong hand wrapped around her arm and pulled her to a stop.

"The mistake would be leaving."

His words washed over her, his breath tickled the side

of her neck, the heat from his body enveloped her. Darcy closed her eyes.

"Colin," she whispered. "I can only be here for Iris. Nothing more."

"You deny yourself too much." His thumb stroked over her bare arm. "The car, new clothes…my touch. I've tried to ignore the power you have over me. I've tried, but there's only so much a man can take. You're driving me crazy and I'm taking my frustrations out on you when it's my fault I can't deal with how much you get under my skin. I snapped at you earlier because I'm angry with myself."

Darcy gasped at his raw honesty.

"Tell me you don't want me to touch you," he whispered.

"I'm not a liar," she informed him. "But I can't let you. There's a difference."

Colin turned her around so fast she fell against him. Instantly, her hands came up to settle on that hard chest she'd been lusting after. Why did she have to have such strong feelings for this man? And why was he so forceful, so dominating and constantly arousing at every single moment of the day?

"Being alone with you is not a good idea." Her defense came out weak, and the smirk on his face told her he wasn't buying it, either. "I need this job, Colin. I can't afford to…well…whatever you have in mind."

With a low growl from deep in his throat, Colin framed her face with both hands, forcing her to look only at him.

"*Moro*, you have no idea what I have in mind."

Moro. What did that even mean? Something Greek, she assumed. Coming from his lips, though, it sounded sexy, naughty.

No, she didn't want to appreciate the seductive terms rolling off his tongue, dripping with a toe-curling accent.

With taut skin beneath her palms, Darcy was fighting the urge to dig her fingers into his heated skin, rise on her toes and take what he was so blatantly offering.

"This isn't professional." She focused on his face, wondering if he was having doubts, but all she saw staring back at her was desire.

Had a man ever looked at her in such an arousing way before? If she had to ask herself the question, the obvious answer was no.

"No, it's not," he agreed, still holding her face in his hands. "But damn it, the more I fight this, the more I crave it. Do you want to quit working for me?"

"No."

"I'm not about to fire you." His thumb stroked over her bottom lip, back and forth. "So that leaves us here, fighting an urge that's only gaining momentum. What do you want?"

Was he mocking her? What did he think she wanted to do? She wanted this ache to cease, but she didn't want to be so clichéd as to sleep with her boss.

"I think you need to keep your hands off me," she whispered. "I think we need to focus on Iris and I think we need to be adult enough to have self-control."

Colin slid his hands back through her hair, tipped her head up and inched even closer, leaving only a breath between their mouths.

"I didn't ask what you thought. I asked what you want."

With her hands trapped between their bodies, his firm grip on her and air barely passing between them, Darcy did the only thing she could think to do…she kissed him.

Instantly Colin took control, pushing her back against the wall. Her hands fell away and just as she tried to grip his shoulders, he grabbed her wrists, jerked them away from his body and had both arms pinned up over her head. She was at his total mercy, at his command. His mouth covered hers, dominated, possessed and every part of her wanted more, wanted him.

Her body arched into his. The sensation of those hard planes against her had any feeling of self-consciousness disappearing. Apparently Colin didn't seem to mind his woman a little on the curvy side. If his arousal was any indication, he actually preferred a little extra flesh.

With one hand gripping her wrists, Colin's other hand found the hem of her shirt. His fingers slid beneath the cotton and found her waist. His palm flattened against her heated skin as he brushed his thumb along the satiny barrier of her bra. Such a thin layer, yet it proved to be quite a hindrance. She wanted his hands on her, all over her.

Darcy groaned as his hips pushed against hers; his thumb glided back and forth over her breast. He utterly consumed her with the simplest yet most demanding of touches and she still burned for more.

Wait. What was she saying? He was a widower. He'd been married and his wife had passed not too long ago. So, what did that make Darcy? The rebound? A fling to help him recover from a broken heart?

Wasn't that precisely what Colin was to her? Hadn't her own heart—and apparently her common sense, too— taken a hit from her failed relationship? Were they using each other as stepping-stones to get beyond the hurt?

With her arms still locked above her head by Colin's firm grip, Darcy tore her mouth away, causing his lips to land on her jawline.

"Colin," she panted. "Wait…just…this is…stop. Please."

He froze. His hand fell from her shirt as he slowly backed away. The second he released her arms, Darcy pulled some much needed air into her lungs.

With a curse, Colin raked a hand through his damp hair and turned away. Darcy watched as he walked over and sank onto the weight bench, rested his elbows on his knees and dropped his head between his shoulders. Apparently he was at war with himself.

Unsure of what to do next, Darcy remained still, hoping he'd say something to cut through this instant strain that settled between them. "Go upstairs, Darcy."

The angst in his tone had her glued to the spot. He may want to be alone, but she didn't think he should be. How could she just walk out after what they'd experienced? Ignoring it would only create more friction.

"I'll go," she informed him, smoothing her hair away from her face. "But you need to know something first."

Darcy risked walking toward him and rounding the bench to talk face-to-face, even though he still kept his focus on the ground between his legs.

"I won't be used as someone to pass the time and I won't be anyone's rebound. Yes, I'm attracted to you, but I can work and put that aside." Pulling in a deep breath of air and straightening her shoulders, she pushed forward. "What I can't do is get wrapped up in an affair that will leave me wanting more because I've been hurt before. I'm not going to lie, I'm still recovering from that betrayal. Right now I have to look out for myself because I have no one else. And as much as I'd like to take you up on what you were offering, I can't sacrifice my heart. I'm not a fling type of girl and I know what might be temporary pleasure to you would be much more than I can handle."

Slowly, Colin lifted his head, sought her gaze and nodded. "I won't touch you again. I won't kiss you and I'll make sure not to put you in a position where we're alone. Iris will be our focus. I have enough going on in my life without adding more complications."

Darcy fisted her hands at her sides. This is what she wanted him to say, right? She wanted him to treat her as a professional and not make her choose between her morals and her desires.

Yet now that he'd pulled up this invisible wall between them, Darcy couldn't help but wonder if she'd just be on the outside looking in at what she could've had. And this incident confirmed he was looking for an emotional crutch. Trouble was, she was, too, and hadn't even realized it.

Colin came to his feet, keeping his intense gaze on her. "You need to know that I never meant to make you feel like you were passing my time. I haven't been this attracted to a woman in years and damn if this timing isn't inconvenient. You're my nanny, for pity's sake. But I need to clarify one thing before you go upstairs and we table this discussion."

Darcy swallowed. "What?"

Softly, gently, Colin eased forward and touched his lips to hers for the briefest of moments before easing back. He touched her nowhere else, but just that simple kiss packed as much of a punch as when he'd practically taken her standing up.

"You deserve more than a fling, more than a quickie against the wall." His whispered tone washed over her. "There are just some promises I can't make."

Sliding her tongue over her bottom lip, she savored him. "Why did you kiss me again?"

Bright cobalt eyes locked her in place. "Because I'm selfish and I wanted one last taste."

Heart in her throat, Darcy resisted the urge to reach up and touch her tingling lips. He'd told her he had nothing else to give but a fling and she refused to settle for a few moments of pleasure. She was worth more than that and she'd promised herself after Thad left her with nothing that she wouldn't succumb to passion and charming men again.

On shaky legs, Darcy skirted around Colin and headed out of the gym. By the time she hit the steps, she was nearly running.

What would tomorrow bring, she wondered as she closed herself into her suite. Could they truly put every kiss, every touch behind them? Could she forget the fact she'd felt proof of his desire for her? That he'd touched her breast? They'd crossed into another level of intimacy and that wasn't something Darcy took lightly.

She was just about to change into her pajamas when a piercing cry came from the monitor.

Duty called. She only hoped duty wasn't calling up Colin, as well.

Eight

"How's the nanny working out?"

Colin cringed at his brother's question. For the past three days he'd managed to keep his promise to always have Iris present if he was in the room with Darcy. On the night he'd all but consumed Darcy, right after she had left the gym and Iris had started to cry, Colin had made his way upstairs and waited for a moment to make sure Darcy went into the nursery to care for his little girl.

Being so close, inhaling her fruity scent, seeing her handle Iris in such a loving, caring way, had had him questioning his sanity. They still had months to go and he was no closer to controlling his hormones than he was the moment he opened his door to her. But how could he kick her out when she and Iris were obviously the perfect pairing?

"That good, huh?" Stefan chuckled.

Colin gripped the phone, hating how his brother was across the globe and could still hone in on the truth.

"She's amazing with Iris," Colin stated. "I'm surprised how fast she's has taken to Darcy. Most times Iris prefers Darcy over me when we're playing a game. She climbs into her lap. It's like she's already choosing sides."

"And how have you taken to Darcy?" Stefan asked.

"She's the nanny. That's all."

Stefan's mocking chuckle filled the line. "Pretty defensive. I admit, I'm happy to hear it. I worried about you after Karina's death and then the backlash and speculation from the media. You closed in on yourself for a bit, but with this nanny, you sound a bit…agitated. You're showing signs of life again. You must like her on more than a professional level."

Colin watched out his office window as Darcy and Iris splashed around in the pool. Why did he torture himself by standing in here staring at her? Why did her faded, plain black one-piece do ridiculous things to his libido?

"That doesn't mean anything is going on with my nanny," he grumbled. Maybe he was so moody because nothing *was* going on with the nanny.

Darcy lifted Iris into her arms and climbed from the pool. With each step up, water sluiced off Darcy's curvy body. Watching as she bent to retrieve Iris's towel was pure hell. For several moments Colin took note of how Darcy cared for Iris, drying her off and making sure she was warm before focusing on herself.

And those few minutes were more than enough to have his body responding. He never should've gone so far the other night because now when he saw her, he could actually *feel* her. The combination was killing him.

"The ball is less than two weeks away," Stefan went on, oblivious to Colin's state. "If you're not here, the media will only try to crucify you more. Even though they won't be inside, they'll be hovering outside the palace to see who's here. Besides, word will get out and rumors will fly."

"I'm well aware of how the media would handle my absence."

Colin turned from the window. The last thing he wanted to think about was returning to Galini Isle for a ball hosting the monarchies from surrounding countries. The only bright light was that his best friend, Luc, would be in attendance, and since the man had recently gotten engaged Colin wanted to congratulate the happy couple in person.

But right now he wanted to forget all duties, all pressing issues that demanded his attention. Still, if he didn't go, Stefan was right, it would be like throwing gasoline on the proverbial fire. He just wished he weren't so confused. He was happy here, albeit sexually frustrated. He enjoyed living in California, but he also missed his brother. And being away from his duties had Colin wondering what his late parents would've thought of his actions. Would they support his decision if he chose to walk away? Would they be disappointed?

If he ended up going to the ball, he'd have to reveal his true identity to Darcy. Traveling back for the event would be tiring and he'd want her with him to help with Iris. A small sliver of him wanted her to know, he wanted to see how she'd treat him if she knew the truth. He liked to think she'd still be the same Darcy he'd come to respect and desire.

"I'll let you know what I decide," Colin stated as he headed down the hall and upstairs to his bedroom. "I'll give you a few days' notice for security."

"They're already on standby," Stefan confirmed. "They're ready to come to LA and hover over you. I had to tell them to stand down more than once."

"Keeping my identity a secret would be kind of hard with royal guards surrounding the perimeter of my home."

"Which is why I'm honoring your wishes and letting you have some privacy. But you'll have to make some decisions soon and I'm not just referring to the ball."

Colin closed his bedroom door and toed off his shoes. "You'll be the first to know what I decide. Right now I have more pressing matters to deal with."

Stefan chuckled. "I'm sure you do."

Colin disconnected the call, cutting off Stefan's mocking laugh. Quickly changing his clothes, Colin decided he was taking charge of everything in his personal life starting now. He was torn up over the decision involving his royal status, but he refused to have his libido all out of control, too. He was going to take what he wanted… and he wanted Darcy Cooper.

How would he know if whatever they were feeling was something real? Colin had told her he couldn't give her more, but those words had been spoken out of fear. He didn't want her to think he was using her, but he ached for her in ways he hadn't known possible.

Lust was something he remembered from his bachelor days, but Darcy was worth more than that shallow emotion and damn if it wasn't complicating everything right now.

He'd given her the space he promised. He'd watched her, kept his hands to himself and had not made any innuendos whatsoever. His self-control was choking him to death.

Their connection was obvious. Why couldn't they spend these next few months enjoying each other? Surely by the time he was ready to move on they'd be tired of each other.

Seduction would be the key to winning her over and he had every intention of pulling out all stops and making her just as achy and needy as he was. This entire plan was a risk because he knew he wanted to explore more, but what would happen if they reached the point of no return?

Iris wasn't acting sleepy at all after the swim and brief snack, so Darcy slipped back into the pool. Schedules were important for babies, but so was soaking up all the fun and memories they could. Delaying Iris's nap by half an hour wouldn't hurt. The other day the nap had been put off for too long, hence the mega tantrum, but Darcy had learned what Iris's nap meltdown threshold was.

Easing Iris into her baby raft with canopy, Darcy held onto the side and swished the float around in the water. Iris squealed and clapped her hands with each twist. Her little legs were working back and forth beneath the water. Darcy couldn't help but laugh as an immeasurable amount of joy filled her heart. There truly was nothing like a baby's sweet laugh. Darcy watched Iris's face as she led her further into the pool. Those bright eyes really sparkled in the sunlight…and reminded Darcy how much Iris looked like her daddy.

Dunking down lower to get her shoulders wet, Darcy tried her hardest to keep images of Colin from her mind. Of course the harder she fought, the more he kept creeping into her thoughts. It was so, so difficult to keep her professional feelings separate from her personal ones.

Darcy loved Iris, enjoyed every moment she got to spend with her. But she also thoroughly enjoyed Colin's company on a level that she hadn't expected. Her mind and her heart were in agreement for once, telling her that feeling anything for the man was a bad idea.

A flash of him doing chin-ups with one muscular arm, the memory of how he'd stared so intently into her eyes the instant before he claimed her mouth flooded her thoughts. Then there was the other side of him that also played through her mind. The man was an amazing father, always wanting to give Iris her bath, wanting to spend so much time alone with his little girl. The smile he gave Iris was unlike anything Darcy had ever seen. The man was truly in love with his daughter.

How could Darcy not be attracted to all facets of Colin? He may still be quite mysterious, and he still had that expensive SUV in the drive waiting for her to drive it, but he had her so torn up, she had no choice but to want to know more.

For the past three days he'd stayed away from her unless they were with Iris. Part of her hated the barrier she'd placed between them, but the other part knew the separation was the best thing for her. Between focusing on her business and reminding herself she needed to guard her heart, Darcy couldn't afford to fall into a fling no matter how she desired to do just that.

Memories of how amazing his weight had felt pressed against her as his mouth consumed her would just have to suffice. Unfortunately, right now, all the memories were doing was leaving her achier.

"How can I stay inside and work when there's so much fun going on out here?"

Darcy froze the same instant Iris squealed for her daddy.

No. No. No. She didn't want to turn around because if she did she knew she'd see Colin wearing some type of swimming trunks that only showcased his impressive set of abs and all of his other magnificent muscles.

She wanted to hide, to instantly be poolside and wrapped in a towel so he didn't have to see her get out of the water with her thighs jiggling and her rounded stomach that had stretched her "miracle suit" beyond the promised miracle.

From the corner of her eye, Darcy spotted a flash of black just as Colin dove headfirst into the pool. What was he thinking coming out here with her? Yes, Iris was present as they'd discussed, but he wasn't naive. He knew exactly what coming out here half naked would do to her. What type of game was he playing?

When Colin surfaced, much closer to her than she'd anticipated, he swiped the water back from his forehead and smiled at Iris.

"Hey, baby. Are you having fun?"

With Colin's hands on the raft, Darcy eased back. No way was she going to accidentally entangle her legs with his because she'd quite possibly start to whimper, which would completely override the speech she'd given him three days ago.

"I'll just let you two have some time alone."

Darcy made her way to the steps. There was no good way to get out without Colin seeing her ancient, threadbare suit pasted against every dip and roll. Best to just get out, fake a confidence she didn't own and run like hell for the nearest towel.

"You don't have to get out because I'm here."

Darcy knew full well the man had his eyes on her, but she didn't turn to meet his gaze until she was properly wrapped like a terrycloth sausage.

"I'm not," she told him, lying through her smile.

Colin adjusted the canopy over Iris to keep her shaded. "Are you going to run every time you get uncomfortable?"

Gripping her towel at her breasts, Darcy straightened her shoulders. "I'm not running."

"But you're uncomfortable," he said with a smirk. "Your rules, Darcy. You can cancel them at any time and take what we both want for as long as we're here."

No, she couldn't.

"She'll need a nap soon," Darcy told him, dodging the obvious topic. "Just bring her in and I'll get her all dried off and ready. If you don't object, I plan on making almond-crusted chicken and grilled veggies for dinner."

"No objections here. At least not on dinner."

The man was so confusing. One minute he was moody and kissing her so she had to put on the brakes. The next minute he was agreeing to her terms and then he tried to muddle her mind by flashing that chest that should be enshrined in gold.

Darcy marched into the house, not in the mood to play whatever game he was offering. He had issues of his own, at least he said he did, and so did she. They had a temporary working relationship. Pursuing anything beyond that agreement would be wrong and settle so much awkwardness between them they'd never find their way out.

The last time she'd fallen hard for a man, she'd let him into her life, into her business because her grandmother thought he was perfect for Darcy. Darcy had trusted her hormones and ignored common sense for too long.

She'd let business and pleasure mix once before and she'd be paying for that mistake for the rest of her life.

Nine

Darcy may want him to give up, but until he quit seeing desire in her eyes each time she looked at him, he wasn't backing down. She'd been burned before and now Colin was paying for another man's sins.

She may have asked for space, and he wasn't one to go against a woman's wishes, but that didn't mean he still couldn't get what he wanted.

True, the house was huge so giving her space wasn't necessarily a problem. But their physical connection was so intense that the walls seemed to close in on them.

At first he'd fought the attraction, then he'd resigned himself to the fact it wasn't going away. Then he'd wondered if they could both heal by seeking comfort in each other. But as that thought ran through his mind, he couldn't help but wonder if there was something more building here.

He sounded like a woman thinking through all of his feelings and emotions, but Darcy was bringing out a side he hadn't known existed and he didn't want to cheapen whatever this was to a potential fling. They both deserved more than that, yet he couldn't help but want her and there was no point in trying to fight the tension anymore.

He'd failed in his attempt at seduction at the pool earlier today. He thought for sure spending time with her in a more relaxed setting with Iris would soften her. Now Darcy was up in her room and he was once again in the gym. He couldn't even come into this room anymore without seeing her pressed against the wall, flushed from arousal and looking up at him beneath heavy lids.

There had to be a way to break down the barrier she'd encompassed herself in. There were so many layers he'd yet to peel away. He wanted to know why she only wore three outfits and rotated them. He wanted to know why she was sewing things in her spare time and why she sneaked down to the gym early in the mornings before Iris woke when she thought he was still asleep. On a rare occasion he would catch her searching the internet for more recipes. Seems that cooking wasn't just a fun hobby for her as she'd stated, but a true passion.

Still, she'd made it apparent she didn't want to be alone with him so talking to her was damn near impossible, because when Iris was around he wanted to devote his time and attention to his daughter.

Colin pushed the bar back into locked position and sat up on the bench. Swiping a hand across his forehead, he cleared away the sweat as a brilliant plan entered his mind. He was going to have to get creative, to make sure there was no way she could run from what was happening between them. And something was happening whether she wanted to admit it or not.

Sliding his cell from his shorts pocket, Colin quickly did a search for the number he'd used when he'd first contacted her and placed the call. "Colin?" she answered, confusion lacing her tone.

He chuckled. "Yeah."

"Why are you calling my cell?"

A nugget of doubt slid through his mind, but he pressed on because he'd never backed away from a challenge.

"To talk."

Silence settled over the line. Maybe this was a mistake, but it was a risk he was willing to take. Hadn't he always been a daredevil? Hence his accident and recovery. "Darcy?"

"I'm here." She let out a sigh and a faint sound of sheets rustling filtered through the line. "What do you want to talk about? We're in the same house. You *are* in the house, right?"

He came to his feet and reached for a towel hanging over a weight machine. "I'm in the gym." Colin mopped off his face and neck, and flung the towel into the bin in the corner. "Did I wake you?"

"No. I had just turned off my light and crawled into bed."

Closing his eyes, he could easily picture her spread out on his guest bed, her dark, rich hair spilling over the crisp, white sheets. What did she wear to bed? A T-shirt? Something silky, perhaps? Nothing?

"Is everything okay?" she asked. "I'm a little confused as to why you're calling me."

"I want to hear your voice."

Colin shut off the light in the gym and headed toward his office. Only a small desk lamp lit the room. He knew he had to keep control of this conversation or she'd hang up.

"Tell me about your life before you came here."

Darcy laughed. "What about it? I work with kids and love to cook—that's about as exciting as I am."

She was so much more and he'd be the man to show her. Whoever she'd been with last was a jerk who hadn't realized what a treasure he had.

"You have friends, yes?" he asked.

"Yes. I was living with my best friend before I came here. What about you? You're from Greece, you're an amazing father, you keep simple working hours, but that's all I know."

"I'm not talking about me." He sank onto the leather sofa, leaned back and shut his eyes. He wanted to hear all about her, wanted her sultry, sleepy voice to wash over him. "We're talking about you."

"This Q and A can go both ways," she replied with a hint of a challenge. "How about we take turns? I'll go first. Why are you still trying to seduce me?"

"Wow. You sure you don't want to lead in with something lighter? My favorite color is red and my favorite sport is rock climbing."

"You're dodging the question," she stated. "You are the one who started this game."

"Fine. I want you." He shifted on the couch and propped his feet up on the cushions, then leaned back on the arm. "Why are you afraid to be alone with me?"

"Because you're sneaky and I wouldn't be able to resist you."

Colin smiled, settling a hand on his bare abs. "I'm not sneaky, I'm honest."

"That's debatable." She sighed and Colin imagined her upstairs in the dark, aching for him as much as he was for her. "It's my turn. How did you injure yourself?"

"I was rock climbing and made an error in judgment. Trusted the wrong rock."

Darcy's gasp had his own gut clenching. He was actually glad for the head trauma because he didn't remember the fall in any way. A minor blessing.

"You could've been killed," she cried.

"I nearly was. The doctors weren't so sure at first, but once they knew I would live, they told my wife I would never walk again."

"You're remarkable," she whispered.

As much as his ego loved her stroking it, Colin really didn't want her pity because of his accident. He wanted her, no question. But he understood she was burned in the past and he knew she was struggling for money, so she definitely had more at stake than he did.

"Tell me about the jerk who broke your heart."

Darcy groaned. "Why don't you ask something else?"

"Because my backup question is me wanting to know how fast I can be in your room with nothing between us but the darkness."

"You're not playing fair," she muttered.

Colin gritted his teeth. "Baby, I'm not playing at all. I'm tired of playing. We've danced around this attraction for too long and I'm going insane."

"Fine. We'll discuss the ex."

He didn't know if he wanted to laugh or cry at the reply.

Darcy's deep inhale had Colin eagerly waiting, but knowing he'd probably want to hunt this guy down and make him pay. Colin had no reason to be jealous, no reason to be so territorial…yet he was.

"My ex took every single dime I had to my name. I trusted him with more than my heart, he was my new business partner after my grandmother passed, and he betrayed me. Apparently he had another girlfriend and was using my money to buy her presents. And by presents I mean trips, a car, a condo." Darcy paused and Colin wasn't sure if there was more or if she was waiting for him to reply. After another soft sigh, she continued. "He not only ruined my business, he killed my dream of adopting a child."

Colin tamped down his anger. Whoever this bastard was, Colin loathed the man and wished for about five minutes alone with him. The fact he'd stolen all of her money was a sin in itself, but to know Darcy wanted to adopt was a morsel of information he was shocked she'd revealed.

Did she have a dream of adopting because she was compassionate toward kids and wanted to save them? Did she not plan on marrying? Or was there something medical that prevented her from having her own?

She'd answered one question and triggered a multitude of others.

But now he realized why Darcy had so little with her, why she was so upset over the new car and him having hers taken away without asking first. Her ex had thrown money around, albeit hers, and had used the funds to further his own desires. This woman was a fighter and she wasn't about to take handouts from the likes of Colin. How could he not admire how strong-willed she was?

Fortunately, he'd gotten her car back, now fixed, and it sat in one of the bays of his second garage behind the house. But even though he'd smoothed things over with Darcy, Colin didn't want to stop there. He was already in deep with her, so why not keep going to satisfy his curiosity?

"What's his name?" Colin asked.

"I'm sorry?"

Colin fisted his hand over his abs. "The lowlife who stole from you. I want his name."

"It's not your turn."

Her tone left no room for argument, so he waited for her to ask her question.

"You're a man of mystery. What's your profession?"

"I'm a CEO of sorts." Okay, there was no good way to answer, but he was a leader…for now. "I manage a large group back in Greece."

There. That sounded believable, didn't it? It was his turn to ask a question, but he wasn't wasting it on her ex's name. He could find that out later and take care of things. Right now, he wanted to dig deeper, to get to the point of his call. Priorities.

"What are you wearing?" he asked.

Darcy's soft laugh enveloped him as if she stood before him. Damn, he wanted to touch her, to kiss her, to feel her beneath him. He'd only known her several weeks and she all but consumed him. Obviously she had no clue the power she held over him.

"Are we playing that game now?" she all but mocked. "I'm wearing a black, silky chemise that leaves very little to the imagination."

Colin swallowed, the image now burned in his mind. "You're lying."

"You'll never know. What are you wearing?"

"Shorts and sweat. I just finished my workout where all I could do was see you pinned against the wall with your eyes closed, your mouth on mine and my hand up your shirt."

Darcy sighed. "What are you doing to me?" she whispered. "I can't keep up with how quick you turn me inside out."

"That goes both ways, *erastis*."

"What does that mean?"

"Come down to my office and I'll tell you." More like show her.

"I can't, Colin. You're making this so difficult for me. You have to understand that just because I want something, doesn't mean I can take it. Apparently you're used to getting what you want."

"I always get what I want."

"Sounds like a threat."

Colin smiled. "It's a promise."

"Tell me about your wife."

Colin eased up and shook his head. No way was he getting into how he'd let his wife down when he'd lived his reckless lifestyle and then pushed her away when he'd truly needed her most. He totally took the blame for their failed marriage because he'd been too proud, too stubborn to let her just help him through his rough time. Which was beyond ironic since he'd hired Darcy to assist him because he'd finally come to the realization he couldn't do it all.

Maybe it was time to break the cycle. To finally let someone in and keep his stubborn pride on the back burner. But, right now he had other, more pressing matters.

"Let's table that discussion for another time."

"Count on it," she said around a yawn.

"I'll let you go," he told her. "I need to hit the shower before I head to bed."

"I'll just be lying here in my chemise, dreaming."

Colin fisted his hand and came to his feet. "You're getting too good at this. Better watch what you say, you're playing with fire."

"You lit the match."

When she hung up, Colin stood in his office with a painful arousal and a ridiculous grin on his face. Yeah, he was used to getting what he wanted and he wanted Darcy in his bed.

And he would have her there. It was only a matter of time.

Darcy hadn't slept at all. Once Colin had started with the "what are you wearing" game her mind had formed so many fantasies, leaving her restless and aroused.

She hadn't lied when she said she was lying in her bed wearing a black chemise. She actually owned two. Sleeping in something so soft, so flawless gliding over her skin always made her feel more feminine. After dealing with children all day and spending most of her waking hours dealing with various problems and parents, she had to stay in touch with her femininity even if she wasn't sleeping with anyone.

Which was why last night's little chat with Colin left her aching in ways she'd never thought possible. She'd been with one man, and even during their intimacy Darcy had never felt an inkling of what she'd felt last night on the phone with Colin.

The man wasn't just chipping away at the defensive wall she'd erected, he was blasting through it with a sledgehammer. He'd started opening up just a touch over the past several weeks and he'd become playful, flirty and flat-out blatant regarding what he wanted.

Because she hadn't slept very well, she was awake even earlier than usual and in the gym. Of course, during her entire workout all she could picture was Colin down here last night. How long had he been sweating and working out while thinking of her? Did he regret calling her? Had he assumed she'd come running to him and they'd enter into this affair without giving the consequences another thought?

When she glanced at the time on her phone, she realized she'd been working out for over an hour. A great improvement over the first day. Granted, she'd had a hard time concentrating with Colin flexing his perfectly honed muscles all over the place.

If she could keep up this regime while she was here and continue eating healthily, she just may be on the fast track to getting her life back. In such a short time she already felt better about herself and had more energy.

More energy was something she would most definitely need if she was going to continue to battle Colin and his bold advances.

Darcy headed back upstairs, careful as always to be quiet while Iris and Colin slept. Grabbing a quick shower would give her time to get her thoughts in order before facing Colin. She knew the mutual desire would not go away. And as if fighting her urges wasn't enough, he wasn't playing fair. How could she keep putting up a strong front when he'd pretty much laid his cards on the table?

Lathering up her hair, she slid the strands through her fingers beneath the spray. She'd been worried about getting entangled with Colin after her last romance debacle, but Colin was so different from her ex. She only had to look at his interactions with Iris to see how loving he was. And he wasn't out to use her for anything because at this point he knew she had nothing to give.

Maybe he wanted her for no other reason than to satisfy his curiosity…just as she felt with him.

Darcy rinsed her body and shut off the water. Quickly she toweled off. She'd just pulled her hair into a messy topknot when fussy noises blared through the monitors.

Iris was crankier in the mornings than any other baby she'd dealt with. Of course, Darcy hadn't personally worked with a vast number of children under two, but Iris was certainly special. The toddler was happiest when she got her food. Darcy could totally relate.

Darcy wrestled her sports bra back on and yanked up her shorts; she didn't have time to find something else. When she turned the corner of her room and hit the doorway of the nursery, Colin was lifting Iris from her crib. That toned back with ink scrolling over his shoulder continued to mock her, because every time she saw it, she wanted to trace it…with her tongue.

The way he gently spoke to Iris, the way he held such a delicate little girl against his hard, strong body really hit

Darcy. Even rumpled from sleep, Colin Alexander was a man who demanded attention without saying a word.

When he turned and caught her gaze, his eyes did some evaluating of their own. Darcy was reminded she stood before him in only her sweaty sports bra and shorts. Not her best look, considering she wasn't perfectly proportioned or toned in any way.

"I just got out of the shower and threw on the closest thing," Darcy stated, keeping her eyes locked on Colin as he continued to close the gap between them. "Give me one minute to change and I can take her and feed her."

Colin's limp was a bit more pronounced this morning. Most likely he'd slept wrong. How had the man slept after that call? Maybe she was more revved up with this sexual tension than he was.

"You're flushed." His eyes traveled to the scoop in her bra and back up. "Looks good on you."

"Colin—"

"Go change," he urged. "I'll feed Iris and you better be fully dressed next time you're around me."

Darcy stared at him for another minute, which was a minute too long because he reached out, trailed a fingertip across her collarbone.

"Go, *erastis,* before I take what I want."

That was the second time he'd called her that and she wanted to know what it meant. She had a feeling it was a term of endearment or something sexy because his voice took on a whole other tone when he said it. She was drowning where this man was concerned and she knew it was just a matter of time before she succumbed to all of the desire and passion that kept swirling around them.

Darcy turned and all but ran into her adjoining bath. The man was killing her. She dug out a pair of jeans and her favorite pink T-shirt before heading back downstairs, praying she'd have control over her emotions. She should be praying Colin would have control over his.

She didn't see them in the kitchen, but the sound of the patio doors sliding open drew her attention. Through the wide window she spotted Colin with a banana in one hand and Iris holding onto the other as he led her out onto the stone patio. He'd just placed her on the settee when he lost his balance and went down. Darcy ran out the door and was crouched at his side in an instant.

Had he reinjured himself? Worry flooded her. How she would get him back up without hurting him further?

With a muttered curse in his native tongue, Colin pushed her away. "Don't. Just take her inside and feed her."

Darcy reached for him. "Let me help you up."

"Leave me be," he shouted, meeting and holding her gaze. "I'm not paying you to coddle me, I'm paying you to care for Iris."

Darcy jerked back and came to her feet. Iris started to climb off the chair and Darcy reached down, taking the little girl's hand.

"You're right," Darcy replied, swallowing the hurt. "I'll remember my place from now on."

Colin shifted and stood, wincing as he did so. Even though his jab sliced deep, Darcy waited until he got his bearings. Just as he opened his mouth to speak, Darcy turned.

"Come on, baby girl." Darcy swiped the banana from the ground where Colin had dropped it when he fell. "Let's get you some breakfast."

No way would Darcy make the mistake of trying to get close and help Colin again. If he wanted to run hot and cold with his emotions, he could do so with someone else. Darcy wasn't here as an outlet for his frustrations and anger over his accident.

Ten

Disgrace was a bitter, nasty pill to swallow.

After his spill that morning, Colin didn't know what he was angrier about, himself for falling and possibly hurting Iris or the fact that Darcy was there to witness his humiliation. He'd taken his anger and embarrassment out on her for no reason.

Hadn't he hired a nanny in case something like this happened? The real possibility that he would fall in the presence of, or God forbid, while holding Iris, had been his main concern. What he hadn't planned on was having his hormones thrown into the mix. And he hadn't been forthcoming with Darcy about his injury because he'd prayed there wouldn't be a mishap while she was here. He didn't want to be seen as weak or crippled.

Colin sneaked into the house through the back door after Darcy had taken Iris in for breakfast. After he'd showered and gotten his damn leg and back under control with some stretches his doctor and therapist had shown him, Colin felt somewhat human again.

This morning his goal had been to carry on the plan of seduction that he'd started on the phone last night. Then his past had come back to bite him when he'd fallen, completely erasing any impact he may have had on Darcy last night because of his inability to handle this entire situation like a mature adult. Wow, wasn't he just the king of all things sexy? Now instead of Darcy viewing him as a strong, confident man, she saw him as a cripple, as someone who couldn't even care for himself, let alone a child.

If the paparazzi back in Galini Isle ever caught a glimpse of his inability to stand on his own two feet at times, he'd be ridiculed, questioned and thrust into the limelight even more. They'd already speculated that he and Karina were falling apart, but since her death, they hadn't left him alone and he was sick of the pity, the way they portrayed him as helpless and lost.

He was an Alexander. They were strong men, determined and focused. Nothing would stand in the way of him getting everything he wanted.

Needing to get back on track and spend time with his daughter, Colin figured today would be a great day for a little outing. Darcy might not like men who threw their weight and money around, but he wanted to treat her. Out of every woman he'd ever known, Darcy most definitely deserved to be pampered, even if only for a few hours.

If she was working for him, then she was going to be treated like royalty.

Which reminded him, he needed to have a serious talk with her. He'd decided to attend the ball and he wanted Darcy to come with him. That conversation would have to take place at just the right time. He didn't want her to feel as if he'd lied to her…though he had by omission.

Just as Colin reached the bottom of the stairs, he heard

Darcy's laughter and Iris's sweet giggle. That combination slid a new emotion through him—one he wasn't sure he could identify and one he wasn't sure he wanted to.

When he found them on the floor in the living room, Colin stopped in the wide, arched doorway to take in the scene. Days ago the sight of freshly picked flowers, obviously from the landscaping, all over his floor would've had him enraged. But now, seeing those vibrant petals in Darcy's and Iris's hair had him smiling. These two were like kindred spirits and he could easily get wrapped up in watching them.

There he went again, sliding down that slippery slope even further toward Darcy. He had lost control somewhere between opening the door that first day and the first time she'd verbally matched him with her banter.

"Daddy!"

Iris squealed, scooped up all the flowers her little hands could hold and sprinkled them on top of Darcy's head.

"Deedee pitty," she exclaimed, clapping her hands.

Darcy glanced his way, but quickly darted away. "I'm Deedee. It's much easier for her to say."

Colin hated how Darcy wouldn't even look at him. He'd done that to her when he'd sworn he wouldn't hurt anyone again over this injury. Because of his inexcusable actions, he'd driven a wedge between them.

The fact his daughter had adopted a nickname for Darcy added another layer of bonding that was already wrapped so tightly around them. All part of the nanny-child relationship, nothing more—or at least that's what he needed to keep telling himself. Darcy wasn't part of this family; her presence was temporary.

"Darcy, go get yourself and Iris ready. We're going out for the day." He moved into the room and slid his hand over Iris's dark curls. "I'll work on cleaning this mess up."

Darcy came to her feet, catching the flowers as they

fell down her chest. "I'm sorry. We went for a little walk and picked some flowers from the gardens. I planned on cleaning—"

Colin held up a hand, cutting off her words, and offered a smile so she didn't think he was angry or a complete jerk after how he'd treated her earlier. "I've got it. Really. Go on."

"Okay." She bent down, lifted Iris into her arms and turned back to him. Finally, she met his eyes with a worry he didn't want. "Are you feeling all right?"

She didn't come out and ask about the fall, but he knew that's exactly what she was referring to.

He gave her a brief nod. "Do you want to know where we're going?" he asked.

Darcy's lids lowered. "My place isn't to ask questions. You're paying me to care for Iris, so I'm going to get us ready."

Colin absolutely loathed the words he'd spouted off to her earlier out of anger and humiliation. There was no taking them back now that they were out in the open. All he could do was show her he wasn't the ogre she thought he'd become.

Darcy left the room without another word. He needed to apologize, but words would only go so far. He would show her that he wasn't a terrible person. He'd make her see that she didn't have to work her butt off for nothing.

And by the time she left him at the end of her term, she'd never have to worry about her business or her finances again. If he did nothing else, he'd make damn sure of that.

He had to be kidding. That dress—as stunning as it was—cost more than an entire month's worth of groceries. Colin had talked her into shopping, but she'd had no idea he'd pull her into the most expensive store she'd ever seen in her entire life.

After working for him for several weeks now, one would think she'd have the courage to stand her ground and decline.

On the flipside, though, she'd discovered with each passing day that Colin was impossible to resist.

"At least try it on," he urged, holding up the elegant, one-shouldered, bright blue dress.

Darcy wasn't in the mood to be shopping, but Colin had claimed this was just another work incentive and he truly wanted her to have new clothes. After the morning they'd had, she really had no clue why they were here.

"I won't wear that dress," she told him, though she loved it. Being stubborn could go both ways.

On a sigh, he hung the dress back up and inched closer. "I already apologized, but I'll keep saying it until you realize I am honestly sorry for how I reacted. I know you were only trying to help, but my pride usually doesn't allow me to let others come to my rescue."

That she could understand. She, too, had her pride and he had come and apologized shortly after she'd completely ignored him.

"I just find it convenient you're getting me clothes today and calling them incentives," she shot back, talking quietly so the salesclerk didn't hear. Iris squealed and chewed on the baby doll in her stroller, oblivious to the turmoil.

"I'd planned on this anyway," he told her. "The timing is just wrong. If you're not in the mood, we can do this another day. I figured we could both use a break and to get out and do something fun."

Something fun? What man found shopping fun? Darcy chewed on her bottom lip as she considered how to approach this. She could be childish, the way he had been the other day, or she could accept the olive branch he was extending.

"Fine," she conceded.

With a wide smile, Colin lifted the dress back off the rack. "What size do you need?"

Darcy laughed, gripping the handle on the Cadillac of strollers. "Nice try, buddy. I'm not telling you my size. It's not in the single digits and I doubt that dress will look good on my frame."

His eyes scanned her body. "Your frame looks fine and you'll never know how it looks if you don't try it on."

Darcy shook her head and turned toward another rack. "Everything in here is so pricey. Why are we even here?"

Colin's hand came around, gripping hers over the handle. Darcy threw a glance over her shoulder and saw he was much closer than she'd thought.

"Pick out whatever you want." He held up a hand when she started to argue. "I'll take Iris to the toy store next door. Text me when you're done. The clerk has my credit card number."

Darcy closed her eyes. "There's nothing I need that will take me that long. Just give me a couple minutes."

"You may not need it, but you deserve it." His thumb stroked over her hand. "I'm not trying to buy you. I'm trying to put a smile on your face, to let you have whatever you want for the entire day. I'd bet my entire savings that you haven't bought anything for yourself for years."

Darcy glanced down to their hands. The contrast between his dark skin and her paleness was minor in comparison to their many differences.

"I'm not sleeping with you."

Colin jerked her around, his fingers digging into her shoulders. "I'm not offering this shopping trip as a bribe, Darcy. You going to bed with me has nothing to do with this. I'm here because I want to give you nice things while you're with me. If you want to leave everything when you go, then do that and I'll donate the clothes to charity. You were told up front you'd be getting bonuses along the way. Don't argue."

"Yet again, does anyone ever tell you no?" she asked.

A smirk flirted around the corners of his mouth. "You're the only one who keeps trying."

On a sigh, Darcy closed her eyes and nodded. "Fine. I'll pick out a couple of things. Seriously, though, we could find a cheaper store."

His eyes traveled over the racks, the displays and mannequins. "Do you not like this store?"

Darcy laughed. "Everything in here is gorgeous. I just think we could find one with smaller numbers on the price tags."

"Don't look at the price tag. Focus on how stunning you'll look, how beautiful you'll feel." Colin's intense gaze lasted a minute longer than she was comfortable with before he moved around her and gripped the stroller. "Take your time. I've got Miss Iris."

Darcy stared at his retreating back. He paused at the counter and spoke to the pretty female employee. Of course she batted her lashes and laughed at whatever Colin said before he slipped out the front door. The man seemed to have that effect on every female.

Colin was way too charming. Not only did he have that devastatingly handsome, sexy arrogance about him, he had a beautiful baby girl. All he had to do was be the loving, doting father he was and women's ovaries started weeping.

The burn in her throat had her swallowing. Colin and Iris were missing the female figure in their lives and Darcy was missing the family she'd always dreamed of having. Yet they could never mesh together because... well, just because.

She was his employee, she had goals of her own and right now she needed to get her business back up and running. Added to that, Colin made it clear he would probably be leaving in a few months to go back to Greece.

Darcy nearly laughed. She'd never have the chance to set foot on Colin's home turf. If he wanted to treat her like Cinderella today, she would let him. For once she would let someone else take care of her, do something nice for her.

By the time Darcy finished trying on clothes, she had way more in her want pile than in her "no" pile.

"Miss Cooper," the clerk called from the other side of the thick floor-to-ceiling curtain. "I have some shoes pulled and jewelry for you to look at once you're done. Can I get you any other sizes?"

Shoes? Jewelry? When had she ever purchased an entire outfit complete with head-to-toe accessories?

"My sizes are fine," she called back. "I'll be right out."

When Darcy stepped out of the dressing room, she resisted the urge to adjust her simple V-neck T-shirt. She didn't fit in this place and the clothes she'd tried on certainly wouldn't work for her daily activities relating to Iris's care. But if she left with nothing, she knew Colin would drag her somewhere else.

"What can I take to the counter for you?"

Darcy glanced to the perfectly polished clerk with her carefully applied makeup and elegantly coiffed hair. Darcy glanced back into the dressing room where she'd hung everything up.

"I'll take that blue dress for now," she told the clerk. "I need to think about everything else."

She hated to admit it, but the blue dress did hug her curves and made her feel beautiful. She didn't mind said curves or her figure so much, and with her workout sessions she was actually starting to see a difference in her body. The extra boost of confidence had her smiling.

Colin had liked the dress, so that's what she'd go with for now. And damn if he wasn't right. It had looked good on her, better than she'd ever imagined...not that she'd admit such a revelation to Colin.

"What size shoe are you? I was guessing a seven."

Amazing how the woman was dead-on, but Darcy shook her head. "Oh, I couldn't—"

"Mr. Alexander made me promise to add shoes and any jewelry you wanted to the outfits you chose." A soft smile spread across her face. "He also said not to argue and worry about the cost."

Darcy couldn't help but laugh. Colin thought he had all his bases covered. Biting her bottom lip, Darcy pondered what she should actually do versus what she wanted to do. She could go ahead and get the things Colin requested. If she didn't wear anything, he could return them and get his money back.

"I should also tell you, he also made me promise you'd leave with no less than three outfits." With her hands clasped in front of her bright pink capris and crisp white shirt, the clerk nodded toward the dress in Darcy's hand. "He also said you weren't leaving without that blue dress, so I'm glad you already chose that one."

Three outfits? The staggering cost of all that would be beyond ridiculous. Outfits, as well as accessories and shoes. What else did Colin have planned for her? Buying clothes and loaning her a brand-new car were both so personal. When he'd initially said bonuses, Darcy had assumed he'd meant the monetary kind. She really should've asked him for specifics, but she'd been too concerned about keeping her job and making it past the trial period.

"To be honest, I don't have a need for fancy clothes," she told the clerk. "I love everything in here, but I'm a nanny and caring for a child doesn't necessarily require bling and stilettos."

The clerk laughed, reached out and patted her arm. "Tell you what, let's look around and I'm sure we can find something to make you both happy. You can still be fashionable and comfortable while caring for that sweet baby."

An hour later the young worker, whom Darcy now knew as Carly, had delivered on her promise. New shorts, basic tops and adorable sandals were neatly wrapped in tissue paper and placed in two large bags…along with that blue dress Darcy would never have a use for. She had drawn the line at jewelry, though. There was no need for earrings or a necklace for Iris to tug on, not to mention Darcy wasn't preparing herself for a fashion show.

She shot Colin a text, telling him she was finished and she'd come to the toy store to meet him. After thanking Carly for all of her help, Darcy headed out the door. So much money spent for two bags worth of clothing, but he'd insisted, and to be honest she'd never let someone splurge on her before. Colin had been adamant he wanted to do this for her and she was done being stubborn.

Perhaps she was being selfish, but life had thrown so much crap at her, it was nice to have someone refreshing waltz into her life. She truly believed he wasn't buying her to get her into bed. If he'd pursued harder at home, she would have caved and they both knew it. Getting new clothes certainly didn't make her want to jump him. No, she'd wanted to do that from the second he'd opened his door and greeted her.

The bright sun warmed her face as soon as she stepped onto the sidewalk. A familiar scream of delight had Darcy turning her attention down the sidewalk to where Iris sat in her stroller, hugging a brand new elephant in one hand and a waving rather large lollipop in the other. Seeing the big, wide smile across her precious face, Darcy didn't know if she'd ever seen Iris happier.

Colin, on the other hand, looked as though he could use a stiff drink. His hair stood on end as if he'd run his fingers through it for the past hour, his lids were heavy and he appeared to be in a daze.

Darcy held back her laugh, but couldn't stop from smiling as he moved closer. "Looks like you had a good time at the toy store."

Colin's eyes snapped to hers as if he'd just realized she stood near him. "Do you know what they have in that place?"

"I'm assuming toys," Darcy stated.

"From floor to ceiling." He continued to stare as if he'd been traumatized. "But it's not just toys. There's candy. Everything lights up or sings or dances to get your attention. It's not even safe to walk through the line to check out. She was reaching for everything. It's like they don't even care about the parents."

Darcy did laugh now. "Surely this wasn't your first trip to a toy store with her."

Colin blinked, raking a hand over his face. "Actually, it was."

The statement shocked Darcy. Perhaps his late wife had always taken Iris toy shopping. Maybe they had another nanny where they'd lived before and she did all of that. Or maybe someone just delivered toys and they hadn't taken Iris to any stores yet.

"Why don't you take these bags and I'll push Iris." She didn't wait for him to answer as she thrust the sacks into his hands. "Let's head home and I'll start dinner. You look like you need to get back to safer territory. We can't have all those plush toys terrorizing you anymore."

Colin glared at her. "Now you're mocking me. We don't

need to go home. I just needed to escape that store with my life."

Darcy started pushing Iris down the sidewalk toward the SUV—the one he'd bought for her use. Yes, the man was used to getting what he wanted, in one sneaky way or another.

"I'm not mocking you," she told him. "I'm just stating a fact based on the evidence you presented to me." Colin grunted in response. Darcy smiled as she loaded Iris into the car seat. "What do you say we head over to the park and let Iris play while you recover? Then we can go home and I'll make dinner."

Colin seemed to think about the suggestion before a wide grin spread across his face. "That's a great idea. It's a beautiful day. We might as well spend it outside."

Elation pumped through Darcy. She was seriously having such an amazing day with them and it had nothing to do with her new purchases. Being out with Iris and Colin was just fun and broke up the monotony of being in the house. Darcy had been so dead set on not letting Colin buy things for her, yet here she was watching him load the new clothes he'd purchased into a vehicle that he'd also bought for her.

She was not a shallow woman and she certainly wasn't hung up on material objects. But, if she was going to be spending months with Colin and Iris, they would be leaving the house at various times and she couldn't very well keep going out in her ratty old clothes. Granted she didn't need thousands of dollars' worth of clothes, either, but she'd lost that fight. She also planned to leave them behind when her term was over because she didn't think it would be fair to keep them…not unless something deeper happened between her and Colin. And at the rate they were edging closer together emotionally, she wondered how they actually would end up at the end of the six-month term.

As they all settled into the car and Darcy climbed in behind the wheel, she realized the main problem. She was getting too comfortable with this family. Not comfortable the way she had on other nanny jobs, but comfortable as in she'd started envisioning this little family as hers. The thought alone was utterly ridiculous, but she couldn't stop the daydream any more than she could control her hormones around Colin. Everything about this family struck a chord so deep within her, she knew she'd carry them with her for the rest of her life.

Darcy was completely in love with Iris. The little girl could easily melt anyone's heart.

As for Colin…she knew she wasn't in love with the man, but she did have feelings for him. Feelings that had no place in her life or in this professional atmosphere.

Now if she could just keep telling herself that, maybe she'd believe it. But would she stop fantasizing about him?

Eleven

He had become a creature of habit at a young age, due in part to his royal status. Schedules were a normal part of his life and without them, the members of the palace's security team would not have been able to do their jobs efficiently.

And here in the United States he found he was no different. He was in the middle of his nightly workout, which meant he was sweaty, breathing hard and still aching for the woman who lately occupied his every blasted thought.

Today had been amazing and seeing Darcy's face light up was worth the sacrifice. He knew she wasn't easily bought and that was definitely not his intent.

He treated her just as he would any other employee. Colin and his brother were always quick to supply anything the members of their staff needed. Just because he was in the United States, away from the palace, didn't mean he wouldn't treat Darcy like any other member of his staff.

Except Darcy had become more than an employee the second he'd plastered her up against the wall and kissed the hell out of her.

Last night their phone conversation had stimulated him in ways he hadn't expected. Sleep had been a long time coming and he had a feeling he'd be in the same predicament tonight. For the next several months, in fact, if they didn't end up just giving in to their desires.

He needed to get his head on straight and figure out how to tell Darcy about this trip. He actually loved the thought of taking her to his home country. He could only hope she'd take the news of his royal status well and agree to go with him. Colin had just started doing squats with the weight bar across his shoulders when his cell chimed from the bench behind him. Of all his exercises, this was the one that nearly killed his back and leg so he welcomed the distraction.

Dropping the bar back into place, he turned and smiled when he saw the name on the screen. He should've expected this.

"Is this going to be a ritual?" he asked in lieu of saying hello.

Darcy's soft laugh greeted him. "I just wanted to tell you again how much I appreciate the clothes. You didn't have to do anything like that for me, and saying thanks seems so inadequate, but…thanks."

Colin gripped the phone, wishing she'd come down and thank him in person. From her soft tone, he knew she was feeling a bit insecure, most likely about the money, which meant absolutely nothing to him. He had an exorbitant amount of it, so why shouldn't he be able to spend it on people he cared about?

"You're more than welcome," he replied, playing it safe instead of telling her what he really wanted to say. "But you don't have to keep thanking me."

"Maybe I just wanted to hear your voice."

Colin froze as she tossed back the words he'd given her last night. "You hear my voice all day."

"It's not the same with Iris around."

Closing his eyes, Colin reached out and rested his arm on the cool bar. He dropped his head and contemplated how to approach this shaky ground, because each step could set off a series of events he either didn't want or wasn't ready for. "You can come to the gym if you want to hear my voice," he said, hoping she'd take him up on his offer.

"No. This is best. I just…this is so silly."

"What were you going to say?"

Her pause had him lifting his head, listening for the slightest noise in the background. Was she already in bed? Had she lain there and thought of him?

"When I talked to you on the phone last night it was as if we were alone, just without the pressure of being alone." She laughed, then let out a groan. "Forget it. I'm not making sense."

She made perfect sense. Everything about her and this crazy situation made sense to him at this point in his chaotic life.

"Maybe we should pretend we're alone and we don't have to have any boundaries," he stated, his mouth spouting off words before he could fully filter his thoughts. "What if you were here with me now? Or what if I was up there with you? If we were just two people who met and there was nothing holding us back from taking what we wanted, what would you do?"

Silence greeted him and he knew without a doubt images were flooding Darcy's mind because they sure as hell were playing through his.

"What would you do if I showed up at your bedroom door right now?" he whispered.

He knew he was torturing himself. Unfortunately, he fantasized about Darcy whether he was speaking the words aloud or keeping the thoughts to himself.

"If nothing stood in our way, I'd let you in."

Colin wasn't sure whether to be thrilled or angry at this torturous piece of information. At least she came right out and said the words, but words meant nothing without action.

"What would we do after I came in?" he asked.

Her soft laugh enveloped him. "I'm not having phone sex with you."

"I wasn't headed there." Though now that she'd put that thought in his mind, he wouldn't object to a little phone sex. "Tell me, Darcy. Once I came to your room and you let me in, what would happen?"

"Everything I've been dreaming about," she whispered. "But dreams aren't always meant to come true."

That sad tone of her voice said so much more than her actual words. He knew she'd been saving for an adoption. He wished he could be the man to give her what she wanted, but he was in no position to give anything unless it was financial or sexual. All superficial things, yes—anything involving his heart or too many emotions, hell no. He wasn't naive. He figured if things were different they may actually have a shot at something special, something more meaningful than intimacy. But how could they pursue anything beyond that when she had no idea who he was and he had no idea who he wanted to be?

A muffled sniff slid through the phone and Colin gripped the device tighter. "I'm coming up."

"No. Colin, you can't." Another sniff. "This is good, just talking. I haven't really talked about my feelings for a long time."

"You're crying."

He hated the thought of her lying up there upset, most

likely over a bad memory that had been triggered by what he'd said. Colin wanted her happy, wanted that light in her eyes he'd become familiar with and he wanted to break down every damn wall she'd erected between them.

"I'm fine," she assured him. "It's getting late and I need to get up early for my workout."

"You have a standing invitation to work out with me."

"I know."

She still wouldn't take the offer, but he had to remind her anyway. He wanted to be here for her, to give his support, and that thought scared the hell out of him. Taking on someone else's problems was not going to help him solve his own and would only push him deeper into Darcy's life…a place he couldn't allow himself to be.

"Good night, Darcy."

"'Night, Colin."

He disconnected the call and resisted the urge to throw the phone across the room. This was a dangerous game he was playing with her. Not only were her feelings obviously involved, he had a sense her heart was teetering on the brink, too. That wasn't his ego talking, either. He didn't know if he had it in him to give her his heart. He knew he wanted her on a primal level and he was fully aware that his emotional connection with her was stronger than he'd intended, but there were so many uncertainties.

On the other hand, he wasn't too keen on the idea of another man capturing her heart, either, which left him in quite a predicament.

He had some decisions to make in his personal life here and back on Galini Isle. No matter what path he chose, Colin feared he'd be making a mistake and now there were even more lives—and hearts—on the line.

Colin kicked a ball to Iris, and just as she went to raise her leg the ball rolled right by her, causing her to laugh hysterically just like the past seventeen times he'd purposely kicked it by her.

Darcy swallowed the lump in her throat. A child's laughter was the sweetest noise, and by the looks of Colin's little game, he thought so, too..

The day was too beautiful for them to eat inside so Darcy had decided to set up lunch in the outside eating area. The father-daughter duo was having so much fun, they hadn't spotted her yet and Darcy was enjoying the view. Colin epitomized what fatherhood was all about. Spending time with his child, putting work on hold and not caring if he was getting texts or emails.

Exactly what Darcy would want for the father of her child if she could've had children. But she had to wonder what profession allowed him to have such flexibility. He'd mentioned that he managed a large group back home. Maybe he delegated most of his tasks. She could totally see him in a position of power and authority.

After pouring fresh iced tea into two glasses and placing a sippy cup of juice on the table, Darcy stood back and double-checked to make sure she hadn't forgotten anything. She was trying out a new recipe on Colin and she hoped he'd like it. Finding healthy dishes that weren't an all-day task to prepare was proving to be more difficult than she'd thought.

Smoothing her hands down her new mint-green shorts, Darcy headed out into the yard. Blades of grass tickled her bare feet as she crossed the lawn. Shielding her eyes from the afternoon sun with her hand, she continued to take in the beautiful image of the sexiest man she'd ever met playing with the sweetest little girl she'd ever cared for.

To look at them right now, one would never know a piece of their life had been ripped away when his wife passed. On a positive note, Iris wouldn't remember the pain of losing her mother. But she wouldn't have any mother-daughter memories to cherish. Darcy's mother hadn't died, but she had abandoned her at a young age. Still, Darcy's grandmother had always been there and was an amazing role model.

Colin glanced up, catching her gaze and pulling her from her thoughts. "You come out to play?" he asked.

"I set up lunch on the patio," she replied, rushing to play on Iris's side. Darcy kicked the ball back to Colin. "I figured we could eat out here today."

Iris clapped as Colin sent the ball back. "Deedee kick it."

For the next couple minutes, Darcy and Colin carried on a game. Before she knew it, the competition had turned serious and she was all over the yard, rounding him with the ball, dodging any attempt he tried to get back control. Colin thought he could outmaneuver her. Wasn't he in for a surprise? She was no stranger to kicking a ball around.

Finally, Darcy had mercy on him and she kicked the ball hard, sending it soaring through the air. Colin jumped, his arms extended above his head, and caught it with his hands.

"I'm raising the white flag," he panted.

Darcy resisted the urge to bend at the waist and draw in some much-needed air. She'd gotten in her second work-out of the day, but she wasn't about to admit she was still out of shape and thrilled he'd called a halt to their impromptu game.

"How about we eat?" she suggested, reaching down to take Iris's hand. "I have fresh tea and I desperately need a drink."

Once they were all settled, Darcy sat next to Iris to help her with her food if necessary. Colin took a look at his plate and smiled.

"This looks great."

His verbal approval shouldn't have had her so excited.

She'd only grilled some pineapple and chicken and put a homemade glaze over it. Nothing too fancy.

"Were you an athlete in school?"

Darcy sipped her glass of tea, welcoming the cold, refreshing drink. "I played soccer, actually. My school was big, so we had our own girls' team."

"You were pretty quick out there."

Darcy shrugged, even though a bit of pride burst through her at his statement. "Not as quick as I used to be. After graduating and helping Gram full time, I lost most of my stamina. As I've said before, I'm pretty out of shape now."

"I've already told you, your shape is just fine."

Darcy expected to look up and find him staring at her, but he was cutting into his chicken. Apparently the comment he kept throwing her way didn't affect him the way it did her. He tossed the words out so matter-of-factly, yet they meant so much to her. More than he could ever know.

"Your new clothes look nice on you."

Iris kicked her little feet in the highchair, causing the whole thing to wiggle, sending her sippy cup to the ground. Darcy retrieved it and set it back on the tray.

"For what you spent, they better," she joked.

Silence settled in for a bit before Iris started gibbering. Darcy didn't mind the quiet meal. There was no awkwardness surrounding them, only the peaceful, bright sunshine and the beauty of the lush backyard. It was times like this that Darcy could imagine slipping into the role of something so much more than a nanny.

"Did you play any sports in school?" she asked, trying to distract herself from her wayward thoughts.

Colin's fork froze halfway to his mouth, a naughty smile flirted around his lips. "I pretty much concentrated on girls and defying my father."

Darcy could easily see that. "What about your mother?"

"She was killed in an auto accident when I was younger."

Darcy's heart ached for him. He'd lost his mother and his wife? How much could a man take in one lifetime? So much heartache, yet he still smiled, still pushed forward and created a wonderful life for his own daughter.

"I shouldn't have asked," Darcy stated, slicing into her pineapple. "That was rude."

"You can ask me anything you want," he told her. "There's no need to be sorry. You didn't do anything wrong."

"No, but I don't want to bring up bad memories."

With a slight shrug, Colin reached for his tea. "The memories are always there. Not talking about them won't make them disappear."

Once Iris was finished, Darcy tidied her up and wiped off the tray. After taking a load of dishes into the kitchen, she came back out. Colin had pretty much cleaned up the rest and had his own stack of dishes in hand.

"I would've gotten those," she told him. "Just set them inside and I'll clean up later."

He didn't say a word as he passed. Darcy pulled Iris from her highchair and took her back out into the yard to continue the game of ball before the toddler went in for her nap.

Running in the grass, laughing and playing with a little one may have been something Darcy had dodged for years, but honestly this was exactly what she needed.

But the way they'd settled in almost like a family terrified Darcy because falling for a baby was one thing, but falling for the baby's father was another problem altogether. Yet the more time she spent with Colin, the more she saw what an amazing, giving man he was and the more she wanted him.

She was done denying herself.

Twelve

For the past week, Darcy had spoken to Colin on the phone every night before bed. There was something soothing about hearing that low, sultry voice without having to look him in the eyes or be distracted by that hard body. She loved their talks, which ranged from joking to flirting to borderline naughty.

They'd also had some serious moments. Moments that probably wouldn't have happened in the light of day or face-to-face. For some reason saying personal things on the phone was relaxing—almost therapeutic. She'd shared memories of her grandmother and he'd shared stories about how he and his brother used to rock climb together.

Darcy shifted against the sheets, the satin of her chemise sliding over her heated skin. Her gaze traveled to the phone on her nightstand. They'd already hung up for the night, but she needed more.

Before she lost her nerve, Darcy picked up her phone and called him back.

"Forget something?" he answered.

Oh, the replies she could throw back.

"I wasn't ready for bed." At least not alone. "Mind talking a bit more?"

"Not at all. You're a welcome distraction from this office work."

Darcy slid from bed and padded down the hall, careful not to speak when she passed Iris's door. For once she was going to be spontaneous, she was going to take what she wanted and live for the moment because there was no way she would walk out of here with regrets when her term ended.

There was only so much a woman could take.

"Something specific on your mind?"

Easing down the stairs, guided by only the soft glow of the dimmed chandelier in the foyer, Darcy smiled. "Too many things to list."

Some shuffling and cursing in his native language had Darcy pausing, her hand on the banister at the base of the steps. "Everything okay?" she asked.

Colin laughed. "Yeah, just making a mess here."

Darcy knew that as soon as she hit the hallway he'd hear her talking, so she took a seat on the bottom step, curled her feet up onto the step below and looped her arms around her knees.

"If you wanted something more than anything in the world, but there were obstacles in your way, what would you do?"

"Are we going to pretend we aren't talking about you?" he asked.

"I'm pretending," she said with a smile, even though he couldn't see her. "You don't have to."

"Then pretend it's me," he told her. "When I want something, I find a way to claim it at any cost. I may not get it in the time frame I want, but eventually with enough patience, I make it mine."

Closing her eyes, Darcy let his strong words push through that wall of fear she'd tried so hard to hide behind.

"What if time isn't on your side?" she whispered.

"What is it you want, Darcy?"

His question, nearly a whisper, too, told her he knew exactly what she wanted…or whom she wanted.

"I started to come to you." She gripped the phone tighter as if she could somehow pull strength from him. "I'm afraid."

Admitting that really humbled her because she didn't want to be seen as weak or vulnerable. Colin was neither of those things and she didn't figure he'd find a woman who was so indecisive and fearful attractive.

"You think I'm not?"

That voice was in full surround sound. Darcy jerked her head up to see Colin standing before her, phone still to his ear. The glow from the light illuminated him, making him seem even larger than life.

Darcy laid her phone beside her on the step. "You're not scared," she countered, unsure of what else to say at this point.

Crouching down with a slight wince, Colin placed his phone next to hers before laying his hands over the arm that was still wrapped around her knee. "Just because I'm scared doesn't mean I'll let the fear control my emotions. I want you, and the second you said you were coming to me I had to meet you halfway."

The man truly didn't let anything get in his way, not fear, not worry for the unknown…absolutely nothing.

"Maybe—"

He cut her off as he claimed her mouth beneath his. His hands instantly cupped the side of her face and tipped her head for better access. Colin's body eased forward and

Darcy realized he'd placed his knees on the bottom step, so she spread her legs to accommodate him.

The moment her bare thighs slid against the side of his ribs, she groaned into his mouth. She'd never been this turned on, this ready for a man, and he'd only started kissing her. Granted, she'd only been with one man in her life, but there was absolutely no comparison between this passionate moment and anything she'd experienced before.

Breaking away, Colin peered down, stroked her bottom lip with his thumb and held her gaze. "Never hold back with me. I want it all."

At that firm command, he took her lips again. Shivers coursed through her as Colin trailed his hands down her bare arms then slid them around her waist. With only the silk of her chemise providing a barrier, the warmth of his hands seared her skin. Arching into him, she wanted more and she wanted it now.

In one swift move, Colin picked her up and changed their positions so he sat on the step and she straddled his thighs.

His eyes roamed over her body. "You really do sleep in a black chemise."

Without comment, Darcy did what she'd wanted to do since day one. She leaned forward and trailed her tongue across that ink scrolling over his shoulder and down to his pec. The muscles clenched beneath her touch and a low growl erupted from Colin. His hands came around to cup her backside, jerking her closer against his arousal.

Darcy trembled, clutching his shoulders. An ache even fiercer than before spread through her. There was nothing outside this moment. Not her financial issues, not her infertility, not the mystery surrounding Colin, because if she were honest, that only added to his allure. They were both taking what they wanted.

Colin moved one hand around, splaying it over her

upper thigh. His thumb teased just beneath the edge of the lacy trim on her panties, each stroke coming closer to the spot where she needed him the most.

Forgetting the torture of tasting his inked skin and chiseled muscles, Darcy dropped her head to his shoulder as he finally slid his thumb inside the material. Those slow strokes over her heated center were going to be the death of her. Darcy tipped her hips, silently demanding more. She'd denied herself this pleasure for so long, she simply couldn't take much more.

Her breath hitched as he eased inside her, her fingertips curled into his skin. He continued to torture her slowly, yet with so much control and power, Darcy was having a hard time getting her mind around the emotions tugging her in all different directions. But what if she wasn't enough for him? What if she disappointed him once they really got down to it?

She froze, not wanting this moment of blissful perfection to end, because it felt too good, too perfect. Too right.

"I told you not to hold back with me again," he growled in her ear. "Stop tensing up and let go."

With one hand still stroking her, he used the other to jerk down the top of her chemise. The strap snapped apart as his mouth settled over her breast. Darcy arched back, crying out as the full-on sexual encounter washed over her, sending her spiraling into the most intense climax of her entire life.

Before her tremors could cease, Colin was shifting beneath her and she realized he was working his shorts from side to side to get them down. Quickly she assisted him and found herself hovering right above a very naked, very aroused Colin. Then he slid his other hand between them and gave her chemise a tug, tearing apart the seam in the middle.

"I owe you another shopping trip," he muttered against her lips. "This time I'll be in the dressing room."

Oh, mercy. Shopping for lingerie with this man would be…heaven. They'd never make it out alive.

"I have protection in my office and in my room."

Darcy held his gaze, her mind trying to process the words because she was still in a euphoric state.

"I've been anticipating this moment so I was prepared." He nipped her lips, shifted his hips so his erection nudged her. "You have about two seconds to decide where this will happen."

"Whichever one we get to fastest."

Colin came to his feet, causing Darcy to stand on her not-so-steady legs. She didn't have to worry, though, because Colin lifted her once more, not in the romantic scoop she'd always read about or seen in movies, but hooking her legs around his waist, forcing her to wrap her entire body around him. Oh, yeah. This was the experience she wanted. Nothing mushy here, but full-out want, need and the snapping of the control they'd both been barely holding onto.

He moved down the wide, darkened hall toward his office. Only a small bronze desk lamp cast any light on the room. Still, with her wrapped all around him, Colin jerked open a drawer and tossed a foil package onto the glossy surface of the desk. Darcy nipped at his shoulder, earlobe and jawline. With protection taken care of, she wanted him. Now.

When he sat her on top of his desk, he eased back, taking her face in his hands. "You're sure?"

Darcy nodded. The intensity of his gaze and the way he held his lips firm told her he may have more to say, but instead he tore open the wrapper and covered himself before pulling her to the edge of the desk.

Darcy leaned back on her elbows, staring up at him

and watching as he gazed back down at her. Colin's hands gripped her hips as he slid into her. When he caught her gaze, a tick visible in his jaw, she smiled. "Don't worry about going slow."

Something must have snapped because the next thing she knew he wasn't holding back…in any way.

Darcy's head fell back as pleasure engulfed her, as Colin claimed her. She'd never experienced anything so perfect, so all-consuming in her entire life.

Their frantic pace sent something from the desk crashing to the floor, but she didn't care and the commotion didn't slow Colin down, either. She barely noticed papers shifting beneath her. With the way Colin's eyes were locked on hers, the way he held her waist with his strong hands and took her as if he owned her, Darcy didn't think she'd ever care about anything else again. He was completely ruining her for any other man.

Another wave crested over her and Darcy cried out, her legs tightening around Colin's waist. He jerked once more and stilled, his fingertips bruising her sides.

After they stopped trembling, Colin leaned over, his forehead resting against her shoulder.

"I haven't done that since before my accident," he muttered. "I was afraid I'd hurt you if I carried you and fell, but I had to try. I wanted you in my arms. I want to be the man you need."

He was that man and so much more. Darcy had wondered if her heart would get swept away with Colin because of his single-father status, but what she felt for him had nothing to do with his child, his finances or anything other than the fact that he alone turned her inside out and made her feel things she'd only ever fantasized about. He made her come alive in ways she never had before.

"If you give me a few minutes, I'll take you up to my

room." His lips cruised over her damp skin, causing her to already want him again. "I need you in my bed."

Darcy didn't say a word. She would follow him to his bed. She'd follow him anywhere he asked.

Darcy's hair tickled the side of his face, but there was no way he was moving. She fit perfectly against his side, tucked snugly into him, as if she was made to be there. But right now, after taking her on his desk, and pleasuring her again once they'd arrived in his room, Colin didn't want to think any deeper than this blissful, sated feeling. He couldn't, wouldn't dive into that black hole of thoughts where all of his worries and fears about committing to another woman lived.

For the first time in months, he let loose and enjoyed his time with a refreshing woman who pulled him back to basic life…exactly what he'd been searching for.

With Darcy's arm across his abdomen and her leg across his thigh, the woman was staking her own claim and he had to admit, he liked it. He liked her. To know she wasn't into one-night stands completely humbled him. She'd been brave to initiate the encounter.

"I have a trip I need to take in a few days." His words cut through the darkened silence. "I'd like you to accompany me."

Sliding her fingertips up and down his abs, she asked, "Where are we going?"

"I need to go back home for an event," he told her, unable to reveal the rest of the details. "We will only be gone a few days."

Darcy shifted, easing up on one elbow to look down at him. His eyes had adjusted to the dark, plus the soft glow from the security monitors offered a dim light.

"Do I need to pack anything in particular?" she asked with a smile. "I've never been out of the country before."

She'd need a passport if she didn't have one and that could be problematic unless his assistant pulled some strings. They'd be flying in the palace jet, but still there was customs. He'd have his staff figure out the details.

"That blue dress would be a nice start," he told her. "But just be yourself. That's all you need to do."

She didn't have to go, she could stay behind, but he wanted her there. Granted he had a whole host of people who could care for Iris—maids, butlers, assistants, his sister-in-law. The list truly was endless.

But he wanted Darcy on his turf, he wanted to see how she fit into his life.

Colin nearly gasped as a realization dawned on him. He was falling for this woman in his arms. He was falling so hard, so fast, but he couldn't admit it fully, because what if she rejected him?

"You mentioned your parents had passed. Do you have siblings other than the brother you've mentioned?"

Her question pulled him from his thoughts.

Being here with Darcy, going into public without guards or paparazzi snapping photos was so different, so refreshing and so damn freeing. But he still felt as if he was letting down not only his country but Stefan. His brother was all Colin had left and putting the entire future of Galini Isle on Stefan's shoulders wasn't fair.

"Just Stefan and his wife Victoria."

"And they live in Greece?"

"Yes," he replied, fully enjoying the way her fingers continued to travel over his exposed torso. "What about you? No siblings, I assume."

"No. It was just my Gram and me after my parents split town. Apparently they weren't into the whole parenting thing and my Gram wasn't about to let me go into the foster system. I lived with her, worked with her and learned everything I know from the most amazing woman in the world."

No wonder Darcy was such a fighter. She'd had one person to depend on her entire life…a life spent caring for others. Colin had a whole army of people he depended on back home and he was running from them.

"Did you once mention wanting to adopt a baby of your own?" he asked.

A soft sigh escaped her, tickling his shoulder. "I would love to adopt, but it's expensive and my business needs to get back on track again. I'm afraid by the time I get all settled financially and go through the process, I'll be too old."

"You're young enough."

Her fingertips traced his tattoo the same way her tongue had earlier. She'd damn near had his eyes rolling back in his head.

"I know, but given the experience I had with my ex… it just hurts." She settled her head back in the crook of his arm, but continued to run her hand over his chest and abs as if she couldn't get enough…which suited him just fine. "To know you share your dreams, open your heart to someone and have them lie and betray you like that. I'm not sure I'll ever get over that pain. My dreams were put on hold and I'm not sure I'll ever get them back."

Colin swallowed. He wasn't the same as this ex, so he shouldn't feel guilty about lying.

Still, he wanted to clear the air about something.

"The last woman I was with was my wife," he told her, hating this topic in bed, but needing to get it out. "I know I mentioned that before, but I wanted you to know I may have been reckless as a teen and into my early twenties, but between marrying, the accident and then Iris, I've calmed down. I didn't want you to think I was using you because you were here and convenient."

"I know you're not," she murmured. "I've only been with one man before you. I just don't take the time to date and a fling is not something I can do."

Colin laughed, earning him a smack. "Sorry," he chuckled.

"You know what I mean," she defended. "I'm going to be here several months, so I hope tonight wasn't a one-time thing. I mean, I guess that should've been discussed, but I assumed—"

Colin rolled over, pinning her beneath him and cutting off her words.

"I plan on having you as often as you'll allow me to," he told her. As he looked into her bright eyes, he knew he had to tell her the rest. "I need to tell you why we're going back home."

She stared up at him, her eyes locking directly onto his. "Let's not talk right now." She spread her legs so he could settle firmly between them. "I only want to think about right now, with you, in your bed."

The trip could wait.

Colin smoothed her hair away from her face, nipped at her lips. "Maybe I want you to just lay back, think of absolutely nothing but how good everything feels."

He didn't wait for her reply as he started kissing his way down her body. When Darcy clutched the sheets, he smiled as he continued his path.

The next few months were going to be amazing.

Thirteen

Darcy wore only Colin's T-shirt as she maneuvered around the kitchen getting breakfast ready. She'd skipped her early morning workout and opted to stay snuggled next to Colin's warm, strong body. Of course she'd gotten enough of a calorie burn last night, in the middle of the night and again this morning.

Not only had he ruined her for any other man, he'd ruined her for any other workout. Why exercise with some cold piece of machinery when she could get a thorough workout with a hunky man ready to meet her every need?

Iris sat in her high chair, tapping her spoon against the tray and babbling. Every now and then a coherent word would slip out, but she was mostly just entertaining herself while Darcy cooked up some pancakes.

Colin had wanted to shower early, so he should be joining them soon. Everything about the morning after wasn't at all uncomfortable the way she'd heard people say. If anything it was very…domestic and normal.

The chime at the gate jerked Darcy from stirring the pancake batter. Who on earth was trying to visit this early in the morning? As long as no one on the inside of the house buzzed the guest in, they wouldn't get beyond the gate, unless they had the code. Darcy wasn't allowing anyone to pass through because Colin hadn't mentioned he was expecting a guest and this wasn't her house.

A moment later Colin came down the steps wearing a pair of running shorts and nothing else but a tan and the tat. She'd explored that body, tasted and touched it, yet the sight of him still had her knees weakening. How had her life gone from being so bleak, so depressing, to something that sparked hope and new life?

"Was that the gate alarm?" he asked as he bent down to give Iris a kiss and ruffle her curly bedhead.

"Yeah. I didn't answer the call because I didn't know if you were expecting anybody or not."

Darcy went back to mixing, wondering how she should act this morning. The entire scene seemed so family-like, so perfect, and she feared she'd make a mistake and this dream would be over.

"I'm not. Wonder who wanted in this early in the morning?" he mumbled. "I take it you weren't expecting anyone."

Darcy laughed as she poured the batter for several pancakes onto the warm griddle. "Do you honestly think I've invited friends to come over?"

"You can, you know."

She glanced his way and rolled her eyes. "I may take you up on that. I've texted my friends, but I've just been too busy to entertain."

"You can entertain me anytime." He crossed the spacious kitchen, rounded the island and slid a hand up beneath the T-shirt she wore. "You look better in this shirt than I ever did."

How could she not get swept into the fantasy this whole scene represented? She had to keep everything separate—her attraction for Colin in one part of her heart, her love for Iris in another. And there was no room for this family bonding. Colin and Iris weren't her family no matter how much she wished they were. Being swept into a love affair was already uncharted territory, but allowing her heart to get caught up in this fantasy was only going to crush her in the end when she walked away alone.

The doorbell chimed, causing Darcy and Colin to freeze. His hand slid out of the shirt, leaving her cold where his warmth had been.

"Stay here. There's only one person who has this code besides us."

Colin didn't look happy. Who would have the code? They'd been here for two months and nobody had used it yet, so why now?

As soon as the front door opened, another male voice filled the home. She pulled the pancakes off the griddle and set them aside on a spare plate. After flicking the griddle off, Darcy cut up a half of a pancake for Iris. Raised voices from the foyer had Darcy plucking Iris from her highchair.

Who was here? Should she try to go out the back and get to a neighbor for help? Darcy cursed herself for only wearing a T-shirt. She scooted closer to the side of the kitchen that was closest to the foyer to see if she could hear better but not be seen since she was hardly dressed for company.

"Are you going to let me in?" an unfamiliar male voice asked. Whoever this man was, he had the same sexy accent as Colin.

Colin spoke vehemently, again in Greek—what sounded like a curse. Moments later the door closed. Whoever was here, Colin knew him but he was a stranger to Darcy.

Great. Her attire screamed that she'd just gotten out of bed...her lover's bed.

"Nice place," the other man commented. "But are you ready to come back and forget this notion of living in the States?"

"You should've called," Colin replied, his tone implying the guest still wouldn't have been welcome.

"We've talked nearly every single day. I wanted to surprise you."

Footsteps echoed, growing louder. Darcy moved toward the island and put Iris back into her high chair. She'd just taken her seat when a man who could be Colin's twin stepped into the room, Colin right on his heels.

"Stefan, this is Darcy."

She hadn't been able to hide behind the island in time and the man's eyes traveled over her, taking in her oversized T-shirt, the hem of the boxers peeking out from beneath it and her bare legs before going to Iris and then back to Colin.

"I'm sorry," he said, turning back toward Colin. "I didn't know...wait, is this your nanny?"

Darcy cringed and turned to concentrate on cutting up Iris's food. Whatever was going on with these two, she wanted no part of it. Clearly they had issues that didn't involve her. Well, maybe they did now.

"Stefan," Colin growled. "Not a word."

"I'm just trying to figure things out." Stefan shook his head and propped his hands on his hips. "Are you giving up your title, turning your back on your country and the throne for someone you barely know?"

Darcy froze. *Title? Throne?*

Slowly, she lifted her gaze to Colin. He stared back at her as if he was waiting to see her reaction, too.

"Shut the hell up, Stefan," Colin nearly shouted. "Apologize to Darcy. She has nothing to do with my decision and you know I'm taking the full six months to think this through."

"My apologies," Stefan said, turning and tipping his head toward Darcy. The worried look etched across his face told Darcy he was sincere. "I mean no disrespect to you. I was just taken aback. I've been waiting for my brother to come home, and I knew he'd found a reason to stay for now. I certainly didn't mean to take my shocked state out on you. Actually, Mikos has told me quite a bit about you and I want to thank you for being so kind to my niece."

"There's nothing to worry about with me," Colin cut in before Darcy could respond. "I'm still unclear on my decision."

"Mikos." The other man stepped closer to Colin. "Are you seriously that happy here that you're still confused? Have you not missed anything about Galini Isle or the people who love you?"

Darcy swallowed, terrified to ask, but needing to know. "Why is he calling you Mikos and what does he mean by throne and title?"

Colin's eyes closed on a sigh, but before he could answer, the other man turned to face her completely. "I'm calling him Mikos because that's his name and he's a prince from Galini Isle, a small country off the coast of Greece."

Darcy had no idea what to say, what to do. All those times they'd talked, every single day they'd shared together over the last two months and he couldn't find it in his heart to tell her any of that? Not even his real name?

Tears blurred her vision, but even through the hurt and confusion, she had a baby to care for. That was what he was paying her for, right?

Whatever game he was playing by seducing her, it was clear that she was pretty much just hired help. Had he ever seen her as anything more or had he been laughing at her this entire time?

"Darcy—"

With a jerk of her head and a glare, Darcy cut off whatever Colin, Mikos…whoever, had been about to say.

"You haven't told her?" the other man asked. "Classy, Mikos. Real classy."

Colin was seriously fighting the urge to punch his brother in the face. First of all, to show up unannounced was rude even for Stefan. Second, how the hell did he fix this with Darcy now? The last thing he wanted was for her to be hurt, for her to feel as though she'd been betrayed again.

But he'd lied because been so dead set on keeping his identities separate. He'd gotten so wrapped up in her, in this life, that he hadn't given much thought to consequences. He'd been thinking only of himself. Just as he had with Karina, and look how that had turned out.

"Let me feed her," Colin offered, stepping forward. "You go change."

Her hands shook with each bite she put in Iris's mouth, but Darcy didn't even turn to answer him.

"Darcy." Stefan also stepped forward. "I apologize for coming in like this and dropping a bomb on you. I'd assumed my brother would've told you about his status. Why don't you go change and I'll feed my niece? I haven't seen her for a long time."

Now Darcy lifted her head, gave a slight nod and headed out of the room, careful to go around the island to avoid getting too close Stefan and Colin. She didn't say a word, didn't look either of them in the eye.

Her pain lingered after she was gone. Colin would never forget the angst that had washed over her face right before she slid up that invisible wall and avoided looking at him. Good God, what had he done?

"I could kill you for that," Colin muttered.

Stefan leaned his hip against the island and forked up another bite for Iris. He made an airplane motion and some ridiculous noise to get her to open for him. Of course she clapped and kicked her feet, oblivious to the turmoil going on.

"Don't be angry with me that you kept the truth hidden. If you like the woman, and I have to assume you do because you're still here, then she deserved the truth."

Colin slammed his fist onto the counter. "You have no idea what has happened so don't even think about assuming you do." But Stefan was absolutely right. Why hadn't he seen this coming?

"It's about time you're showing emotion for someone else." A smile spread across Stefan's face. "I'm glad to see you're living again. Are you and Darcy serious?"

Colin rolled his eyes. This wasn't up for debate. He went to get a plate, but suddenly he wasn't hungry anymore. Right now Darcy was upstairs, most likely angry, hurt, maybe even crying, because he thought he could keep all the balls in the air and have control over every facet of his life.

"I don't know what we are," Colin defended himself. He thought he knew what he wanted, but would Darcy ever speak to him again? Did his wants even matter at this point?

Stefan paused, bite in midair. "She's wearing your shirt and whisker burn, cooking your breakfast and caring for your child. I'd say that's pretty serious. Yet you still lied to her. It makes me wonder why."

"I'm paying her to care for Iris."

Stefan glanced around the island, found a sippy cup and passed it to Iris before turning his focus back to Colin.

"And the rest? I know you're not paying her for that, and this is the first woman you've shown interest in since Karina."

"I don't give a damn what you think right now. I was planning on coming home for the ball, you didn't have to show up unannounced."

Stefan shrugged. "Last time we spoke you told me you weren't sure if you were coming back. I merely came to talk some sense into you. Victoria had to stay behind to get last minute things prepared for the event or she would've been right here with me."

Colin raked a hand over his still damp hair. "Watch Iris for me. I need to go upstairs and talk to Darcy. Stay down here and shut the hell up next time you see her. You've done enough damage."

Colin didn't wait for Stefan to confirm anything, he just turned and stormed from the room. His back was killing him, as was his leg after all the extra activities he'd participated in last night, but he was determined to march right into Darcy's room and set things straight.

He had nothing planned to say, had no clue what state he'd find her in or what was even going through her mind. He was about to enter unstable territory and it terrified him because he realized that what she thought was important.

Not only did he not want to be the one to hurt her, but he also wanted to be the one she counted on. So many people had turned away from her, betrayed her in one form or another.

And he'd just added his name to the list. Surely he could make this up to her somehow.

Yet he stood outside her bedroom door, staring at the barrier as if the inanimate object could offer insight. What a mess he'd made, all because he'd been too self-absorbed, too wrapped up in Darcy and his hormones to truly see the big picture. Not that he saw any clearer now, but he did know one thing, he still wanted Darcy and he'd make damn sure he would fix this disaster he'd caused.

Colin tapped his knuckles on the door. It hadn't latched completely so the weight of his hand eased it open just enough for him to see her standing across the room, her back to him, as she looked out onto the backyard.

"I know you want to be alone," he started, staying in her doorway. "But we need to talk."

Darcy's shoulders stiffened, the only sign she'd even heard him. Silence settled heavily between them, when only an hour ago they were lying side by side in his bed. At least she'd thrown on some pants so he didn't have to be tortured further by the sight of her bare legs. He could still feel them wrapped around him, entwined with his.

"I didn't set out to lie to you, even though that's how it looks." He had to keep talking. If she wasn't ordering him out, then he knew she was listening. "I have a lot going on back home, so much that I didn't want to talk about it with anyone. I wanted to separate myself from that part of my life for a while to get my head on straight. I had to put Iris's needs first and keeping our identity a secret was one of my top priorities."

He paused, giving her a chance to speak if she wanted. When she remained silent, he pushed on.

"I wish I could blame my brother for barging in here and dropping that bomb like that, but it's my fault you didn't know." Taking a risk, Colin stepped further into the room, raking a hand down his face as he carefully chose the right words. "You matter to me, Darcy. More than I want to admit and more than I thought someone could after Karina. I don't want this to come between us."

Darcy whirled around. The tear tracks on her cheeks crippling him in ways words never could.

"You mean you don't want your lies to keep me out

of your bed?" she threw back. "Because isn't that all we have between us? Our arrangement was never meant to be more than temporary. So, for once since I've known you, be honest."

Colin swallowed the fear, the anger. He'd brought it all upon himself. He had to stand here and take it like a man. He deserved every word, every bit of rage she wanted to fling at him.

"You're only up here because you want to continue what we started last night." Darcy shook her head and laughed, swiping at her damp face. "I was such a fool. You were probably laughing at me the entire—"

She gasped, her eyes darting to her closet before her face crumbled. Turning away, she let out a low moan as she hugged her arms around her midsection.

"You knew I had nothing and there you were, throwing your money around," she whispered.

Colin started to cross to her because he couldn't stand the anguish lacing her voice, but she spun to face him, holding him with her hurt-filled stare. He stopped only a few feet from her.

"Did you get a kick out of giving to the needy?" she asked, her tone nothing but mocking. "Did you enjoy knowing you had everything, while I had absolutely nothing? Money, power, control. You literally played me, never once thinking how this would affect me."

"I never played you," he corrected. "I wouldn't have told anyone I employed here about my life on Galini Isle. And I damn well did worry about you. Every single day we grew closer I worried how this would affect you, but I didn't know what to say or how to even approach it."

Her eyes narrowed. "Because you're a coward. Apparently running from the truth is what you do. You fled your home when you obviously didn't want to face responsibilities there."

How could she ever understand that he hadn't been strong enough to face his royal duties as a widowed father, trying to bring up a duchess? How could she ever grasp how much was involved in being a prince raising a child in the kingdom? What if Iris didn't want the title that came along with her prestigious family name?

At some point this getaway had turned from him finding himself to him deciding what was going to be best for the future of his daughter.

"I have to go back in a couple days," he told her, forcing himself to put up a strong front because the sight of her so broken was damn near crippling. "I still want you to come with me."

Pain-filled laughter erupted from Darcy. "You're insane. I'm not going anywhere with you. This isn't some fairy tale, Colin or Mikos or whatever the hell you want to be called. This is my life and I'm not just running to some island in Greece because you snap your fingers and expect me to."

"I want you to go to be with Iris," he explained, hoping she'd cave because he didn't realize how much he needed her to be there on his turf until this moment. "She's used to you, she's comfortable with you and I'd rather have you caring for her than any of my assistants."

Throwing her arms in the air, Darcy pivoted and moved around him to stand on the other side of the room. "You're something else. You probably have multiple people at your disposal, yet you continue to want to torture me. Why? Are you enjoying this power trip?"

Clenching his fists at his sides, he watched as she began to pace. "I'm not enjoying any part of this."

"You're using Iris as a bargaining tool." She stopped and propped her hands on her hips. "You're using her to get me to come with you."

"I'm being honest," he told her. "You wanted honesty,

I'm laying it out there. I tried to tell you this morning. I know that's a convenient thing to say considering the timing, but it's the truth. I want you to see my country. I want you to be the one to care for Iris while I'm home because I will be facing many challenges there."

He didn't want to get too far into everything that he was running away from. Darcy wasn't in the right frame of mind to hear it and he wasn't ready to admit how weak and vulnerable he truly was.

Darcy pursed her lips together, then nodded. "Fine, but if you want to throw that money around so much, then I want double my original pay for the entire six months. If I'm traveling, then I deserve to be compensated accordingly."

This was probably not the time to say he was proud of her for standing up for herself, for playing hardball and fighting for what she wanted. Most women would've packed their bags and left. He'd always known she was a fighter and she was coming back at him full force.

She was the only woman who'd ever challenged him. What would he do on Galini Isle without her by his side? He wasn't about to find out.

"Done," he said without second thought. "On one condition."

She quirked a brow. "What?"

"When we're at the palace, you have to do what I say. No questions."

"I don't think—"

"Do you want the money?"

Darcy stilled, and her nostrils flared as her cheeks reddened. "You're despicable."

No, he was desperate, but he'd never admit that aloud. "We'll leave Sunday evening and sleep on my jet."

"Of course you have a jet," she muttered before moving toward her door. "We're done here. I'll take care of

Iris, I'll do everything a hired nanny does and she will be my number one priority. That doesn't include sleeping with my boss. From now on our relationship is strictly professional."

Crossing the room, Colin kept his gaze locked onto hers. As he neared, her eyes widened but she never looked away. He stopped only a breath from her, then leaned down to whisper in her ear.

"I never set out to lie to you, Darcy. You have to believe me."

As he spoke, his lips caressed the side of her cheek. Just as she shivered, Colin eased back. Her hand came up to slap him, but he quickly gripped her wrist in midair.

"You're angry. Don't do something you'll regret later." Although he knew he deserved it.

Her eyes flared, filling with unshed tears. "I hate you."

He yanked her forward to fall against his chest. With one hand still holding onto her wrist, Colin hooked an arm around her waist. "There's a fine line between hate and passion," he said with a confidence he didn't quite feel.

Unable to resist temptation, Colin captured her lips, but let the brief kiss end for fear she'd bite him. He smiled down at her.

"Make sure to pack the blue dress for our trip."

He'd barely made it out her door before it slammed at his back.

Damn it. He had to do something. Somehow he had to make this up to her. Losing Darcy was not an option, but he'd messed up. He didn't deserve her forgiveness, but that wouldn't stop him from doing everything in his power to earn it.

Fourteen

Darcy could dwell on the fact that her parents had abandoned her at a young age. She could also hone in the fact that the man she'd thought she loved had stolen every last penny she had to her name. She could even focus on her most recent betrayal: Colin keeping the colossal truth that he was a freaking prince from her. But Darcy opted to go a different route.

From now on, she would choose anger, because if she even attempted to shut it out, all she'd have left to face would be soul-crushing hurt. There was no time for that because there was an innocent child in all of this…a child Darcy had been hired to care for.

As much as Darcy wanted to take the initial half of her pay and leave Colin, she wouldn't abandon Iris. Darcy couldn't walk away, not when she knew all too well the feeling of rejection. But what would Colin do at the end of the six months? Did he have other arrangements set up or was he going back home? Did he even know himself?

Darcy continued to stare out the window of the car that had been waiting for them when they'd arrived at the private airstrip on Galini Isle. Iris had been sitting, securely strapped in, between her and Colin, and since they'd left LA Darcy had barely spoken a word to him unless it involved the baby. Nothing else needed to be said at this point, the damage was done.

Iris continued to sleep, which was a blessing because the poor thing had cried a good bit of the flight. Most likely the pressure in her ears had been getting to her. Even though exhaustion threatened to consume Darcy, too, she was too angry to be tired.

Beyond the obvious anger toward Colin, she was furious with herself because of her reaction to his parting shot in her room about still wanting her. He'd known just what to say, exactly the right way to deliver the words for the most impact.

Colin may have been a different man when he was with her, a man he'd made up, yet she still wanted him. Nobody had ever made her feel more beautiful, more wanted than he did. He'd wrapped his arms around her and kissed her as if he had every right in the world.

But that was all part of his game. He'd created a new life in America and she was just another prop. More than anything she wished she could switch her emotions off to avoid the hurt, but she simply wasn't wired that way.

The chauffeur pulled into a drive. Darcy noted the gate, guards and white columns as the car made its way onto the estate grounds. What was she doing here? She was going to spend the next few days in a palace. *A palace.* Only a few months ago she'd had to sleep in her car because she'd lost her condo, and now she was going to be staying in a freaking mansion in another country. She'd never even set foot outside of California before.

When they came to a stop, Darcy started to open her

door, but Colin leaned a hand across where Iris slept and laid his other hand over Darcy's arm.

"They'll get your door," he told her.

Rolling her eyes, Darcy jerked from his grasp and opened her own damn door. Once she stepped out, she turned and reached in to gently unfasten and pull Iris from her seat. She slept on as Darcy cradled her against her shoulder.

"Ma'am." The driver held her door, tipping his head toward her. "I'll make sure your bags are brought in."

She nearly laughed. Her bag, singular, was still her ratty old suitcase that didn't suit palace living at all. Of course the clothes inside certainly did, considering they were purchased with royal money.

Ignoring Colin's attempt to put his hand on her and guide her, she stepped to the side and shot him a glare. "Just have someone show me where the nursery is and I'll take her in."

"I'll show you."

His tone left no room for argument. Whatever. She wasn't going to fight, not with sweet Iris in her arms. Darcy truly wanted the best for Iris, even if her father was a lying jerk.

The three-story mansion stretched along the grounds farther than any "home" Darcy had ever seen. Lush plants and vibrant flowers surrounded the palace, edged along the circular drive and flanked the steps leading up to the entrance. Guards in full military-looking uniforms stood at attention on either side of the door.

This world was definitely not hers. Everything about her life had been transformed the moment she'd met Colin. From the new clothes, her emotional state, her sexual experiences…every single aspect of her personal and professional life would never be the same.

Passing by guards, entering a grand home with a tiered

fountain inside the entryway—*inside* the entryway—was stunning. Darcy shook her head as she followed Colin closely. As they passed random people…maids, men in suits, servants? Darcy noted that Colin would nod in greeting while the others would slightly bow. People actually bowed to the man.

Yes, they were worlds apart in every sense of the term because Darcy was on the same level as these people bowing to the man she wanted to throttle.

Colin led her toward a grand staircase that would make the iconic home from *Gone with the Wind* seem miniscule.

Colin turned before ascending the steps. "Why don't you let me carry her up?"

"I've got her and your back has been bothering you."

The corner of his mouth tipped as if he were holding back a smile. "You know me so well. And you care."

Darcy moved around him, refusing to even look at that handsome, sexy grin, those mocking, alluring blue eyes. "I saw you cringe when you stepped off the plane and again getting out of the car. And I only care about Iris."

As she started up, she knew he was behind her, most likely eyeing her rear end. That was fine, she couldn't stop him from looking, but she could prevent him from touching.

She had to prevent him from touching because if the man even tried to come on to her, she'd have a hard time holding it together. She couldn't ignore her emotions or hormones, no matter how much she wished her body would stop betraying her.

Once she reached the second floor, she turned back to see Colin gripping the banister, taking the steps more slowly than she'd thought he would. An unwelcome tug on her heart revealed the anger still rolling through her.

With one arm securing the sleeping baby, Darcy eased down a step and reached out her free hand. Colin froze, glancing from her hand to her face. She thought for sure his stubborn pride would have him swatting her away, but he put his hand in hers and squeezed. He climbed the last few steps with her support, without comment.

Once he righted himself, he moved down the hallway and Darcy was relieved they weren't heading up to the next floor because she highly doubted Colin could make it. Being on the plane for so long had most likely agitated his injury. His limp was a bit more prominent as he moved down the wide hallway. She wanted to reach for him again, but…she couldn't. Focusing on following him, she took in the luxurious surroundings.

Gold sconces adorned each section of wall between each door. The ceiling had scrolling artwork that she would have to admire later because Colin had neared the end of the hall and was going into a bedroom.

Bedroom was seriously too loose a term. The area she entered was a condo all its own with a formal sitting area, open bedroom tucked away in the far corner and two sets of French doors that opened onto a balcony offering a breathtaking view of the ocean.

"This is the nursery?"

"This is your room. I've asked for Iris's stuff to be put in here so you can stay close to her and you won't have to be near me or anyone else."

The crib was nestled in the opposite corner along the same wall as the king-sized bed. Moving across the wide room, Darcy gently laid Iris in the crib, surprised when the little one nestled deeper into the mattress and let out a soft sigh.

Once Darcy was sure Iris was going to stay asleep, she turned and moved back to where Colin remained standing. His eyes were fixed on hers and, try as she might, she couldn't look away. She both hated this man and found herself drawn to him for unexplainable reasons.

"We'll be fine now." She hoped he'd take the hint and leave. "I'm assuming someone will bring our things to this room."

Colin stepped closer to her, closing the gap between them. Darcy had to tip her head back to look up and hold his gaze.

"The formal ball is tomorrow night," he told her. "I want you there. With me."

This fairy tale was really starting to get out of control. She only wanted to be here with Iris. Getting dressed up and playing any other role wouldn't be a smart move.

"I'm your child's nanny," she informed him, forcing herself to ignore the thread of arousal winding though her at his intense stare. "I'm not your date for hire or one of your assistants you can order around. Everything changed when you opted to keep the truth from me."

A smile spread across his face, showcasing that dimple she'd once found sexy.… His palms slid up her bare arms, curved over her shoulders and glided on up to frame her face.

"You forget you agreed to do what I want while we're here."

The reminder was the equivalent of cold water being thrown in her face.

"You can't use me like this," she whispered.

"I'm not using you," he replied, his face now hovering just above hers. "I'm simply taking what I want and I want you on my arm during the ball."

Another layer of anger slid through her. "Is that why you told me to pack the blue dress?"

"No. I don't want anyone else to see you in that dress." His thumb stroked her bottom lips, his gaze honed in on her mouth. "That dress is for my eyes only. You'll wear it for dinner tonight."

"I don't want dinner with you," she threw back, though

her voice wasn't as strong as she'd hoped it would be. "You said I didn't have to leave my room if I didn't want to."

That thumb kept sliding back and forth with just enough pressure to have Darcy nearly begging him to kiss her. Darn hormones betraying her common sense.

"You're not leaving your room," he stated. "Dinner will be delivered."

He stepped away, leaving her aching, wanting more and all he'd done was use that low, sultry voice and fondled her lips. How pathetic could she be?

"Be ready by seven."

With that he turned and walked out of the room. Darcy continued to stare at the door long after he'd left. How dare that man expect her to just be at his beck and call? If he wanted to have dinner with her, fine, but she had a surprise of her own for him and it sure as hell didn't involve that sexy blue dress.

Darcy was playing hide-and-seek with Iris—which was quite easy in a room of this size with the adjoining bath and colossal walk-in closet—when someone knocked on her door.

Iris squealed and ran to the door, standing on her tiptoes to try to reach the knob. Darcy laughed and eased Iris back so she could open the door.

Darcy was greeted by one of the most beautiful women she'd ever seen in her life. The stranger was holding a long, white garment bag.

"Hi, Darcy," the woman said with a wide, radiant smile. "I'm Victoria Alexander. I'm Stefan's wife. Would you mind if I came in for just a moment?"

Iris sneaked around Darcy and started reaching for Victoria.

"Hi, sweetheart." Victoria bent slightly, shifting the

bag to the side so she could give Iris a kiss on her head. "How's my big girl? I missed you so much."

Darcy stepped aside and let Victoria pass through. Victoria crossed the room and hung the garment bag over the door leading into the closet area.

When she turned back around, she scooped Iris into her arms and squeezed her. The instant burn to Darcy's eyes was unexpected. Iris obviously had so many people who loved her, who needed her. Darcy had to face the harsh reality that she was just a random employee of the prince passing through. The impact on Darcy was huge, life-altering, but Iris would never even remember her.

"First of all, let me tell you how sorry I am about this whole thing." Iris wiggled in Victoria's arms until she was let free. "Stefan explained everything to me and I am embarrassed that he dropped what I'm sure was shocking news when he visited. I'm even more embarrassed that my brother-in-law took it upon himself to lie to you by omission. The Alexander men can be infuriating and you were dealt a double dose."

Darcy clasped her hands in front of her, not quite sure how to take this woman, but from the looks of things, she could be an ally.

"I'm from LA, too, so I know this whole royalty thing can be overwhelming at times," Victoria went on, offering a sweet smile. "I just want you to know that while you're here, please feel free to let me know if you need anything. Stefan and Mikos can be quite…difficult to communicate with at times. They seem to have their minds set on certain agendas and tend to let nothing stand in their way."

Darcy laughed. "That's one way of putting it."

"Mikos really is an amazing man." Victoria's eyes darted to where Iris was running around the spacious room, dodging the chaise longue, weaving through the sheers by the patio doors. "He's a wonderful father and he's been through so much. Don't be so quick to judge him when he's clearly made a drastic mistake."

Darcy shook her head and sighed. "I'm just the nanny. It's not my place to judge."

"If you were just the nanny, I wouldn't have spent the last two days making a dress for you to wear at the ball tomorrow." Victoria pointed to the garment bag. "Once you try it on, let me know if it needs to be altered. Mikos was pretty specific in his instructions."

Darcy stared at Victoria, then to the bag. "What? You made a dress?"

"I'm a designer. It's what I do." Victoria shrugged. "Sounds silly, I know, considering I'm also the queen, but that's just a title. I was designing dresses before I ever married into the Alexander family and I didn't want to lose my identity."

A bit taken aback, Darcy made her way to the garment bag and slid the zipper down. Peeling away the protective plastic, she gasped at the shimmering, pale blue formal gown. With one shoulder open and the other covered in clear crystals that were heavy at the top and tapered off toward the ruched waistline, Darcy didn't know if she'd ever seen a more beautiful dress.

"You made this?" she asked as she stared over at Victoria. "In two days?"

Laughing, Victoria nodded. "I did and I have to say, I think you'll look stunning in it."

Darcy's eyes locked onto the dress. Colin had requested this for her? He'd not only requested it, he'd been specific about what he'd wanted.

Darcy swallowed, unable to even comprehend this world she was temporarily living in.

"Would you mind if I took Iris out for a walk?" Victoria asked. "Stefan and I were going to go down to the beach before the guests start arriving and things get crazy around here."

Still in a daze, Darcy turned back to Victoria. "Oh, sure. Of course."

Victoria lifted Iris into her arms and kissed her neck until the baby giggled. "Let's go get some sand between our toes."

"Thank you," Darcy said before Victoria cleared the doorway. "The dress is spectacular, so 'thank you' seems so inadequate."

Victoria nodded and grinned. "It was my pleasure. I'll bring Iris back shortly. You look like you could use some time to let all of this sink in."

Just as Victoria reached the doorway, she turned and glanced over her shoulder. "I know it isn't my place, but I can't let this go. Mikos left here because he couldn't face being a widowed father. Between all of the responsibilities and losing his wife, he was severely broken. He was only looking out for Iris when he left. She's always been his number one priority, so whatever he said or didn't say to you, was only to protect her in the long run."

Victoria slipped out the door, shutting it with a soft click. Iris's squeals could still be heard, but Darcy was stuck on Victoria's parting words.

A new plan started to form. Colin was coming for dinner and he expected her to wear the other blue dress.

What was it with him and blue? Apparently that was his favorite color.

She shook her head and focused on her plan. She'd wear the blue dress, but she was going to make him suffer. He might think he had control here, but they both knew she carried the power right now. She'd seen the vulnerability in him when she'd helped him up the steps and she'd seen how much he fought the weakness that continued to plague him.

But as far as their relationship went, she knew he still wanted her and most likely he'd planned dinner in her room as a way to seduce her. He may have started off lying to her, he may not have meant to hurt her, but he'd had ample opportunities to tell her the truth before taking her to bed.

If he wanted her for more than a romp, she wasn't going to give in so easily. She'd make him beg if she had to, because she was worth it.

Tonight she'd see what they both were made of.

Fifteen

Colin wanted to get to the room before the dinner arrived. He'd also asked Stefan and Victoria to keep Iris for a few hours this evening. He hated incorporating them into his plan, but he had to call for reinforcements because time was not on his side.

Taking a deep breath and willing his damn nerves to settle, Colin knocked on her door. He wanted time alone with Darcy, wanted to be able to let her into his life, his world because he'd come to realize she mattered more than he'd ever thought possible. At first the instant physical attraction had eaten at him, but he'd soon come to the conclusion that she was much more than someone he wanted to sleep with. Darcy was honest, invigorating and perfectly suited to him…someone he could spend the rest of his life with. The woman had woven her way into his world just when he wanted to be left alone the most. She'd awakened something fresh, something new inside of him he'd thought was long dead and gone.

When the knob turned and the door eased open, Colin's breath caught in his throat as his eyes traveled over the stunning image before him.

"I didn't think you'd actually wear it."

His eyes raked over the bright blue dress that wrapped over Darcy's breasts, dipping low enough for him to see the swell, then securing at her waist where her classy figure dipped in just above the flare of those hips that drove him insane with want and need.

She'd left her hair down, silky and straight. The barest of makeup made her seem so natural, so beautiful and so seamlessly matched to what he wanted but hadn't known he was looking for.

"Why wouldn't I?" she asked, gesturing for him to come on in. "You requested it. You are paying me, after all."

Cringing as he walked in, Colin hated that he'd thrown money in her face once again. He'd been so low as to dangle the very thing she needed and then relished his delight when he got his way.

He was no better than her ex and deserved nothing at all from the woman he'd found himself falling for.

Before he could say more, another knock sounded on the door and a member of the waitstaff rolled in a covered cart. He took it on out to the patio, bid them a good evening and was gone.

"Shall we?" she asked.

Not giving him a chance to answer, she headed toward the open doors that lead to the terrace. The ocean breeze slid through her room, bringing that familiar saltwater scent he'd taken for granted as a kid, but positively loved now. And he realized how much he'd missed the island now that he was back.

White table linens, gold candlesticks and a cluster of white roses adorned the table set for two. Darcy went to take the cover off of one of the dishes on the cart, but Colin stepped in front of her, blocking her action.

"You look beautiful," he told her, needing her to know how he felt, that he believed what he was saying. "You're more than I deserve right now."

She tipped her chin, leveling his gaze. "I'm your nanny, Colin. Or would you prefer Mikos? Perhaps Your Highness. What do your other servants call you?"

"You're not my damn servant." Colin gritted his teeth. She was mocking him. "You can call me Mikos or Colin. Either would be fine."

She bowed and something in him snapped. He gripped her shoulders and gave her a slight shake.

"Don't bow to me. Ever."

Her eyes widened as she ran her tongue over her plump, glossy lips. "I'm your employee, am I not?"

"You're more, damn it, and you know it."

She stiffened beneath his touch. "Do I? Because I assumed even friends were up front with each other. Employees and employers keep their private lives separate, so excuse me if I'm a little confused."

He needed some space to cool off and she needed to get used to the fact that he wasn't going to give up so easily.

Releasing her, he pulled out a chair. "Sit. I'll get your dinner."

Surprisingly, she obliged. Once he'd served the meal, they ate in strained silence. Thoughts, possible conversations played over and over in his mind. There was so much he wanted to say, needed to say. But would she hear him, would the words penetrate into her heart where he needed them to go?

Pushing away from the table, Colin came to his feet and moved to the rail of the terrace. Watching the water ebb and flow against the shoreline calmed him. He absolutely loved his home, loved this view he was blessed to wake up to every day. It was all the hype around his name, his title that he could live without. He wanted a simple family life and the ability to live without the media snapping photos of him and his daughter, splashing whatever headlines they chose.

Stefan and Victoria had managed to attain such a life. They were making it work with their titles and they always managed to find time to themselves, away from all the hype and press. Could he have that, too? Could he attend to his duties and actually have a family?

His heart clenched. He hadn't known how much he wanted a family…a family with Darcy and Iris.

"I stared at this view for hours after I came home from the hospital," he started as he kept his back to her.

He hadn't counted on talking, but he couldn't keep her shut out of his world…not if he truly wanted her to be a part of it. And now more than ever he knew what he wanted.

"I'd sit out on the balcony off the master suite and curse that damn wheelchair. Karina was pregnant and all I could think was what type of father I could be to our child when I couldn't even stand or put on my own pants."

Darcy's chair scooted against the tile, but Colin kept his back to her. He couldn't turn and look her in the eye, didn't want to see pity staring back at him.

"I gradually got stronger, but I was too busy working on myself to realize I had to keep working on my marriage. Karina went through the pregnancy pretty much alone because I devoted all of my time to my recovery. I was determined to be on my feet when our baby came."

From the corner of his eye he saw Darcy step up to the rail, but far enough away that she was just out of reach. Probably for the best. With his emotional state, if she touched him, if she offered compassion right now, he'd break down, and baring his heart was about all the vulnerability he could handle. No way in hell did he want to be that man who clung to a woman, sobbing…which is exactly what he feared would happen if he didn't concentrate on the words and not the feelings of the past.

"When Iris came my whole outlook on life changed," he went on as he watched a palace guard pass by below. "The media wanted pictures of her, wanted photos of the happy family. It was then I realized we weren't a family. Karina had started sleeping in another room, she started distancing herself more and more from me and I can't blame her."

"It takes two to make a marriage work," Darcy added, her soft voice hitting him square in the heart. "You can't take all the blame."

Risking a glance over his shoulder, Colin met her intense gaze. No pity lingered in her eyes, if anything he saw understanding.

"I abandoned her long before she decided to leave," he replied. "After she suddenly passed away, I couldn't handle the strain of my life here any longer. It's no secret to my family that I've never wanted to be Prince of Galini Isle. I didn't want that weight on my shoulders. Stefan took the lead as king, which was fine with me, but if anything happens to him, I have no choice as long as I retain my title."

The familiar twinge in his back started out dull, the way it always did before blowing up into something major, so Colin pushed off the rail and stood straight, twisting at the waist to keep the muscles warm.

"Are you okay?" she asked.

"Fine. Just needed to move."

She stared at him another minute before looking back out to the water. "I have no clue about the life you were running from. I see this place and I think you have it all. But then I hear the pain in your voice and I know you are torn. I know you don't take this for granted and you're seriously worried about what step to take next."

Turning to fully face her, Colin took a step closer. "I'm not only worried about the title, Darcy. I'm worried about us."

Shaking her head, her lids lowered as she bit her lip for a moment before speaking. "How can *us* even exist? There was one night. One amazing night, but it was built on lies."

He started forward again, but halted when she held out her hand. With a deep breath, she turned to face him. "You don't understand how deeply you hurt me. You can't imagine what it cost me to come to you that night. I kept avoiding you because you had everything I always thought I was looking for and I was terrified if I let my guard down, I would want too much. I would love too much."

Breath caught in Colin's throat. "Darcy—"

"No." She shifted, backing up a step as if she feared he'd reach for her. "Whatever I felt wasn't real because I developed feelings for a man who doesn't exist."

Swallowing hard, damning any risk he was about to take, he closed the distance between them and gripped her arms. She fell against his chest, her mouth opening in a gasp.

"Does this feel fake to you?" he demanded, holding on to her a little too tightly. "Every time I kissed you, touched you, did all of that feel like a lie?"

Her intense gaze held his as he continued to loom over her. She'd cracked open something deep within him, something he hadn't even known he was holding back. His heart was wide open for her and she just needed to walk through. Damn it, he needed her to.

"You were so brave, calling me, wanting to come to me." He softened his voice. "You realized what we had was worth putting yourself out there for and you were ready to take a chance. Don't back away now, Darcy. Don't make judgment calls until you really see the big picture."

With the way he stood over her, her body arched against his, Colin couldn't avoid temptation another second. Nipping his lips against hers, testing to see if she'd let him continue, he nearly wept with relief when she didn't pull away.

As he wrapped his arms around her, pulling her hips flush against his own, he covered her mouth completely and deepened the kiss. Darcy's hands remained at her sides, though her mouth opened, inviting him in. For a split second, she froze, as if her mind were starting to override her emotions.

"No," he murmured against her lips. "Don't think. Feel. I never lied about how I feel and you know that. Everything we shared with our bodies was real. Everything I ever told you about how I felt was real."

With her eyes closed, she licked her swollen lips. "I can't do this, Colin. I'm here for Iris."

"Well I'm here for you," he whispered.

Not giving her another chance to speak, he claimed her mouth once again and ran his hands around to the front of her dress. He gave each side of the material a yank to expose her lace-covered breasts. On a gasp, Darcy tore her mouth from his and he feared he'd gone too far, but she tipped her head back and groaned. Colin stole the chance to trail a path of kisses down her silky skin until he reached the edge of the lace bra.

Darcy's hands fisted in his hair as he turned and backed her up against the smooth stone next to the patio doors. The last thing he wanted was to stay close to the rail and have one of the guards look up. Darcy was his and sharing even a glimpse of her was not an option.

Colin reached down, bunched up the bottom of her dress and slid his hand over her heated center. She adjusted her stance as he tore away her lacy panties and he had no doubt they matched the bra he was about to remove.

With a flick of his fingers, the front closure sprang open. Colin feasted on her while his hand continued to pleasure her. Her heavy panting quickened as her body arched against the stone. This is how he wanted Darcy, delirious with passion, aching with a need only he could provide because he was the only man for her.

"I pictured this the moment I saw the dress," he murmured against her heated skin. "It was made for you, made to drive me insane with wanting you."

Her hands went from his hair to his shoulders. Fingertips dug into him, but he continued, ready to feel her release, to watch her come apart in his arms.

As her hips bucked against him, Colin lifted his head to see her face. When he glanced up, her eyes were on him. The intensity of her gaze flooded him with a hope he wasn't sure she even knew she was offering.

Within seconds she was flying apart, calling his name. Colin gritted his teeth, concentrating on making this moment all about Darcy, no matter the cost.

As her trembling ceased, Colin slid his lips against hers. "You're mine for the ball tomorrow."

When she started to speak, Colin laid a finger against her lips. His other hand smoothed down her skirt as he kept his eyes on hers.

"Whatever you may think of me, know that I want you and I don't just mean physically. Yes, I lied. I did it to protect Iris because in the beginning she was all that mattered. But now you matter, too, more than you could ever know, and I'm giving you the chance to see everything about me without any guard on my heart. I want you to take it all in before you decide anything."

With shaky hands, she refastened her bra, pulled her

dress back into place. "What about…you're not leaving now, are you?"

He smiled. "You mean why aren't we having sex? Is that what you want right now, Darcy?"

Her eyes held so much heat, so much desire. "I don't know what I want," she whispered. "I thought I did."

As much as it cost him, he took a step back. "I'm not staying and I'm not making love with you. Tonight was all about you. I wanted you in that blue dress because I knew you'd feel beautiful. I wanted you out here on the balcony for dinner because I know you normally eat fast to get back to taking care of children. And I wanted you to come apart in my arms without giving anything in return to me. From here on out, everything in my life will be centered around my daughter and you. Take all the time you need to think about what that means because I'm not going anywhere."

Her chin quivered. If she started crying, he'd have to hold her and he wasn't sure he was strong enough to wrap his arms around her and not take more than she was ready for at this point. Never in his life had he been this scared of losing it all. Even when he'd battled with his duties or being confined to a wheelchair, nothing had put fear in him as much as the thought of losing Darcy.

"Not all guys take everything, Darcy. Don't compare me with the jerk who shattered your dreams." He started toward the open French doors, but stopped at the threshold to look back at her. "I may just be the guy who can make your dreams come true if you'd take the time to look beyond the anger."

Oh, how he hoped she would do just that. Living without Darcy was simply a life that was unthinkable.

Sixteen

Colin swirled the amber liquid around in his glass, resisting the urge to throw it across the room. He hadn't heard a word from Darcy since leaving her room last night. The ball was in a few hours and he honestly had no idea if she was going to be there with him or not.

But right now he couldn't care less about the ball. He wanted to know where he stood with Darcy. He'd bared his soul to her, he'd passed all power over to her and now he had to wait. This was not how he lived his life...ever. Power and control were staples in his life, ingrained in him at a young age. But Darcy was worth giving all of that up for. She was worth every sacrifice.

"You're going to drive yourself mad and drinking won't help."

Colin didn't turn at the sound of his brother's useless advice. "If I want to drink, I will."

Standing on the balcony off his suite, Colin wasn't calmed by the water rushing the shore. For the first time in his life, he was consumed by emotions he had no control over: fear, frustration, worry.

"Luc just arrived." Stefan's shoes scuffed over the tile as he leaned against the rail beside Colin. "I told him you'd be down shortly."

Colin wanted to see his best friend, especially since he hadn't met Luc's fiancée yet. But he had to get his head on straight first. He couldn't go down to the ball with this much emotional baggage. Even if the media had not been permitted inside, he didn't want fellow dignitaries to see him so vulnerable.

"What have you decided?" Stefan asked.

Tilting back his glass, Colin welcomed the burn of the whiskey. "I haven't decided anything."

"Because of Darcy?"

Colin shifted, leaning one elbow on the rail as he stared at his brother. "You were a mess on your coronation day, if I recall. I know I was fresh from the hospital and in a wheelchair, but I remember how you were torn up over Victoria leaving you."

Stefan nodded. "She was my wife."

"Only because you needed her to be," Colin corrected. "You married her for one reason and fell in love with her later. It's no different with Darcy and me. She started out as Iris's nanny, but…"

Stefan's eyes widened. "Are you saying you're in love with her?"

Colin swallowed, afraid to say the words aloud. He merely nodded because the first time he admitted the truth verbally, it would be to Darcy, not his brother.

"And you're waiting to see what happens with you two before deciding whether to keep your title or not?"

Colin glanced out to the ocean, contemplating his next decision because no matter what he chose, the outcome would be life-altering.

"I'll remain on Galini Isle if Darcy stays with me." Colin pushed off the rail, began to pace in an attempt to release some tension. "I can't do this alone, Stefan. Raising Iris, helping you reign over this country. I won't leave Iris to be raised by staff, not when I have a woman I can't live without, and Iris loves her. I've realized that Iris is happy here or in LA but she is really attached to Darcy. And so am I."

Stefan smiled. "Then maybe you should tell her how you feel. I'm not the one you need to be selling this to."

Colin stopped in front of his brother. "You think she's a good fit for me?"

"I think Victoria is crazy about her and it's obvious Iris is, too." Stefan slapped a hand on Colin's shoulder. "And I've never seen you this torn up over a woman. I've also seen you face cliffs that would make even the most experienced climber cringe. Even after your accident you wanted to get back out there. You were angry the doctors wouldn't allow it. So the fact this woman has you in knots, yeah, I think she's a perfect fit."

"Then I need your help."

Colin laid out his plan, ready to fight for the woman he loved…the woman who completed his family.

The risk he was taking was huge, but the payoff would be substantial if every part of his plan fell into place.

Victoria had delivered Colin's message to Darcy that he wanted to meet her in the south hall, just outside the private entrance into the ballroom. Now he paced as Iris sat on the gleaming marble floor, playing with the simple doll Darcy had given her that first day.

He'd battled over whether or not to have Iris present for this moment; he didn't want Darcy to think he was using his child. But he needed Iris here because they were a package deal, they were a family.

The soft click of heels echoed behind him. Colin took in a deep breath, willed himself to be strong and prepared to fight for what he wanted.

"Deedee pitty!" Iris exclaimed before she jumped to her feet.

"You are beautiful." Darcy's upbeat voice gave him hope that she wasn't miserable, that she wasn't dreading tonight. "Your gold gown is so pretty, Iris. What a big girl you are tonight."

Pulling up a courage he'd never had to use before, Colin turned and was nearly brought to his knees. Darcy stared across the open space. She wore the gown he'd asked his sister-in-law to make, she'd pulled her hair back into something sleek and fit for a princess and she wore the diamond earrings that had been his mother's. Obviously Victoria had delivered those along with his message, but Colin hadn't expected her to wear them, though he was so glad she had.

Yet, as breathtaking as Darcy was right at this moment, it was the sight of her holding Iris's hand that stole his breath away. The two most important women in his life stared back at him, waiting for him to say something, but he was utterly speechless.

"Thank you for the dress." Darcy took a step forward, and Iris, still holding onto her hand moved with her. "I've never felt so…I don't know what the word is."

"Breathtaking," he murmured. "You're positively breathtaking."

Her eyes widened. "I could say the same for you. I've never seen you in something so formal."

The standard royal uniform of a black double-breasted jacket with gold buttons, his medals for various works and services and his signature blue sash meant nothing to him. His entire life on Galini Isle meant nothing without this woman by his side.

"Are you ready to go in?" she asked, smoothing her hand down her gown as if nerves were getting to her, too.

"Not just yet. I wanted a minute alone with you before we go inside."

Darcy glanced down at Iris before meeting his gaze again. "I actually wanted to talk to you, too."

No. He refused to hear her say she couldn't do this anymore. He needed to tell her everything he'd planned before she made any decisions.

"Let me start," he told her.

"Me, me, me." Iris let go of Darcy's hand and extended both arms up. "Deedee hold me."

Laughing, Darcy swung Iris up into her arms. Colin wanted to capture this mental picture of Darcy in that pale blue gown and Darcy in her gold dress with matching gold headband, both of them laughing and smiling at each other. The bond those two had formed had been instant.

Colin zeroed in on the doll Iris clutched. He'd frowned upon it at first, but realized now how much it represented. Life could be simple, he could still have a normal existence, as long as Darcy shared it with him. Every relationship took work and he was ready to put forth every effort to make sure Darcy was in his life and happier than she'd ever been...if she would have him.

"Colin." Her eyes held his as she stepped forward. "What did you want to say?"

"I love you."

Darcy jerked, her gasp audible in the nearly empty hall.

He cursed beneath his breath. "That's not how I wanted to tell you. I wanted to lead into it by telling you how you've changed my life, how you've brought out something in me I thought was dead."

Colin closed the last bit of space between them, placing a hand on her arm and another on Iris's back. "I wanted to tell you how being without you all day has nearly killed me and how going to sleep at night without hearing your voice has left me feeling empty. I needed you to know how much you mean to me, how much you mean to Iris before I told you how deeply I've fallen in love with you."

Unshed tears swam in Darcy's eyes. "You're going to make me ruin my makeup."

He gently swiped the moisture just beneath her lashes. "I want to be the man who ruins your makeup for all the right reasons. I want to bring tears of joy to your life, I want to lie by your side every night, knowing you're happy and that I've done everything in my power to give you all the love you deserve, all the happiness you can handle."

Darcy bit her lip and lowered her lids as Iris laid her head on Darcy's shoulder and cuddled in closer.

"I can't give you any more children," she whispered. "I know you'll want more heirs."

He shut her up with a soft kiss to her lips. "The only thing I want is you and Iris. You both will complete my family."

She glanced up at him, one tear trickling down her cheek. Colin swiped it away with the pad of his thumb and cupped the side of her face.

"We can adopt, too." He watched as her eyes widened, her breath hitched. "I'll adopt as many babies or children or teenagers as you want. I'm not above giving children a home. I love that you have such a strong will to help others and I know you'll make an amazing princess of Galini Isle."

"Colin," she whispered on a gasp. "What—"

"I want you to marry me."

Darcy wrapped her other arm around Iris and continued to hold his stare. Iris's eyes were slowly drifting closed, as this was her bedtime, but between the ball and Colin wanting her to be part of this monumental moment, he couldn't just leave her to sleep in her room.

"Have you thought about this?" she asked. "Have you thought about what having someone like me will do to the media you tried so hard to dodge so you could find the life you wanted?"

"I found the life I wanted," he told her, stroking her damp cheek. "I found you. I wasn't even sure what I was looking for, Darcy. I wanted to be alone, I wanted to figure things out, but you kept working your way deeper into my heart and I can't be without you now. No matter where we live, I want to be with you. Facing this country, standing by my brother's side is what I'm supposed to do. I just don't want to do it without you."

"I have a life in America, Colin. I have a business I'm trying to save because of a promise I made to my grandmother. I can't ignore who I am, I can't lose my identity."

Colin nodded. "I understand. You will restore Loving Hands to its former glory. I don't want you to lose your identity, either, because it's what made me fall in love with you to begin with. See what staff you can hire back and have someone manage the office while we are here. So much can be done online, but I'm assuming you have someone you'd trust to run the office?"

Darcy nodded, her eyes darting away as if she were already thinking through the plans that would need to be made.

"Tell me we can make this work," he pleaded. "We can even keep the home in LA to use when we go back."

"You'd come with me when I go to check in on Loving Hands?" she asked, her eyes wide, brimming anew with unshed tears.

Colin wrapped his arm around her waist, tucking her side against his so he didn't squeeze Iris too much now that she was sound asleep. So much for her taking part in his epic moment.

"I have to admit, I'm quite fond of those steps," he muttered against her mouth before he slid his lips across hers. "I think keeping that house is a great idea."

"I'm still under contract, you know. What happens at the end of my six-month term?"

"We can make it our wedding date, if you'll have me."

Darcy sighed into him, opening her mouth beneath his. Everything about her felt right, perfect. How did someone from a completely different world fit so effortlessly into his?

He eased back. "I should tell you, I allowed a trusted media source into the ballroom. If you agreed to stay with me, I wanted to be in control of who revealed our good news first."

She froze, her eyes searching his. "I thought you hated the media."

"I hate the stories they make up and how they were portraying Iris and me as broken. We're a strong force, and with you by our side we are even stronger."

Darcy smiled. "You're an amazing father. I love you, Colin."

He'd never tire of hearing those words. "What was it you wanted to talk to me about?"

Her smile widened. "I was going to tell you I wanted to give us another chance."

Shocked, Colin eased back. "You mean you let me go through all of that knowing you were giving me another chance?"

With a shrug, she shifted Iris a bit higher in her arms. "I wanted to know how far you'd go. I needed to see you grovel, just a bit."

Sliding a hand around her waist, Colin leaned in to whisper in her ear. "You want to see groveling? I still owe you a shopping trip and I plan on helping you in the dressing room. We'll see who's groveling then."

Before she could utter a word, Colin wrapped his arms

around his girls and ushered them out. After putting Iris in her bed with a staff member close by the nursery, Colin whisked his future princess into her first royal ball. The first of many royal gatherings they'd be attending as a family.

* * * * *

MILLS & BOON®

Desire™

PASSIONATE AND DRAMATIC LOVE STORIES

A sneak peek at next month's titles…

In stores from 19th June 2015:

- **Claiming His Secret Son** – Olivia Gates
  and **Seduced by the Spare Heir** – Andrea Laurence

- **Pregnant by the Cowboy CEO** – Catherine Mann
  and **Lone Star Baby Bombshell** – Lauren Canan

- **The Billionaire's Daddy Test** – Charlene Sands
  and **A Royal Amnesia Scandal** – Jules Bennett

Available at WHSmith, Tesco, Asda, Eason, Amazon and Apple

Just can't wait?
Buy our books online a month before they hit the shops!
visit www.millsandboon.co.uk

These books are also available in eBook format!